WRECKED

Also by E. R. Frank
Friction · America · Life Is Funny

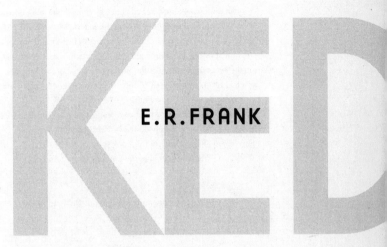

E.R.FRANK

A RICHARD JACKSON BOOK
ATHENEUM BOOKS FOR YOUNG READERS • NEW YORK LONDON TORONTO SYDNEY

Atheneum Books for Young Readers

An imprint of Simon & Schuster Children's Publishing Division

1230 Avenue of the Americas, New York, New York 10020

Book design by Kristin Smith

The text for this book is set in Aldine 401.

Manufactured in the United States of America

First Edition

2 4 6 8 10 9 7 5 3 1

Library of Congress Cataloging-in-Publication Data

Frank, E. R.

Wrecked / E.R. Frank.— 1st ed.

p. cm.

"A Richard Jackson Book."

Summary: After a car accident seriously injures her best friend and kills her brother's girlfriend, sixteen-year-old Anna tries to cope with her guilt and grief, while learning some truths about her family and herself.

ISBN 0-689-87383-2 (ISBN-13: 978-0-689-87383-6)

[1. Traffic accidents—Fiction. 2. Death—Fiction. 3. Grief—Fiction.
4. Guilt—Fiction. 5. Brothers and sisters—Fiction. 6. Self-acceptance—Fiction.
7. Family problems—Fiction.] I. Title.

PZ7.F84913Wav 2005

[Fic]—dc22   2004018448

For Jim

BEFORE

THE DAY I KILLED MY BROTHER'S GIRLFRIEND STARTED WITH ME handpicking leaves off our front lawn.

"Did you lose an earring, Anna?" Mrs. Caldwell called. She was wearing navy blue sweats with white racing stripes up the sides.

"Um," I called back. "Yeah." She stepped onto our brick pathway, probably to help me look.

"Oh," I said, loud, before Mrs. Caldwell could get too close. "Got it." I held my hand high in the air, as if I was showing her something I'd found. She nodded and then turned around right as my brother, Jack, backed the Honda out of our garage, music blasting.

"You want to help?" I called. I mean, he could have helped.

"Nope." He let the car roll slowly backward. "Sorry." He didn't sound sorry. But still. I guess I wouldn't have helped either. He cranked the music up even louder.

"What is that?" I shouted. He's always listening to bands nobody's heard of.

"Barking Duck!" Which is what it sounded like.

"Do you like it?" he asked, turning the volume down.

"Very funny," I said. "And don't forget, I have the Honda tonight."

"You won't need it if you don't finish the lawn."

And then he left me there, picking up crunchy brown leaves the size of hair clips. Picking them up, one by one, and dropping them into a plastic grocery store bag. Exactly the way my father had insisted. Not raking, because that might damage the grass. Not leaf blowing, because the noise was too loud and the gas smelled. Not watching some crew, because why should my father hire other people to do his lawn work when he had two perfectly able-bodied teenagers?

My mom poked her head out our front door, holding my cell. Damn. I thought I had it clipped to my back pocket. "It just rang." She had the top flipped up. "I think it was Ellen."

I blew out a big breath of air and straightened.

"Do you want company?" She has a bad back, so it went without saying that she wasn't going to help.

"No, I don't want company," I snapped. "I want not to do this."

"Is it such a big deal?" My mom handed me the cell.

"It's ridiculous, Mom." I put a lot of emphasis on the *dic* of *ridiculous*.

"Well," she said. Then she went back into the house.

I picked up two more leaves and dropped them with the others. And then something weird happened. I didn't plan it. I hadn't even been thinking about it. But all of a sudden I opened the plastic grocery bag, turned it upside down, and dragged it through the air. I watched the leaves scatter sideways and then spiral downward toward the wispy blades peeking up from where my father had made Jack sprinkle seed last weekend. How do they say it? *In one fell swoop.* Well, in one fell swoop I dumped out all those leaves I'd been so stupidly gathering up. Just dumped them right out.

I remember that moment as clear as the accident. Sometimes clearer. Who knows why.

WE'RE AT ELLEN'S. SHE'S FLATTENING HER BROWN HAIR, SLICKING
it back into one long ponytail.

"It's too early to leave," she's saying. "Things won't get going
until at least twelve."

"Well, it's twelve now," I tell her. "And we're still not ready."

"You want to call Lisa and them, and see where they are?"

I dial, and some guy answers. "What's up?" There's giggling
in the background.

"Seth!" the giggler goes. I think it might be Lisa. "Give it
back!"

"Is Lisa there?" I ask.

Ellen and I are sort of between groups right now. Last year
we hung out a lot with this other Anna, and Katy and Slater and
Kevin and Trace. But the other Anna switched schools, and
Katy and Slater started wearing black lipstick and shaving their

heads and telling us we were conformists, and Kevin and Trace started dating each other and never hanging out with anybody else, and things just sort of dissolved from there.

"Give it!" I hear Lisa shouting over her own giggles.

"What's going on?" Ellen asks.

"I think it's Seth. That guy who wears the sleeve," I say. A sleeve is this thing that looks sort of like a combination of a glove with no finger coverage and a sock that fits all the way up to your elbow. Other than the sleeve, Seth's pretty cute.

"Oh," Ellen goes. "Sleev-eth."

"Listen," I tell the phone. "Could you put Lisa on?" I try to sound sarcastic and bossy, but I'm not so good at that. Ellen is slightly better at it than I am. Neither of us is nearly as masterful as the Ashleys. Which is fine, because we have no desire to be complete bitches. Just to know how when necessary.

"Who's this?" Seth asks.

"Who is it?" I hear Lisa say.

"Give her the phone, man," some other guy complains.

"This is Anna," I say. "Ask Lisa if she's going to the party at Wayne's."

"Yeah." It's still Seth. "We're going. Is this Anna Lawson?"

I cover the phone with my hand. "Ellen," I whisper. "Sleev-eth knows who I am."

"Good," she goes.

"How do you know who I am?" I ask into the cell.

"It's me," Lisa says. I guess Sleev-eth gave hers back. "We're leaving in fifteen minutes."

"Us too," I say. "Ellen's taking forever to do her hair."

"I am not," Ellen goes. "Ask if they have beer." Ellen's developed a taste for alcohol lately. I haven't. I don't like beer, for one thing. For another, I do like knowing what's going on.

"Do you guys have beer?" I ask.

"Yeah, plus Jack Daniel's."

"They've got Jack Daniel's," I tell Ellen.

"Where did they get that?"

"Anna?" It's Sleev-eth again.

"Seth!" I hear Lisa scream. Then the signal goes dead.

I flip down my phone. Ellen tugs at her ponytail and then turns from her mirror to look at me.

"You don't want to go, do you," she says.

"Yeah I do."

"You wanted to bitch some more about your father and then see *Rocky Horror*."

"Maybe. But it's too late." *Rocky Horror* always starts at midnight.

"I kind of like parties now," Ellen tells me. Neither of us used to. Last year we would go to the mall instead. Or to Top Hats, our favorite diner. We thought parties were stupid up until about a month ago.

"I like parties too," I lie.

"No you don't. You always nurse a beer and stay in one place the whole time."

I don't know what to say to that. Ellen's been my best friend since we were nine. She knows me better than anybody. Really, anybody.

"You don't like me anymore," I sulk. "You're going to get in with the Ashleys and break them up and be one of their best friends and dump me." I'm only half kidding.

"Don't be stupid," she goes. "I just want to have some fun."

"Well, I do too," I say.

"Since when?"

"Since today."

"Oh, yeah?" she asks. "Do I have your dad to thank for that?"

"Whoever you want to thank," I tell her. "But I'm going to have fun flirting with Sleev-eth. And I'm going to have fun drinking."

She's always said I'm more of a stoner than a drinker, if I ever had the guts to do either. I've always said it's not about guts. It's just that I don't want to do drugs because if I got caught or something bad happened, my father would kill me. That's where Ellen usually rolls her eyes, and I wonder if she actually knows me better than I know me, and then I get nervous if I don't switch the subject in my head.

"Well, don't have too much fun," Ellen's warning me now, "because one of us has to be able to drive."

"Okay," I say. "Then, I'll just flirt."

"Good," Ellen goes. "Let's leaf now."

"Ha," I tell her.

Wayne's house is sort of like mine. Old and big with a huge front and back lawn. Which makes me think about my father and the fight we had before I left.

"You will not leave this house until that grass is taken care of," my dad said. He isn't used to me not doing what he asks. I'm not used to it either. But whatever it was that made me dump out those leaves earlier wouldn't let me give in.

"No," I argued. I was already late. I'd told Ellen I'd be there ten minutes ago. I was working hard to keep my head from going fuzzy, the way it gets when my father has me trapped somehow. Because even though I'm usually sure that it's something the matter with him that starts it all, I always end up feeling like there's something worse the matter with me for not seeing things his way.

So I tried to sound reasonable. My dad likes reasonable. "I'm sorry I didn't do it already," I said, as calm as I could. "But it's dark out now. Plus, it doesn't make sense to hand pick up leaves. I'll rake tomorrow, but tonight I'm going to Ellen's." Then I held my breath and started walking through the kitchen. Jack was at the table, waiting for his girlfriend to come over and typing some new movie review, probably, onto his Web site. Or maybe checking his UCLA admissions status.

"Stop," my father ordered. I didn't stop. "You stop right there." The fuzz went black while he moved in front of me to block the mudroom door. Jack didn't even look up. He can get so absorbed in whatever he's doing that he wouldn't notice if a hurricane hit.

"Dad!" I said.

I heard my mother's hard-soled shoes clack on the stairs. My father was standing so close I could feel the heat of him on me. "Give me the keys," he ordered.

"No. You're being totally unfair!" The black was getting worse, the way it does when he won't back off, which is all the time, and you can't do anything, you're just stuck, and everything turns into a massive knot of confusion. Jack glanced up at both of us right then, but only for a second.

"Harvey," my mother said, clacking into the kitchen. "What's going on?"

"She didn't pick up the leaves." The vein over his left eye was popped out. His face was shiny.

"I saw her pick up the leaves," my mother told him in that ultrapatient tone of voice she gets when he's like this. His jaw muscles started jumping.

"So did I." Jack snapped closed his laptop, scraped back his chair, and walked out.

I tried to clear the messiness in my head. It works better if you stay calm. Even though my father never does. His face was turning purple. I looked at my mom. "I told him already," I said evenly. "I'll rake tomorrow."

"Not rake!" my father exploded. He was frothing at the mouth. Seriously. Spit was gathering at the corners like he had rabies or something. "Not tomorrow. Pick. Up. Now!"

My mother was just standing there, lips in a tight, straight line. That *This is not right, but there's nothing I can do* look. I couldn't take it. I wasn't going to let him ruin my whole night. Make me get on my knees under the spotlights out front, as if I were some kind of psych patient, when he was the insane one.

I stepped around my father and through the mudroom, into the garage.

"If you leave this house, you will be extremely sorry!" he shouted right as I was yanking open the car door.

I jumped into the Honda. "If I come back to this house," I shouted back through the open window, "you will be extremely lucky!" And then I cried the whole way to Ellen's.

Wayne's got two sound systems going: one on the third floor and one on the first. Outside you can hear them both. House from the top. Disco from the bottom. They don't mix too well.

"See anybody we know?" I ask Ellen. We're trying to make our way inside. Ellen's always cold, so unless it's seriously summer, we never stay outdoors.

"No." She weaves through the crowd. Then when we walk in through the garage, she points. "There's Jason." I don't really know Jason. He's this guy in her history class Ellen has a crush on. He sees us and waves us over.

"Lisa and her friend were looking for you," he tells Ellen. "They went up to the third floor."

"Come with us," Ellen invites him. "This is Anna. Anna, this is Jason."

"Hi," we both say, and then we all start trooping upward.

On the stairs someone has taped signs that read, PLEASE DO NOT PARTY ON THE SECOND FLOOR. They're written in red marker on graph paper.

"There they are," Lisa says when she sees us. We're in a bedroom. Wayne's probably. It's got posters of bands and supermodels all over the place and beer-can pyramids everywhere. Lisa and Seth and a couple of other people are sitting on the bed. The house music is pounding. You can feel it buzz in your chest. *Thrum, thrum.* "You want some?" Seth offers us a bottle of Jack Daniel's with his right hand. With his left he's eating a peppermint patty.

"You guys know Jason?" Ellen asks, taking the whiskey. Everybody nods. My whole body keeps thrumming with the beat of the music. *Thrum, thrum.* "Where did you guys get it?"

"Bought it," Lisa goes. "Seth's got a fake ID." He does look sort of old. Not twenty-one, exactly. But with a fake ID I guess he can pass.

"You're Jack's little sister, right?" Seth asks me. This never used to happen.

"Where's your sleeve?" I ask him back.

"We convinced him to lose it," Lisa says.

"How do you know my brother?" I ask, even though I know how. But Seth's popped the rest of the peppermint patty into his mouth, so he can't answer.

"Ohhh," Jason goes instead. He takes a drink of Jack Daniel's. "Jack Lawson? You're Jack Lawson's little sister?" I still can't get used to having a brother who, practically overnight, has become a household name.

"Everybody knows your brother this year," Ellen tells me, like she's reading my mind. Which she kind of does a lot of the time.

"Cameron," I guess. Seth sighs. Jason and Lisa nod.

"Cameron Polk," they all say at once. *Thrum, thrum.*

Cameron Polk is Jack's girlfriend. His first girlfriend ever. They've been dating since the second week of school.

"Late," I said to Jack from his bedroom door, on the night I found out. He was sitting on that ergonomic chair in front of his laptop with the phone in his hand. He looked a little out of it. "Dinner," I said. "It's three minutes past." My parents had sent me to get him. My father wouldn't let me yell up the stairs. I had to walk up.

"Cameron Polk just agreed to go out with me Saturday night," Jack said.

"Really?"

He nodded. As far as I knew, he hadn't asked anyone out

since he was in the eighth grade, when Trisha Todd told him no because he was too short. He'd grown more than a foot since then, and mostly I thought of him as this annoying, gawky guy who lived in my house. Nobody ever messed with him exactly, and he and his best friend, Rob, weren't total outcasts or anything. But it wasn't like people loved Jack either. Then again, when I thought about it, looking at him with the phone in his hand, I realized that a lot of kids had started talking to him at the end of last year. Had he been getting cool, and I hadn't noticed it?

"*The* Cameron Polk?" I asked him.

She moved here the last month of school last year. She's one of these girls that you sort of can't believe. Nobody could stop looking at her. She's got smoky skin and shiny blond hair and this square jaw, with a little bit of slant to her eyes. She transferred into all the honors classes, and she seemed actually nice. No attitude. It took only three days before the Ashleys asked her to sit with them at lunch. She did a few times. But she sat with other people too. You can't get much classier than that.

"We're in French Five together," Jack told me.

I noticed that his shaggy hair and something about his jeans and T-shirt looked like this ad I'd seen in some magazine lately. Those ads where the guys never seem as if they care what they look like, but they look good anyway. Weird.

"Saturday's my night for the car," I reminded him.

"I know." He looked at the phone in his hand. "But."

"Anna!" we heard my dad yell up the stairs. "Jack!" He had that edge to his voice. It meant he'd be screaming for five minutes once we got down to the dinner table.

I stood there trying to think over the noise of my dad. I should let Jack have the car. It was a date. It was Cameron Polk. Obviously I should. It was just that I'd promised to drive to Jake Lowell's party so that Ellen could drink, and I didn't want Ellen to be mad. . . .

"Forget it," Jack said, and he had that expression I hate. That one where it's obvious he thinks I'm a disgusting human being. "Get out of my room."

"Anna!" my father shouted. "Jack!"

"Get. Out." When I didn't move, he stabbed a key on his keyboard, stood up, and brushed by me into the hallway.

"All right," I said to his back. "Fine. You can have the car on Saturday."

"Jack!"

"You know what?" my brother said, stopping at the top of the stairs. "Sometimes you are so small."

So now I get it. "Is that how you know who I am?" I ask Sleev-eth. He's holding out the whiskey, and I take it.

"Are you really going to drink tonight?" Ellen asks me.

I ignore her and keep talking to Seth. "Because you know who Jack is because everyone knows who Cameron is?" Then I take a huge, and I mean huge, swallow. And nearly choke to death. Jason kindly pounds me on the back for a while.

Ellen says, "Take a smaller swallow and go slower."

While I do, Seth goes, "No. I'm always seeing your hair in the hall." *Thrum, thrum.*

I have copper-colored corkscrew hair. No joke. Coils and coils of the stuff. It would be bad enough to have just the color.

And bad enough to have the corkscrews. Having both is the worst. Ellen and my mother say it's "adorable" and "striking." Right. Try *freakish*.

"I've been dying to pull it all year," Seth says. Then he reaches out, grabs a curl, stretches it down straight, lets it go, and watches it bounce right back.

"Supreme," he says.

"If we were in third grade," I inform him, "you'd so be in the corner right now."

"If we were in the third grade," Seth informs me, "I'd so be kicked out of school right now." He reaches out and pulls another curl.

"I hated that in the third grade," I warn him.

"She loves it now," Lisa says with a smirk. As if she even knows me.

I hold out the bottle to Ellen. She takes it and drinks.

"We're co-opting your liquor," I tell Sleev-eth. I'm having fun.

Here's when I first noticed Jack trying with me, after a lot of years of not. It was this past summer, the first Friday of our annual two-week beach vacation at Commons End. We'd just arrived at that year's rental house after a five-hour drive. Which should have been three hours, but the shortcut my father thought would shave off ten minutes ended up getting us lost. So whatever.

"Anna," Jack called up to me. I was on the elevated deck, hauling my suitcase and my mother's. It was dusk but still hot from the sun of the day. I could feel my skin prickle from sweat and aggravation.

"What?" I asked him.

"You want me to unpack so you can go check out the water?"

"Huh?"

It's always Jack and me who have to take everything out of the car and indoors. My father usually insists on packing the trunk before we leave, which involves a lot of impatience and yelling because he's sure that not everything will fit. Then, on the arrival end, he never helps unload. And with her bad back, my mom can't do much either.

"I'll unpack," Jack said. "You want to go see the ocean before it's dark, right?"

It was something we usually raced each other for. Who would get their half finished the quickest, jog the two blocks, scramble up the narrow dune path, and reach the peak first. Who would get to throw off shoes, slip-slide down, pad across the warm sand, and wade into the undertow, looking out onto the choppy green water, before the other one even showed up. It was usually too late to actually swim. But most years getting that first piece of the beach on the day we arrived was a part of starting things off.

"You mean, you'll unpack the whole car?" I asked Jack.

"Yeah." I watched his face, trying to figure out the trick.

"Okay," I said finally.

When I got back, we ate dinner, and after that Jack wandered through my door, listening to his iPod. My room had twin beds with ugly flowered curtains that matched the bedspreads, and a fake bamboo chair. I was on my cell phone, lying on the floor with my feet up on one bed. Jack did the same next to me. Not knowing what else to do, I said to Ellen, who was planning to come down three days later, "So, this is weird. Jack just came into my room and, like, made himself comfortable. He doesn't even have his laptop with him or anything."

He didn't so much as blink, and with his music on I couldn't even be sure he'd heard me. When I hung up with Ellen a few minutes later, Jack said, "Do you like Straw Man Proposal?"

I rolled my eyes. "You know I've never heard of them."

"Listen to this," he said instead of telling me what a moron I was. And he leaned over to plug his earphones into my ears.

I listened. It wasn't bad.

SOMEHOW ME AND ELLEN AND SETH AND LISA AND JASON AND these two other guys and this one other girl wearing a hot pink jean jacket end up in Wayne's basement playing pool. Which is fun, especially since I'm sort of good at it, and Sleev-eth and I are on the same team, and he's good too. Three swigs of the Jack got me way drunk for a few hours, but now I think I'm sobered up. For a while there I thought I was going to puke, but Ellen walked me twice around the entire house, even all around the second floor.

"Walking off too much alcohol doesn't exactly count as partying," she said when we passed some of those red-markered signs.

"Yeah, but we're not supposed to be here," I moaned. "The second floor! Wayne will be soooo mad."

"Wayne is soooo stoned right now he wouldn't be able to tell the second floor from the fifteenth," Ellen told me. "Now, keep walking."

"Do you think I'm going to pass out?" I was sort of hopeful. I'd never passed out before.

"Nah," she said. "If I thought you were that far gone, I'd throw you in the shower." That probably got me sober faster than anything.

"You're the best, El," I told her.

"Ugh," she said. "You are not a cute drunk."

But now I'm fine, and Ellen is having a hard time holding her pool cue. She had four beers on top of three shots of Jack Daniel's, all in the last hour and a half. And right as I'm realizing that I also realize our curfews are way over.

"Oh my God," I say, scratching my shot.

"What's wrong?" Sleev-eth asks. He's finishing another peppermint patty. I think I've seen him eat four tonight. And he's not even a little bit fat.

"Ellen, we have to go." I stand up and hand off my pool cue to Jason. "I'm in such deep shit."

"About time," Ellen says to Jason and the others. "She never does Anna-thing wrong." It's hard to believe she can do her word thing so drunk. Then again, *Anna-thing* is an old one.

"You have to go now?" Seth sounds bummed, which is nice.

"Just stay," Lisa goes. "You're already late anyway."

"You don't know my dad," I tell her.

"You're not driving," Jason warns Ellen.

"I am," I say, pulling the keys out of my back pocket. My key ring is a teeny, tiny glow-in-the-dark planet Earth. If you sit in the pitch black with it, it's got all the greens and blues and whites and the shapes of the continents and everything. Ellen gave it to me the day I got my learner's permit. "Now you've got the world at your fingertips," she'd said.

"Bye," I tell everybody. Seth pulls one of my curls.

"See ya," they say.

"Bye." Ellen flaps her hands at them and stumbles.

"Come on," I go, and I lead her from the pool table, up the stairs and out the front door, down the street, to the Honda.

"Eech," Ellen goes on Ocean Road.

"You want me to pull over and walk you around a little?"

"Eech," she says again. Then she leans over and against her seat belt to crank up the radio. It's that old U2 song. That ancient one: "Hoow loong to sing this soong? Hooow looong, hooooow looong, hoow loong . . ." Ellen cranks it loud, and then she turns to me and she goes, "Do you think—"

And then there's this deafening smacking sound and the smell of new plastic, and Ellen in my lap, dripping with blood, and there's pieces of something falling and all this dust everywhere and chips flying up from the floor, and Ellen bloody with her head pressed hard against my collarbone, and the sharp brush of her ponytail sticking my right eye. "Hooow looong, hoow loong, hoow loong . . . ," and the sound of somebody screaming and screaming and screaming, and then somehow my door opens and I fall out with bloody Ellen half on top of me and her ponytail still sticking me in my eye, and I think, *How could she be in my lap and how could we fall out with our seat belts on?* And I keep hearing that screaming and screaming and screaming and screaming, and then I hear the screaming stop, and instantly I vomit all over myself and all over Ellen's head. "To sing this sooong?" And a man's voice says, "Three seven oh one," and there's a siren and somebody's holding a blanket, and another man's voice says, "Can you talk?" and I say, "My friend is bleeding," and then Ellen slides away, and her ponytail slides away with her, and the music stops, and then there's three policemen standing over me, and one of them wears Harry Potter glasses, and one of them is licking his lips, and the other one is saying something, only I can't make out the words, and I go, "I can't hear you," and I see the glow-in-the-dark earth dangling from somewhere really high up, and I'm looking at it and telling the cop, "I was going to do it tomorrow. I swear. I was going to do it tomorrow," and he stops talking to me, and he looks at the other two, and the Harry Potter one pulls off his glasses and turns away, and the one who was licking his lips turns with him, and I'm watching the earth swing gently back and forth, and that last cop leans down to me and tries again, and this time I hear him, and he's saying in this really friendly voice, "Okay. Okay. Okay. Okay."

3

I WANT TO VOMIT, AND MY RIGHT EYE THROBS. I GO TO TOUCH IT, when I hear someone say, "Don't do that." I open my eyes, except only the left one seems to be working. A nurse calls out to someone behind her, "She's waking up."

I feel panic spreading through my blood, like ink in water.

"Anna?" It's my mother.

"What are you wearing?" I go. Even with one eye I can see her long raincoat over pajamas.

"Anna," she says again. Blue-and-white-checked cotton. A raincoat over pajamas? Something is very wrong. I reach up again to my eye, but Mom grabs my hand.

"Don't," she says. "You have a shield on it. Leave it."

"Is Dad mad?" I say, and she starts to cry. Seeing that is so strange it makes me remember everything. Scattering the leaves in one fell swoop, and Ellen bloody in my lap. And screaming, stopped.

"Ellen." The panic is seeping everywhere. "Is Ellen okay?"

"She has a collapsed lung," my mom tells me. "And some broken bones." She blows her nose. The nurse fiddles with something above me, and I notice I've got a needle sticking in my arm. An IV.

"A collapsed lung?" I go. "That's bad, right?"

My mother nods.

"Is it days later?" I ask. I think it is. I think the accident must have happened at least a week ago.

"No, Anna," my mom says. She picks up my hand and squeezes it. "It's the same night. It's five thirty in the morning."

"What bones did Ellen break?" My eye is killing me. The throb fills up my entire head.

"Some ribs and her leg."

"Did I break anything?" I ask. Because it's hard to tell.

"No," my mom says. "You just injured your eye."

"My body hurts."

"Where?" Mom asks.

"Everywhere."

"We'll get the doctor. He'll want to talk to you."

"Where is Ellen?" My mom's chin starts to work a little again, and I feel the ink oozing into my chest.

"Intensive care," my mom finally says.

Maybe it's going to be Ellen who will wake up days later.

"Is she in a coma?" I don't know why I ask that exactly. Maybe because that's what usually happens on TV. My mother shakes her head and lets go of my hand to stroke my left arm. The one without the IV. Sometimes people don't wake up from comas. Sometimes people just stay vegetables. Ellen. A vegetable. I can hear her say it: *veg-Ellen-table.*

"Is she going to die?" I ask.

"No," my mother says. "She's not in a coma, and she's not going to die." Suddenly I'm really tired.

"She better not," I say. It's hard to get the words out. To speak.

"She won't," my mother says. It doesn't sound like she's lying, but a collapsed lung is bad. I'm pretty sure that's bad. And there's something else going on, something to do with the panic. I can't relax.

She's still stroking my left arm.

"Mom," I say, *why are you petting me?* But I don't have enough energy. "Mom" is all I say.

Later I still feel sore all over, and my eye throbs along with my whole skull. There's a sideways sliding tray set up in front of me. Scrambled eggs, toast, a small cup of purple jelly, and orange juice are sitting on it. I have to pee. Badly. I shove the tray out of my way and realize there's no needle in my arm anymore.

"Hello?" I go. The door to my little room is open, and with my left eye I can see nurses and people walking back and forth. "Hello?"

My mother rushes in. Now she's wearing regular clothes. Her light leather jacket, jeans, and clogs.

"Anna?" she says.

"I have to go to the bathroom."

She helps me. It's strange to stand up. It makes my entire

head pulse, for one thing, and my legs feel wobbly and splayed, like a newborn foal's. I have to lean on my mother to walk the five steps to the toilet. Which is strange too.

There's a mirror above the bathroom sink. My mom hustles me through washing my hands, but I see myself long enough to get nauseous again. My hair is a mass of orange snakes. The thing on my eye looks like a miniature spaghetti strainer. Silver-colored metal, pricked with little holes. Around the sticky, white-tab edges of it my skin is swollen and blue. I try not to imagine what's underneath.

"Is it Sunday?" I ask after I'm safe back in bed. My mother sits in a chair next to me. For some reason I still feel like I must have blacked out, and for much longer than she's saying.

"Yes."

"Last night was the accident?" I ask, just to be sure. She nods. "Where's Dad and Jack?"

My mother looks awful. Huge gray circles under her eyes, white lips, stringy hair. Like she hasn't slept all night. Which, now that I think about it, she probably hasn't. "Mom?" I say again. "Where are they?"

"Anna," she says, taking my hand again.

"What?" I won't let her hold it. Something's not right. That ink seeps through me. I can't relax. "Dad's really, really mad, right?" I say, but some part of me knows that's not it.

"Do you remember what happened last night?" she asks.

"Yes," I say. "What does that have to do with Dad not being here?" The aching in my eye and head drops straight to my throat. My body starts to tremble. My whole body. It just starts to shake.

"Do you realize that there was another car involved?" my mother goes.

There was screaming. Screaming and screaming and screaming. It wasn't Ellen, and it wasn't me. *"Hoooow looong, hooow loooong . . ."* And then the screaming stopped. It stopped because the life stopped. Somehow I knew it then. I know it now. I don't need anybody to tell me. I heard the life stop.

I feel the ache come out of both my eyes in tears, and I try not to cry, but it's hard not to cry, and it makes me shake more. My mom sees it. The shaking. My teeth are chattering. She climbs onto the bed. She spoons behind and wraps her arms around me tightly to try to keep me still. But I can't stop shaking.

"Anna, listen to me," she says. Her breath is warm on my neck and in my ear. "The driver of the other car died."

"I know," I try to tell her, but my jaw and mouth are chattering so much, I can't make the words.

"Anna," my mother says. She pulls her arms even tighter, and I'm glad because I think I might shake myself right off the bed onto the floor if she weren't here, holding me together. "It was Cameron Polk," she says. *Cameron Polk.* "Do you understand?" *Cameron Polk. Cameron Polk.* I make myself understand.

"Yes," I say, shaking.

"Do you understand?" she says again.

"Yes," I say.

4

THE NURSE IS EXPLAINING ABOUT MY EYE. ONE DROP A DAY TO help the pain, and another drop of something else to keep my pupil dilated so that there won't be rebleeding. Somehow I register the word *rebleeding,* and I wonder, vaguely, what that means. The nurse might be trying to tell me what it means, but I can't really understand what she's saying. I see her mouth moving, and I see my mother's listening face, and I even hear words, but it's like I'm underwater on Mars. Everything is blurry and foreign and floating.

Things get slightly more clear and still and in focus after my mother leaves me to call my dad and check on what's happening with him and Jack. I wobble out into the hallway and ask another nurse where intensive care is, and she tells me, even though I think she won't. While she's saying I should go back to my room and wait for my mom to come get me, I get myself into the elevator and hold on to the metal bar on the way up to the fifth floor. Right as the elevator door opens I see the Gersons rushing down the hall in the opposite direction from me, so I make my way to the end of the hall where they were coming from, and I check a few doors, and the third door is where I find Ellen.

Even with half vision, from ten feet away, feeling like I'm still underwater, I can see she's messed up. I ache all over, and I'm stiff as anything, and my whole head is pounding, with the center of the pound right in the middle of my right eye, even with the drops for pain, so it takes a while to get near Ellen's bed.

Besides two IVs, one in each arm, there's a tube that goes from under the covers to a bag with what I'm sure is pee in it. She has a bandage on her left cheek, a big blue tube in her mouth that looks like a sicko accordion straw designed to choke you to death, and another tube that's attached to her somewhere, only I can't tell where because it disappears under the hospital blanket and sheets. She's asleep, I guess, only I'm worried she's in a coma. How do you know the difference, anyway?

"You look like shit," I tell her. She turns her head the littlest bit. "I threw up on you." She opens her eyes, and for a second I think she sees me, but then she closes them again. I hear this slow whooshing sound, but I can't tell which machine it's coming from.

"Hey," a male nurse says, walking in. "You're not supposed to be here."

Ellen is really still now. The whooshing keeps going, though.

"You need to leave," this nurse says. He's got hair the same color as mine. "What floor did you come from?"

"I killed Cameron Polk," I whisper to Ellen.

Nothing.

I'm sitting in a wheelchair, waiting for my parents to come get me. The hospital doesn't let you walk out. They make you wheel out. I'm thinking about how stupid that is and trying to block the screaming, stopped, out of my head, when my dad walks in.

"Hi," I say.

My heel starts uncontrollably tapping the footrest of the wheelchair.

"Anna," my dad says, and the next thing I know, he's kneeling and hugging me hard, careful not to touch my right eye.

"Is the Honda totaled?" I ask.

"I don't care about the car," he answers, which is a complete lie and really nice of him to say. Especially because he hugs me tighter when he says it, even though it's hard to hug when one person's in a wheelchair and when you can see that her heel is clattering like a mini jackhammer.

Driving home, it's mostly my father who talks. My mom lets me sit up front in the Audi and stays quiet.

"Jack is . . ." My dad stops and clears his throat. "Jack's not doing well," he tells me. I try to picture my brother. It's hard, for some reason. "He's pretty broken up." My mother's hand finds my shoulder and rests there. I look out the window and wonder how long she's going to keep it there, warm and light, and notice how the shield over my eye itches me around the edges.

"Was it my fault?" I ask. My father doesn't answer right away.

He turns left on Pelham, taking the long way home. "Was it my fault?" I ask again. "The accident?"

"She was on your side of the street," my father says. She was? "Were you speeding?"

I shake my head. He makes a left onto Ladyshire. And then I figure out what he's doing. He's avoiding Ocean Road. He's avoiding where it happened.

"Were you drunk?"

"I don't think so," I say.

"What do you mean, you don't think so?"

I feel black fuzz start to mix with the ache behind my eye, and I try to stay clear.

"I had two shots of Jack Daniel's a long time before I drove," I say, waiting for the yelling. "Two or three hours before."

"Your blood-alcohol level was under the legal limit." My father's not raising his voice. He doesn't mention anything about the fact that I shouldn't have been drinking at all. "Were you speeding?" he asks again.

"I don't think so," I say. "I was about to pull over for Ellen. We thought she might be sick."

"Her blood-alcohol level was three times the legal limit," my father informs me.

I'm not surprised. Everybody's quiet for a while. And I still need to know for sure.

"So." I'm kind of shaking again. My fingers are quivering. "Was it my fault?"

"No." My mother's hand tightens on my shoulder before my dad can answer. "She was in your lane."

When we come around the curve in our street, so that I can see my house, there's a figure kneeling on the grass. As we get closer and pull into the driveway I can see that it's Jack.

"What's he doing?" my mother asks. I look out the window with my one good eye, and Jack glances up with his two.

He's picking leaves off the lawn.

5

WHEN WE WERE LITTLE, WE GOT ALONG REALLY WELL. ESPECIALLY at the beach. Every day of our two-week summer vacation at Commons End we would play in the surf, facing the choppy green expanse for hours. Our parents would be lying on the shoreline, under the shade of two umbrellas, covered with sun-block, broad-brimmed hats, and wraparound sunglasses. They'd be reading in low-slung chairs, legs outstretched, bottoms of their feet encrusted with wet sand.

My brother and I would locate ourselves exactly in the path of the breakers, giddy with the challenge of negotiating those endless waves. We'd dive into a curl and pop up and out the other side, braced for the next. We'd shoot our bodies vertically over a crest, letting the edge of it slap hard at our necks. Lie on our backs, feet forward, bobbing toward the sky with a slow-moving swell. Duck low and deep when our timing was off on a rough rogue, holding our breath beneath the frenzy, desperately waiting for it to pass over. Bodysurf until our bellies scraped sand, then fight the tide to get back in. Wipe out every now and then, the ocean flinging us underwater into a spinning knot of suffocating, airless panic. Bump and slip and hurl ourselves into each other's bony arms and legs. And then, dozens and dozens of waves later, with blocked ears, salty, snotty upper lips, and burning eyes, Jack would look at me and say, "I'm going to stop the ocean."

He'd face the surf, plant his feet wide, all lean limbs and spiky hair and shiny skin. "Watch." He'd raise his arms, palms flat forward, a wave bearing down on us. "Stop!" he'd yell in his deepest voice. "I command you to stop!"

And for a second I'd think he could do it. I'd think the wave would freeze in its curl, cartoonlike in its obedience to my brother's power. But then it would be on us, tumbling our bodies under its smack, daring us to find our legs again.

"Stop!" he'd order the second one, arms out, like a traffic cop. "Stop! You will stop now!" But that one wouldn't stop either, and then, hurrying before the next hit, he'd pull at my shoulder, lining me up right next to him. "Anna," he'd say. "You've got to help." So I'd plant my feet wide, just like his, and throw out my palms, and I'd shout at the next wave, "Stop! Stop!"

And the two of us, blue-lipped and drenched, worn out and determined, would yell over and over and over, wave after wave after wave, "Stop! We command you to stop!"

6

THEY LET ME SLEEP LATE ON MONDAY. I SLEEP HARDER AND deeper than usual. When I wake up, I'm so groggy it takes a while for me to figure out that the heaviness in my blood and the dread in my chest are because two nights ago I killed somebody. *Cameron Polk is dead.* And Ellen. Jack.

My eye is killing me. I sit up in bed, peel off the spaghetti strainer, and reach for the eyedrops. It's hard. I miss a few times with each bottle, and the liquid drips coldly down my cheek.

Things are clanging downstairs. Silverware drawer opening and closing, dishes dropped into the sink. I press the shield back into place, drag myself out of bed, and pull on jeans and a zip-up sweatshirt.

My parents are in the kitchen drinking coffee and wiping instant-oatmeal dust off the table.

"Don't you have classes?" I ask my mother. I rub my left eye. It has tons of crust in the corners. Gross.

She reaches to hug me. "Never on Mondays." She holds on for a long time, careful of my right eye. It's strange but good, like when she held me in the hospital bed. It's not that we don't get along, so much as we're not that close, I guess. The truth is, before yesterday I don't remember the last time we touched. "Just office hours," she's saying now, sipping at her mug. "Which I've cancelled."

She teaches Web design and computer skills at the community college. She always gets the highest marks on her student evaluation forms at the end of each semester. She has Jack or me look at them and give her the results because she says it's only a matter of time before her luck changes and they all start to hate her.

I wander over to the kitchen table, near my father. "I thought Russell was incompetent."

My dad works in finance. He invests other people's money, and he has this male secretary who he doesn't much like and who he thinks is going to accidentally bankrupt the clients and ruin us all forever.

"Russell is incompetent," my father says. "Which is why I'm going to work." He checks his watch. "In about five minutes. I just wanted to see you first."

"Here I am," I say. And then I want to cry, but my father doesn't like crying, so I look away. Still sitting, he pulls me in by the waist and doesn't say anything, which makes not crying harder.

"Why don't you just fire Russell?" I ask into the air over his head. It's an old question. It feels good to ask it, like everything's normal, like today's just another day. My father releases me.

"Because everybody's incompetent," he says. "And I'd rather deal with familiar idiocy than with unfamiliar idiocy." It's what he always answers, and it helps me pretend that my hands aren't trembling and that I'm not sore all over and that I didn't kill anyone.

"How does your eye feel?" my mother asks. Which begins to ruin my pretending.

"Like it has a toothache," I tell her.

"We leave for the ophthalmologist in half an hour."

"Okay," I say.

"Then we'll see if you can visit Ellen." Now my legs are trembling a little too. I sit down and cross my legs and arms, try to hold everything still.

"Can I go wake up Jack?" I ask.

"No," they both say, right at the same time.

Dr. Pluto is all business.

"Hyphema," he tells me and my mom. He looks more like a football player than an ophthalmologist. His whole head is shaved, and he's huge. When he puts my face in this vise, his hand palms my head the way I'd palm a tennis ball.

"Are you still here?" I ask the room. Because I can't turn my head now.

"Behind you," my mom says from behind me and to the left. I didn't care if she came in or not. She wanted to, though.

First Dr. Pluto uses this machine to shine a vertical yellow light right at my eye.

"This is called a slit lamp," he tells me, even though I didn't ask. When he's done with that, he puts a drop in my eye, tells me the next procedure won't hurt, and fiddles with the vise a little.

"Does that feel okay?" he asks.

"I guess," I say. I mean, my head is in a vise.

Now it's a different machine. It moves closer and closer and closer, until it touches my eyeball really fast and there's this beautiful bright blue light everywhere, and then it's done.

"I'll need to see her every day to monitor the pressure and to make certain there's no rebleeding," Dr. Pluto tells my mother while she helps me get the strainer back on. "A hyphema is really just blood in the anterior chamber. It's a tear in the eye, probably from the air bag."

My mom asks him something, but I stop paying attention.

The air bag. The smell of new plastic. *"Hooow looong, hoow loong, hoow loong . . ."* Screaming, stopped.

Ellen's mom owns a women's clothing store called Cinnamon Toast. According to the tags of speckled brown paper on each item, Cinnamon Toast specializes in flowing styles and natural fibers. Usually Mrs. Gerson is wearing something in flowing style and natural fiber, and today is the same as always. Muted green slacks and a pale lavender blouse. She reaches for my face as soon as I walk into the fifth-floor waiting room. She cups my cheeks in her palms.

"That thing is awful," she tells me, meaning the shield, and she pulls me into lavender. "I'm so glad you're all right." She smells like Ellen's house: lemons and perfume. It's nice but embarrassing to be in her arms, so I ease away after a second.

"Are you all right?" Ellen's father asks, holding me, straight armed, by the shoulders and staring at my face. Aching in my eye. Aching in my throat.

"Yeah," I tell him. His eyes are swollen and bloodshot. "How's Ellen?"

"Well," Mrs. Gerson answers in this bright, fake voice. "She's got a tube in her mouth to help her breathe, a tube in her chest to reinflate her lung, an IV for antibiotics, an IV for pain, a catheter to help her pass water, a cast on her leg, and nothing for her ribs. They'll heal on their own."

"A collapsed lung is bad, right?" I say. Mrs. Gerson's attitude is confusing me. It doesn't match Mr. Gerson's face.

"She's going to be fine, Anna," Mrs. Gerson tells me. I see a nurse behind that long counter glance up and try to make eye contact with her, and I see her refuse to make eye contact back. That starts me shaking so hard both of the Gersons notice. Ellen's mom takes my hands and rubs them.

"She's going to be fine," she says again, loud.

"I'm really sorry." My teeth are chattering again. My eye radiates ache through my head. "I'm really, really sorry."

"It's not your fault," Mr. Gerson says. "They say there was a tree branch. Cameron must have swerved to avoid it."

A tree branch. I hadn't heard that yet. But if Cameron swerved to avoid a tree branch, couldn't I have swerved to avoid Cameron? I start to think about the alcohol and how drunk I was at first, and then how drunk Ellen was.

"Ellen doesn't have a drinking problem or anything," I tell them. "I mean, sometimes this year she would get pretty drunk at a party, but only twice." Oh my God. She's going to kill me for telling them this.

"Okay," her father says to me. His red eyes start welling up.

"We were always careful, though," I go on. I can't seem to

help myself. "We always were with each other, and we never drank with anybody we didn't know." Well. Almost never.

"Okay," Mr. Gerson says again. His eyes are all wet, but he doesn't cry.

He works for the same bank as my dad, only in some other area. Something higher up, I think. I don't know. They don't ever see each other at work. They have totally different responsibilities. And even though Mr. Gerson's got some big job and isn't a teller, I suddenly imagine how calm he'd be during a robbery. Some guy with a stocking over his head would be pointing the gun right at Mr. Gerson, and Mr. Gerson would just face him squarely, all steady.

"And she doesn't do drugs or anything, and it's not like she needs to drink when we go out. She doesn't do it at every party." Which, now that I hear myself saying it, might be sort of a lie.

"Okay," Mr. Gerson says a third time.

"Don't be mad at her," I tell them. When I say that, Mrs. Gerson starts to nod, but then her face collapses like Ellen's lung, and she's crying, and seeing Mrs. Gerson afraid is almost as shocking as Cameron Polk being dead.

"It's okay," Mr. Gerson tells her. He turns from me to face her. "It's okay."

He sounds like that policeman from the accident: "Okay. Okay. Okay. Okay." But it's not okay. Nothing is okay.

The Gersons let me see her for ten minutes. They leave the room for five.

"I called you," I tell Ellen. That whooshing sound would put me to sleep if it weren't paired with all those tubes and things, snaking right into her body or disappearing under the blanket. Today her left leg is over the covers. There's a bright white cast from just above her knee all the way to her toes.

"I left a message. Actually, I left eight. Did you get them?" I know she didn't because cell phones aren't allowed in hospitals. There's no phone in here. She can't talk anyway, with that tube in her mouth.

Her hair is dirty. It looks like somebody brushed it, but it really needs a shampoo.

"Pretty soon it's not going to be cell phones anymore," I say. She makes a sound, and I lean forward to listen better, but then she stops. I notice this other machine. A squarish clear plastic box with water in it. The water is making all these bubbles. I can't figure out what it's for.

"It's going to be these little chips that get implanted behind our ears. I read about it just now, while I was waiting to have my eye checked out. They didn't have any *People* magazines, so I had to read *Scientific American* instead. Actually, I didn't really read it. Mostly just the headline. Things are blurry up close with my right eye. But I'm allowed to use my left one. And TV is okay."

Ellen opens her eyes, and I move to where it seems like they're focusing, but by the time I adjust my position, they're closed again.

"No school for a week," I say. "I'm supposed to stay really still, and I have to wear this shield thing when I'm asleep and in a car." Now she moans. Definitely a moan. She moves her head a little. "El?" I go. She's still again. "I'm supposed to try not to sneeze," I say. "If I sneeze, it might tear inside my eye again, and then everything gets worse. Only, once you have to sneeze, it's impossible to stop yourself, you know?" She opens her eyes and looks straight at me. "El?" She stays looking at me. "Hi, Ellen," I tell her. I move closer. She keeps her eyes open for a second longer, and then she's gone again.

"I was thinking I should send Cameron's parents a letter or something," I say, listening to the whooshing and watching the bubbles in that plastic box. "That's what you think I should do, right?" I wait, and I hear the screaming, stopped, and try to shake it out of my mind. "My father is being slightly less of an asshole." I walk nearer to her bed. I touch her cast, by the ankle. It's hard and cold. "I'm going to write something on this," I tell her. I look around for a pen. There's one attached to a clipboard hanging from a peg on the door. I slip it off and think about what to write. I think and think and think, and I'm still thinking when the Gersons walk back in.

"I can't think of anything to write," I tell them when they see me at the edge of the bed with the ballpoint in my hand.

"How could you?" Mrs. Gerson says as if it's an argument and she's taking my side. She hands me a cup of coffee. I don't really drink coffee, but I like the heat in my palms. "For God's sake."

My mom and I get lunch out after the hospital, and she keeps touching my hand or my arm or some part of me, which is still so different from our usual, and we don't say a whole lot, which is the same as our usual, and she drives really, really slowly on the way home.

We don't get back until about three. Jack is in the family room, watching TV. Not watching a movie on DVD. Watching an actual television show. I walk in, my chest hot and pounding, and then I notice Rob is here.

"Hi," I say.

Rob nods. He's not a big talker.

"Thanks for coming over, Robert," my mother says, stopping in the family-room doorway. She stares at Jack, slides her palm along my arm, and then walks away.

"Why are you guys watching TV?" I ask. I can see the TV fine with my left eye. The throbbing is still pretty bad, though. It passes through my head like a steady wave.

Rob shrugs.

"You hate TV," I tell Jack. He picks up the remote and aims it at the screen. The TV goes black. Now my brother looks at me. I want to say things, but it's hard with Rob here. He's staring at my eye. He points to it and tilts his head.

"It's called a shield," I say.

"Why are your teeth chattering?" Rob asks next. His voice is really deep. I always forget how deep it is.

"They're not chattering," I lie, and then I clamp my jaw tight to stop them from doing it.

Jack's still looking at me. I guess I'm going to have to ignore Rob.

"Jack," I go. "I . . ."

He just looks.

"I didn't have time. I mean . . . I didn't even see her when . . ." Rob's face is turning red. Jack's face stays exactly the same. Why doesn't Rob just leave?

"Jack," I try again. But the words won't come.

Jack looks back at the still TV. "I'm glad you're okay," he says. His voice is as blank as the screen.

• • •

Cameron was good for us. I didn't get it then, but even from the first time I really met her, she helped Jack and me. It was just some school-day afternoon, right after they started going out. It wasn't any big deal.

"Oh my God," I yelled, throwing my hands over my ears. The kitchen looked like a war zone. "What happened?"

Pots and pans and flour and chocolate splotches and bunched-up dishrags and eggshell slime all over the place. Plus the smell of something burned, and what looked like soil sprinkled all over the kitchen floor, and some horrendous, unbelievably earsplitting music.

"Hi!" Cameron called to me. She was on her knees trying to sweep up the soil with the edges of her hands. "I'm Cameron!" As if I didn't know. "You must be Anna!"

Jack clomped in from the family-room side of the kitchen, hauling the vacuum cleaner. He was moving his mouth along with what I guessed were supposed to be lyrics. He stopped clomping and lip-synching the second he saw me. Then he was saying something, but I couldn't hear a word.

"What?"

He tried it again.

"What!"

Jack dropped the vacuum cleaner and hit the stop button on the CD player. I lowered my hands from my ears, and Cameron stood up.

"What happened?" I asked again in a normal voice.

"We're making a chocolate cake," Cameron said. Then she laughed. Not giggled. Laughed. One of those big, joyful, from-your-gut kinds of laughs. It was totally contagious. Well, it would have been with anybody other than Jack and me. He stood there looking bummed. I stood there feeling awkward. Cameron stopped laughing.

"Since when do you bake?" I asked Jack.

"Since today," he told me. "Weren't you going to the mall with Ellen?"

"We went," I told him.

"That's going to be much better," Cameron said about the vacuum cleaner.

"Did you drop a plant?" I asked them.

"We dropped the cake," Jack said.

"That's sweet," Cameron said. "Your brother is so sweet. *I* dropped the cake."

"Was it burned?" I asked. "It smells like something got burned."

"The first one burned," Cameron said. Then she started laughing again. "We kind of forgot about it, if you know what I mean."

Jack turned red. I think I did too.

"So. Good-bye," he said to me. He flicked the CD player back on. I clamped my hands over my ears again, and right away Cameron leaned over and turned it off.

"What's that about?" she asked Jack.

"What?"

"Can't your sister hang out with us?"

Jack and I both looked at her like she had four eyes and antennae.

"Now?" Jack asked.

"Um. Yeah," Cameron said. I didn't know what to do. On

the one hand, I really wanted to hang out with Cameron. On the other hand, that meant hanging out with Jack.

"We don't really hang out," I said finally. "Not since we were little kids." She curled a strand of shiny blond hair behind her left ear and then kept her fingers on her earlobe.

"Seriously?" she asked. It was embarrassing. All of a sudden I felt like there was something really wrong with us. Maybe Jack felt that way too, because he started humming. Just like my father does when he's tense. I guess Cameron heard a tune somewhere in there.

"Bid List?" Cameron asked him.

"Yeah," he said, smiling. It was this smile I sort of knew but sort of didn't. It reminded me of when he was a lot younger. "You know Bid List too?"

"I'm telling you," Cameron said. She was finished fiddling with her ear. "You better get into UCLA. Everybody in California likes the music you like."

"Nobody here has ever heard of it," I told her.

"That's what Jack says."

"Yeah, well. He's right." He looked at me, and I looked at him. Cameron looked at both of us and went to work on her earlobe again. Her left one.

"You're probably not as different from each other as you think you are," she told us.

"We're pretty different," Jack said. What was that supposed to mean?

"I'm not sweet," I told Cameron. "According to Jack, I'm small."

"Sometimes," he added.

She turned her back on us to start washing a cake pan at the sink.

"You guys even look alike," she said. "Except for the hair." We don't look anything alike. He's all dark skin and eyes and everything, and I'm orange and pale and blue.

"She's crazy," I told Jack.

"Hey," he said. But he was joking. "Don't call my girlfriend crazy."

She splashed water at him from the sink. Some of it splattered me. "Your girlfriend?" she said. "I have a name, you know."

"Yeah," I said to Jack. "She's got a name."

"You've got to vacuum, for that," Cameron told him. "I'll clear off the counters and start a new cake." She laughed again. "Third time's a charm. Anna, you wash."

So I swapped places with Cameron, and she let Jack put the music back on, only not so loud, and we all sort of did our thing in silence. When Cameron poured fresh batter into the pan I'd just cleaned, she said, "So, what's the deal?" She dipped a pink, pretty finger into the pan and then reached over to feed Jack, who had just stepped on the vacuum to turn it off. Oh my God. I looked out the window. I was not about to watch my brother lick cake batter off his girlfriend's finger. Off Cameron Polk's finger. "Do you guys hate each other or something?" she asked.

I waited awhile and then risked a glance at them. It seemed safe again. Jack was sitting on one of the counter stools, and Cameron was using the back of a spatula to spread batter evenly in the pan.

"Of course we don't hate each other," I said.

"You don't?" Jack asked.

"Do you?" I asked him back.

"Are you two kidding me?" Cameron said.

"No," we both said at the same time.

"It's Ellen. Leave a message. If this is Anna, try back in five minutes."

It's totally good to hear her voice, even though it's not live. I'm lying in my bed with my legs drawn up and one ankle resting across the other knee. It's late, and all my shades are down, and the only light in the room is the quiet blue from my cell phone. Before I would have my glow-in-the-dark key chain hanging off my big toe, and I'd be gazing at the earth. But that was before. It's lost now.

"Hi, Ellen. It's Tuesday. Everybody's totally psyched. They took that breathing tube out, which is a good thing. In a couple more days, after they're sure your lung isn't collapsed anymore, they'll take out the chest tube. I haven't been back to school yet. I'm bored out of my mind. Plus, I look like a cyborg with this shield thing I have to wear over my eye. Jack is freaked out. My father is being sort of nice and sort of not. After we went upstairs at Wayne's, I got really drunk and then you got really drunk and we were playing pool and then we were late, and I drove us home, and they say she swerved to avoid a tree branch, and it happened really fast, and I think you passed out right away. Your parents don't seem mad about the drinking. I told them not to be. You know it was Cameron, right? If they haven't told you, or if you think you dreamed it or something, it was Cameron in the other car. She died, Ellen. Just so you know. Call me as soon as you get this."

7

"YOUR BROTHER WAS REALLY GOOD," LISA GOES AFTER SHE HUGS
me, carefully, at my locker. The smell of shoes and hand lotion
and the sound of locker doors slamming make me feel a little
more normal than I've felt in a while. Maybe I'm not even
shaking all that much.

"Thanks," I say. Even though I was still just getting to know
her as of the night of the party, I'm really glad to see her now.

Dr. Pluto checks me every day with the tonometer—the
machine with the beautiful blue light. Last Friday he said
everything looked good enough that I could go back to school.
I have to wear the shield, though, and I have his note ordering
teachers to let me leave classes early so I can walk in quiet halls
and not get my eye whacked again by some joker tossing
around his backpack or a Frisbee or whatever. I decide I'll use

the note just sometimes. When I'm in a boring class. Like history, for example.

Jack started back last Thursday. Friday there was an assembly in honor of Cameron. Her funeral will be in California, where she used to live and where her parents have already returned. People are saying they couldn't stand to stay where she was killed. *Killed.*

Jack spoke at the assembly Friday. I only know that because my mother told me. Jack isn't not speaking to me exactly. But when he does, it's only for polite reasons. "Excuse me," he said yesterday as we brushed by each other going in and out of the first-floor bathroom. "Excuse me"? We'd never said "Excuse me" to each other in our entire lives.

"That memorial link to Rosebud Is a Sled is an amazing idea," Lisa tells me. Link? I don't know what she's talking about. I do know that Rosebud Is a Sled is Jack's movie review Web site. He designed it last year, and once I heard him tell Rob he'd gotten more than three thousand hits. I guess that means people actually use it. "Can he really get it ready that fast?" Lisa's asking me. "He said by next week."

"Yeah." I'm wondering how long I can get away with one-word responses before Lisa figures out that I don't know what the hell she's talking about.

"I'm not sure if I should post anything," Lisa's going. "I was thinking about it, except I didn't really know her. Then again, maybe I should just do a sentence or something so they get the five dollars." Five dollars? "Is Jack going to pick the charity the money goes to, or are Cameron's parents going to do that?"

"I don't know," I say. How could he have done that

already? How could he have thought of it and started it? "I think they're still figuring it out." How could the brother I saw less than a week ago on our front lawn–turned–psych ward have already spoken to the entire school and planned an entire link? An entire memorial Web site? I need to write a letter. I need to write Cameron's family a letter. Screaming, stopped. My eyes throb. Both of them.

"Are they letting people visit Ellen?" Lisa's asking me. Jason yanks at his lock across the hall, making sure it's locked, and then heads our way.

"Just family. She can talk now, but she's on serious drugs." Her parents said I could see her the day before yesterday, but when I got to the hospital, the doctor was there and he vetoed me for some reason.

It was weird to see the Gersons in the hospital but not to see Ellen. What made it weirder was the way the waiting room was decorated. It was strung with orange and black streamers and cardboard cutouts of black cats and broom-riding witches and a white ghost with big, friendly dimples. Halloween. I'd forgotten it was almost Halloween. I must have looked right at home with my robot eye.

"Hey," Jason goes, and he hugs me too. He has strong arms, and he holds on for more than a second. It feels good. "How are you?"

"Alive," I start to say, but, mortified, I stop myself and mumble some nonword instead.

"Does your eye hurt?" Jason asks, looking at my shield.

"No." I'm deciding right here and now that I won't complain again, ever, about anything that hurts me. That just seems like the right thing to do. If Cameron can't complain, why should I get to?

Everybody's quiet, and I don't like it. So I think of something to say. "Did you understand the math homework?" I ask Jason. He has precal fourth, and I have it fifth, but it's the same teacher. At our school if you miss a day, it's murder. I don't know how Ellen's going to catch up. I don't know how I am either. It's hard to read with just one eye.

"Not remotely," Jason says.

"Seth has been really worried," Lisa tells me.

Katy and Slater slide through the crowd of kids and walk over. Katy hugs me as if we've never stopped being friends. Is everybody going to hug me today?

"It's really good to see you," she goes. We nod in the halls this year, but we haven't really spoken at all.

"Thanks," I say. Her fingernails are polished black to match her lipstick, and she has a ring through her eyebrow. I'm nervous Lisa and Jason will think she and Slater are losers, which might make them think I'm a loser.

"That thing on your eye is excellent," Katy tells me.

"Tell Ellen we say hi," Slater adds. He's completely bald except for an orange tuft at the top center.

"Okay." I sort of just want them to go away, they're so weird. "I definitely will." They leave.

Lisa looks at me.

"Ellen and I were friends with them for a long time," I explain.

"Whatever." And then I feel bad because I think Ellen will be happy they stopped me the way they did, and I'm not happy about it and I know that's sort of mean, but I can't help it.

"You know where that guy is going to be ten years from now?" Jason says. He means Slater.

"Who cares," Lisa goes.

"In a manly office, in a manly business suit, with a manly haircut, and a thing for men."

"Slater?" I go. "You think he's gay?"

"I do," Jason says. I guess he should know, since he's gay himself. According to Ellen, anyway.

"Do you think he's cute?" It didn't occur to me that anybody would actually look at Slater these days.

"Ech," Lisa goes.

"He could be cute," Jason says. He eyes Lisa. You can tell from his look that he doesn't like how she's being bitchy. "You just have to see underneath."

I wonder for a second why I'm not worried what people think of Jason being gay, but maybe not everybody knows, and anyway, you can't tell that Jason's different just by looking at him, the way you can tell a mile away that Katy and Slater are complete outsiders. Besides, Jason doesn't go around being the gay guy. He just goes around being Jason.

"So, why is Seth worried?" I ask Lisa, noticing that my shakes are back somehow.

"He gave out the alcohol," Jason says. Lisa nods.

I cross my arms to try and hide the trembling. "But I wasn't drunk."

"Well, that's good," Jason goes. And he's right. If I hadn't been sober, all of this would be worse. A lot worse.

"Even if I was drunk, it wouldn't be Seth's fault."

"I know," Jason says, arching his left eyebrow. "But still.

I'm glad nobody has to deal with that." I'm glad too.

"He's coming now," Lisa says. "Stop talking about him."

The hall's emptied out a little. I think I heard the bell ring a second ago, but I wasn't really paying attention.

"Hi," Seth says. He looks right at Lisa. "I totally heard you."

"It wasn't your fault," I tell him, while Lisa turns red. Seth looks sort of surprised. He glances at Jason.

"She wasn't drunk," Jason explains.

"Plus, they're saying there was a cinder block in the middle of the road," Lisa adds, recovering. "Right, Anna? Cameron was swerving to avoid it."

"A tree branch," I say.

"Your brother was really good Friday," Seth tells me.

"That's what I heard."

I won't tell them. I won't tell anybody, except maybe Ellen sometime ten years from now. I won't tell them that when we got out of the car, home from the hospital, Jack wouldn't get up off his hands and knees. That he wouldn't stop dropping earth into the grocery bag. That he was picking up a lot more soil and new grass than leaves, and that my mother talking to him softly and my dad jabbering at him and me wailing like some kind of animal wouldn't budge him. I won't tell them that my father finally had to pull my brother up by his armpits and drag him into the house.

They're all staring at me. Seth puts his hand out like he's going to touch my shield, but then he stops.

"Does it hurt?" he asks me.

"Just looks weird," I say. "And my eye waters a lot."

"It doesn't look weird." He pats my shoulder.

"Didn't the bell ring?" I ask them.

Jason gives me a ride home. We're quiet practically the whole way. I notice a bunch of books scattered all over his backseat. Something called *I Am* and something called *Tragic Sense of Life*. Also, there's *From Socrates to Sartre* and *Man and His Symbols*. I've at least heard of that one.

"You're into psychology?" I ask.

"Philosophy," Jason goes. I know exactly nothing about philosophy.

"So, how did you and Ellen get to be friends?" I hate silence. It always makes me think there's something wrong.

"I liked the way she says things," he tells me.

"You mean the way she plays with words?"

"No," Jason says. "Not that. That's annoying, to tell you the truth."

"What do you mean, then?"

"She just seems like she's actually thinking some of the time."

I kind of get what he's talking about, and I kind of don't. And I want to ask him if he thinks it seems like I'm thinking sometimes. Only, I already know that probably he doesn't see me that way, and for some reason it matters, and I feel embarrassed.

"Thanks for the ride," I tell him.

"Any time."

When I walk into our house, my father's Tumi suitcase is packed and sitting by the mudroom door. Everybody's in the kitchen. I know Rob probably gave Jack a ride home, only Rob's car isn't out front, and Rob isn't in here.

"What's going on?" I ask them. My brother takes a gulp of chocolate milk straight from the bottle.

"Use a glass," my dad tells him. My dad never comes home early from work.

"Jack's going to California," my mother says. "Will you be okay here alone for a few hours? We're driving him to the airport." My dad never lets anybody use his luggage, either.

"Why are you going to California?" I ask Jack. He takes another gulp, so my dad answers for him.

"Your brother wants to pay his respects."

"Oh," I say. "Should I go?" They all look at me. "Oh." I guess not. Jack grabs the Tumi handle. "Are you coming back?" I ask him.

"Wednesday or Thursday," my dad says. "Depending." Depending on what?

"You'll miss more school," I say.

Jack doesn't look at me. He wheels the suitcase though the mudroom and then lifts it down the three steps into the garage.

"Take care, Anna," Jack says finally. It's way worse than "Excuse me."

Two weeks after Jack and Cameron started going out, I was sick. As a dog. My father thought it was food poisoning, and my mother thought it was the flu. My dad yelled at me for eating the half tuna sandwich he'd left out on the counter, which he'd forgotten to put in the fridge after he wrapped it that morning. He shook his head with amazement that anybody would eat a tuna sandwich not cold from the refrigerator. It didn't help.

I was in bed with the wastebasket nearby, too wiped to get up, but thirsty and hot and miserable. And then Jack walked in.

"Hi," he said.

"Where's Cameron?" I asked. They'd been joined at the hip.

"Helping her mom shop for her little brother's birthday party. You need anything?"

"Huh?" I just wasn't used to him going out of his way to be nice. Even with how much more it seemed like he was trying with me since the summer. I was still suspicious.

"Do you need anything?" he repeated.

"Um . . . some ginger ale maybe. And crackers."

He left and came back five minutes later with a tray. "Provisions," he said, putting the tray over my legs. I smiled. At the beach, when we were little, we used to play sailor underneath the houses. We'd pack plastic bags of crackers and pretzels and butterscotch candies, and we'd have bottles of water. Those would be our provisions—we loved saying that word—and we'd fight pirates and sea monsters and starvation on desert islands.

"Thanks." I sat up a little on my pillows and took a sip. "It must stink in here."

"Kind of," he said. "Want me to open some windows?"

"Yeah."

He started with the one over my desk. The fresh breeze felt good. When he was done with the other two, at the head of my bed, he sat on the floor with his back against my dresser.

My cell rang. I grabbed it and flipped up the top. It was Ellen. It kept ringing.

"It's Ellen," I told Jack. He just looked at me. Normally I'd answer it and forget all about my brother. But there he was being so decent to me, so instead I snapped the top down and let the cell drop onto my bed somewhere in the covers.

"Jack," I said. "I'm not trying to be mean or anything." I took a sip of ginger ale. He waited. "But . . . why do you think Cameron went out with you, in the first place?"

He sighed and looked out the newly opened window. I knew what he was seeing: a telephone wire, that big maple tree, and the streetlight. He started humming.

"What?" I wasn't trying to be rude. I was really wondering about it.

Jack stopped humming. "Nothing." He shrugged. "But you are really superficial."

I felt my face get hot. "What's that supposed to mean?"

"Listen," he said. "You just implied that there's something about me that is lesser than Cameron." I opened my mouth to argue, but he kept talking. "That's what I mean. You think about things that aren't important. Like who's got more status than the other person." I started feeling nauseous again. "And you make your decisions about that based on things like clothes and friends and where people sit in the lunchroom and who people hang out with. And if people aren't just like you, you think they're not worthy and that nobody else who matters to you thinks they're worthy. And so you write those people off." I thought I might throw up. "I remember when you weren't like that. I remember when you cared about things that mattered and when you weren't always sizing everything and everyone up all the time. And I liked you a lot then." He stayed where he was, leaning against my dresser, butt on the floor, knees up.

He wasn't giving me that disgusted look. He didn't have that disgusted tone of voice. He was really talking to me. Trying to tell me something. I sat there a long time, feeling smelly and nauseous and awful. I didn't know what to say. I just sat there. And so did Jack. We sat there and sat there. My phone rang again. I rummaged around in my sheets and flipped up the top. It was Ellen again. I didn't answer it. We sat there some more.

"So, how old is Cameron's brother?" I finally said.

"Nine on Thursday."

"Does Cameron like him?" I asked.

"A lot," Jack said.

"Do you like him?"

"He's a cute kid," Jack said.

We got quiet again.

"What are her parents like?" I asked.

"Her mother's really hyper all the time," Jack told me. "But not like Dad. She doesn't have to have everything be a certain way, and she doesn't yell at the drop of a hat. She just hovers a lot."

"Hovers?"

"Yeah. Hovers."

"Maybe because she knows you two are in love," I said. "Parents worry about that, right?"

Jack smiled. That big, wide smile. The one I used to know really well, which looked totally the same on his face now as it did when we were little.

"Yeah," he said.

8

"I'M CALLING ELLEN," I TELL JASON AND SETH AND LISA. WE'RE in the lunchroom.

"Again?" Lisa asks. "She's going to have about fifty messages from you the first time she checks her cell." It's Tuesday. Ten days since the accident.

"I don't think anybody would mind fifty phone calls from their best friend after they've almost died," Jason goes. He stares at Lisa with this look of his. It's not exactly a nasty look, just one that commands respect. Lisa blushes and bites into her pizza slice.

I dial the hospital number first. I've never gotten Ellen on that phone, but a couple of times a nurse answered and told me Ellen was too doped up to talk. This time it rings forever again, so I hang up and dial her cell. Call number seventy-three or something.

"It's Ellen. Leave a message. If this is Anna, try me back in five minutes."

"Hi, Ellen. I'm sitting here with Lisa and Seth and Jason at school. We're missing you and we want you to call as soon as you're feeling up to it. I snuck in—sorry, *sneaked* in—to see you the other day, and you were in your new room with practically no tubes or machines, and somebody had washed your hair and you didn't look too bad, and I wanted to write you a note or something on your cast, only there was no pen anywhere. Anyway . . ." Lisa and them are looking at me like I'm nuts. "The Ashleys keep saying hi to me in the hall, and Kevin and Trace called to ask how you were doing, and then they broke up and then got back together again. Lisa's getting a Mac instead of a Dell, and we're waiting for you to get out of the hospital so we can start an SAT study group, and did you know that Seth eats a different candy bar each week, like all week, and this week's is Caramel Crunch, and I've seen him eat three already, and it's not even twelve thirty? And there's a rumor starting that Jason and Sleev-eth are going out, only Seth swears he's not gay, and Jason swears that even if Seth was gay, Jason wouldn't date him for a million dollars, which is an interesting question. The question being, What would we each do for a million dollars?"

I hold my cell out to everyone. "Anybody want to leave a message?"

Lisa takes the phone. "Anna is crazy, Ellen, but you must already know that. Get better! We miss you!"

She hands it to Jason. "The only way out," Jason says, "is to simply observe." Then he passes the phone to Seth.

"Get well soon. We need you for vocabulary." Seth hands the phone back to me.

"Bye," I say.

"The social worker at the hospital suggested we get some counseling," my mother tells me.

I'm in the family room, channel surfing. I'm used to having one eye right now, only I'm just a little worried it's making me bend my head in a weird way.

"You don't need counseling, though, right?" my dad adds. They've sat down on the L of the couch next to me. They never sit on the couch in here.

"I don't know," I say.

"I think it's a good idea," my mother says.

"Really?" I'm not even sure what counseling would be like. "Why?"

"Right," my dad tells my mom. "That's what I think."

"The social worker thinks differently," my mom says.

"Did the social worker suggest Jack get counseling?" I ask.

"She suggested it for all of us," my mother goes. "But especially for you and Jack."

"Dad doesn't think we need to, though," I say. "Right?"

"I don't really see the point," my father says. "We go through difficult times. We live. We learn. We move on."

"If she wants to go," my mother says to my father, "she'll go."

"Right," my dad says. "If she really wants to."

"Does Jack want to?" I ask.

"We haven't asked him yet," my mother says. "We're waiting until he gets back."

I stay quiet. I'll do whatever they tell me to do. But I don't really care.

"All right, then." My father stands up.

"I think we should talk about this more," my mom says. He makes this huge, exaggerated sigh.

"It's fine," I say to my mom. To keep them from arguing. To keep him calm. "I don't really want to go."

Besides music Jack loves movies. Films, he would say.

"We're not watching this," I went one afternoon, years ago, as soon as I saw words on the bottom of the screen.

"But it's a classic," Jack said. "It's *The Four Hundred Blows*."

I was too young then to make an obscene comment about that title. But I was old enough to know it wasn't going to be as good as the top countdown on MTV.

"It's in French," I said.

"So?" Jack argued. "The French make really good movies. Just give it a chance."

"Watch it in your room, then."

"My screen's too small in there," he told me. "You have to see this stuff on a big screen."

"Mom!" I yelled. "Jack's hogging the good TV again!" Which wasn't even fair of me, because we'd already made a deal about whose day was whose.

"Work it out," she yelled back from her office upstairs.

"It's Thursday," Jack reminded me. Thursday was his. We'd agreed.

"But the top ten is a special today," I complained. "This month's mystery host is going to be on." I wanted to relax before dinner the way I wanted to relax. I couldn't explain why exactly, but I was in a bad mood, and it mattered.

"That's not a special," Jack said. "That happens every month. And it's never a mystery anyway. It's whoever won last month's vote. Just watch this with me. You might like it."

I hated those old movies. I hated subtitles. They make you work too hard. I didn't want to work.

"If I wanted to read," I told him, "I'd get a book."

And then I went to my room, mad at him and mad at the small screen on my dresser and just mad.

Later, at the kitchen table, my father said, "So, tell me something you learned today, Anna." Ever since I'd woken up, I'd had a feeling he might ask that night. You never knew exactly when he would, but it had been a bunch of days. You always had to be prepared. Only somehow, no matter how prepared you were, it never went well.

"Fractions," I said.

"What do you mean, 'fractions'?" my dad asked. "There's a lot of different elements to fractions."

"I learned that if you add fractions, you have to find the same numerator."

My father was serving himself rice. He stopped with the serving spoon in mid dump. "I hope you didn't learn that," he said.

My brain started blinking. "That's what we learned." I was pretty sure I was right, even though my father was already making it seem like I was wrong.

"I hope not," my father said. "Think about it." He put the serving bowl back down on its hot pad.

I felt my mind go fuzzy. "If you add fractions, you have to find the same numerator," I said again.

My father placed his fork on his plate, wiped his mouth with his napkin, and glared at me. "Why are you repeating the same incorrect information?" He had that irritated tone of voice. The tone that comes right before the mad one, and the yelling.

"That's what we learned," I insisted, only now I wasn't so certain, and the fuzziness got fuzzier.

"Harvey," my mom said.

"Think about it again, Anna," he ordered. "Put down your glass, straighten yourself up in your seat, and take a minute to think."

So I put down my glass without drinking, and then I couldn't think at all. I was sure I had it right. I remembered learning it and practicing it and planning that it was what I would say if he asked the question that night. Only, now it wasn't right.

"I'm thinking," I said. Was it a trick question? "But that's what I learned."

"She meant denominator," Jack mumbled.

"Why?" my father asked him. Jack looked down at his plate. The vein in my father's temple pulsed. "Why do you do it?"

Jack kept looking at his plate. I was so thirsty.

"You could see that I was trying to help Anna figure something out for herself, couldn't you?" my dad asked, only it wasn't a question. Jack looked up at him and then back down again. "Why did you interfere?" With my dad looking at Jack, I figured it was safe to pick up my glass. I did. I drank.

"Is this really necessary?" my mom tried. But Dad never listens to her.

"Well, what did you learn today?" my father asked Jack. "Since you're eager to share what you know."

I took another drink, glad he wasn't on me anymore.

"I learned that sometimes a script is better if there's not very much dialogue in it."

My father stared at Jack. "What?"

"Did you ever see *The Four Hundred Blows*?" Jack asked. "I learned that less dialogue is better from watching *The Four Hundred Blows* today, plus from watching some other films this week and thinking about it a lot."

"You watched another movie?" my dad said. "What have I told you about watching all that TV?"

"It wasn't TV," Jack said. "And I did my homework first."

"Did you watch it on a TV screen?" my father asked him. Jack nodded. "Then, it's TV."

"No," Jack said quietly. "It's not."

"Don't argue with me," my dad said. So Jack shut up.

I don't recognize the number on my cell caller ID. But I answer it anyway.

"A million dollars?" Her voice is soft, and the edges of it don't quite meet.

"Ellen!" I yell. I'm sitting in front of the TV on the L-shaped couch in the family room, not doing my SAT prep handbook.

"The problem with a million dollars," she tells me in that voice, "is that after taxes it's really only half a million." She still sounds like her, only way, way tired.

"Ellen!" I yell again. I picture her, sitting up maybe, in her hospital bed, a tan phone pressed to her ear.

"And half a million dollars really isn't that much money these days."

"How are you? How's your lung? How are your ribs? How's your leg?"

"My leg is really heavy. My ribs and the place where they had the chest tube is brutal if I laugh. I made this funny nurse leave this morning."

"Does everything hurt that much all the time?"

"Not so much. Painkillers."

"You drug addict."

"Yeah."

"You sound dreamy," I tell her.

"That's about right," she says.

"Everybody's asking about you all the time. Have you seen all the cards and stuff?"

"Yeah," she says.

"The bear is from Jason."

"Isn't it weird how much like Whitey it looks, only bigger?"

"Totally."

"Isn't Jason so cool?"

"Totally," I say again.

"I wish he wasn't gay."

"I know."

"How are you?"

"I don't know."

"How's Jack?"

"I don't know."

"Did your father have a conniption?"

"I don't know," I say. "You're fading."

"Yeah," she says. There's this silence. I can hear her breathe. Then she goes, "Ten million. Ten million would be a different story."

"Ten million?" I ask.

"I'd probably do just about anything for ten," she says, and suddenly I know for sure what Jason was talking about earlier. She's got this thinking tone of voice. This tone where she's taking an idea seriously, turning it over in her mind. Paying attention. "Yeah," she goes. "Anything. Except kill, injure, or molest somebody."

"I did that for free," I go, before I even realize what we've just said.

And then I start crying. So hard I don't make a sound. There's this long silence while I lose it. My SAT book slips off my lap and thunks onto the floor. "Are you still there?" I finally manage to choke out.

"Hmm, Anna," she says, and then I think she falls asleep.

9

WEDNESDAY NIGHT. ELEVEN DAYS SINCE I KILLED CAMERON.

I sit on the L of the couch and try to study. I have a biology quiz tomorrow, and I need to get a good grade on it. It's hard to focus. I mean, my right eye can't focus, obviously, because of the drops to keep my pupil dilated, but my brain has no excuse. *The key to speciation is reproductive isolation.* I've written it in my spiral, circled it, and starred it, so it must be important. I open up the textbook and try to find *speciation. The key to speciation is reproductive isolation.* Ms. Riffing gives us rhymes to help us remember. She puts tunes to them to help us more. She's a great teacher, and even though I don't like biology, I love her class. *The key to speciation is reproductive isolation. The key to speciation is reproductive isolation.* I hear my mother's footsteps on the third-floor stairs, heading down. I look at the clock. Twenty minutes have passed, and I don't know what the hell I'm reading.

"I can't concentrate," I tell my mom when she walks in. She sits on the edge of the couch.

"You're not worried about it, are you?" she asks. I don't know what she means by "it." Failing the quiz? My eye? What?

"A little," I say anyway.

"There's nothing to worry about!" That's my father, yelling from his spot at the kitchen table. It's where he likes to play poker online. He sets up his laptop and plays for hours. His favorite game is called Texas Hold 'Em. He plays for real money. He has a rule for himself that he's not allowed to keep playing if he loses more than a thousand dollars in one year. I don't know what he does with the money he wins. I don't even know if he ever wins. I just hear him cursing a lot and yelling at the screen.

"You're worried about Ellen, too, I guess," my mom goes.

"And other stuff." Things I can't say out loud to her because I don't have any practice saying anything important out loud to her. Like, *I killed somebody. How do you make the fact of something like that go away? How do you make the fact of something like that not nag and poke at you, like some kind of virus that's stuck in your blood, stuck in your cells, stuck in who you are and who you will be forever?*

"Would you leave her alone, please?" my father shouts from the kitchen again.

"I'm not bothering her," my mother calls back. "We're talking, Harvey." She says *talking* as if it's a word my father doesn't know the meaning of. Then she looks at me. "I'm not bothering you, am I?"

"Amanda!" my father yells while I shake my head. She's not bothering me exactly, but then again, I'm not used to her trying to talk to me so much either. We both hear my father stand up and start walking toward the family room.

"Well," she says, "come upstairs if you want. I'll be in my study." I never go up to the third floor. I think the last time must have been when I was about ten.

I hear her pass my father in the hall on her way to the stairs. She hisses something at him, and he snaps something right back, and when I can tell he's resettled himself with poker, I get off the couch and go up to my room.

I sit cross-legged on my bed, staring at a sheet of white stationery edged in silver. I'm trying to think of what to write to Cameron's family. I can't think of anything beyond *Dear Mr. and Mrs. Polk.* After that I just start to hear screaming, stopped, and I'm shaking so hard I don't think I could write a word anyway.

So I stand up and cross my arms tight and pace the room. I make three laps back and forth before the shaking slows down. I land in front of my mirror.

"Listen, Jack," I say to my reflection. My curls are tied back in a mass of metallic spirals, and my skin is so pale it's almost the same shade as the stationery. I don't have to wear the spaghetti strainer at home unless I'm sleeping, so I can see that my eye is almost back to normal except for a greenish tint to the skin around it and my enlarged pupil. "I can't believe that . . ." I stop. That sounds too fake or something. Plus, I never knew the left side of my mouth twitches when I talk. Ugh. "Jack," I say again, trying to keep my mouth moving evenly. "When I was driving home that night, I had no idea . . ."

I shut up and watch my reflection give me the finger. "Try it again, and come up with something decent," she tells me.

"Look. Jack," I try again. "You must be feeling . . ."

But it's too hard. How are you supposed to put into words something so awful there are no words for it at all?

I do a search on the Internet. There's a lot of sites for if you're dying. They give you links and medical information about what happens if you have this kind of cancer or that kind of heart condition, and what medications and operations you can have and your chances of getting any better. A bunch of other sites are for if someone you love dies. They're about mourning and grief. I read some of them, and it seems like nobody really knows all that much about it, even though they all have a lot to say. If you're mourning, it's like there's no rules about what you're supposed to feel when, or for how long. Sometimes you feel better if you can talk to other people who are also mourning, and sometimes that makes you feel worse. All the postings seem really confident, like they're the ones with the right answers, but then the next one will just as confidently say something totally different. I try to decide how much I'm mourning Cameron, and it's hard to figure out. She wasn't my sister, or even my friend really. I don't think I miss her exactly. It's more like I'm horrified every time I think of her, and I feel this dread and guilt that's a part of that ink in my blood all the time.

I think about forwarding some of the grief sites to Jack where he would see them out in California, but then I'm not sure if I should. So I don't. Instead I keep searching. These other sites come up about if you want to die. Some of them tell you all the reasons why you shouldn't commit suicide. Because you'll go to hell, which is worse than whatever you're unhappy about here on Earth. Because other people will be hurt and will miss you. Because it's wrong. Because you don't really want to die, but you just want help to feel happier. Then other sites tell you exactly all the different ways you can kill yourself. They tell you about the best way to hang yourself, the most effective method to slash your wrists, which pills to take if you're serious about dying. I don't like those sites. They make me nervous. Besides, I don't want to commit suicide.

Mostly I want to find out what you're supposed to do when you've killed someone else. What you're supposed to do for all the people who really loved her. And also what you're supposed to feel.

But I can't find any sites about that.

If I were Jack, I'd probably create one. Except I'm not him. I'm only me.

Somehow I fall asleep, and it feels like I've slept for hours, only when I wake up, on top of my comforter, the clock tells me it's forty-five minutes later.

I can't fall back asleep, and I can't concentrate on anything that requires my brain, so I decide maybe I'll clean. At least you don't have to think when you clean.

My parents collect glass. Blown glass. They have vases and paperweights and sculptures all over the house. I'll go around and dust them. When they're totally clean, the pieces by our windows change colors with the light somehow. Most of the them have a lot of orange and red in them. But the newer ones have more blue and purple. They're kind of cool.

I get myself downstairs and into the kitchen, rummage around underneath the kitchen sink, and find a relatively clean rag and some Windex.

My father doesn't say anything, but he does start to shuffle his real deck of cards while he stares at the laptop screen. He shuffles like a professional, making the cards whir and jump and fan without even looking at them.

"God damn it," he mutters. Then he starts to hum.

I start in the living room, where the most fragile pieces are. Spray and wipe. Wipe and spray. They're not so dusty to begin with, but I can tell they look better after I've gotten to them.

"What are you doing?" my dad finally calls to me.

"Cleaning," I tell him. I notice that if I slow my hand to stop a rag over the glass, my hand buzzes just the littlest bit, as if it were resting on the sill of a moving bus or train.

"Cleaning the glass?" my father asks.

"Yeah," I say. I imagine him cutting his deck of cards over and over and tapping at his mouse.

"Remember when Jack broke the bud vase?" he calls.

We were ten and eleven, and we were playing indoor baseball. That's when you pull the pom-pom off the tip of a knit cap, you make chair cushions the bases, and the fireplace is home plate. You bat with your palm, and you use ghost men. It's a good game when it's raining out, or when you're bored at night. We weren't supposed to be playing it because of the glass.

I was up. I smacked the pom-pom over Jack's head. He had to turn to chase it. I ran like mad to first and slid off it toward the blue armchair cushion for second. Rounding that, I slipped on the wood floor and grabbed at the window seat, trying to stop myself. The bud vase went down. And shattered.

"God damn it!" my father yelled from somewhere in the house. We heard his feet pounding the hallway above and then pounding the stairs. "That better not be glass!" He charged into the living room and saw us stuck, frozen. His face was pink. He scanned the room, taking in the cushions, the pom-pom lying innocently in the corner, the fragments of glass, like a kaleidoscope exploded.

"Did you do this?" he asked Jack. Instead of answering, my brother took a step forward and half leaned down. I stood very still, hoping my dad wouldn't ask me if I had done it.

"Stop," my father said. Jack straightened up fast.

"I was going to clean it up," he tried to explain. I held my breath, waiting for my turn.

"You don't clean broken glass with your hands," my father told him. "What is the matter with you?" Jack stood still again. My father stared at him, jaw muscle jumping. "What is the matter with you?" he said again. "I want an answer!" Jack stayed quiet. "What is the matter with you, Jack!"

"I don't know."

I started breathing again. Maybe my dad wouldn't notice me as much as Jack this time. You never knew.

"Harvey?" My mother had arrived at the living-room door. "Oh." She stared at the shards on the floor. She looked around the room, checking the paperweights and vases and sculptures. "The bud vase?" she asked.

My father pointed at Jack. "Don't just stand there. Get the broom and the dustpan." But then, before Jack could move, my father said, "What were you thinking?" Jack didn't answer. "What were you thinking?" my dad asked again. His eyes were wide open with lots of white showing, like the Black Stallion, upset. Jack stayed quiet. "I'm asking you a question, Jack. What. Were. You. Thinking?" That vein in his forehead started hopping.

"Harvey," my mother said. "Calm down." I inched toward

the door. I wanted to get to the hall, the stairs, my room. Away from my dad, away from his making you feel stupid and wrong.

"I'd like to know what he was thinking!"

Tears began to bloom out of Jack's eyes. My mother's mouth set itself into a thin line. She couldn't do anything. I inched farther.

"Stop it," my father said. He hates crying. "Stop it now." Jack's tears didn't stop. My father shook his head and snorted through his nose. "Get the broom."

About an hour later Jack banged through my closed door and marched right up to me. I was leaning against two pillows on my bed, braiding beads into my hair and trying to stay invisible. He was sweaty and tearstained. He didn't say a word. He just punched me hard twice in the arm. Really, really hard.

"Dad," I call back into the kitchen. I tuck the Windex under my arm and shake out the wet rag. "Jack didn't break that vase."

I hear him drum his fingers on top of his deck. "Okay."

"Okay?" I stay where I am and keep talking loud so he'll hear me. "Did you just say 'okay'?"

"Anna, I'm in the middle of a game."

"But what does 'okay' mean? Did you know that he didn't break it?"

"I don't know. Probably. I don't really remember."

I walk over to stand in the kitchen doorway. He's got his feet up on the seat of a chair and his laptop propped on the lazy Susan, which is so old it doesn't spin anymore. "Why did you punish Jack and not me?"

He sighs and keeps his eyes on the screen. "I didn't punish Jack," my dad says.

"You yelled at him," I remind him.

"Yelling isn't punishing," my dad says. I can see his eyes moving across the screen.

"Yes, it is." I know that what I'm saying is true. I'm sure of it.

"No." He taps his mouse and looks up. He lifts his glasses to rest on the top of his head. They get buried in his hair. It looks stupid. "Yelling is just being angry. Punishing is giving a consequence. Like docking allowance or TV."

"But you made him stay and help you clean it up, and you didn't make me."

"I remember both of you helping to clean it up."

"I didn't help."

He lowers his glasses. "Anna, please. This isn't a good time for either of us to have this sort of discussion. Understand?" He looks down at his deck of cards and then back at me. I can see him working to keep the irritation out of his voice. "You're trying to have a quiet night after a difficult week. I'm trying to also. I'd like to play some poker. Do we have to have this conversation?"

"You brought it up."

"No, I didn't."

"Yes, you did. You said, 'Remember when Jack broke the bud vase?'"

"Fine," he smiles a strained smile at me. "Okay. But now I want to go back to my game." He clicks himself on and drops one of his legs off that chair.

"Yelling is punishing," I tell him.

"Hmm," he goes, scanning the screen. On it clusters of cards pop up, surrounding a green poker table.

"Dad," I say. "Yelling is punishing."

10

JACK GETS HOME WHILE I'M IN SCHOOL ON THURSDAY. WHEN I
see him, he's not as blank or stiff as he was before. He's sitting
cross-legged on his bed, clattering away at his laptop.

"Writing another movie review?" I ask him.

"Yeah." He doesn't stop typing while he's talking.

"What's it called?" I ask.

"*Eternal Sunshine of the Spotless Mind.* I watched it in the hotel."

But I'm not really interested in his movie review. "How was
the funeral?" What a stupid question. How was the funeral?
How about, *It sucked, Anna.*

"In the words of Cameron's little brother," Jack says, looking
up, "not what I expected." And then he goes back to his keyboard.

It's almost dinnertime on Friday. I'm in the Gersons' downstairs
guest room waiting for Ellen to get home. I took her pillows and

comforter and her stuffed animals and vanity table and all her clothes and the little round crystal hanging in her window and her TV and everything from her bedroom, and I tried to set it up exactly the same down here. And I fixed up the guest bathroom. I took all her grapefruit shampoo and conditioner and kiwi bath oil and body scrub and arranged them by the sink along with her Sonicare toothbrush. I set up her crutches by the bed, and I'm just wondering how she's going to shower with the cast on her leg, when the Gersons wheel her in.

"Surprise." I give her a hug. Which, as I already know, is hard to do when one person's in a wheelchair.

"This looks terrific," Mrs. Gerson tells me, meaning the room, and then she and Mr. Gerson leave, saying something about getting Ellen food or ice chips.

"Wow," Ellen goes, looking around. She's way pale. There's a scab on her cheek where that bandage used to be, and her hair seems longer.

"You lost weight," I tell her. She's pretty thin to begin with.

"Yeah. Hospitals are great for that." She eyes my shield.

"You like it?" I ask her.

"You look like C-3P0." It could be worse.

"I brought homework and movies and ingredients for chocolate-chip cookies, or we could call Jason and those guys, and they said they would come over."

Ellen closes her eyes for longer than a blink and then opens them. "Actually," she says, "I'm pretty tired."

"Oh," I go, feeling stupid.

She wheels herself over to the bed. "I kind of want to take a nap."

"All right."

"Um," she goes. "I'm sick of my mom. Could you help me?"

She shows me how to help lift her from her chair onto the bed. Her leg is heavy and clumsy. We have to sit her on the edge of the bed first and sort of lean her back. Then I have to lift her cast up after the rest of her. She winces and her face grits itself in pain.

"Aagh." I think it's her ribs more than her leg, but I'm not sure, and I don't know what to do. Ellen does, though. She lies still for a bunch of seconds, and then her face relaxes. "Thanks for remembering Whitey." She picks up her polar bear. She's had him on her pillow since she was born. He's all worn out and gray looking now. She rubs him across her chin. "Thanks," she says again, yawning and then immediately wincing. About a minute later she's asleep.

I wake up to my own voice. I'm making this moaning, calling sound. It's still coming out of my mouth as my light snaps on, and then my father and Jack are standing at the foot of my bed.

"Stop it, Anna," my father's saying. "Stop it now."

My blankets are all over the place. The back of my tank top is sticking to my skin. I'm shaking. The eye shield is falling off. My mother rushes in.

"Anna?" She sits on the edge of my bed and puts her hand to my forehead.

"She had a nightmare," Jack says.

"You're all right," my father tells me.

"She's trembling," my mother says.

"She's fine." His gray hair is in complete bed head. He touches my sweaty shoulder. "You're fine," he says again.

"I'm fine," I say. My father leaves, and Jack snaps off the light. You can still see, though, from the light in the hallway.

I'm in my room, not on Ocean Road. I'm in my room, not in the street with Ellen in my lap and a ponytail, sharp as glass, in my eye. I'm in my room, not out in the middle of the road, huddling near Jack, who's huge as a giant, tree trunk legs planted wide and firm, tree limb arms and branched hands raised up and out. I'm in my room, not in the darkness with policemen and screaming, stopped. I'm in my room, I'm in my room, I'm in my room.

"I need water," I say. Jack gets it for me. I wait, the shaking slowing down while my mom sits close.

"Thanks," I tell Jack after I take a swallow.

"You're welcome," he says.

There was this one night, back when we got along. That year's beach house was called Porpoise Swim. I had run into my room to pull on jeans and a sweatshirt, even though it was so hot out. I hate bug spray and won't use it. I could hear my family's voices clear as anything as they trooped down the stairs from the upper deck, under the house, and out to the driveway.

"And then they cut to something else," I heard Jack saying, "and then they slice up her eyeball, only it's a special effect, so it's not really her eyeball."

"That's disgusting," I heard my mom go as I pulled the hood of my sweatshirt up. Mosquitoes will get your ears if they can't get anything else.

"Really, it was a cow's eye, except you couldn't do that today because of animal rights and all," Jack explained. It sounded as if they had reached the bottom of the stairs. "You never heard of it?"

"No," my mother said.

"But it's famous," Jack told her. "They're showing it at the museum next Saturday. Could we go home a day early so I can see it?" I walked down the hall toward the great room.

"You know we don't leave until Sunday," I heard my dad say. Then he went, "Is that dripping?" He meant the outdoor shower underneath the house, where we were supposed to rinse the sand off before we came upstairs and inside. It was always dripping. "Damn it," my father said. "It is."

"Yeah, but it would just mean leaving one day early, and you can't rent it." It sounded like they were almost at our driveway. I stepped out onto the deck through the sliding glass doors.

"We're not leaving one day early so you can see *Anderson's Dog,*" my father said. I could see the flashlight beams bouncing around out near the street. "Anna!" my dad called as I stepped onto the top stair.

"It's *Andalusian,*" I heard Jack say. "Not *Anderson's.*"

"Turn the shower all the way off when you come down!"

My father had been standing right there looking at it. Why couldn't he have turned it off?

"Whatever it's called," my father told Jack, "we're not driving back a day early for it."

They were all the way out of our driveway and down the street by the time I got to the dripping shower. I could see them stepping in and out of one another's shadows. I reached for the little blue on-off wheel, bent down, and twisted it to the right. And in that exact moment there was this flash of light and something hit me hard, and then I was on my back on the sandy ground at the edge of where the driveway began and the underneath of the house ended. A crash of thunder. More lightning streaking the sky. Another bang. And then driving rain.

By the time Jack and my parents were back under the house with me, I was sitting up, moving each arm and leg one by one to make sure I wasn't half dead, or something. My heart was pounding. I couldn't believe that a second ago I had been leaning under the dripping shower, and now I was sitting all the way over here. I couldn't believe how fast it had happened. How I hadn't even had time to scream.

"I think I just got hit by lightning," I told them. They were soaked.

"What?" My father was frowning at the exposed stairs, probably trying to figure out how to get up them without getting more drenched.

"I mean," I said, "I didn't get hit exactly, but my hand was on the metal thing for the shower. Maybe lightning hit the house and it went into the metal, and since my hand was on it—"

"Anna, I'm dripping wet," my father said. "What are you talking about?"

"Mom," I said, I thought I was okay. Nothing hurt exactly. "I think I got electrocuted or something."

"Are you all right?" she asked.

"I don't know," I told her. "It was really weird."

"Can you move everything?" my father asked. He'd finally looked at me.

"I think so," I said.

"Are you burned anywhere?" He walked over and touched my head, my arms, my back. My mother looked too, over his shoulder.

"I don't think so," I said. He stepped away and began squinting at the rain and the stairs again. "But it knocked me all the way over here."

"Anna, it couldn't have knocked you that far. Come on, now. Don't exaggerate."

"I'm not," I told him. "It really—"

"I'm making a run for it," my father interrupted. My mom glanced at me and followed him up. Jack stayed where he was.

"Did you really get electrocuted?" he asked.

"I swear," I said. Why didn't they believe me? I don't make up stuff like that.

"What did it feel like?"

"Like you tackled me."

"Really? Let me see your hand." We both looked at my hand. Maybe it would be black. But it wasn't. "You were just touching this?" Jack asked, and he pointed to the blue on-off wheel.

"Yeah," I said. "Right when that first big lightning happened."

"Cool."

"It kind of scared me." As soon as I said that, I started to cry, which was embarrassing.

Jack looked away while I pulled my fist across my eyes. He waited awhile before he said anything. "Are you okay?"

"Yeah." I sniffed.

He watched me finish sniffing. "Maybe you'll end up with special powers."

"You mean like a superhero?" I asked.

"Yeah." He walked to the space underneath the deck, where there was more height. "Like that. See if you can fly."

"I can't fly." I followed him.

"Just see." He made a scoop out of his hands, lacing them

together, palms up, and locking them. "I'll give you a boost." So I backed up to him and stepped my right foot into his scoop.

"One," Jack said. "Two. Three!" He threw me upward, and I leaped and fell right back to the ground.

"Nope," I said.

"Nope," he said back. "It's still cool."

"Do you think I'm okay?"

"Yeah. You're fine."

"What's Andalusian?" I asked him. He thought about it.

"I forget," he said. "Either that, or I never looked it up in the first place."

After they leave, and it's dark in my room again, and I'm sipping from the water Jack brought, I think about all that. I don't know why exactly. But I remember how it felt like I'd been hit by a truck, and I remember how scared I was when my parents didn't get it. And how Jack didn't mind that I cried, and then made that step for me out of his hands to see if I could fly, even though we were both too old to really believe I would. I don't know exactly why I'm thinking about all this, except it has something to do with how Jack brought me the water just now. He filled it three-quarters full so it would be enough, but not so much that I'd spill, and he waited to let go of his grip on the glass until he was sure I had it firm in my shaking hands. He was the one in the nightmare trying to stop something terrible from happening, and he was the one in real life double-checking that my hand wasn't blackened, burned to a crisp, and letting me feel scared without minding.

11

JASON AND SETH AND LISA AND I TAKE TURNS MAKING SURE
Ellen gets to and from classes okay. She'll be in her chair for at
least another two weeks, and she moves really, really slow. When
we're just sitting around, Jason massages Ellen's earlobes.

"That feels so completely amazing," Ellen goes every time he
starts. You can see just how amazing in her face, and I don't
think it's only because she has such a thing for him. Her eyes
and her cheeks and her whole face and neck relax.

Sometimes, out of the blue, she'll wince, as if someone's hit
her, and then she'll hold really still for a few seconds.

"It's not my leg so much as the ribs," she tells me the third
time it happens. "And especially by my boob, where that
goddamn chest tube went in."

Technically I'm supposed to be wearing my strainer in

school, but I'm not following that particular rule anymore. Yesterday at Dr. Pluto's I had a gonioscopy. He put some sort of special contact lens in my eye and then vised my face and used the slit lamp to look at things. The blood was totally gone, he told me, and the tear was tiny and basically healed. I have to take atropine—that's the drops to keep my eyes dilated—for a few more days, and then I'm done.

"I'll see you in a week," Dr. Pluto said, palming my head.

Now Ellen and I are making our pathetic way through the humanities hallway. The only problem is, the armful of helium balloons Lisa tied to Ellen's chair keep popping and startling us, which is a pain in the ass, plus if Ellen jumps, her face grits itself in pain and she has to hold still for a while before she can move or talk or not look like she's dying.

"Lisa's not around, right?" Ellen asks.

I take a quick glance up and down the hallway, which is pretty crowded. "Yeah," I say. "I think she turned left for Spanish."

"Okay, stop," Ellen says. We stop. "Let's just pop the rest of these." There's three left. She pulls at one of the strings so she can reach a balloon. I pull at the other two.

"Got a pen?" she asks. I hand her a pencil. She stabs a few times, but the pencil is dull, the latex is tough, and Ellen's stabs are weak, I guess because of her ribs.

"What about a nail file?" I dig one out of my backpack side pocket. "Here." I stab at a red one, and it pops. A couple of kids jump.

"Excellent," Ellen goes. "I mean, no offense to Lisa. But do another one." So I pop another one. Some other kids yelp. Ellen starts gnawing on the strings.

"Wait, wait," I go. "Let me untie them." So she lets them go, and I start to untie. I'm good at that, actually. Any time somebody's chain gets knotted, they ask me for help.

"It's freezing," Ellen says.

"You're always cold," I tell her.

She yawns this huge, loud yawn and then winces. "Ow."

"You okay?" I ask.

"I'm just really tired. And then it hurts to yawn."

"It's your first day back," I remind her.

"I know," she says. "I just didn't think I'd be so tired."

She doesn't sound good. "Do you want to go home?" I ask. It's not like anybody's going to stop her. The teachers are being pretty nice to both of us. I can't remember the last homework I completed. And I've failed two tests and a quiz already—that biology quiz, actually—and everybody's let me take them over.

"Mostly it's that I keep thinking about Cameron," Ellen tells me. "You know?"

"Yeah," I answer. Only, I can't stand to think about it, so I say, "Can I pop the last balloon?"

"Go ahead."

I pop the last balloon. A few kids jump, and this one girl screams a very loud, very long scream, and the second she stops, I make this gasping sound, and then I think I'm going to vomit, only I don't, and I'm shaking so hard I drop my backpack, and Ellen's asking what's the matter, and I can't get my mouth to work, and Ellen's grabbing my hand and asking why it's all sweaty, and my heart is pounding and I think, *Oh, my God, I'm having a heart attack, but sixteen-year-olds don't have heart attacks,* and Ellen's telling me to stand up already, just stand up, and our biology teacher walks by and she's going, "Girls? Are you all right? Girls?" and she stays with us while I get my breath back and get my heart to slow and while Ellen sinks lower and lower into her chair with her eyes closed and these tears just sliding out of the corners and down her cheeks, and then Ms. Riffing checks with the junior-class vice principal and then calls Ellen's mom, who says we're like soldiers battling shell shock and we should both go right to bed, and drives me home.

Instead of getting into bed, I'm sitting at my desk, staring at the cover of my history book. I hear Jack's step, walking into the kitchen from the mudroom and then on the stairs, and he stops at my door. He takes the earphones out of his ears. I can hear squawking coming from them. I swear he's going to be deaf before he's twenty-one.

"Your friend Jason told me you and Ellen freaked out in the hall today before sixth period," he says. He needs a haircut, and he has this line between his eyes I've never noticed before, and the whites are sort of bloodshot.

"Did people see?" I ask. But I don't really care.

"I guess," he says. "Jason seemed pretty worried. That guy Seth was with him. They both went out of their way to find me."

"Oh," I say.

"They seem pretty cool, those two," Jack tells me.

"Oh," I say again.

"Do you want to go to Top Hats?"

"With you?" The idea of going anywhere with Jack is so strange I can hardly picture it.

"Yeah," he says. "I'm sick of being cooped up in this house."
Even though he just got home.

"How would we get there?" I ask.

"I heard Mom drive in when I was walking upstairs," he says.
We still have only one car. The Audi. "We could tell her we'll
pick up Dad from work." They're going to buy another Honda.
They're not sure if insurance will cover it, and my dad's been
yelling at a bunch of people over the phone about it.

"I'm really behind on my homework," I tell Jack.

"Bring it," he says. "I'll bring my laptop. We can hang out
there until dinner."

In the garage he hesitates on the third step from the mudroom. "Who's driving?" he asks.

"You," I tell him.

Dr. Pluto warned me that outside during the day without the
shield my eye may be sensitive to the sun. This is the first time
I'm trying it, and he's right. As soon as we're out of the garage,
I have to cover the eye with my hand. I haven't dug up my sunglasses yet. So I have to keep my hand there until we're inside
the diner.

I order onion rings and a Coke. Jack orders fish sticks and a
Diet Coke.

"Gross," I say about the Diet Coke. It's not like he's got a
weight problem. "How can you drink that?"

He shrugs. "I like the taste."

The waitress comes over to refill our water glasses, even
though they're still about half full. "Where's your friend?" She
remembers Ellen and me from when we used to come here all
the time.

"She broke her leg," I say.

"Same time you broke your eye?" the waitress asks.

"Yeah," I say, and I guess something about my face makes her stop asking me about it. Instead she goes, "This your boyfriend?" Jack snorts Diet Coke out his nose. Nice.

"My brother," I say. Jack's wiping himself off.

"Should have guessed," the waitress says as she walks away. "You two look alike."

It reminds me of when Cameron said that, and I wonder if it reminds Jack, too, when he sticks his earphones back into his ears and taps his iPod and won't look at me. Which makes me start to shake again. My wrists mostly, stuttering on the edge of the table.

"Jack," I say.

He picks up a fish stick, dips it in ketchup, and then puts it back on his plate.

"I just wanted to tell you that—"

"Don't," he interrupts.

"But I never really—"

"Don't, Anna!" he goes again, and he thumbs his iPod, scrolling up the volume.

I reach over and try to pull an earphone out of his ear. "After the accident I thought you—"

"Stop it!" He whips his head up and away from my hand. His face is thin. Like Ellen's. It's filled with that disgusted look, that one that tells me how unbelievably small I am.

"Okay." My chest is filled with ink. "Let's just go home."

I've barely even started my onion rings, but I put a twenty on the table, grab my backpack, and walk out. Jack's right behind me. He slides into the driver's side as I'm snapping on my seat belt one-handed so that the other can cover my right eye. Jack starts the car and smacks the CD player on, turning up the volume on some band he must love. After two seconds of driving I turn the volume way down. He turns it back up. It's a good ten minutes before I notice we're not going anywhere I recognize.

"Where are you going?" I ask. We should be home by now.

"Nowhere," he says.

"Why are you so mad?" I ask him.

"Why are you such a bitch?"

It digs this big black hole right into my gut, and there's nothing to say back. I just sit here, feeling inky and heavy and horrible, while Jack keeps driving.

"Do you even know where we are?" I ask.

"No," he says. Great. He takes an exit, and we start passing gas stations and fast-food restaurants.

"What music is this?" I ask.

"Spoonerism," he tells me.

"Spooner what?"

"Spoonerism."

We sit here and listen.

"Did Cameron like this song?"

"Yes. Shut up. I'm not talking about her with you."

"I wasn't trying to get you to."

"Yes, you were." He pulls into a gas station.

"No, I wasn't."

"You're full of shit," he tells me, easing the car up next to a pump.

"And you're being an asshole."

"I'm fucking *sad*!" he explodes at me. "Do you understand?" And he leaps out of the car and starts walking. Just walking. He's headed for the road. The gas station guy is pumping gas. I don't know what to do. I have only five more dollars on me and no credit card. My parents don't give us our own. And Jack's walking—more like slamming—away down this street, and it doesn't look like he's turning around anytime soon.

"Stop," I tell the attendant. He's pumped three dollars. He stops. I get out of the car and pay him. I have to take my hand away from my eye. I try to close just the right lid against the light. It's hard to close just one lid. I end up sort of squinting both eyes instead. The attendant gives me the change. And then I run after Jack. It takes me a good few minutes to catch up to him. For one, it's hard to run with a hand over your eye. But also, I'm wearing these slip-on shoes with no back, plus I'm not exactly an athlete.

"Stop," I huff at him when I finally catch up.

He keeps walking. I'm out of breath and wiped out. I have to half jog to stay near him. I drop my hand and go back to squinting.

"Jack."

"What?" he says. I'm right on his heels, like a dog being walked. I reach out to grab his arm.

"Come on," I say.

He stops, curses, kicks the ground, and turns around. His face is like a mask. Like one of those painted demon masks you see from Africa. All big, wild eyes and stretched-out, gaping mouth and insanity. I take a big step backward, away from him, and cover my right eye with my palm again. We stand here staring at each other.

"Somebody's going to steal the car," I tell him finally. It's still there, with the key in the ignition, by the pump. "We've got to pick up Dad."

Jack must hear something in what I've said that makes his mask shift a little. He bends down and grabs a handful of thistle and pebbles and dirt, and he hurls it. He grabs another handful and throws that, and then another one. He's crouching, and cars are driving by, and I still don't know what to do. After a few more grabs and throws Jack stops but stays crouched. He puts his head in his hands, and I don't think he's crying, but I kind of wish he were, because somehow that would be easier than this.

"I don't want to deal with Dad," Jack says. "I do not want to deal with Dad."

He wipes his face with his hands.

"You've got dirt on your face," I tell him.

He stands and starts walking toward the car. Then he stops again, and I nearly run him over, I'm so close behind. I could have damaged my eye all over again.

"I can't stand this," Jack tells me. "Seriously, Anna." He nods, as if I've said something to agree with him somehow, and then he starts walking again.

When we're pulling out of the gas station, I turn his music on for him. I turn it up really, really loud. He changes the CD from Spoonerism to some other band. I close my eyes against the brightness. It's all I can do not to cover my ears now. Partly because the music is so unbelievably loud, and partly because it sucks. Instead I tuck my hands under my thighs and grit my teeth. I stay like that, eyes closed, hands jammed, jaw locked, all the way to the bank.

12

"THAT'S EASY," LISA SAYS. "LIKABLE. EXTRA LIKABLE."

We're at Ellen's studying for the SATs, which are totally screwed up this year. Instead of being on the first Saturday of December, like always, they're the Saturday before Christmas. So that gives everybody two extra weeks of anticipatory agony. Because at my neurotic school, people start studying early and worrying earlier.

"Popular," Seth says. He's sitting next to me on the floor at the coffee table in Ellen's living room. He's half concentrating on what the rest of us are doing and half writing something on a piece of paper he's hiding underneath his thigh. Every now and then he rubs his calf on my ankle. I try to see what's got him so interested on that piece of paper.

"*Charisma* means 'popular,'" he repeats.

"It's more than that, though," Jason says from the couch next to Lisa. "Right?" He's asking Ellen because it's the sort of thing she would know. "Doesn't charisma have something else to it?"

She's been getting quieter and quieter since she got home. Not as quiet as Rob, but noticeable. At least, I can tell Jason's noticed. He's always making a point of directing what he says to her. Maybe to get her into things again. I don't know.

She's sitting in the wheelchair with her leg propped on an ottoman right next to the coffee table and a huge chenille blanket wrapped around her shoulders. We've got a bunch of markers out, and every time we review a word, someone makes up a sentence with it and then writes the sentence on Ellen's cast. The word has to be in a different color than the rest of the sentence. So far we've got *Ellen's cheeks are* gaunt *from the shitty hospital food* and *The pornographic cable channels present* tawdry *options for the masses,* and a few more like that.

Ellen shrugs at me and Seth. "What do you guys think?"

Seth looks up from whatever it is he's working on underneath his leg. "I thought charisma had to do with how people look, too," he says. "Don't you have to be hot to be charismatic?"

"Read the definition," Jason tells Ellen. Seth pulls a Tootsie Roll out of his pocket, unwraps it, pops it into his mouth, and then picks up the bowl of sour-cream-and-onion potato chips and passes it to me. I grab a bunch and pass the bowl to Jason. It goes around the circle while Ellen reads. Seth rubs my ankle again. I rub back.

"'A personal magic of leadership arousing special popularity or enthusiasm.' That's One. Two is 'a special magnetic charm or appeal.'"

"But people who are charismatic are always good-looking," Seth insists.

"I thought we just disabused ourselves of that," Ellen says.

"Disa-what?" Lisa asks her.

"Proved ourselves wrong." Ellen sighs.

"Whatever." Lisa leans back onto the couch in a huff. I don't blame her. Who but Ellen would know a word like *disabuse*? The SAT people, I guess.

"So it's not attractiveness," Ellen says, holding the bowl and then not taking any chips. "It's some other thing. Some other quality. Like . . . like . . ." Then she shrugs again and gives up. Before the accident Ellen was not a shrugger. Or a giver-upper.

"Weirdly sexy?" Jason offers.

Ellen perks a little. "Yeah," she says, and she sort of straightens. "Think about it. Who are the most long-lasting celebrities or politicians? Some of them are objectively hot. But most have this weirdly sexy thing happening. Charisma." We all sit there and think about it. It seems sort of true.

"That girl in those frozen-dinner commercials," I say. Everybody nods.

"Bono," Lisa goes.

"They're not pure good-looking," Ellen says. "But they're weirdly sexy, and they have that magnetic charm and appeal."

"But just because you're good-looking doesn't mean you have charisma," Jason says. "That's the point."

"Cameron," I say. I've been thinking it since before Ellen even read out the definitions. Everybody gets quiet. I look over at Ellen. She nods and stares at her cast and then at the dictionary. She kind of sags, like a balloon, deflated.

"Let's do a sentence with her," Lisa says. "Anna, you write it."

Lisa hands me the box of markers she was holding. I look at all the colors for a while, trying to decide. I end up choosing black.

"Do you have a sentence?" Seth asks. I'm not sure. I sit here, the tip of the marker poised over Ellen's cast. It trembles, so I pull it away and cap it while I think. Everybody's waiting. "Cameron," I finally write, "= charismatic." It's the first sentence I've done today. The lines are jittery and wavery. They're strange next to Lisa's bold, curvy letters and Seth's wiry chicken scratch. It makes me not be able to look at Ellen, or at any of them, for some reason.

"That's not exactly a sentence," Lisa finally says.

"'Without the desire to see there is no seeing,'" Jason tells her.

"And that means what exactly?" Lisa goes.

Jason arches his left eyebrow. "It means shut up."

My cell rings. I toss the marker onto the coffee table and flip up the phone. "It's my mom."

They wait politely, smashing open a bag of baked corn chips, while my mother talks. She says I need to get someone to drive me home to pick up the Audi to drive to the car dealer on Bateson Avenue to pick her and my dad up because the new Honda they were supposed to buy today got accidentally given to someone else.

"Can't Jack do it?" I ask my mom.

"We called you first," she says. "You're closer than he is. He's at Rob's."

"Rob's isn't that much farther," I say.

"Anna, please."

"Why is the Audi at home?" I ask. "Why don't you or Dad have it?"

"We miscommunicated," my mom explains. "I thought Jack was taking it, so I got a ride with Phyllis. Your dad thought I was taking it, so he got a ride with Russell."

"I'm in the middle of studying," I say.

"Anna, this isn't an option. We're stuck here," my mom says.

"Is she giving you a hard time?" I hear my father ask in the background.

"I can't—," I start to tell my mother.

My dad gets on the phone. "Get over here now," he says. And he hangs up on me.

"What's the matter?" Seth asks. "Your teeth are chattering."

"No, they're not," I say. They all look at me funny.

"Can someone give me a ride home?"

Seth does. I have to direct him because he's never been to my house.

"Are you okay?" he keeps asking. I keep nodding behind my sunglasses. I'm going to need them for at least a few more weeks. Even though I stopped using the drops a couple of days after that gonioscopy.

"What happened on the phone?" Seth tries.

"Nothing," I say. "My mom just needs me to pick her and my dad up." I pull my arms around myself, and he drops it.

"So, what was that piece of paper you were so interested in at Ellen's just now?" I ask him. My teeth are chattering, and it's not even that cold out.

"My next big thing," he says.

"Your what?"

"My next big thing." He grins. He has sort of a goofy grin. "You need a big thing every now and then," he goes. "To keep life from getting boring." He reaches into the pocket on his door and grabs a Tootsie Roll.

"Here," I say. "You're driving." I unwrap it for him. Instead of holding out his hand, though, he opens his mouth. I ignore that and toss the naked Tootsie Roll into his lap, so that he has to fish for it. "So, what's a big thing?" I ask him.

"My first one was in seventh grade," he says, rolling the candy between his front teeth. "You know that huge water-wheel moat thing by the library?"

"Yeah," I go. "The one somebody made into a bubble bath about four yea . . ."

He's rolling and smiling.

"Oh my God," I go. "That was you?"

More rolling. More smiling.

"What about the colors?" I ask him. "That started later, right? Like, a year later?"

"Food coloring," he goes. "My favorite was the purple."

"Mine too!" I go. "How did you not get caught? I mean, they could have arrested you or something."

"Yeah," he goes, tucking the Tootsie Roll into the side of his cheek, making a little bulge. "Life without parole."

"Don't make fun of me."

"Never." He chews and swallows. "I'm glad you don't have that robot eye anymore during the daytime," he says as he turns onto my street. My arms have become uncrossed somehow, only I'm shaking again, so I recross them.

"Because I've been wanting to kiss you, only that thing was messing up the physics of it."

"The physics?"

"Who have you gone out with, anyway?"

I cross my legs now too. "Nobody," I say.

"I thought you and Paul what's-his-name were a thing."

"No," I say. We're around the curve now, almost at my driveway. "He liked me, but I didn't like him back."

"Why?" Seth asks. I don't really know why. He was cute and cool, and he played soccer, and Ellen thought I should like him. "And what about Rothman?"

I roll my eyes. "Rothman is ridiculous," I say. "Here." He pulls into my driveway. I unknot my limbs and get out of the car. I try to seem calm while I make myself walk around to his side.

"Why do you like me, Seth?" I ask through his rolled-down window.

"Am I ridiculous if I don't have a reason?"

I shake my head. He reaches out and pulls a curl. And doesn't let go.

"Let go," I tell him.

The truth is, I've been kissed by only two guys. Paul what's-his-name and Rothman, and I've never really had a boyfriend, and I'm sort of old not to have ever had a boyfriend, and it's embarrassing and the idea of dealing with it all just makes me shake, only I've been shaking for weeks anyway, so maybe it's hard to know exactly what the shaking is about.

"Lean down," he says, keeping gentle hold of my curl.

"You never said what your next big thing is," I tell him.

"Lean down," he says.

"I'd really like to know."

"Lean down," he says again.

"I didn't say you could kiss me," I tell him. He keeps hold of my hair.

"Lean down." He's like a broken record. "I'm going to kiss your other eye."

I lean down. He lifts himself through the space of the window and very gently raises my sunglasses.

"Hmm," he goes. And then he very, very gently kisses my left eye.

"See ya," he says, and he's out of here. I'm shaking and shaking and shaking.

I get to the end of my block. That's how long it takes before I lose it. Chest leaping, body shuddering, sweating like I'm running a marathon. *Something happened to me in the accident,* I think as my slick palm slides all over the steering wheel. *I got injured somehow that nobody realized. My heart got hurt, and now I'm having a heart attack.* I manage to weave the Audi over to the side of the road and pull out my cell phone. I call 911. I stumble out of the car and think I'm going to vomit on the street, only I don't. I collapse onto the pavement, but by the time the ambulance gets here six minutes later, I'm almost fine, and Mrs. Caldwell is sitting with me in that navy blue sweatsuit with the white stripes up the sides.

"She was in a car accident about a month ago," Mrs. Caldwell explains to the EMTs. So even though they don't see anything obviously wrong, they decide to take me to the hospital. Mrs. Caldwell picks up my parents at the Honda dealership and drives them home. And Jack is at the house by then, and my whole family drives to the hospital in the Audi to get me, and I'm fine.

On the way home again, Jack and I sit in the back, with my parents up front, and it's like a trip to the beach, because when else are we all in the car together these days? My father's humming. Jack's got his earphones in and turned way up. I can hear that squawking sitting next to him. My mother keeps twisting around with this concerned expression.

"Okay, look," my father says finally. I tap Jack and nod at the back of my father's head, at his mass of gray hair. Jack pulls out his earphones. But then my dad doesn't say anything else.

13

SETH AND JASON AND LISA BRING TWO MOVIES OVER TO ELLEN'S.
Her mom has to go into her room to wake her up about three
times before Ellen finally wheels out with her hair messed up
and the same sweatshirt she wore yesterday.

"We got them both off Rosebud Is a Sled," Jason tells her.
"They're in Jack's top fifty list." I flop onto Ellen's couch next
to Seth. He puts his arm across my shoulders while we look.

"*My Life as a Dog*?" I say, looking at one of the DVDs. "What
is that? My brother is so weird."

"*Big*," Seth says, crunching into his Toffee Crisp and reading
the title of the other movie. "Which one should we watch
first?"

"*My Life as a Dog* will make you cry," Ellen's mother informs
us, walking through the family room to get to the stairs.

"Out, Mom," Ellen tells her, loud, and then she winces. Her ribs and the spot where her bra strap meets the cup must still really hurt. It creeps me out to think a tube poked right into her body there. I've seen the aftermath, once, when Ellen changed her shirt in front of me. It's all this gauze and white tape and a wettish spot in the middle. She has to change it twice a day. Ugh. Poor Ellen. I saw her laugh at something Jason said at school earlier, and then immediately grit her face and almost cry.

"I never weep at movies, Mrs. Gerson," Seth is saying now.

"Weep?" Lisa goes.

"Am I allowed to respond?" Mrs. Gerson asks Ellen.

Ellen shrugs. "A-parent-ly."

"That movie will make every single one of you cry," Mrs. Gerson announces. Then, at Ellen's look, she speeds up, saying, "Yes. Yes. I'm going."

So we watch *Big*. Seth keeps his arm around my shoulders the whole time. Ellen doesn't even seem to notice. I stick my tongue out at her to make her notice.

"Mature," she says out loud to me, but not like she cares.

"Shh," Lisa goes.

Later I can tell that Ellen's not even paying attention. Once, I see her eyes on the TV screen, but they're all spaced out, and another time she's braiding the tassels on the scarf around her neck.

Jason's not into it either. He wanders around the Gersons' bookshelves halfway through and pulls out something to read. When the movie's over and everybody's getting ready to go, Lisa starts teasing him.

"Since when are you such a bookworm?"

"That movie sucked," Jason says.

"Are you kidding?" Seth goes. "That movie rocked."

Jason slides his book back onto the shelf, using his body to hide it so that we can't tell what it was.

"What were you reading?" Lisa asks.

"You'll never know," Jason tells her.

"I can't believe you actually sat here and read a book while we watched a movie."

"Anna's walking me out," Seth announces. "Don't follow us. We're going to be fooling around."

"If you're lucky," I tell him, but I follow him to his car. We get in, and he leans over to kiss me.

"Don't," I say.

"Oh." He sits up straight again. He looks bummed. I'm not really sure why I stopped him. I want him to kiss me, but when I think about him kissing me now, I think about us kissing later, and us being boyfriend and girlfriend, and I get tired. And then I think about Ellen and how tired she is all the time, and how, truthfully, she's seemed not okay somehow, and I get more tired.

"So why did you come into the car with me?" Seth asks after a while.

"Because I like you," I tell him.

"Oh."

"It's just . . . there's a lot going on." I'm not really sure what I mean.

"Cameron?" It's the obvious thing.

"I guess," I say.

"I know." He looks at me sideways. "Did you see her?" At first I think he means did I see her car swerving. But then I realize he means did I see her dead.

"What kind of question is that?" I ask him.

"I just . . . ," he starts.

"Does it matter if I saw her?" Does he only like me because I'm some sort of reverse celebrity now? Because I'm some story?

"Anna. Whoa. I didn't mean to . . ."

"Does it matter if I saw her!" Does he think he gets status if he can go and tell everybody all the gory details? "Seth!" I'm shouting. Really shouting. "I'm asking. You. A question!"

He looks like I've just smacked him. "I was only . . ."

"Forget it," I tell him, opening the car door. "Just forget it."

The others are gone when I get back inside. Ellen and I set up our sleeping arrangements in her temporary downstairs room. Actually, I set things up, while Ellen watches and rubs Whitey across her chin over and over. She gets the bed, obviously. I sleep on the blow-up mattress, inside a sleeping bag.

"I saw which book Jason was reading," Ellen goes after we've turned out the light.

"What was the book?"

"The Bauble."

"The what?"

"Think about it, Anna."

"I'm not in the mood to think. Just tell me."

She sighs. "The Bible."

"Oh."

"Yeah."

"Is he religious?"

"I have no idea."

"He's into philosophy, you know."

"I know. And stealing."

"What?"

"He didn't put it back. The Bible."

"He didn't put it back on your shelf?"

"Nope."

"But we saw him put it back."

"It's not there now."

"Are you sure?"

"Yeah."

We're quiet, and I think she's almost asleep, but she's not.

"Let's not tell anyone," she says. "Okay?"

"About Jason?" I go. "Of course not."

"It's a weird secret to keep for someone," Ellen says. "You know?"

"Yeah."

"That they were reading the Bible."

"Yeah."

"That they stole a Bible."

"Right."

"But he definitely didn't want us to know he was interested in it. And he'd never tell something we wouldn't want him to tell, you know?"

"Yeah."

"Besides," Ellen adds. "Nobody in my family's going to notice a missing Bible anyway."

We're quiet again, and this time I'm sure she's asleep, only I'm wrong.

"Did you and Seth have a fight?" she asks.

"We're not even really going out to have had a fight."

She's too smart to buy that. "What was it about?"

I feel how wide awake I am. "The accident."

"How could you have a fight about that?" Ellen asks.

"We just did." Then it doesn't seem fair not to tell her more. We tell each other everything. "He wanted to know if I saw Cameron dead," I say.

"Oh," Ellen says. "Did you?" Coming from her, it doesn't seem like such a bad question. She was there too. She got hurt too.

"No," I tell Ellen. And I can hear the screaming, stopped. I shiver and zip the last part of my sleeping bag to get warmer.

"I'm sorry I passed out," Ellen says.

"What?"

"I'm sorry I passed out." Her voice is sort of breathless, like she's been on a StairMaster or something. "I was thinking that I escaped the worst of it by passing out, and you were on your own."

"No," I tell Ellen. "No way. I never thought of it like that. No."

"I've been sort of thinking that."

"You nearly died," I say, and I concentrate on not starting to cry. "I only got some stupid blood in my eye. Plus, I was driving. I could have done something different."

"I might not have passed out like that if I hadn't been so drunk."

"Even if you hadn't passed out, there's nothing you could have done." I hear her smacking her pillow. She can never get her pillow the way she likes. She's always smoothing it or plumping it or something.

"Were you terrified?" Ellen asks after she settles things with the pillow.

I think about it. I try to think about it the way she would. The way Jack thinks I should, the way Jason likes for people to do. I really think about it.

"I'm more terrified now," I say.

I'm on Ocean Road and there's a glass ponytail slicing into my eye, and there's the earth dangling above me in the dark sky, and there's screaming and screaming and screaming, and there's Jack, giant size, with tree trunk legs planted wide and tree branch hands up and out like a good monster traffic cop's, and there's a tidal wave of salt water and blood about to destroy us, and there's screaming and screaming and screaming, and then the screaming stops.

"Anna, wake up!"

The lights are on. Mrs. Gerson is shaking my shoulders. "Anna!"

"I'm awake," I say. My heart is going wild.

"You're soaked," Mrs. Gerson says. "Soaked." I don't know who she's talking to. I look over at Ellen, half sitting up in bed.

"Are you okay?" she asks me. I touch my face. It's wet. My heart is like a little animal trapped inside my chest.

"Did I wake you up?" I ask. My body is shaking again. From tip to toe. My whole body.

"You could say that," Ellen says sarcastically.

"Was I really loud?" I ask them. *A tidal wave and my brother and screaming, stopped.* I could vomit.

"Freight trainish," Mrs. Gerson says. "Get up, now. I'm running you a bath."

"A bath?" My heart starts to slow down.

"Mom, you can't make her take a bath," Ellen says. The shaking turns more into a slow shudder.

"For God's sake, Ellen," Mrs. Gerson goes.

"It was just a nightmare," I tell her. "I'm okay. Really. I don't need a bath." But actually, a bath sounds sort of good.

"You are not okay," Mrs. Gerson tells me. She looks at Ellen. "And neither are you." She leans over and kisses Ellen's head and then touches her cheek. When Ellen shakes her off after a second, those tears sliding out of the corners of her eyes, her mom sighs at her in this nice way. Then Mrs. Gerson turns to me again, takes my hand, pulls the twisted sleeping bag off my legs, and tugs me to a stand. "Neither of you is okay."

14

I DON'T KNOW WHAT MRS. GERSON SAID TO MY PARENTS, BUT IT'S
a week later, Thanksgiving is in five days, and Jack, Ellen, Mr.
and Mrs. Gerson, and I are all on a plane to Florida. We're
going to some resort "to get away and recuperate," as Mrs.
Gerson puts it.

"Isn't it weird," Ellen's saying to Jack, "how Anna and I have
been best friends for years, and you and I have barely ever said
a word to each other?" Her back is to the window and her leg
is stretched out in my lap. That cast is heavy. We got to board
first because of it, and we'll get off last.

"Same with Anna and Rob," Jack answers. He's across the
aisle from us.

"That's only because Rob never talks," I say.

"He talks," Jack says.

"Barely," Ellen goes.

"I hate peanuts," Jack tells us, holding his mini package of them by the edge.

"Since when?" I ask him.

"Since always."

"I didn't know that," I tell him. "I hate peanuts too."

"So does Mom."

"Ellen loves them," I say. "Give her yours."

Jack gets his own room. Ellen and I share. There's a pool with purple and red tiles checkered around its sides and a swim-up bar where you can buy drinks and sandwiches and chips. The beach and ocean are through a gate and down a stone path. There's a huge, round floating trampoline anchored beyond the breakers pretty far out. We never had that when we were little. It looks like fun.

The Gersons keep their distance from us, except at dinner-time, when we all go out to eat. They let us order wine, and I notice Ellen motioning the waiters to fill her glass every time it gets near half empty. Other than dinner, when they pass by us, Mrs. Gerson makes either a shooing motion or else puts up her hands, as if we're throwing eggs at her.

"Recuperate," she orders. "Recuperate."

Mr. Gerson brought a Monopoly game, which I never would have thought of, but we take it from him and set it up by the pool. We arrange things so that Ellen can prop her leg in the shade but sunbathe the rest of her. She still has a jumbo-size square gauze bandage underneath her bikini where the strap meets the cup, but it's not as bad as it seemed a few weeks ago. It's smaller and cleaner now. She and I make Jack shuffle over every twenty minutes so we can stay in the sun and maximize our tans. When Jack and I get hot, we jump into the pool and then come back to shake our wet hair onto Ellen. We cover her leg with a cut-out piece of blue tarp to protect the cast. We all bought sunglasses in the airport. The wire-frame-with-colored-glass kind. Ellen bought a shade of light blue. Jack bought orange. I think his are weird, but Ellen says they're funky and cool. So whatever. I'm working on trying not to worry about things like that. I bought as dark a pair as I could find. My right eye still hurts when the sun hits it. Ellen and Jack and the mirror tell me that the pupil's dilated, only not to the degree it was before. Also, it's not round so much as vertically oval. All I know is Dr. Pluto said not to worry, and I'm allowed to swim.

"Seventy-eight entries," Jack announces right after his turn at Monopoly. He's been taking his laptop with him everywhere. Since UCLA's deadline was so early, and since you can use the same essay for different schools, he's pretty much through with college applications. Deadlines for NYU and Brown aren't until January anyway. So mostly he's not working, but checking his Web site and the Cameron link. "Two new ones today." He means memorial posts for Cameron.

I roll, land, and then go directly to jail.

"I thought that one written by Shelly was really nice," Ellen tells Jack. I didn't know she'd gone to the site.

"Did you write one?" I ask her.

"Didn't you see it?" she asks me back.

"Ellen's was great," Jack tells me sort of softly. I try to think of a quick lie, but my brain won't work fast enough.

"You've looked at the site, right?" Ellen asks.

I shake my head. Ellen rolls the dice and gets really busy moving the hat.

"I'm hot again," I say to Jack. "Want to jump in?"

"It's just weird," he tells me. "You haven't even looked?"

"Hotel," Ellen tells Jack. Then she winces. "Aaagh."

Jack and I have gotten used to seeing her pain come suddenly. It's the chest tube wound, mostly. Her ribs aren't as bad. We've learned to wait it out with her. So now, within a few seconds, she relaxes and hands him some of her colorful cash. He hands her a little red building in return.

"You haven't even looked at it?" Jack asks again. I stare at the red and purple tiles in the pool and feel small.

"Not yet," I say.

It's a wave made up of tree branches, millions and millions of them in all shapes and sizes, and it's bearing down on me, and somehow it's clear water, even though it's tree branches, and I can see my father behind the wave in the distance, and I can tell he's just hurled the wave at us, and I look around for my mom, but I can't find her to help, and there's screaming and screaming and screaming, and the wave is rising and curling, all those tree branches interwoven and meshed together, and the screaming and screaming, and a jagged glass ponytail splashes out of the tree branches and latches on to my eye, and then Jack is next to me, feet planted wide, hands up and out, and I know he'll be able to save us, and he's shouting loud, "Stop, stop," but the wave keeps coming, and it's the screaming, it's the screaming and screaming and screaming that stops.

I sit up fast, my heart racing, and my stomach rising into my throat and mouth and then falling again, and I'm breathing really loud, and it's dark, and then something hits me, and it's Whitey, the polar bear.

"Ellen?" I say. I fumble for my lamp and turn it on. She's half sitting up, which is actually sort of how she sleeps these days anyway. She's got the phone in her hand.

"Don't call anybody," I tell her. My entire body is shuddering.

"What's the nightmare?" she whispers.

"Don't call your parents." My heart starts to slow. "Come on. It's embarrassing."

"What's the dream?" she asks, hanging up the phone. I swallow to get the sour taste out of my mouth.

"It's just a bad dream." I peel off my nightshirt. An extra-large T that says TALK TO MY AGENT across the front. Ellen got it for me as a gag last Christmas. Now it's wet with sweat.

"Nice apples," Ellen tells me. My heart's regular now, but my curls are matted to my skull.

"Apples?" Underneath the damp sheet I wiggle out of my sweaty underwear. "You are so weird."

"What's the dream?" Ellen asks me again.

"What do you think?" I ask her back. She slumps deeper into her covers. "I'm sorry," I say right away. "I'm sorry." I toss Whitey back to her, but gently. She rubs him across her chin with one hand and starts plumping her pillow with the other.

"Do you ever dream about it?" I ask. I move to a cooler, drier spot in my bed. It feels better.

"No," she says, pounding and smacking. I like the sound. "I just dream that I'm a mermaid mummy."

"A mermaid mummy?"

"Don't tell anybody."

115

"I won't."

"In the dreams my torso is all taped up in this tight gauze and my legs are fused together, and I'm on land, and I can't move."

"Oh."

She smushes and whacks a few more times.

"Tell me when you're ready for the light off," I say.

She tugs and flattens. "Leave it on," she goes. So I do.

"Your friend Seth called," my mother says over the cell phone. "He says he's had trouble reaching you."

I unfurl a towel with an underwater scene on it. "I'm not picking up when it's him," I tell my mother. Ellen shakes her head, and Jack gives me the thumbs-down. We're in the hotel gift shop. It's drizzling outside, so no pool or beach this morning.

"What should I tell him if he calls here again?" my mom asks.

"Just don't pick up when it's him," I say, rolling the towel back into a sausage and returning it to the shelf. "Check the caller ID." Ellen picks out a seashell anklet and gestures for me to put it on her good ankle.

"Oh, Anna, I'm not going to remember to do that every time I pick up the phone."

I get Ellen to hold the cell to my ear while I lean down to clasp the anklet on. "Do I have any mail?" I ask. Which is a ridiculous question. What mail would I have?

"No," my mother says. "But your teacher Ms. Riffing called to say that she can work with you after school to catch you up after Thanksgiving."

I stand and take the phone back from Ellen. "Are we going to Buck and Jerry's?" That's my uncle and aunt. Jerry is a woman.

They don't have any kids, and we usually spend Thanksgiving with them.

Jack's holding a huge conch shell. The kind you blow into to make a sound like a horn.

"We'll see," my mother says. It's what we do every year.

"What do you mean, 'we'll see'?" I ask her. Jack holds the conch to Ellen's ear. She smiles. They get along pretty well. They went for a walk alone the other day. Well. A walk and a roll. "Rock and roll," Ellen said later. I was napping, and when I woke up, they were gone. Not that Ellen can get so far. I felt left out and uneasy, which is stupid, I guess. But I couldn't help it.

"We'll see if we're all up to it," my mother says. "Dad was suggesting we just stay home."

"I don't want to stay home," I say. Now Jack has the conch up to my ear. I can hear the ocean on one side and my mom's faint breathing on the other. The idea of what she's saying makes me nervous. Just the four of us, home together having dinner on Thanksgiving? Alone?

"Well, I'll tell Dad that."

"Is he there?" I ask, moving away from Jack and the conch. I'm surprised I've asked, because I never talk to him on the phone when I'm away. She puts him on.

"Hi," he says.

"Hi," I say.

"Are you kids going to buy anything?" the saleslady goes. Which, if you ask me, is pretty rude behavior for a fancy hotel. We all ignore her.

"See any porpoises?" my dad asks.

"Not yet," I say. "Can I go hang gliding?"

"Absolutely not," he says. "Are you using sunblock?"

"Yeah."

"What number?"

"Fifty," I lie.

"Put your brother on the phone."

I hand the phone to Jack. He hands me the conch.

"Hi," Jack says. He waits a second. "Yeah," he looks at me. "We're fine."

Ellen's been napping a lot. A whole lot. But now, for some reason, she's getting stir-crazy. When I walk out of our bathroom, she's sitting in her wheelchair in front of my queen bed, holding up her dad's car keys. Rental-car keys.

"What are those?"

"You know what they are," Ellen goes. "Come on. Take me for a drive."

Jack's in his room watching movies or maybe listening to music.

"I'm not in the mood," I tell Ellen. "Besides, your parents will kill us. How did you get those, anyway?"

"They always leave them in the bottom of their pool bag," Ellen says. "I fished them out this morning. Come on." She jangles them at me.

"Are you crazy?" I say. "If something happens, your dad could be liable for a ton of money."

"Nothing's going to happen." Ellen tosses the keys in my direction. I let them fall to the floor, while she winces.

"Please?" Ellen goes a few seconds later. "I can't swim or anything. I'm bored out of my mind."

"All right," I say. "If we get Jack to drive."

Ellen gives me a long look.

"What?" I say.

"I want to go, just you and me."

"You don't like Jack?"

"You'd rather I didn't like him, but that's not it."

"What do you mean, I'd rather you didn't?"

"You wouldn't want him and me to be friends. But that's a different subject. You're changing the subject. Anyway. It's not that. I want you to drive." She starts to wheel herself.

"I'm not changing the subject," I say. "You brought it up. And how come you want me to drive?"

She pauses at the hotel dresser and grabs her white, floppy hat.

"I just do," she goes, adjusting the hat on her head, wincing with how it hurts when she raises her arms like that, and then gliding her chair across the room.

"I don't care if you and Jack are friends," I tell her, even though now I'm not sure if that's true.

"Good," she says. "Don't forget your sin-glasses." She's got the door open, only it's one of those heavy ones that close on their own, and it looks like it's about to smash her, so I have no choice. I scrape the keys up off the knobbly rug, snatch my shades off the bedside table, and grab the door from Ellen.

"I feel kind of sick," I say, following her out into the hallway.

"You'll feel better once we get outside," she tells me. But I don't. I feel worse in the elevator and way worse in the hotel lobby.

"It might be heatstroke or something," I worry as we pass

by doormen, or porters, or whatever they are, and rock and roll outside.

"Come on," she says. So we keep going. In the parking lot Ellen eases herself into the backseat. I fold her chair, which takes me less than fifteen seconds now, lift it into the trunk, and then slide behind the wheel.

"I feel really sick," I tell Ellen. Maybe I'm going to throw up. My hands are jiggling on the steering wheel. I can't drive. There's no way I can drive. Ellen waits for more than a minute while I sit here shaking and sweating. Then she gives up.

"I knew it," she says, and I can see her face in the rearview mirror, completely disappointed.

15

THE SUN COMES OUT, AND IT'S LIKE IT NEVER EVEN RAINED, so we go to the beach. We always pick a spot far from the water and close to the path because it's nearly impossible to roll a wheelchair on sand. I carry all our stuff.

"I'm going to swim out to the trampoline," I tell her when we finally settle.

"Do you feel up to it?" she asks.

"I'm fine now," I say. And I am. "It must be something I ate."

"But that was just a few hours ago," she points out. "If it was something you ate, wouldn't you still be sick?"

I swim out, wearing my sunglasses. It's a long way, and I'm breathing hard by the time I reach the ladder. I hang on to it for a while before I even try to climb up. There's nobody else here, even though it's big enough to fit about ten adults comfortably.

All along the rim is this rubber bumper, I guess so you only go over the edge when you really mean to. I can't figure out how the thing is anchored so far out, so deep. But it is.

For a minute I think about jumping, but I didn't check out jumping with Dr. Pluto, so I wave at Ellen and then just lie flat and feel the sting of the sun on my face and belly.

Then I hear giggles, and two little kids monkey up the ladder. A brother and a sister. About nine and ten. Nut-colored hair, eyes, and tan. I scoot over to the side bumper of the trampoline. They start jumping right away.

"Higher!" the girl screams. "Higher!"

"Watch this," the boy goes, and he falls on his butt and bounces up to his feet.

"Higher!" she screams again.

"Look," the boy goes. "You can make it spin!" and he starts running around the bumper edges, which makes the trampoline spin in place. She follows him. I sway to the side a little when they get near, and they do a little hop so they won't run right into me.

"Faster!" she yells. "Faster!" They've got us spinning in the water pretty fast. Then the boy stops.

"I'm going to push you in," he tells the girl.

She shrieks. "No! Jeremy! No!" Before she can get in another no, he's scampered right to her and shoved her over the edge. I can hear her shrieking a beat after she disappears. Then I hear a splash. Jeremy grins at me, holds his nose with one hand, and then leaps off after his sister.

Two minutes later Jack climbs on. "Did you see those kids?"

"Yeah," I say. "Cute."

He doesn't jump. He lies on his stomach, leaning up on his forearms so that he can stare out at the horizon. "Ellen said you got sick or something."

"Yeah." The sun has me sort of dopey. "I feel better now."

I roll over onto my stomach. The plastic of the trampoline smells like seaweed. It's warm and damp under my right cheek.

Jack gazes out at the water.

"See any riptides?" I ask him.

"No," he goes.

"Good."

My father was cursing and struggling to get the umbrella raised. I looked around for my mom. She was already on her raft, swimming out to brackish green infinity. On calm days she would even bring a book out there with her. She likes true stories about survival adventures. Mountain-climbing accidents and shipwrecks and campers lost. Sometimes she'd float so far out, the lifeguards would stand up on their white towers and start whistling and waving their arms at her. Then she'd have to paddle closer in. But today was too rough for books. My mom had her hands full just paddling out past the breakers.

"Hey," Jack said, squinting at the lifeguard tower to read the squiggled-chalk report on swimming conditions.

"Don't drop the chairs like that," my dad said, finally clicking the umbrella's canopy into place. "You'll break them."

"Dad," Jack said. "Mild riptides today. It says so on the board." He pointed.

The lifeguards sat up pretty high, white zinc on their noses, with dark sunglasses, orange swimsuits, and binoculars dangling around their necks. They were always blackly tan, with maybe some white peel spots on their shoulders or faces. They posted the water temperature and the time of high tide each day in white chalk on the board. And they wrote up warnings of small riptides. If the rips were really bad, the lifeguards spiked red flags up and down the shoreline. It was against the law to go into the water if there were red flags out.

"I don't want you throwing down our chairs," my father said, ignoring Jack and letting his fall to the ground. He spotted my mom and waved his arm at her as he walked into the surf. She was facing land, so she probably saw, but she didn't wave back. She paddled herself sideways and then around and headed straight out to sea.

About an hour later Jack and I were in the breakers, trying to stop the ocean without much luck. Every now and then, when we drifted to the left, I could feel a mini riptide. They don't let you make any progress when you try to swim or walk back to shore. Even if land is just a few feet away, the weight of the current keeps you from moving. When people drown, it's because they get so tired fighting. They see the beach is only an arm's length off, and they keep swimming straight in and getting nowhere. Then they exhaust themselves and that's the end.

But my dad had taught Jack and me what to do in a riptide. As soon as you realize you're in it, you let it take you out to sea. It's counterintuitive, my dad explained, meaning it doesn't make sense to your gut. But if you let the tide pull you out to its triangle tip, even if you're really far out, then all you have to do is swim parallel to shore until you're beyond the rip's boundaries. After that you can swim straight back in to land.

It's important not to panic, because panicking makes you tired. And it's important to pace yourself. That's what my father always said.

"Hey," I called to Jack, only he wasn't there. He'd timed things wrong on the last wave and was tumbling underneath the water somewhere. *Dad looks weird, doesn't he?* That's what I was going to say. Because he did look funny. Off somehow. *He's in a rip,* I thought, and he was. Right in the middle of a small, dark triangle with ripples on the surface, like scales on a fish, going at an angle against the rest of the ocean. He was swimming and swimming and swimming and getting nowhere. There were surfers all around him, in every direction, but they were on their boards on the surface of the water, skimming above the current.

"Dad!" I yelled. Only he was too far away. And Jack had wiped out all the way back to shore. I spotted him sitting on his butt in the undertow, getting his bearings. I looked back at my father. He was still trying to swim. He was working hard, shoulders straining.

"Hey!" I tried to yell to one of the surfers. It was useless. "Dad!" I yelled again. I turned for the lifeguards up high on their platforms. I waved my arms in a crisscross over my head to get their attention.

"Hey!" I yelled. "Hey!" One was holding up the binoculars, but he was facing the other way.

So I started swimming toward my father. If I could get close enough, I could remind him just to tread water and rest, or I could get a board from someone for him to hold on to. I was a good swimmer. We all were. But I couldn't swim fast enough. I saw my father's head go under and then pop back up, and he was spluttering. Why wasn't he staying calm, like he'd told us to do? Why wasn't he realizing he was in a riptide?

"Dad!" I yelled. "Dad!" I stopped to rest and waved my arms in a crisscross again for the surfers, for the lifeguards. For anybody who would notice. Nobody did. I scanned the horizon for my mother on the raft, but I couldn't even see where she was. I looked back at my dad. He was still trying to swim straight in. "Stop!" I yelled. He went under again, and I was furious. How could he be so stupid?

I swam as hard as I could. "Hey," I breathed, kicking my way to the first surfer who might hear me. "Hey! Help!" I pulled at his leg the second I was close enough.

"What?" He was a teenager, and he looked annoyed.

I pointed to my father, who was going under again. "He needs help," I said. "He needs your board."

My father was flipping his head up and out of the water. His eyes were wide, mouth round, and you could see how hard it was for him to lift his arms.

"Hurry!" I yelled to the teenager.

He did. He paddled fast.

By the time I caught up, my father was clinging to the board, just outside of the rip.

"You scared me, dude," the surfer was saying.

My dad was breathing really heavy. The vein in his forehead was pulsing.

"Got a little rip going there, man," the surfer went. "Listen, when you get in those, you want to relax, you know?"

My father gulped in air and wiped his mouth. He didn't

even notice me there, treading water behind him. He didn't notice me following as the surfer paddled and then pointed his board straight in to shore while my dad hung on. I was right behind them.

"I'm okay," my dad breathed. "Thanks."

"You sure?" the teenager asked. "You seem kind of tired." My father nodded and let go of the board. He started swimming. I swam after him. He was going slow. His arms looked heavy. We passed my brother.

"What's going on?" Jack asked me.

"Dad almost drowned."

Jack followed me following my father. I watched my dad climb onto the beach, his dripping body bent, drooped. On the sand he wobbled, like he was drunk, and he kept wobbling all the way back to our blanket and umbrellas. Jack and I followed.

"What happened?" my mom asked. She must have swum in without anybody noticing her.

My father flapped his hand back toward the water and didn't answer. He was still breathing really heavy.

"You look ill," my mom went. "What happened?"

"He almost drowned," Jack told her.

"I did not almost drown." My father sank down hard onto his chair, making a smacking sound, and rubbed a towel over his head and face.

"Yes, you did," I insisted. Why was he lying?

"I'm fine," my father told me.

"I saw you." I remembered his face. The way it had kept going under. The way his eyes and mouth had been so round. I started to cry.

"Harvey?" my mom said. Jack was looking back and forth at my father and at me, all worried. I couldn't stop crying, and I was waiting for my dad to yell at me for it, which made me more mad and more scared.

"He did," I sobbed. "I saw it with my own eyes. He almost drowned."

My dad didn't yell. He pulled me to him and onto his wet lap.

"It's okay," he said, real gentle. "I'm all right."

"You're remembering Dad, right?" Jack asks me now.

"Yup," I say.

"Was he really drowning?"

"Yeah." I sit up and look out toward the brownish horizon. There's a ship way off in the distance. And a hang glider above us. "It was so weird, with all those people around." The hang glider is bright yellow and orange. It's peaceful to watch it.

"You saved his life," Jack tells me.

"Not according to him," I answer.

Now Jack sits up. "Isn't it interesting how you and I deal with what a pain in the ass he is?"

"What do you mean?"

"I get so into my music and movies. You know? I get so into it, he could be yelling or being a jerk right in the same room, and I'd barely hear him."

"Aren't you just that way naturally?" I ask.

"And you," Jack goes on, ignoring me and standing up on the trampoline. "You get so uptight you skim the surface of everything."

"What do you mean, I skim the surface?"

"You get nervous so quick you forget to stop and breathe."

"Breathe?" I snort. "That definitely came from Cameron." Then I smack my hand over my mouth. "I'm sorry," I say. "I'm sorry."

Jack starts jumping. "That's okay," he tells me. And half of his face smiles while the other half cries. "It did come from Cameron."

He jumps lightly, the bottoms of his feet just barely leaving the rubber on each ascent. Really it's more of a bounce.

"I'm not nervous," I say cautiously.

"Not nervous exactly." Jack bounces. His face readjusts back to normal. "Just . . . not relaxed."

"That's not true."

I stand up.

"It's not a criticism," Jack says. "It's a constructive observation."

He bounces for a while, facing me. The hang glider is circling over us. I'm thinking about a lot of different things all at once.

"Will you ever stop being sad?" I ask him. He doesn't stop bouncing, and his face flashes to that half-crying–half-smiling mask and then back to normal, and then he shoves some of the dark, damp hair out of his face.

"No," he says. "I don't see how."

Back on the beach Ellen says, "Sea-rene."

"What?" I squeeze my hair to get the water out and lie down on my towel.

Jack's spreading his at my feet.

"Everything looked so serene," Ellen says. "You guys out

there on the trampoline. That ship way off on the horizon. That hang glider. It was like watching a silent movie."

"Do you like silent movies?" Jack asks her.

"Jack says I'm superficial," I interrupt, "and I only skim the surface of things because of my father."

"She's not superficial exactly," Ellen tells Jack.

"Oh, thanks," I say.

"She's just scared."

"I know." Jack squirts sunblock onto his hand and starts to rub his arms and chest with it.

"I'm not scared," I say. They're pissing me off. I don't even know what they're talking about. Besides, Ellen is supposed to defend me. "I'm dumping you for the Ashleys," I tell her.

"That's what I mean." Now Jack's rubbing his legs.

"What?" I say.

"You're the only one who calls them the Ashleys," Jack tells me.

"That's not true." I look at Ellen through my sunglasses. "Everyone calls them the Ashleys."

Ellen rolls her eyes.

"What?" I say. "You call them that."

She shakes her head. "You came up with it."

"Maybe, but you use it."

"Actually," she says very carefully, "I don't."

I stop to think about it. I'm sure I've heard her say "the Ashleys" before. I'm sure of it. I watch Jack get rid of the excess sunblock by wiping the webs of every two fingers onto his chin.

"Do you know that Ashley Jasper has a little brother who's retarded?" Ellen asks me.

"Is that Ashley One or Ashley Two?"

"See?" Jack says to Ellen.

She won't look at me.

"I'm not superficial," I argue at them. They don't argue back. "I'm not scared, either," I say. "The Ashleys are bitchy snobs. What would I be scared of?"

"It's more complicated than that." Jack lies back on his towel.

"Like you know so much," I tell him.

"I just see more of the big picture," Jack says.

"So you're better than I am," I say.

"Could you guys stop it?" Ellen asks. Her voice is off. Raggedy somehow.

Jack and I both squint at her. She's staring up at that hang glider, biting her lip.

"Sorry," I mutter.

"It doesn't matter what you were scared of before," Ellen says. "You're scared now, and it's messing you up."

"I'm okay," I tell her.

"No, you're not." Ellen's still gazing at the sky. "My mother was right. Shell shock. I think she's right about all three of us. But especially about you."

"What do you mean?" I say. "You were in the car too. You got hurt way worse than I did. And you're tired constantly, even when it has nothing to do with your leg or your ribs, so don't even say that's it, and you space out and get bored all the time. And Jack." I look at him, lying on his back with his eyes closed. "Jack's going to be sad for the rest of his life."

Ellen answers in this really gentle voice that's not like her at all. "Jack and I can sleep, and—"

"You sleep too much," I interrupt.

She waits for more than a second before she speaks again, and when she does, her voice stays soft, careful. "And we can drive. Well, I'll be able to as soon as my leg heals. Plus, we can concentrate usually."

"It's all of us," I argue. "It's bad for all of us. Jack cries all the time. I see him." He doesn't move. On his back, with his eyes closed, tanned skin glistening in the sun, anybody who didn't know would think he was dozing. "I see you," I tell him. He starts to hum.

"What are you humming?" Ellen asks him.

"Guid Merge."

"I see you crying sometimes, Jack, when you don't think anybody is looking or can tell. And I hear you in your room at home. I heard you two nights in a row last week." He keeps humming, eyes closed.

"We don't shake," Ellen tells me quietly. "We don't have fake heart attacks every second and nightmares."

"I have nightmares," Jack says. No more humming.

"Okay," Ellen agrees. "So do I. But we don't wake up screaming and freaked out. We wake up sad."

"I'm sad," I say, and it sounds ridiculous.

"I know, Anna," Ellen says as nicely as she's ever said anything to me. "But also you're really messed up."

16

THREE HOURS AFTER I GET HOME, SETH IS ON OUR DOORSTEP.

"Anna!" Jack yells, even though I'm right there behind him.

"Hi," I say to Seth.

Jack steps aside.

"Hi," Seth says to me. "I like your shades." He holds out his hand, palm up. M&M's.

I don't take any. My brother takes a few. "Are you going to invite him in?" Jack asks.

"Would you like to leave now?" I ask Jack back.

"Delighted," Jack goes, and he nods his head at Seth and disappears up the stairs.

"Okay," I tell Seth. "Come in."

I lead him to the family room and plop myself down on the L of the couch. I keep my sunglasses on, even though I don't need them indoors.

He stays standing. "Anna, I'm sorry I was such an idiot that night."

"It doesn't matter," I go, even though it does matter.

He sits down, but as far away as possible. "I'd been wanting to say a lot of stuff to you about the accident for a long time," Seth goes. "But . . . it's . . . you know . . . I guess the way it came out was . . . well, stupid."

"The truth is," I tell him, "we don't even really know each other."

"We were starting to," Seth says. "All of us, I mean. Jason and Lisa and Ellen."

"Who did you used to hang out with?" I ask Seth.

He digs into his pocket and then feeds some M&M's into his mouth. "Leo Feld and Rimi and Justin and that crowd," Seth says, crunching. "We still hang out sometimes."

"Ellen and my brother tell me I'm all messed up," I say. "I don't think I'm such great girlfriend material right now."

"Maybe that's just a way of saying you're not into me," Seth goes.

"Maybe."

He looks bummed, and then he starts to smile a little. "You're sort of a bitch," he tells me.

"Screw you," I tell him back.

"Okay," he goes, and he scoots over next to me. Then he lifts the sunglasses off my face and holds my cheeks in his hands. He doesn't kiss me. We just look at each other for a while.

"You got tan," he goes.

It's hard not to smile. His hands are big and warm.

"And your hair is the color of fire now."

He has pretty eyes. Brown with black rings around the outside.

"You've got a cat's eye," he tells me. He pulls his head back and squints. "Your pupil is vertical."

"I know," I say. "It might never get round again."

"Supreme." He smiles.

He doesn't let go of my face. My heart starts to beat fast. "My brother told me no girl can resist this move," he says finally, his face inches away from mine.

I knock his hands away. "Your brother doesn't know anything," I lie. But I keep hold of one of his index fingers, between us.

"So, what's going on?" I ask. He pulls a curl with his free hand. Then he pulls another one. I shake him off. "What's all this stuff you've wanted to say to me since the accident?"

"I really, really love your curls."

"I'm serious," I tell him. "What did you want to say?"

He sits up straight and scoots back a little. Shoves his free hand into his pocket and pulls out two M&M's. A green and an orange. "I just . . . um . . ." He slips the M&M's back into his pocket, and we listen to them click against each other. "I just feel . . . bad for you. Really, really bad."

"Oh," I say.

My uncle Buck is a gourmet cook. My aunt Jerry takes in foster dogs. Besides a Great Dane named Mamie they've had forever, there's always a few greyhounds and a mutt or two.

We hear barking even before we're out of the car.

"Welcome to the zoo," my father mumbles. Which is what he says every year. My mom and I carry two pumpkin pies and a bowl of stuffing, but still the dogs jump all over my father. Dogs love him for some reason.

"Off, Cyrus!" Aunt Jerry yells. "Off, Nixon! Off, Lucifer! Off! Off!"

"Lucifer?" Jack asks her. Aunt Jerry grabs me and Jack at the same time. She's the only one so far not too careful about my eye.

"I'm sorry, you guys," she whispers to us. "I'm so, so sorry."

"Get away!" my dad's yelling at the dogs. "Get away!"

"You have to say 'off,' Dad," Jack tells him, pulling free of Aunt Jerry, his face that half-and-half mask.

Mamie is too old to be a jumper. She lies right in the doorway between the kitchen and dining room, so you sort of have to leap over her. She's almost the size of a small pony.

"God damn it," my dad mutters when he spills some of his beer, stumbling over her. Mamie licks it up and then goes for his hand. He spills more beer trying to avoid her big head.

We sit down to eat almost right away. The table is covered with soups and salads and pumpkin breads and cranberry dishes and sweet-potato purees and two bowls of rice with flower petals garnishing the tops. We'll never finish it all, and Aunt Jerry will take the leftover main courses and half the fresh desserts to a soup kitchen later tonight. She'll make Jack and me come with her. She does that every year.

"There won't be any lawsuits?" Uncle Buck asks while he carves the turkey.

"No," my father says, shoving Nixon's head out of his crotch. I hadn't even thought about that.

"It wasn't Anna's fault," my mother says. "It wasn't anybody's fault. It was an accident."

"Not even a civil suit?" Uncle Buck asks. He puts the dark meat on one platter and the white meat on another. I pick up two big serving forks, waiting to add them when my uncle is done carving.

"No, Buck," my mother says. She sounds mad. "There won't be any lawsuits."

"Lucky," Buck says. "That's lucky."

"Stop that, Anna," my father tells me.

"Stop what?" I ask him. Everybody looks at me. I don't get it at first. Then I notice: The two forks are clacking together in my hand, making a fast, metallic rhythm, like a pair of castanets. I drop them onto the table and shove both hands in my lap. "Sorry," I say.

I'm refilling the water pitchers in the kitchen halfway through the meal. Aunt Jerry and my mother are pulling more bread out of the oven. It's infused with some sort of garlic pumpkin flavor, and Uncle Buck won't allow us to eat any that's not warm.

"It's called EMDR," Aunt Jerry's saying. "It's a kind of therapy for trauma survivors. I really think you should try it for her."

"For me?" I ask. "Are you talking about me?" Am I a trauma survivor?

"Get away!" I hear my father yelling.

"Off, Lucifer!" Uncle Buck and Jack yell right after that. If I hadn't just been called a trauma survivor, I'd laugh.

"Dad doesn't want me in therapy," I tell them.

"Your father is clueless," Aunt Jerry says, annoyed.

"Jerry," my mom goes. "You don't have to—"

"Just look at her," Aunt Jerry tells my mother. "Look at her!"

My mother looks at me. Aunt Jerry looks at me. I wonder if this is how the dogs feel when Jerry goes to pick one out.

What do they see?

Lucifer comes with us in the car. Everybody else stays home. Uncle Buck will get the desserts ready—the ones we haven't taken along with the leftovers—while my parents moan about how sick they feel from eating so much.

"So, how have you been really?" Aunt Jerry asks Jack.

He shakes his head. "I don't know. You should ask how Anna's been."

"It's obvious how Anna is," Jerry says. "You. You're less obvious."

"He's sad," I say.

"Shut up," he tells me, but not mean.

Lucifer is a mutt. He's small and energetic. He keeps trying to lick our faces. He wiggles from the front to the backseat, back and forth, first to me, then to Jack, then to me. If I'd been prepared for Lucifer, I'd have dug up my eye shield.

"And how have the two of you been together?" Jerry asks. She's my mom's older sister, but she's different from my mother. She gets right to the point. She doesn't let things go. She reminds me a little bit of Ellen's mom, actually, only not so stylish. To be honest, with her short hair and boxy body and something about her skin, she sort of looks like a man.

"What do you mean?" I ask.

"I think you know what I mean," she says. I glance at Jack. He's staring out the window.

"You mean that I killed his girlfriend," I tell Aunt Jerry.

"Shut up," Jack tells the window.

"That's not exactly what I mean," she goes. "And that's not exactly the truth of it either." She glances at me in her rearview.

Lucifer leaps from Jack's lap back to mine.

"Let me tell you what I wish for you," Jerry says after Jack and I stay quiet. She pulls into the Salvation Army parking lot. "I wish that when you're the ages of your mom and me, you see each other more than Thanksgiving and Christmas each year. I hope that you talk to each other a lot, about real things, the things that matter, and that you're involved in the lives of each other's children." It's embarrassing. How serious she's being. How . . . I don't know. Earnest.

Lucifer's on her lap now, snuggling in, even though we're all about to get out of the car. Jack glances back at me. His face is red.

"Siblings should be friends," Aunt Jerry says. "The two of you, especially, should be friends." Why us especially?

"Okay," Jack says.

"Okay," I say. I think we both just want her to stop.

"You didn't kill Cameron," Jack tells me suddenly, twisting all the way around from the front seat to see me.

"Yes, I did," I tell him back.

"No, you didn't," he says.

"Yes, I did."

"Stop it," Aunt Jerry says. "We have to bring the food in."

So we stop.

. . .

Back at the house, in front of the dessert spread, with steaming cups of coffee and cappuccino and exotic teas, Uncle Buck doesn't let us dig in until we say what we're thankful for. We do it that way every year. Nothing before the main meal. No prayers or toasts or anything. Thanks always come just before dessert. It's mandatory. Uncle Buck tells my dad to begin. My father puts his palms on the table and looks around at all of us.

"Get away!" he yells when Lucifer tries to climb on his lap.

"Off!" Uncle Buck pulls Lucifer back by the collar. My dad takes a deep breath. The vein in his forehead starts pulsing.

"Well," he says. "We have a lot to be thankful for this . . . ," and then he stops talking. He looks at me and Jack, and he tries to say something, only instead his face crunches inward and goes pink. He turns to my mother and makes a snorting sound, and then he looks at me and Jack again, and he shakes his head, and he stares at the middle of the table, and he goes, in this awful, high-pitched voice, "I can't." And he just sits there, shaking and then crying, while we watch, frozen, and Mamie lurches to her feet from the foot of his chair and whines and starts to lick his face, and Uncle Buck yanks her away, and it's almost as bad as the screaming, stopped.

17

"YOU HAVE SOMETHING CALLED POST-TRAUMATIC STRESS DISORDER," the therapist tells me. Her name is Frances. She's about my mom's age, and she's got a lot of freckles, which are sort of cute and funny-looking at the same time.

"Nightmares, startle response, panic attacks, inability to concentrate, avoidance behaviors."

"Avoidance, like avoiding driving?"

She nods. "Those can all be symptoms of PTSD."

"Did you buy that at Cinnamon Toast?" I ask her. She looks down at her flowing clothes in muted colors.

"Uh . . . ," she goes.

"My best friend's mom owns that store," I say. "Ellen. The one who was in the car with me."

"Oh," Frances says.

It's the third time I've seen Frances in two weeks. My parents have seen her once, together.

"How come Ellen doesn't have post-traumatic stress whatever?"

"Disorder," Frances reminds me. "PTSD. She might have it. But I don't know Ellen, so I couldn't say."

It's not that I don't like Frances. She's okay. It's that I'm embarrassed about being in therapy.

"It means I'm crazy, right?" I say. "Jack and Ellen think so. They think I'm completely and totally insane."

"Do you think you're insane?" Frances asks.

"I don't think most sixteen-year-olds go around feeling like they're going to die from heart attacks every time they get near a steering wheel," I say. Not to mention shaking practically all the time and nightmares every single night.

"Actually," Frances tells me, "in your case that's a normal reaction to an abnormal life experience."

"If it's so normal, why isn't Ellen having the same reaction as I am?"

"First of all, she wasn't driving. But also, Ellen was drunk and then passed out," Frances says. "Her brain was having an entirely different experience from yours."

"We were in the same car," I say. "We were in the same accident."

"Were you?" Frances asks.

Now I'm thinking she's the insane one. If I were a little younger, I'd probably look at her and go, "Duh." But I just stay quiet.

"Anna. There's nothing crazy about you. Listen." She leans

forward, and her freckles slightly change color somehow. They get darker. "When a trauma occurs, it seems to get locked in the nervous system with the original pictures, sounds, and feelings. A part of the brain that's involved in handling thought and language shuts down. Another part of the brain that knows only body sensations and emotions gets lit up. Way up. If those two parts of the brain don't find a way to reconnect, we can end up with symptoms like the ones you have."

She stops talking and leans back in her black leather chair. I'm sitting at the corner of her couch. It's red and has these small, cream-colored suede throw pillows, which are really, really smooth. I can't stop stroking them, as if they're little pets or something.

"Well, how do I get the two parts of my brain to reconnect, so I'm not such a head case?" I ask.

"There are different ways to treat PTSD," Frances tells me, "including taking medication for the anxiety and panic-attack part. There's also something called exposure therapy, which would involve getting you behind the wheel of a car before you really want to, and then making you drive. Then there're ways of making use of body sensations. We'll use elements of that today. And there's something called EMDR, which is my vote on what's most likely to get your brain reconnected."

"I don't want to drive." It's the only part of what she's just said that I hear. *Getting you behind the wheel of a car again.* I feel my heart chipping away at the inside of my chest, just at the thought.

"All right," Frances says. "We won't do that, then."

My heart's still pounding, though.

"What's going on?" she asks.

"What do you mean?"

"Your face is red, and you're sweating."

I wipe the tops of my thumbs down my temples, which are hot and damp.

"That's your body's response to the memory of the accident," Frances says. "You were thinking about having to drive, right?"

I nod.

"See how you're physically reacting to that thought?"

"I guess," I say.

"What kind of feelings are you having, thinking about it?" she asks.

"Shaking. Sweating. Hot," I say. "Kind of like I could throw up."

"Okay. Those are body sensations. What kind of emotional feelings are you having?" she asks.

"Scared. Embarrassed. Nervous," I say. I am crazy. I must be.

"Put your feet flat on the floor." Frances sits up straight, uncrosses her legs, and does it herself. "Like this. Really feel the bottoms of your feet supported by the rug and the wood beneath."

I untangle myself and copy her. I slide my butt to the edge of the couch and flatten both my feet inside my black leather boots with the zippers up the sides.

"Press down a little bit and see if you can feel the ground pressing back, solid under the soles of your feet."

"Okay," I say after a second. I'm a little calmed down, I think.

"Now take a couple of deep breaths," Frances tells me. "Like this." She breathes in really, really slow through her nose. She holds it a second and then blows the air out through her mouth, long and deep. It's a little weird. It looks like Ellen's mom, sort of, on her yoga mat.

But I do it anyway. I take a breath.

"Slower," Frances tells me. "Go slower." So I do. "How does your body feel now?" she asks after I blow the air out.

"I thought therapy was about talking," I say. "Not breathing. Or . . . you know . . . feet."

"This is uncomfortable for you," she tells me.

"Kind of." But as weird as it is, having my feet solidly on the floor and breathing deep like that does make me feel better. "I guess I'm not feeling as embarrassed," I admit to Frances.

"Good," she goes. "So you get a sense of how your body can cue emotions, and how emotions can cue your body. Right?"

I nod.

"So if you notice you're feeling anxious or afraid, you can use this to help soothe yourself. Just put your feet flat on the ground and breathe."

"Uh-huh," I say. "But . . ." I stroke the cream-colored pillow, worrying that the nightmares are too big and the shaking is too strong to be fixed so fast by some new way of sitting and breathing.

"What is it?" Frances asks.

I stop stroking and look at all the certificates on her wall. There're a bunch of them, and the one on the left middle row is crooked. "Am I going to be okay?" I think about how mad my dad is at how messed up I am now, and I feel that thick ink in my chest. "I mean, really okay?"

"Yes, Anna." I can feel her staring at me, and I pull my eyes from her certificates on the wall to look back at her. Her freckled face is so confident. "You're going to be fine." The ink thins out a lot. Not all the way. But a lot. It's a relief. To hear that from someone who maybe actually knows.

Rob's SUV is the easiest car for Ellen, with her wheelchair, compared with Ellen's mom's Volvo or our new Honda. So instead of going to school separately, Jack and I and Ellen and Rob start showing up together.

"How new is your car?" Ellen asks Rob as Jack helps her into the wheelchair. I'm holding her book bag, and Rob's kicking at the back left tire, worrying it's got a leak. He doesn't say anything. "Because it smells new," Ellen goes. "And it's spotless."

"Rob's a clean freak," Jack says. The air has that December edge to it that turns our breath into mini steam clouds.

"So when did you get the car?" Ellen asks again.

Rob holds out two fingers. We're heading out of the parking lot and toward the school building.

"Two months ago?" she guesses. Rob smiles.

"Two years," Jack corrects.

"No way," I say. I spot Lisa exiting the front door of school and walking down the steps onto the lawn toward us.

"Yep," Jack goes.

Lisa meets us near the flagpole. "They've got prom planning committee posted."

I don't know why she's telling us. We're not planning-committee people. To tell you the truth, we're not prom people either.

"I thought we didn't find out until tomorrow," Ellen says. Before I can even register that one, Lisa's talking again.

"Jack's on music, and so is Ellen."

What? We're walking up the outside double stairs now, and I'm shoving past kids harder than I usually do. Rob and Jack carry Ellen, in her chair, as if she doesn't weigh a thing. They're supposed to wheel her in to the side door, where there's a ramp, but we never bother.

"Rob, you're on theme and decoration."

"Excellent," he says.

"Wow," Lisa goes. "You have a really deep voice."

"You guys signed up to be on prom?" I ask.

We're inside. The bell is going to ring any second, and I just want the day to be over already.

"Not me," Lisa says. "I just passed the posting by accident."

"Hi," Jason goes, joining us.

"I wanted decent music this year," Ellen says. "I told you."

"No, you didn't."

"Take your sin-glasses off." She's supposed to remind me when I forget indoors, which is a lot of the time. Jason's looking back and forth at her and me, trying to figure out what's going on.

She went last year with this senior, Alan Frendleman. They broke up five days later because he decided he was too old to have a tenth-grade girlfriend. Ellen didn't really like him anyway. I mean, she liked him as a friend, but she said he was a bad kisser and worse at other things. Whatever.

"I didn't know you signed up," Ellen's saying to Jack. Then she turns to Jason. "Did you?"

"For prom?" Jason asks.

"Who do you think you're even going with?" I say to Ellen, but Rob's bass voice drowns out mine.

"He did it for Cameron," he rumbles.

We look at him. He looks at Jack.

"She was into it," Jack explains. "She convinced me."

"Duh," Lisa goes. "She would have been voted prom queen."

"Actually," Jack says, "she was going to . . ."

We all stop, as if there's a red light or some sort of signal. We just stop right where we are, in the center of the T intersection of the science rooms and math hall. We stand still and stare at Jack. He stares back, and his face fights itself.

"Anyway," he mutters. He shakes his head at Rob. "Come on." They take off.

Lisa starts walking after a second. Then she stops. Then she starts and keeps going. Ellen and Jason and I stay where we are, watching Lisa's back.

"I even e-mailed Anna about it," Ellen tells Jason. He arches his eyebrow. I see Seth moving toward us from the end of the hall.

"No, she didn't," I say to Jason. "She never said a word."

They start meeting for their stupid committees in, like, February or something. It's stupid. We've always said how stupid it is.

"I did," Ellen argues. "I'm sure of it."

The bell rings. Seth walks up and pulls a curl and kisses my cheek.

I push him off and spin away and don't even wait to see how they're going to get Ellen up the stairs for French IV.

18

SETH FINDS ME DURING LUNCH. I'M HIDING IN THE GIRLS' ROOM
at the back of the back gym lockers. It's a bathroom Ellen and
I never use because it's always filled with smoke and there're
only two stalls and Marcy Cunningham gives blow jobs in here
all the time. Seth marches straight through the door.

"Guy!" some girl waiting yells.

"Come on," he says to me.

"You're going to get into trouble," I say back.

"Life without parole," he goes. "Now, come on."

"Get out!" this girl yells.

Marcy Cunningham walks in. "Get out," she tells everybody.

"Come on," Seth says. I walk out with him.

"So, what's the matter?" He steers me away from the lunchroom and toward the side exit. There's a brick wall out there, and

in the spring all these purple and white flowers sprout up along the face of it. But it's not spring, and when we get to the wall, it's not pretty. It's just brick. "What's the matter?" he asks again.

"Everything," I say. I lean my butt on the low edge. It's cold and sharp.

"Oh," Seth goes. He stands in front of me and starts pulling my curls and letting them bounce back. There's nobody else out here. I let him pull.

"Where are your shades?" he asks. I must have dropped them in the bathroom. It makes me realize my right eye isn't freaking out in the daylight.

"I guess I don't need them anymore," I say.

He keeps pulling. He goes, "Boing, boing," under his breath.

"What's your next big thing?" I ask him. "You never told me. From that day at Ellen's. You know. Charisma. Heart attack."

"Oh, yeah," he says. "Send a dollar."

"What?"

"Send a dollar. I started it already. I put an ad in the *City Trib* classified section. It just says, 'Send a dollar.' With a post office box address. That day at Ellen's I was working on the wording."

"I don't get it," I say.

"I want to see how many people actually send money."

"You're kidding me."

"Nope."

"You have a post office box address?"

"I do now."

"Isn't that expensive?"

"I have a feeling dollars will be arriving shortly to cover the cost."

"Isn't that illegal? Can you just take people's money like that? Doesn't there have to be a cause or something? I mean, you could get into trouble."

"Life without par . . . ," he starts, but he doesn't finish.

"Stop making me feel stupid."

"I'm not making you feel anything." But he is.

"I don't want to like you," I tell him.

"Yeah, you're kind of strange about that."

"I don't know why." It's embarrassing for some reason.

"Me neither," he says. "I'm a good catch."

I take his hands and put one on each of my cheeks. It feels nice. Safe.

"Don't kiss me," I tell him.

"Okay," he says. "Can I kiss you this afternoon, though?" His face is almost touching mine. I can smell his breath. Chocolate and peanut butter.

"No," I say. "I have therapy."

"You can't kiss on the same days as therapy?" he asks. "Is that a law?"

"Yes."

"Oh," he says.

Ellen passes me a note in biology. If Ms. Riffing catches cell phones in use, she confiscates them and then uses them to call parents to tell them how great their kids are. She calls them every day from the kid's cell, and at about day four she'll mention that she'll be keeping the kid's phone until the end of the marking period.

Why are you so mad? Ellen's handwriting slants to the right, and her letters are tall and angled. Not curvy and round like Lisa's.

You never told me, I pass back. *After Christmas you and Jack are going to be hanging out together while I'm doing nothing.*

I did tell you. And I didn't even know about Jack.

Fine, I write. *Forget it.*

You'll get to have more alone time with Seth, anyway.

Big deal, I write back.

Stop moping, she writes. *It's just a stupid prom committee. It's just a stupid prom.*

Exactly! And I draw a frown face.

Oh, come on. She draws a smiley face.

I think about Cameron and know I'm a complete spoiled bitch brat, because I'm alive at least, and I suck up how bad I'm feeling straight to somewhere in the bottom of my stomach.

I'm not moping, I write back. *M. C. was in the science hall bathroom again.*

Which guy?

Didn't see.

I feel sorry for her, Ellen writes.

So do I. So, Jason's not on any prom committees?

I wish. He is so amazing.

He's gay, I remind her.

But he hasn't had a boyfriend since I've known him.

He's not straight, Ellen. He's picky. He's got class.

I know. Okay. What are you doing after school?

Therapy, I write. *You?*

Doctor. I get my short cast soon.

It's been almost two months. I can't believe it.

I know, she scribbles.

SATs are almost here.

I know.

Christmas is almost here.

I know. She draws a face with a half smile, half frown. It reminds me of Jack.

I feel like shit.

Yeah, she writes, and I'm reading it, and then Ms. Riffing is standing over me. She whirls around and around, saying something about the path of mitochondria. Actually, I think she's being a mitochondrion. Everyone is laughing. Ms. Riffing doesn't stop talking or whirling. Just holds out her hand. I have to pass over the note in time with her spin.

She uses the note to be some part of a cell, or maybe an enzyme—I'm not really sure—and then she crumples it up and stuffs it in her mouth and keeps swirling, and Ellen and I pay attention after that.

Frances is trying to explain EMDR.

"Bilateral stimulation of the brain used in a certain way," she's telling me, "seems to unlock the nervous system and to help people with PTSD."

"Wait," I say, holding up a little rectangular box that looks sort of like a gray iPod. "Is this the bilateral stimulation?" It has headphones attached to it and also another set of wires that end in two matching plastic handles, each about the size of a mussel. They vibrate in your hands, one at a time, back and forth, when the little box is turned on. The headphones make this soft snapping sound, one ear at a time.

"Yep," Frances says. "I also use left-right eye movements with a lot of people, but since you've had an eye injury, we won't do it that way with you."

I put down the box, with its headphones and hand buzzers and pick up a suede pillow. "Hearing clicks back and forth and getting my hands buzzed back and forth is going to unlock my nervous system?"

She nods.

"I still don't get how."

"We think it works a little bit like what happens when we're in deep sleep," Frances explains. "We all need a minimum amount of sleep in order not to get too crazy. Right?"

"If you say so," I go.

"Okay," she says. "You know how in deep sleep your eyes move back and forth very quickly?"

"I guess," I say, stroking the pillow.

"It may be that those eye movements are a kind of bilateral stimulation that helps people process daily experiences," Frances says. "That way our brains don't get overloaded from all the stimuli we take in each day."

"So deep sleep is like mini EMDR for everybody?" I ask.

"Theoretically."

I put down the pillow and pick up the gray box again. I take a buzzer in each hand and turn it on. *Buzz. Buzz.* And I thought deep breathing was weird. I turn it off.

"Today we're not even going to work on the accident," she tells me.

"Why not?"

"First we need a safe place," she says, "and then we need

some inner resources for you to call on if you ever need them."

"A safe place?" I ask. "Do my parents know we're doing this?"

Frances smiles. "I explained EMDR to them." She has perfectly even teeth, except for this one that's longer than the others and pointy. A fang. "Why do you ask?"

"No offense," I tell her. "But I have a feeling they'd think this is . . . um . . . like, a waste of time."

"Listen," Frances goes. "If you don't stop having nightmares and the shakes and panic attacks after four more sessions, we'll try something else."

"Like forcing me to drive?" I ask.

"No," she says. "Maybe medication."

"But I don't want medication, either," I say.

"Okay," Frances agrees. "So how about trying something weird instead?"

It's hard to fall asleep because I know I'm going to have one of those nightmares, and they scare me, plus they wake everyone up, and it's embarrassing, even though when my mother comes in, she just stays quiet and strokes my sweaty head. So tonight I try to use what we did in therapy the way Frances suggested.

She had me imagine a place that felt totally safe and comfortable. She made me describe the whole thing to her. Every now and then she'd turn those hand buzzers on—I didn't like the headphones—and they'd vibrate back and forth. It's a pink sand beach I made up. Not Commons End, with its greenish, choppy water. Another place. A Caribbean sea, magical, with dazzling turquoise waves that are steady and even, rolling in from the horizon in a predictable, slow rhythm. Between each wave the water's as still as glass. You can hear seagulls and the lapping of wavelets and the breeze rustling through palm trees. It smells like coconut sunblock and seaweed, and it's warm without being too hot. So now I try to think of that. It sort of helps, but still. It's not like I'm actually in this place. It's not like it can actually keep me from having a nightmare. That much I know.

I think of the other two things we did. Frances calls them inner resources. More weirdness. First she had me create a protector figure. She said it could be real, imagined, dead, or alive. I had to think about the qualities I'd want a protector to have: strong, fast, loving, smart, levelheaded, magical. I picked a dolphin. A big gray dolphin with a white underbelly. So I make myself see him now at the magical Caribbean beach with the dazzling turquoise waves, and I swim with him and feel my body relaxing, but then the minute I know I might really fall asleep, I'm wide awake again.

So I picture my adviser. This one has to be wise and smart and levelheaded and able to see problems and solutions from all angles. I've picked an old woman. She's sort of tall and thin, but not in a scrawny way. More regal, like a queen or something, and she has white hair tied back in a fancy knot, and she's dressed in flowing clothes, and she's got wrinkled skin and this kind, knowing expression. So now I put her on the beach. She sits on a three-legged wooden stool in the shade and watches me play in the blue, blue water with the dolphin.

•   •   •

"Anna!"

My father's sitting on my bed. He hasn't turned the light on, but still I can see that he's got a cup of water in his hands.

"I'm sorry," I tell him. "I didn't mean to wake everybody up again."

A bloody glass wave looming over me and Jack, and screaming shattering out of the wave, and blood splattering our faces, looming and red and wet and huge, and screaming, screaming, screaming.

"Drink," my dad goes, so I take the glass and drink.

A bloody glass wave with my father standing behind it, about to throw another one, and my brother with his hands up and out, and screaming and screaming and screaming.

"I'm going to throw up," I say, and he moves fast to grab my wastebasket and hold it near my face, but I don't throw up after all. "Okay," I say after a minute. "Maybe I'm not." I'm shaking. "Thanks," I say. "Sorry."

"I hate to see you like this," he tells me, putting the wastebasket on the floor and sitting down on the edge of the bed.

"I'm okay," I tell him.

"I wanted you on medication," my father goes. "But your therapist said to give her six sessions first with this EMDR thing."

"I don't want to take medicine."

"You need to be able to drive."

"I know," I say. "I'm sorry."

"You need to stop having these nightmares."

"Yeah," I go. "I know. I'm sorry."

"I want you to put this thing behind you."

"Dad, I'm really sorry."

"Stop saying you're sorry, Anna," he orders.

"Sorr . . . ," I go.

"Here," he says. "Sit up a minute." He straightens and smoothes my sheets and then plumps my pillow, just like Ellen might do it. "Now, lie back." I obey. "Try to get some sleep."

"Dad," I say as he's leaving my room. He turns around, but it's too dark to see his face all that well. "Are you going to get therapy?"

"No," he goes. "Why?"

I'm thinking about Thanksgiving. About his voice, so high pitched and awful. About him crying.

"I don't know."

"Get some sleep, Anna."

"You're not in such great shape either," I tell him through the dark. He pauses, just outside my door. I'm frozen, waiting for him to turn around again and yell at me. But he doesn't. I hear him just standing there for a really long time before he finally moves away and down the hall.

19

IT'S OUR LAST STUDY SESSION BEFORE THE SAT.

"Three hundred and thirty-four?" Jason's asking. We're at
Ellen's, as usual. She and I made chocolate-chip cookies before
everybody came over. Actually, I made them while Ellen sat
in her wheelchair, leg propped up, and drank peppermint
schnapps straight out of her parents' liquor cabinet. While I was
scraping the last cookies off the sheet and onto a plate, Ellen
poured water from my glass into the schnapps bottle to hide
her crime.

"Three hundred and thirty-six," Seth goes, chewing his ninth
cookie.

"What are you going to do with the money?" Lisa asks.

"I think it's unethical," Ellen says. She opens up her study
guide. "It's taking advantage of stupid people." She looks down

at the book. "Ugh," she goes. "I'm going to be so glad when this is over."

"How do you know they're stupid?" Seth asks. "Maybe they're just generous."

"Right," Ellen goes.

"Or bored," Jason suggests.

"Whatever," Ellen says. "Come on. We've done practically no math."

"We spent all last week on math," Jason says.

"Well, it's not enough. We stink at it," Ellen complains.

"I'm going to buy you a good mood," Seth goes.

"What?"

"With the money from all the stupid people," Seth tells her. "I'm going to buy you a good mood."

"I like that idea," Jason goes.

"I'm never hanging with you again," Ellen tells him.

"I like Seth's idea too," I say.

Ellen glares at us. "You people suck."

When I get home, Jack's in the kitchen, working on his laptop. He's got a not-too-bad song on low volume.

"Another review?" I ask him.

He stabs at a key and scans the screen. "No," he goes. "Amen Calling."

"What?"

"Amen Calling," he repeats.

We look at each other for a confused second before I get it. "Oh," I go. "Don't tell me Another Review is the name of a band?"

He gets it too. He laughs and turns off Amen Calling. "Yeah," he says. "It is. I was surprised you'd heard of it."

"Anyway," I go.

He nods at the computer screen. "Postings for Cameron," he explains.

My face gets hot. I remember what Frances told me, and I try to think about what my hot face is letting me know. What my body's telling me. It's not hard: My face is flushed because I feel embarrassed and ashamed because I still haven't looked at Cameron's memorial Web site. Much less written anything for it.

Jack looks up. "You want to see?" He turns the laptop a little toward me.

I shake my head. "I've got to study."

He slides the laptop back where it was. "You'll get to take them again," he says.

"Yeah," I go. "But still." He got 1490 on his. I'll never get that. Never.

"Cameron didn't do so great on them," Jack tells me.

"Really?" I ask. "What's not so great?" I'm thinking for Cameron that probably means at least 1400.

"She had trouble breaking a thousand," Jack goes.

"No way," I say.

"Yeah." He nods. "She did really bad on standardized tests."

I'm not sure what to do. We haven't talked about her at all, and the last time I tried, he lost it. So I stand here.

"She wasn't going to college right off the bat anyway," Jack tells me.

"Really?" I figure it's safest if I don't say too much.

"She was thinking of taking a year off to work."

"But she was so smart," I say. "Even with bad SATs she could have gone anywhere, right?"

"She thought it would be cool to just . . . you know . . . live for a year."

The minute he says it, it's like the room shrinks. Just gets small and cramped. *Live*. It's weird how things come out of our mouths that we don't plan. I look at Jack's mask of a face, and I don't know what to do. He drops his head straight down on the table, next to the laptop. *Live*. His forehead makes a thunking sound when it hits.

"Go away," Jack says. His voice is muffled.

"Jack," I say.

"Leave," he goes.

The first time Jack threw me out was the summer of the sharks. We weren't so young anymore. Eleven and twelve maybe. Twelve and thirteen. I'm not sure.

My father was frowning at the newspaper. "This isn't good."

We were sitting around the table, in front of the glass wall with a view of green skylighted roofs tapering to the gray slate sparkle of the ocean farther in the distance.

"What?" my mom asked. She'd made waffles for us. We always got special breakfasts at the beach. When we were really little, it was the assortment pack of mini cereals. The sweetened kind you can open and pour milk right into the box. Other times my mom made us chocolate-chip pancakes. That day it was peach-and-powdered-sugar waffles.

"Sharks," my dad said.

"Sharks?"

"Apparently small blue sharks have been swimming in shallow waters close to shore." My father was half reading, half telling. "A girl had her calf bitten."

"No," my mom said. She sifted some powdered sugar onto her half-eaten waffle.

"Yes."

"Around here?" I speared my next bite with my fork. "Really?"

"Not so far," my father said. "Near Ocracoke two swimmers were bitten on their lower legs just before sundown." He held out his plate for my mom to serve him another helping.

"Can we still swim?" I asked.

"Don't talk with your mouth full," my father answered. "You're going to choke."

I chewed madly.

"The lifeguards are the experts," my mother said. "They won't let us in the water if it's not safe. We'll read the board."

"They should have flags for sharks," Jack went.

"Does it say if anybody's been bitten at our beach?" my mom asked.

My father scanned the paper. "It doesn't say."

"Are there more waffles?" Jack asked. My mother gave him the last one.

"I'm not swimming with sharks," I said.

"I wouldn't let you swim with sharks," my dad said back. Then he grabbed my leg. I yelped. "Gotcha!" He laughed.

About an hour and a half later my parents were arguing in front of the lifeguard tower. Jack and I had dropped our chairs and bags. Jack's face was this combination of pissed off and bored both at the same time. He got that expression a lot lately, especially when we were around my parents. I was scanning the ocean for fins.

"Ridiculous," my mom was saying. "Other people are swimming, the lifeguards are keeping an eye—"

"I'm not trusting some nineteen-year-old with a shit pair of binoculars," my dad said. "You want the kids' feet bitten off?"

Jack had his earphones in and the volume turned way up. I tried to catch his eye, but he wasn't having it. He had barely talked to me in the car on the drive down. Just had his head buried in his laptop.

"Nobody else looks nervous or anything," I tried to point out, but my parents weren't listening.

"The kids can wade," my dad was saying. "It won't kill them."

"Excuse me," some lady said. She was talking to my father. He was blocking the board. Jack picked up his chair and bag and stomped away from us.

"There're sharks," my father informed her.

"Harvey!"

"Excuse me?" the lady said.

"Sir, we'd appreciate it if you'd move aside," one of the lifeguards yelled down. He had talked to my father forever already, explaining that the newspapers liked a good story and that the shark incidents south of us were too far away to be of much concern here.

"You're going to create a panic," my mother said. Not so quietly anymore.

"Don't you think you should at least post this?" my father called up to the lifeguard, waving the article around. It half fluttered into the face of the lady who was trying to read the board.

"Harvey, please," my mother said. Her mouth was getting tighter and thinner by the second. That *This is wrong, but there's nothing I can do* look. "I'm sorry," she told the lady.

It was embarrassing. I followed Jack and spread my towel out next to his. He was sitting up and scowling at the water.

"Everybody else is swimming." He'd taken his earphones out.

"Yeah," I said. "But what if we get attacked?"

"There's no sharks around here," Jack said. "Those other beaches where people got bit are sixty miles away at least. Dad's being so stupid."

"No swimming today," my father told us, kicking up sand, while he dumped the umbrella and his bag and chair.

"There's no sharks, Dad," Jack said.

"You're not swimming."

"Can we swim tomorrow?" I asked.

"We'll see," he said.

"Mom?" I went. "Can we swim tomorrow?"

She sighed and wiggled her toes in the sand. "I think you'll be able to swim tomorrow," she said.

"Why do you do that?" my father asked her. He had that tone. That edge. I glanced up at him. His face was red. The vein was dancing. My mother didn't answer him.

"Amanda," my dad said.

Jack got up and began to walk away.

"Where are you going?" I asked, but he acted like he didn't hear me.

"Why," my father was saying to my mother. "Do. You. Do that?"

I got up and ran after Jack. "We're taking a walk," I shouted back at my parents. My mother was standing, stiff, a half-folded chair dangling from her hand. My father was behind her, arms waving. You could hear his voice, picking and picking.

We walked all the way to the big fishing pier, which Jack said was close to a mile. It took us more than an hour, and we were hot. Tons of people were swimming, but we just dipped our feet. I splashed water on my shoulders and face. Jack didn't want his CD player to get wet, so he stayed at the edge, with the seagulls and sand crabs, staring out at the brown green horizon.

"I used to think it was under*toe,* as in *toe* on my foot," I told Jack when we were walking back.

He didn't say anything.

"Are you mad at me?" I asked him.

"No," he said, but it sort of sounded like he was mad.

When we plopped down on our towels, my mother was there alone, reading a book. I looked at the cover. It was called *Alive.*

"Where's Dad?" I asked.

"Walking," she said.

"I'm hot," Jack went.

"Don't make a fuss, please," my mom said. "I cannot take another fuss today."

"It's hot," Jack said again. "I'm going in."

"You may not go in. Dad said so explicitly."

"It's not fair," I complained.

My mother didn't answer.

"How come he gets to make all the rules?" Jack asked. "How come everything has to be his way?"

"Don't start," my mother warned. "This is the beginning of our vacation. Let's just have a good time."

"On a vacation," Jack told her, "you're supposed to be able to swim!"

I spotted my father walking toward us along the shoreline, his shaggy head bent down, looking for sea glass maybe. Three kids were jumping the waves in front of us, and not far from them two surfers were paddling. I didn't see fins anywhere.

Jack stood up. "I'm going in."

"Jack," my mother warned.

"Dad said you can't," I told him.

He'd gotten his CD player unhooked and his shirt off. He started walking toward the water.

"Jack," my mom said. "Come back."

"No," he told her over his shoulder. "It's so stupid."

Now my mother stood up. Her book fell onto the sand. Jack started jogging, and then he broke into a run and dived into the first wave, whipping out the other side. I looked toward my father's bent head. Then I looked at my mother, arriving at the edge of the shoreline, hand shading her eyes, calling to Jack. He stayed in the breakers, jumping, paddling, swimming. Mostly I just watched his back. When he leaped up, his slick shoulder blades looked as sharp as knives.

Even from a distance it didn't take my father long to notice. I could hear the shouting all the way from where I was, wiping sand off my mom's book.

"What the hell are you doing!" My dad broke into a run. A little girl in a lime green swim diaper sat back from her bucket and stared. A couple strolling arm in arm stopped.

Jack kept leaping. My dad raced toward him, stopping every few seconds to yell. "Get out of the water! Jack. Get out of the water!"

The three kids who were hopping the waves bodysurfed to shore. Jack kept jumping.

My father launched himself into the ocean, disappeared under a cresting wave, resurfaced right next to my brother, and grabbed Jack's arm. You could see him pulling and Jack shaking him off. Then you could see Jack change his mind and turn toward shore. My father kept grabbing some part of Jack. His shoulder, his arm. His hair. My mom stayed at the water's edge, her hands still shading her eyes. Jack clambered out of the ocean and right past her, my dad at his back, grabbing, while my brother kept snaking out of his hands.

"Don't you walk away from me," my father was shouting. Jack leaned down to grab his towel and shoes. His hair dripped on me. "God damn it!"

For some reason I looked over at the lifeguard tower. Weren't lifeguards supposed to keep things safe? They were just sitting there, staring along with everyone else. My mother seemed stuck at the shoreline, facing us. Her hand was still shading her face, like she'd forgotten it was there.

My dad kept yelling, "God damn it, Jack!" He was yelling so loud the little girl in the lime green swim diaper started to wail, and her mother scooped her up and started packing their cooler. He was yelling so loud that the arm-in-arm couple put their backs to the ocean to watch, as if my father were a geyser or a plane crash. Jack was trying hard to get away, up the dune and over its edge to the street, but my father wasn't letting him. He was stepping in front of Jack, so that my brother had to zig and then zag to make progress up the sandy incline. My father was screaming in Jack's face, and Jack kept moving, like a football player in slow motion. Step left, blocked, step right. Step right, blocked, step left.

Finally Jack faked right and then dodged left and ran hard up the hill, spraying a fan of sand behind him. My father shouted at his back, his voice filling the beach with ugliness.

By the time my dad stormed back to our spot, my mother and I had somehow gotten everything gathered together and were ready to go.

"What?" he snapped at my mom. She and I were filling our arms with chairs and blankets and bags. "What?" my dad snapped again, but my mother didn't answer him, and we trooped past the lifeguard tower and up the dune without anyone saying another word.

When we got back to the house, Jack was in his room with the door locked. My father threatened to break it open, and a few seconds later the knob clicked, and my father went inside. My mother hustled me out of the house, and we went to buy fresh shrimp, and she took a long, long time to decide which brand of cocktail sauce to buy. When we got home, my father was quietly reading the paper in the living room, facing the glass window.

I knocked on Jack's door, and he didn't let me in, but then I realized the door was cracked just the tiniest bit. I stepped inside. Jack was flat on his bed staring at the ceiling. His CD player and earphones were nowhere in sight, and his face was red and sweaty, eyelashes clumped wetly together.

"Get out," he said.

"Are you okay?"

"Get out!"

"Your door wasn't locked," I told him.

"I'm not allowed to lock it," he said. "Get out."

"But—"

"Get! Out!"

"I just want to help," I tried to explain.

He looked at me in a way I'd never seen before. With this expression that was brand-new. One that told me how small and disgusting he thought I was. "You?" he said, with that look. "You?" He snorted. "You're no help."

My mom is driving me to therapy. We tried to change the day because I wanted to be with Ellen when she got her new, short cast, but her doctor couldn't switch and neither could Frances, so that was that.

"Do you remember the summer of the sharks?" I ask my mom, tugging my hat down over my ears.

"That wasn't so long ago," she tells me.

"Dad didn't let us swim for practically the whole vacation," I say. I switch the heater vents to the floor. The air blowing from out of the dashboard bothers my eye.

"You and Jack got very good at paddle ball."

"Nobody else was staying out of the water."

"Well," she says.

"Why was Dad being so mean?"

"He wasn't being mean," my mom says. "He was being protective. Can we turn this down a little?" She's already turning the heat down a notch.

"Protective?" I go. "Try psychotic."

"Oh, Anna," my mother says. "What made you think of that?" She makes a right onto Bateson Avenue. We pass the mall. It reminds me I haven't been shopping in months. I need new shoes. And new underwear. I turn the heat back up.

"How come you let him do that to Jack?" I ask her.

"What?" she goes. "Do what?"

"Don't you remember?" I say. "Don't you remember him with Jack that first morning? Screaming and chasing him and everything?"

"Dad gets carried away," my mom says. "He gets scared easily, and then he gets carried away."

"Scared?" My father scared? No way. "He needs therapy," I say. "There's something seriously wrong with him."

"Did you hear that from Aunt Jerry?" my mom asks. I'm totally surprised.

"No," I say. "Why?"

My mom puts her thumb to her mouth and starts gnawing.

"You shouldn't bite your cuticles," I tell her. She drops her hand to the steering wheel. "Why?" I ask again. "Does Aunt Jerry think Dad needs therapy?"

"Can you get my checkbook out?" she says. I fish around in her purse and pull it out along with a pen. "You write it," my mom says. "I'll sign when we get there."

"You never do anything," I say, writing out Frances's name on the top line. "You never make him stop."

My mother glances at me and then back at the road. "I do the best I can," she says finally.

I fill in the date and the amount, and then I cap the pen and I think about it. What I'm trying to understand is, how can my mother say my father is scared, when really he's just a complete asshole? And how come my mother always stays out of things, reading her books or working in her study or floating out at the horizon, just letting him get away with it?

"I need to go shopping," I say. "I've got holes in my socks, and my boots are shot."

She pulls into the parking lot of Frances's building. "Okay," she says.

20

TODAY FRANCES IS WEARING PALE YELLOW PANTS THAT ARE SO flowy they look like a skirt, and a matching blouse, scarf, and vest. It's pretty. Ellen's mother has the same outfit, only she doesn't wear it together all at the same time.

"I have SATs on Saturday, and then it's winter break," I tell her. "Plus, Ellen's getting her short cast today. And my father says I have to get better."

"Really?"

"He says I have to start driving soon."

"Nightmares?" She's pulling out her EMDR box and wires from a black bag.

"Same," I tell her. "The dolphin and the wise woman help me fall asleep. But then . . . you know."

"Heart attacks?" she asks. We both know they're not heart attacks. They just feel like that in the moment.

"Not exactly," I say. "Just little ones sometimes between classes. I remembered to use the safe place once."

"Your Caribbean sea? The calm one with the turquoise water and the coconut smell?"

"Yeah. It worked when I remembered. But I didn't remember the other times."

"Do you have any idea what's triggering the anxiety?" Frances hands me the buzzers. *Triggering* means something that sets me off, gets me going into a panic.

"The idea of having to drive," I say, "a couple of times when I thought someone would ask me. But that wasn't at school."

"What about at school?" she asks. She helps me untangle the wires.

"I don't know. It's always in the halls, between classes."

We untangle, and she moves her chair forward a little and I pull up my legs, cross them, and put a suede pillow on my lap.

"All right," she says. "Are you ready?" She means am I ready to talk about the accident today. It's what we've been prepping for this whole time.

My heart starts speeding up. "My palms are sweating."

"That's fine," she says.

"No, it's not," I tell her.

"Anna, this isn't going to be comfortable."

"I know," I say. "You keep telling me that."

She puts the EMDR box down on the reddish wood end table beside her and looks at me. "I think you can do this," she goes. "You can ask me to stop or let go of the tappers anytime you want to stop. You have your safe place, if you need it, and you have your protector and your adviser. We told your mom this might be a big session, and she's right outside in the waiting room, right?"

"Yeah," I say.

Frances's waiting room isn't as nice as in here. Just a few hard chairs and a low coffee table with old magazines. I keep meaning to tell her she should get some new subscriptions or something, but then I forget, or I think it's rude. My mother likes the pictures on the walls out there. One is a framed poster of an egg. Just an egg. It is kind of nice. Smooth and white and calm-looking. The other is a black-and-white photograph of the sky with one cloud in it.

"Okay." I know I have to stop stalling. I wipe my palms on the knees of my jeans. "Fine. I'm ready. What do I have to do?"

"I'm going to ask you some questions," Frances says. "I don't want you to think too much about the answers. Okay?"

"Okay."

"At a certain point I'll turn this stuff on."

"Then what?" I ask.

"You just let come up whatever comes up. Images, memories, thoughts, feelings, body sensations. Whatever. There's no right or wrong. Sometimes you may notice something change and sometimes you may not. It can help to imagine that you're on a train, and anything that does come up is just the scenery going by."

"Okay," I say. She's explained it to me before. I've heard the train thing. I know that sometimes she'll turn the buzzers off and ask me what's happening, and then I'll get to talk. I know that I'm not supposed to censor anything or judge what happens. I know all that. It's just hard to do what you're supposed to do the first time you do something.

"So," Frances says. She picks up the EMDR box and leans forward a little in her chair. "Take yourself to the night of the accident." I nod and grip a buzzer in each hand. "Just remember."

"The tappers aren't on," I tell her.

"I know," she says. "That's okay. I'm not going to put them on until a little later."

"Oh," I go.

"Take yourself back to the accident and tell me what picture represents the worst part."

"The whole thing was bad," I say.

"Think of it as a mini movie," Frances suggests. "Watch it from beginning to end. Watch each frame."

"The thing I keep seeing," I say after a minute, "is my key chain dangling over me. It's just there, glowing in the dark, swinging, sort of."

"Okay," Frances says. "Now. What words go best with the image of your key chain that express your negative belief about yourself?"

"What?" I shift my crossed legs and lean harder on the pillow on top of them.

"As you see that picture, what is the negative belief about yourself?"

I have no idea what she means. She can tell.

"It would be a statement that starts with 'I am,'" Frances explains.

"I don't know." Everything was inside of me and outside of me in pieces and sideways and upside down and wrecked. "Maybe 'I am out of control'?"

"All right," Frances says. "And when you see that key chain, what would you prefer to believe about yourself now?"

"That I'm in control," I say.

"So how true do the words, 'I am in control' feel to you now on a scale of one to seven, where one feels completely false and seven feels completely true?"

Okay. For one thing, I'm getting a little sick of all these questions. And for another, I have no clue what she's asking.

"Can you repeat that?" I ask. So she does. The second time I think I understand. How true does "I am in control" feel now when I think about that key chain? Not very true at all, so I give Frances a two.

"What emotions do you feel now?" Frances asks.

Well. I feel the out of controllness and the wreckedness and everything sideways and upside down and in pieces, and it's awful.

"Scared," I tell Frances. "And guilty. Really scared and really guilty."

"On a scale of zero to ten, where zero is no disturbance and ten is the highest disturbance you can imagine," Frances says. Another scale? "How disturbing is it to you now?"

It's pretty bad. "A ten," I say.

"And where do you feel the disturbance in your body?" she asks.

"My heart is beating fast, and my hands are sweaty, and I'm all tense everywhere, and my face is hot." I'm thinking how she hasn't even turned on any buzzing and I'm already hating EMDR.

"Bring up the picture of the dangling, swinging key chain,

and the words 'I am out of control,' and feeling scared and guilty, and noticing your heart and hands and face and muscles, and go with that."

Go with that?

Then she turns on the box.

At first I'm just completely self-conscious. I mean, I'm sitting here with this buzzing back and forth in my palms, and Frances is staring at me, and the whole thing is so out there. Then the *buzz, buzz* in my hands turns into the *thrum, thrum* of Wayne's party that night, and it's not like I'm hypnotized or in a trance or anything. I know I'm cross-legged on Frances's red couch, but my mind speeds up too, and I can feel the *thrum, thrum* and taste the Jack Daniel's and see the signs not to party on the second floor and Seth's peppermint patties, and all these details I'd forgotten about.

"Just notice," I hear Frances tell me, and I realize I've closed my eyes. I keep them closed and keep noticing. It's like a movie on fast forward. Drinking and a pyramid of beer cans and someone wearing a bright pink jean jacket and Ellen walking me around the second floor, keeping everything under control. *Buzz, buzz. Thrum, thrum.*

"Take a breath," Frances says, and the buzzing stops, and I open my eyes and breathe in. "Let it go," Frances tells me, so I let the air out. She waits a second, and then she asks, "What's happening now?"

"I'm remembering the party," I say. "I got really drunk, and Ellen took care of me."

"Go with that," Frances says, and she turns on the box again.

There's Seth at the pool table, and then the green skin of the pool table turns into grass, and on the grass are small brown leaves, and my dad is screaming at me on the lawn, and then the lawn becomes the kitchen, and he's screaming at me in the kitchen, and behind him the laptop on the kitchen table shows the poker game, and the green of the poker table on the screen turns into our lawn, and our green lawn becomes the pool table in Wayne's basement, and I'm trying hard to sink the eight ball to impress Seth.

"Take a deep breath," Frances says, and the buzzing stops, and I breathe in and open my eyes, and she tells me to let it go and asks what's happening now.

"Different stuff," I tell her. Because I can't remember all of it. "I was angry at my father. We had a fight that night, and then I was playing pool. That was right before we left."

"Go with that."

I'm thinking how annoyed I'm going to get with "Go with that," but then I forget about it, and there's me and Ellen across from each other at the pool table, and Ellen saying something about how I'd rather be bitching about my father than be here, and then we're in the Honda, and I'm worrying she's going to throw up in the front seat and if she does, my dad will find out and be pissed off, and I'm going to pull over, even though she says I don't need to, and she leans down to do something to the radio.

• • •

"Deep breath," Frances reminds me, which is good, because it's weird how you can forget to breathe. "And let it go." She waits. "What's happening now?"

"I don't know," I say. My voice is all shaky, and I'm breathing heavy. "We've been hit." I huddle into the pillow in my lap and grip the buzzers.

My body's freaking out, and it's hard to catch my breath, and I'm having a heart attack, and there's sirens and Ellen's ponytail like glass in my eye and the smell of new plastic, and the earth dangling above, and "Hooow looong, hoow loong, how long . . . to sing this sooong?" and I feel Frances hand me a tissue box, but she keeps the buzzing going, and I open my eyes with it all happening so that I can wipe the tears with a tissue, and I just feel scared and ashamed and out of control, and I uncross my legs, knocking away the pillow, and I pull my knees up to my chin and keep hold of the tissues and wipe my eyes, and Frances goes, "Just notice, it's old stuff going by, just notice," so I try to keep noticing, and I get so tired, really, really tired, and then I'm waking up in the hospital bed, and my mother is there in her pajamas and raincoat, and she's telling me I'm okay, and then I'm in the car with my parents, and my father's saying, "She was in your lane, it wasn't your fault, she was in your lane," and then I'm in the hall at school, and Lisa is saying, "It was a cinder block," only I know it was a tree branch, and it was Cameron who swerved, not me, and then I see Cameron's silky hair and smoky skin, and I'm so sad I can hardly stand it.

Frances turns off the buzzing, and I take a huge breath and let it go, and I'm still half crying, and I try to explain, but it's hard.

"It wasn't me," I say. "I mean, I was driving, but it was Cameron out of control, not me. She lost control of her car. And it was out of control. I mean, the accident was an out-of-control thing, and I was out of control, but that's just because sometimes things can't be in your control, you know? And it's just really, really sad."

It's like colors and shapes of sadness and out-of-controlness, and I'm seeing them outside of me and feeling them inside of me, thinking how sad it is sometimes, things can be scary and sad, and I'm just watching it, and I open my eyes and let go of the buzzers.

"So many bad things can happen," I tell Frances. "There's nothing you can do about it sometimes. It's just the way things are."

She nods. "Go with that."

I'm thinking again how irritating it is that Frances keeps repeating practically the exact same thing to me, and then I have this memory of my father, enraged, saying, "Why are you repeating the same incorrect information?" And I get so mad, and I think about the words of the song in the car repeating over and over and over, "Hooow looong, hoow loong . . ." and I'm remembering when my father said, "Stop saying you're sorry," and I think, *I'm sorry, I'm sorry, I'm sorry,* and then that cop is going, "Okay. Okay. Okay. Okay," and then my body feels really heavy.

When Frances stops me and goes through her routine, I shrug. "I don't know," I say. "My bones feel like they weigh a lot, and I keep thinking about things with my father, and I'm sort of mad at him."

"When you think about the original incident," Frances says, "what comes up now?" I think of the image we started with. It's changed.

"The key chain is in the palm of my hand, and it's glowing really bright," I say.

She turns on the buzzers.

The key chain glows brighter and brighter, and it's warm and comforting, and the light of it shimmers, filling my hand with brilliant whiteness, and then the whiteness begins to expand and to hollow until it's a steering wheel made of milky white light, and I'm gripping it and driving, and Ellen's sitting next to me, her brown hair dancing in and out of the window.

"Wow," I go, before Frances can even say anything.

"Take a—" she goes, but I interrupt her.

"I know, I know." I take a deep breath and let it out, and I don't wait for "What's happening now?"

"I'm driving with Ellen and the steering wheel is this white light, and it feels okay."

Guess what Frances says?

We're driving in the sun, and it's this long, windy road, with the ocean along one side, sparkling and calm and clear, and even though I have this little knot in my stomach, mostly my body feels warm and relaxed, with the bright steering wheel solid and smooth in my hands.

· · ·

I open my eyes. "You can turn it off," I tell Frances. She does. "I feel good," I say. "I really do. It's this pretty, curvy road, and I'm just driving with Ellen next to me, and it's totally fine."

"So on a scale of zero to ten, how disturbing is the image now?"

"A zero," I say.

Frances smiles. Her fang is sort of cute. "Do the words 'I am in control' still fit? Or is there another positive belief that fits better?"

"Do they fit with me in general?" I ask. "Or with the accident?"

"With the accident," Frances says.

"I guess. I think so."

"Think of the original incident and the words 'I am in control.' On a scale of one to seven, one being false and seven being true, how true do those words feel to you now?"

I think of the original picture. It's the earth key chain, only now it's dangling from the ignition while I'm driving on that windy road with Ellen and the sun and the ocean and everything feeling okay.

"Maybe it's not 'I'm in control.'" I change my mind. "Because something could happen out of my control."

Frances waits.

"Maybe it's more like 'I can be okay driving.'"

"All right," Frances says. "So I want you to pair your image with the words 'I can be okay driving.'"

She turns on the buzzers, and I go with it, and we're just driving and driving, and the earth key chain is swinging from the ignition, and it's all okay. Frances turns off the equipment.

"It still feels good," I tell her. "Still on that road. It's still sunny and pretty, and everything's okay."

"Close your eyes," Frances tells me. "Bring up the accident and the words 'I can be okay driving,' and mentally scan your body. From tip to toe. And just let me know if you feel anything."

So I do that, and mostly I feel calm, relaxed. "I feel fine," I tell her. "Except my stomach hurts a little bit."

"Go with that." She turns the buzzers on. Which surprises me because I thought we were done.

"My stomach hurts a little more," I tell her after a while. "But I still feel pretty good about the whole thing."

Frances glances at her digital clock on the windowsill and then has me imagine my safe place. I'm tired and time is almost up, so we don't do a lot more buzzing. Just enough to let me relax for a few minutes at that magical Caribbean sea with the dazzling turquoise water.

184

21

MY MOM DROPS ME OFF AT ELLEN'S.

"Where is she?" I ask Mrs. Gerson at their front door.

"In her room," Mrs. Gerson goes. She's smoking a cigarette.

"I thought you stopped," I say, stepping inside. Like, two years ago.

She cups her free hand around the back of my head. "I thought so too." Then she pulls me in a little, holding the cigarette out with her other hand so that smoke won't drift into my face. "See what you can do," she whispers. "She won't let me near."

I find Ellen in her downstairs bathroom, sitting on the lowered toilet seat. All she's wearing is her thick brown cable-knit sweater and her panties. Blue cotton bikini. She's holding a plastic razor in one hand and shaving cream in the other, and the tub is running, and she's crying.

It's bad. I didn't know it would be so bad. Her left leg from the knee down is skinnier than anything you've ever seen. It's about half the size of her right leg, and it's covered in dandruffy skin and dark, wiry hair. On the bony part of her shin a red spot, a sore about the size of a quarter, glares up from underneath the hair.

"I bet you didn't know pubic hair grew on legs," Ellen goes. It doesn't exactly look like pubic hair. But it's completely disgusting anyway.

"I thought you were supposed to get a shorter cast today," I say.

"They decided on that thing instead," Ellen says. "That thing" is a plastic and Velcro ski-boot-looking contraption lying on the back of the toilet. "Because it won't rub my leg as much as plaster, and I can take it off to bathe or whatever."

"Okay, look," I say. I lean down and take the razor and the shaving cream from her. I dip a washcloth under the running water and wipe it over her leg from the knee down. I get it as wet as I can without making a mess. Then I squirt shaving cream into her hand. "Start at your knee," I tell her, "and work your way down. Keep away from the sore." She obeys, still crying, while I fold a towel on the floor and then kneel on it. "Do you want to shave, or do you want me to?"

"I don't care."

"I'm afraid I'll cut you if I do it," I warn her.

"I don't care," she says again.

"Slide down to the edge," I tell her. She leans hard on my shoulder to maneuver her butt to the edge of the toilet seat. She winces, from her chest tube spot and from her ribs, and I wait until the wince is done. Then we stretch her leg over and across the tub until we can get her heel anchored on the built-in soap dish. I'm being as careful as possible because I have the definite feeling she's not even supposed to have "that thing" off for vanity reasons. Not that I blame her. "Here." I hand her the razor. She stops crying and starts shaving. One neat row, edged in dirty lines of hair-tinged shaving cream. Then another. After each one I pluck the razor from her fingers and hold it under the tub tap to clean it off.

"Your mom's smoking," I tell her.

"I know," she goes. "I smelled it."

I hand back the razor. "So. What did the doctor say?"

She starts another row. You can hear the hairs getting sliced off. That's how thick they are. *Snick, snick.* "The dicked-her?"

"Ellen!"

"I hate him," she says. "He didn't warn me about this. All he said—once—once, he said, 'Your leg will have lost a little muscle tone.'"

"How long do you wear the ski boot?" *Snick, snick.*

"He said six weeks," she tells me. Except for the round sore, ringed with a thatch of hair, her lower leg is fully shaved. The naked skin is pale and veined and scaly. "But now I don't believe anything he says. Maybe it'll be months. Years even."

She slowly scoots herself back onto the toilet seat. I reach for the Velcro and plastic thing.

"Not yet," she goes. "I took the dressing off." She means off the sore, I guess. "I wanted to see everything. I've got to redo it."

I bring her gauze and medical tape and Neosporin and let her deal with the shiny spot on her shin and then with the boot, while I mop up stray globs of shaving cream and rinse out the tub. When I'm done, I wipe everything down with the towel I was kneeling on. I throw the towel in the laundry hamper and let Ellen lean hard on me while she half walks, half hops to her room. She collapses on the bed, winces, holds really still for a second, and then breathes out slow.

"So guess what," I finally say.

"What?"

"I think I can drive now."

She gives me a glimmer of a smile. "Did you drive here?"

"No. I wanted you in the car with me the first time. If . . ." I stare at the plastic and Velcro. At how shriveled her leg is underneath. And I get scared a little. I can feel it in my stomach, flipping over. "If you'd be okay with that."

"Let's go to Top Hats," she says.

"Now?" I ask.

"You said you could drive," she tells me. "So, can you?"

"I swear," I tell her. "But my mom dropped me off here. I don't have the car."

"You can drive mine!" Ellen's mother yells from somewhere in the house.

"Were you listening to us this whole time?" Ellen shouts.

"Oh, for God's sake!" her mother shouts back.

There's this long, long silence.

"I can smell your disgusting cigarette!" Ellen finally calls.

"Do you want my keys or not?"

It's not a windy road with the ocean on one side and warm sun making everything shimmer, and there's no white light steering wheel. Instead it's freezing, and Ellen's not next to me.

She's in the backseat, and it took us ten minutes, with her mother helping, just to get her into the car. Ellen's not exactly happy, but I'm driving. I'm driving again, and I'm not feeling any sort of a heart attack coming on. Maybe I'm not in control of tree branches or cinder blocks, and maybe it's not totally okay, because Cameron's still dead and Ellen's lower leg looks like a broom handle, but it's okay enough. For now.

I wait a couple of days until I'm sure. Then I tell everyone.

Seth says, "Does your front seat go all the way back?"

Jason says, "Congratulations, Anna."

Lisa says, "You want to drive us to Patty's Saturday night?"

"Patty's?" I go. The last bell just rang.

Ellen left school an hour ago to get a short cast after all. It took only two days before the doctors figured out she wasn't keeping the ski boot on the way she'd been told to. They were satisfied that her sore seemed better and not infected, but apparently Ellen was unbelievably close to screwing up the break in her tibia all over again by wrenching it around in her sleep. Or trying to walk down the stairs on it in the middle of the night. Or something that pissed off her orthopedist enough he told her mother Ellen wasn't being responsible, and she had to go back to a cast. Something like maybe drinking and walking without the boot, I'm guessing. But for some reason I've kept my mouth shut.

Now the rest of us are at our lockers, filling our knapsacks.

"It's the SAT after party," Seth explains to me. "Patty's parents are going to be in Bermuda."

"Saint Bart's," Lisa corrects him.

"Oh," I say.

"But we don't have to go," Seth points out.

"Whatever." My throat is sort of closing up shop. It's not a fake heart attack. It's just . . . I don't know. It's something else.

"Really," Seth says. "We can hang out. Make out." He sees my face. "Count my send-a-dollar money or do origami."

"Origami?" Lisa asks.

"He's kidding," I tell her.

Jason says, "Forget the party." He swings his knapsack over one shoulder. "It's great that you're driving again." He arches his left eyebrow at Lisa, and she drops it. Then he looks at me. "Can I get a ride home?"

After I drop Seth off at his house, Jason switches from the back to the front seat.

"Ellen's getting a new cast," he goes. I turn right at the light and crank the heat. "You're driving again."

"Yeah," I say. The Honda still has that new-car smell. I like it, but Jack gets nauseous.

"So, I've got some news too," Jason goes.

"What?"

"I met someone."

"Really?" I make a left at Broad. "Where?"

"Taylor Academy."

"No way."

"Yes way."

"How did you meet someone at Taylor?"

"Online," Jason says.

"You're sure he's a kid and not some pervert?" I ask.

"Yeah." Jason nods. "I've already seen him a couple of times."

"What's his name?"

"Turn left at the stop sign. I can't tell you yet. He's not out."

"Oh," I say. I turn onto Bateson. "Ellen's going to be bummed." Whoops. I glance at him. "Um . . . ," I say.

Jason sighs. "It's okay, Anna," he goes. "I've known she likes me for a long time."

"She doesn't know you know, right?" I ask.

"I thought you two talked about everything," he says.

"What do you mean?"

"Take the left fork. She didn't tell you about our conversation?"

"What conversation?"

"Guess not. That's mine. The white one with gray shutters." I slow to a stop. "Ellen got drunk."

"When was this?" I put the car in park and keep it on. For the heat.

"A few weeks ago."

"A few weeks ago? Where was I?"

Jason shrugs.

"Where were you two?"

"My room," Jason says.

"Your room?" I ask. "Who else was there?"

"Nobody," Jason tells me.

"Where was I?" I go again. He shrugs again. Therapy? Was I at therapy?

"Anyway," Jason says. "She let me know then."

"She let you know?" I say. "Let you know? You mean, she told you?"

"Not exactly."

"Oh my God," I go. She made a pass at him. Ellen made a pass at Jason.

"Listen, Anna," Jason says. He turns his vents away from him and toward me. He doesn't know how that bothers my eye, so I punch the button on the dash to make the warm air hit our feet. "You know how much I like Ellen."

I nod.

"She's embarrassed enough as it is."

"She really likes you too," I say. "I mean, not just in a crush way. In a person way. She doesn't want you to be embarrassed either."

"Shit," Jason goes.

"What?"

A woman has opened his front door and is stepping out onto the front porch. She's wearing a long fur coat with a wool shawl wrapped around her head and black ski mittens on her hands. "Who's that?"

"My grandmother," Jason goes. "This is going to be bad."

"Does she live with you?"

"Yeah. I should go."

She's saying something to us. At least, I think she is. She keeps gesturing with her mittened hands.

"What's she yelling?" I ask him.

He looks mortified.

"You want to just get out and I'll go?" I ask. "I mean, I don't care if you have a weird grandmother. But . . . whatever you want."

He doesn't move. He looks at me. "Ellen really didn't tell you about this?"

"About what?"

Jason rolls down his window.

"Don't," I say. "It's too cold."

He keeps it down and then looks at me. Now I can hear his grandmother. She's craning her head at us in the car, and she's still waving her hands in the air, as if she's a preacher or something.

"'With a male as with a woman. It is an abomination.' Leviticus 18:22. 'If a man lies with a male as he lies with a woman, both of them have committed an abomination. They shall surely be put to death. Their blood shall be upon them.' Leviticus 20 . . .'"

Oh my God. I refocus on Jason, who's still looking right at me. He mouths the words exactly along with her shouting from their front porch.

"'Even as Sodom and Gomorrah, and the cities about them in like manner, giving themselves over . . .'"

"Oh my God." Did I say that out loud?

"Exactly," Jason goes. I guess I did.

"Ellen met her?"

"Well," Jason says. "She was sort of drunk." He tries a smile. "Ellen, that is."

He rolls up the window and his grandmother's voice fades, but she stays there, gesticulating on the porch with those mittens and that long coat.

"She lives with you?" I go.

Jason nods.

"She does that all the time?"

Jason nods again. "It's kind of entertaining," he says. He's not convincing.

"What about your parents?" I ask.

He shrugs. "They're not exactly thrilled either." I can't tell if he means about his grandmother or about him.

"That is the Bible she's quoting from, right?"

Jason nods. How can his parents let her do that to him?

"You were looking some of it up that night at Ellen's, weren't you?" My brain seems to be working, even though my heart is sort of stopped.

Jason nods again. "I stole it from the Gersons," Jason goes. "I could have just gone to the library or bought my own, but it was right there."

"Ellen knows," I tell him. "She doesn't care."

"It was stupid," Jason goes. "Cowardly. But . . . I guess . . ." He thinks for a second. "Cowards can be judged only from an unbiased point of view."

"I won't tell anybody," I say, not bothering to ask which backseat book he's quoting from. "I promise. Seriously."

He stares out the window at his grandmother and then huffs tons of breath onto the glass, blurring her.

"Couldn't you even try being straight?" I can't help asking it. "I mean, not that I care. But . . . wouldn't it be easier?"

"I would love to be straight," Jason says to me. "Believe me."

I think about what it must be like to be gay. I let myself really think about it for the first time, without all the jokes and stupid assumptions. Jason pulls the door handle and lets in a blast of cold air and shouting.

"'Men with men committing what is shameful, and receiving in themselves the penalty . . .'"

"I believe you," I tell him.

• • •

Jack and I are eating pizza in the kitchen. Half spinach and mushroom for him, half cheese for me. My mom's at some faculty Christmas party, and my father's working late at the bank.

"I get the car this Saturday." Jack lifts a wedge from the box.

"Okay," I say. "I'll spray it with with that lemon stuff. It still has that smell you hate."

He looks at me funny.

"What?" I go.

"Nothing."

"Why are you looking at me like that?"

"Like what?"

"I don't know. Like that."

"I was just thinking about when we used to fight about the car."

"You mean when I was small?" I ask him. He tears at the crust with his teeth.

"Yeah," he says with his mouth full. "That's exactly what I mean." He's being sarcastic, though.

"You mean," I keep going, "like, less than six months ago?"

"Yeah," he goes. "I guess so."

We chew for a while and wipe our messy hands on paper napkins.

"What are you doing Saturday night?" I ask him.

"Rob's," Jack says. "We might go to Lucas's to hear this band. Frozen Shakespeare. Then maybe we'll go to Patty's."

"You're going to Patty's?" I put down my pizza slice.

"Maybe," Jack says.

"You're going to a party?" Somehow I thought neither of us would ever go to a party again.

"I was just thinking about it," he says. "That's all." It's the first time I've heard him sound guilty about anything. He sits back in his chair, leaving the pizza alone. "It's not like I'm planning on it."

I didn't mean to make him think I was accusing him of something. "You're allowed," I tell him. Because there aren't any rules. "You're allowed to go to a party."

We all signed up for the same location and day. I drive Lisa, Seth, and Ellen. Her new short cast goes from below the knee to the toes, and she uses crutches now. The wheelchair is gone for good.

Jason drives himself and meets us there. Only, he's a little late, and a few minutes after he rushes in, some other guy rushes in too, and they both look red in the cheeks. The guy has a blue sweatshirt on, with black stripes across the chest. TAYLOR ACADEMY is printed down the left arm. I glance at Ellen. She hasn't said a word about her conversation with Jason. I haven't told her about mine. It feels wrong somehow, but then again, so much has been wrong these past couple months that it doesn't feel as big of a deal as it could have, before.

The driving was fine. I can't wait to tell Frances. Only one blip from my chest for a split second and slightly sweaty palms. Other than that, a total breeze.

The testing is hard. At first I think my right eye is acting up again and making things blurry, but then I figure out what's really happening: The screen I have is greasy with fingerprints.

You'd think somebody would Windex them or something. It's a little distracting.

We get one break, during which we all gather in a huddle and share cupcakes. Seth brought them.

"Did you make these?" Lisa asks.

"My mother did," Seth says. "From scratch. Except for the frosting. She wanted to make that from scratch too, but I wouldn't let her. I like the kind from the can better." He licks some right off the top of his cupcake. "I bought a ton of it."

"With your send-a-dollar money?" Ellen asks him.

"Yep," he goes.

"How much have they sent so far?" Jason asks. He's glancing over at the sweatshirt guy. I see the sweatshirt guy glancing back.

"Seven hundred and twenty-one," Seth goes.

"That's a lot of frosting," I say. They look at me and crack up. I wasn't even trying to be funny.

But it's all ruined, after.

Kids are streaming out of testing rooms. It's a lot like the halls at school between classes. Only, everybody's more giddy. Like it's the last day of the year or the day before Christmas break. Stupid SATs.

"I'm driving with Jason," Ellen goes. She's leaning her back against the wall and her armpits on the crutches. Jason seems nervous. He's scanning the hall. This girl is shrieking and chasing some guy past us. She's pretty loud. I watch Jason keep scanning.

Then I get it. Oh my God. He didn't just meet Sweatshirt here. Jason *drove* Sweatshirt here.

"No," I say to Ellen. The guy being chased has buttonhooked back around, toward us again, and the girl is still running after him, screaming. She's screaming and screaming and screaming. "Drive with me," I tell Ellen.

"What's wrong?" Ellen asks.

"Nothing," I say. "Just go in my car."

"Is it the driving?" Lisa asks. "You're all red."

Seth nods and frowns. "You are."

I watch Jason catching Sweatshirt's eye. That girl won't stop screaming.

"I'm not red," I say. The running guy turns again, and the girl follows. Screaming and screaming and screaming.

Jason looks at me now. He seems really worried.

"Ellen's going with me," I say, to try and reassure him.

"You're sweating," Jason answers.

"What's going on?" Seth touches my face. The dark rings around the brown of his eyes are so beautiful.

"Are you okay?" Lisa and Ellen ask at the same time.

The girl chasing the guy is coming toward us again. Screaming and screaming and screaming.

"Would you shut up!" Ellen snaps as the girl passes.

And the screaming stops.

22

IF YOU HAVEN'T EVER KILLED ANYBODY, YOU MIGHT THINK THERE'S nothing worse than shaking and vomiting uncontrollably on the floor of the hall of the SAT building where about two hundred kids, half of whom you don't even know and one of whom is your sort-of boyfriend and one of whom is your best friend collapsed on the floor nearby in a mess of crutches, are staring in horror and have absolutely no idea what to do and will tell the story a thousand times tonight at the after party, without you there because you're home in bed stoned out of your mind on legal stuff, and then they'll tell it a million more times for the rest of your life.

Usually, Frances explains, we pick up where we left off the last time. It's Monday morning. I'm missing school. I'm an emergency. Usually, Frances reminds me, we work with an image. But today we're not going to do the usual. We're going to work with what's happening now. And what's happening now, she says, is not an image. It's the screaming. No, I tell her. It's not the screaming. It's the screaming, stopped. So that's what we start with: the screaming, stopped.

My negative belief about myself is "I am a killer." Frances won't let me use that one, though, because she says the truth is that I was behind the wheel when Cameron died, and even though I wasn't responsible for Cameron's death, EMDR won't change the fact that I was involved. So she asks, if I am a killer, what does that mean about me? I say I am very, very bad. She lets me use that.

Target: the screaming, stopped. Negative belief: "I am very, very bad." What would I rather believe? That I'm good, I guess. Right. On a scale of one to seven "I am good" gets a one. When I think of the screaming, stopped, what emotions do I feel? Terror, shame, helplessness. How disturbing are those feelings? A ten. Where do I feel it in my body? All over, shaking and heart pounding, and nausea and sweating.

"Go with that," Frances tells me. So I do.

23

IT'S DARK, AND SOMETHING IS POKING MY EYE, AND I'M CRUSHED on my left side, and Ellen and her blood are heavy, and the smell of plastic is underneath the screaming and screaming and screaming, and when the screaming stops, my body vomits, telling me that the screaming, stopped, is sickening, is somebody's life, stopped, and I want to wipe the heavy wetness off me and get up and run and make the somebody start screaming and keep screaming, to make them be alive, please, please, please, and it's like a wave of blood frozen in a massive curl, a big "Fuck you" to gravity and nature and everything that's supposed to be, and it's wrong, it should keep going, it should fall and roar over everything, but it doesn't, it's a frozen wave of screaming, stopped, of someone dead.

· · ·

Frances is here, telling me to take a deep breath and let it go and what's happening now, and I see her certificates on the wall, with that left middle one all crooked, and I feel the cool, smooth suede of the pillow under my forearms and there's the red of the couch and the brown of her freckles, and I say, "It's weird how sick and sad I feel but also know that I'm here, and it's over."

And she says—big surprise—"Go with that."

And I'm thinking about how it's over, only it's not over. The screaming is over, and Cameron's life is over, and the beginning of my life is over, along with Jack's and Ellen's and Cameron's little brother's, and I see those two kids on the ocean trampoline, that brother and sister with those nut-colored eyes, and they're jumping, and then I see a little boy who looks just like Cameron, with natural platinum hair paired with dusky skin, and I think, *What's he going to do? What's he going to do without her?* And my brother's bedroom door slams, and I'm left on the other side, small and alone and not knowing what to do, and Frances is handing me her tissue box, and I feel it like waves, just waves of despair washing over me, and I cry and cry and cry, and my bones are soggy, and then I see Jack's head flat on the table, next to his laptop, and broken glass strewn across the living-room floor, and broken glass and flashlights glittering underneath the dangling earth, and the earth turns into soil, and then a blade of grass grows up out of the soil, and it's joined by other blades, and then there are brown leaves and fingers picking them up one by one, Jack's fingers picking up the leaves, and then his face looking at me, his face saying, *If you had just stayed home and picked up the leaves, maybe none of it would have happened,* and Frances turns off the buzzers.

There's all these balls of tissue in my lap, and I shake my head and cry, and Frances doesn't have to ask me to breathe or what's happening because I kind of get the rhythm of it all now, and so I breathe on my own.

"It's my fault," I tell Frances. "If I'd done what my dad told me to do, we'd have gotten to the party later and probably left later or earlier, and we wouldn't have been passing by Cameron on the road right at that second, and she could have swerved and been fine."

She doesn't say anything this time. She just nods and turns on the box.

The thing is, if you don't do what my father asks, he ends up being right, and you end up with serious consequences because you are just wrong and bad, and I see his face screaming and that vein and the spit at the corners of his mouth, and he's screaming and screaming and screaming, and I wish it would stop. I wish his screaming would stop, I wish he would stop. I wish he would die. And if you wish people to die, then you are very, very bad.

"Take a deep breath," Frances says. I breathe in, slow and long.

"I'm so mad," I tell her, and I'm crying again, and I tug another tissue, and she turns on her box, but I drop the buzzers and hold up my hand, and she waits, and when I can find my voice, I add, because it feels important, "And I'm scared of how mad I am. I mean . . . not scared exactly. Ashamed."

The word *shame* keeps marching by, like on a big city building's electronic ticker. *Shame, shame, shame,* just marching by, repeating itself in yellow bulbs over a black background, and it feels like I could throw up again, and my heart is heavy, and it moves across the screen of my mind: *shame, shame, shame.* And then my mother is there, curled around me, holding me tight with one arm and pulling a shade over the ticker with another, and I can feel her warm breath in my ear, and she's not far away in the corner of the house or fuzzy in the horizon, she's right here holding me and saying, "Shhh, shhh. I'm here, I'm here," and then I'm waking up in a twist of damp bedding from a nightmare, and my mother is still wrapped firmly around my back, and my father is there plumping my pillow, and Jack is there, watching from the doorway, and nobody's blaming me or thinking I'm bad, even though the sadness in the room is thick, like another blanket, twisted and heavy and everywhere.

I cry some more, with the buzzers off, and then I get this image with the sound gone, so there's no screaming, and no screaming, stopped.

"It's like a silent movie," I explain to Frances. "Everything is frozen. Ellen's ponytail and the cops, and Cameron lying on the pavement, dead. Even though I never saw her that night. I see her now. I'm sitting up, looking at her."

Guess what Frances says?

Cameron stands up out of herself, the way the movies show souls leaving bodies, and she walks over to me, and she kneels down, and she's all in one piece and perfect with those slender pink fingers and that skin and no blood, and she says, "You two are a lot more alike than you think," and she means Jack and me, and she floats away and up toward a lighted place far above us with a white sidewalk and wet green grass, and the echo of her voice says it again: "You two are a lot more alike than you think," and there's something comforting about what she's said because if it's true—and it must be, because dead people know the truth—then maybe I'm not so bad, because Jack isn't, because he thinks I can fly and tries to stop the waves.

205

"What's happening now?" Frances asks.

"I'm thinking about my brother," I tell her.

I see his shoulder blades, sharp as knives, slicing the water.

"I don't know," I tell Frances. "I'm tired. And if you say 'Go with that,' I think I'll scream."

She just looks at me and turns on the buzzers.

Screaming again, only now the screaming is different. It's not screaming like the way it was that night. The night of the accident. It's screaming like the way kids scream. Little kids. When they're playing. And then there's Cameron, a knobby-kneed girl, missing two front teeth. Her toddler brother is wearing nothing but a diaper, and they're playing in a sprinkler, which is going *snickety, snickety, snickety,* and young Cameron is squealing, the way little kids do when they're happy. And then I see me, and I'm my same age now, only I'm as small as a five-year-old, and I'm on the white sidewalk of this front yard where Cameron is skipping through the sprinkler, and I'm curled up in a ball, crying, and Cameron sees me and stops squealing, and she comes over, and she asks if I want to run through the sprinkler with her, and I ask if my brother can come too, and Jack is there, his age and size now, and he runs through the sprinkler and back, hogging it, and then he grins at us and says, "I can stop the water," and he presses his foot on the spout and the water stops and the *snickety* sound stops, and Cameron and I shriek at him, and her little baby brother stares at us with his droopy diaper, and then Jack lifts his foot and the water shoots out, drenching us all, and that's it.

"We're really little," I tell Frances. "We're playing outside in the summer, and we're all sort of shouting and squealing."

"And when you go back to what we started with, what do you get?"

I take a deep breath, and I try to get it back into my head. "It's hard to hear it," I say. "I mean, I know it happened, but I can't hear the screaming anymore. And I can't hear the stopped."

"What do you get instead?" Frances asks.

I try to think of that night. I try to think of the accident. Of that moment, when Cameron died, and I knew she died, even though I didn't know I knew it.

"It's not Ocean Road at night anymore," I say. "I mean, it is Ocean Road, far away in the background. But sort of in front of it and closer is this empty yard with wet grass and the sound of a sprinkler."

"How disturbing is it to you now?"

"It's still sad," I say. "And . . . I don't know . . . ominous a little bit." A good SAT word. How about that. "I don't know why, but I'm uneasy. But it's not as bad as when we started. So I guess it's at about a three."

"You've done a lot of work today," Frances says. She leans back a little in her black leather chair, and I glance at the clock. We're five minutes over. How weird. It seems like we only just started.

"I'm really tired," I say, surprised.

"Yeah," she nods. "That happens."

She doesn't make me leave right away, even though she probably has somebody else waiting. Instead she lets me close my eyes and imagine my safe place for a minute. We've ended like this before. I like it. The smell of coconut. The warmth of dazzling blue.

24

ELLEN'S BACK IN FLORIDA WITH HER PARENTS FOR THE FIRST week of Christmas break. Lisa went to Cancún with her family, and Rob's visiting cousins in Chicago. That leaves Seth, Jason, and us. Usually my family goes skiing, but not this year. It's not like we discuss it or anything. It's just that it doesn't happen. Instead my father's taking only three days off at Christmas, and my mom's doing a lot of shopping and grading.

Seth brings over a bunch of wrinkled envelopes and a family pack of Hershey's Kisses. We count his send-a-dollar money and eat the whole bag of chocolate and tool around a little. Well, a lot. But somehow I start feeling nervous, and then I get bitchy.

Right as I'm kicking him out of my room, my father's walking up the stairs. He doesn't even wait until Seth's through the front door before he starts.

"What was that boy doing in your room?" my father goes. I'm in the second-floor hallway, and my dad has one foot on the top stair and one foot on the carpeted landing.

"That's Seth," I say. He's a guy. Not a boy. "You've met him before."

"What was he doing in your room?"

"What do you mean?" I ask, even though I know exactly what he means.

"You know exactly what I mean," my dad goes.

I haven't had a nightmare for four nights, and I'm driving fine, and the shaking is gone. Plus, I haven't had any more panic attacks. Thank God. According to my father's initial orders, I have only one session left with Frances, but lately he hasn't mentioned anything about ending my therapy, so that's sort of in limbo.

I guess I thought maybe things wouldn't go back to as bad as they used to be, but now, with this old black knot in my brain, I figure I might be wrong. So I stand here, wondering what he wants me to say.

"Harvey?" my mother calls from their bedroom. She's wrapping presents, I think.

"What!"

"We weren't doing anything," I finally say, thinking about when Seth's hand slid up my shirt.

"Leave her alone!" my mom yells.

And then when that same hand slid down my pants.

"What were you doing in there?" my father asks me again, ignoring my mother.

Sometime between the shirt and the pants Seth placed a chocolate Kiss in my belly button with his mouth.

"We were just hanging out," I say. "Eating chocolate. And um . . . working on a project."

"You're not supposed to have food in your room," my dad says. "Bugs."

"We didn't make any crumbs."

"Or boys in your room."

"Since when?"

"Since now," he tells my mother, who's stepping into the hallway. She has a stray piece of Scotch tape stuck to her sleeve.

"I can't have a guy in my room now?" I ask.

"Harvey," my mom says. "Let's discuss this before we lay down any laws."

"There's nothing to discuss," my father says. "No boys in Anna's room."

"What about Jason?" I ask.

"Who the hell is Jason?" my dad goes. "And no."

"Jason's gay!" we all hear Jack yell from behind his closed door. A second later it opens. "Jason's probably safe, Dad," Jack points out.

My father still has one foot on the top stair and one on the carpet. "Don't get smart," my dad tells Jack. Then to me, "No boys in your room. Period."

"You let Cameron in Jack's room," I argue before I can stop myself.

My insides nose-dive with shame while my father's face goes purple. Jack's staring at the wood floor, smirking, of all things, instead of glaring with disgust at his despicable sister. While I'm trying to figure out how that's possible, my father is looking back and forth at Jack and then at me. "God damn it!" he says. He lifts his back leg and advances. His hand is raised.

"Stop it, Harvey!" My mom steps between us, and I dodge around both of them, down the stairs, to the kitchen, through the mudroom, to the garage, into the new Honda.

And then I just sit here. Because the last time something like this happened . . . well.

I turn the car on for the heat. I didn't grab a coat, and even though it's only three steps away, I'm not going back into the house for one. If I'd thought to bring my cell, I'd call Ellen, but I didn't, so I can't. I think about driving to Seth's, only I'm not up for facing him so soon after he's nibbled a Hershey's Kiss out of my navel. I could go to Jason's, only I don't even know if he's home, and what if he is and Sweatshirt is over there and they're in the middle of their own bag of candy? Or worse, what if he's home and Sweatshirt isn't there, but Grandma is? So I sit here with the engine idling, hating my father and hating myself more and shaking. And then I remember about planting my feet and breathing, and that helps a little.

About fifteen minutes go by. My brother walks out the mudroom door. He's holding my coat and wearing his, and he climbs into the passenger's seat.

"I'm sorry about bringing Cameron into it," I tell him right away. I wiggle my arms into the coat sleeves.

"It's because I'm a guy," Jack goes, completely ignoring the whole Cameron thing. Which makes me feel better. I can feel my gut relaxing a little bit.

"What do you mean, because you're a guy?"

"I'm not going to be getting pregnant."

"Oh, come on," I say. "Neither am I."

"He gets scared," Jack says.

"Where do you people get that from?" I ask.

"What 'you people'?"

"You and Mom," I say. "She says he's scared too."

"Well, he is," Jack tells me. "That's why he's such a mess all the time."

"A mess?" I go. "He's not a mess. He's a dick."

"He's that, too," Jack says. "But it's because he's such a mess."

"You always say I'm the one who's scared and a mess," I remind Jack. "If we're both so scared, how come he gets to be a dick and I don't?"

"That doesn't even make sense," Jack goes. "Do you really want to be a dick?"

"He was going to hit me," I say. "That's abuse. I could call the police on him."

"He didn't hit you," Jack points out. "Mom stopped him."

But I'm too mad at my father to let what my mother did sink in yet. "Are you defending him?"

"It's not about defending anyone," Jack goes. "It just is what it is."

"Since when did you get so Zen?" I ask.

"Since Cameron," he goes.

"You mean, since you knew her, or since she died?" I say it as respectfully as possible so he'll know I'm genuinely wondering and not just being sarcastic.

"Both."

His phone rings. You'd think, him being Jack and all, that he'd have it set on some awful song downloaded from the

Internet, but he doesn't. It's just a regular ring. He glances at the number, presses on the cell, and goes, "Hi, Ellen." Ellen? "Yeah. She's right here."

He passes the phone to me.

"I tried you first, so don't get all weird," Ellen says. "Did you know Jason has a boyfriend?" She sounds strange. Not tired exactly, but something.

"Um . . ."

"I just called him, and I heard someone in the background, and I thought it was you or Seth or something, but it wasn't."

"Maybe it was his mom," I say. Lame. How can I lie to Ellen?

"How can you lie to me?" Ellen goes. "I know you know something."

"I thought you just said you knew . . . ," I start.

"I wasn't sure," Ellen goes, and she starts to cry. "Now I am."

"It's a guy from Taylor." I'm a little surprised she's crying. It's not like Ellen to be this emotional over someone who was never even her boyfriend. "Jason just told me, and he didn't want you to feel bad, so he asked me not to . . ."

I hear Ellen kind of stop crying, and then I hear the slurp and swallow of her drinking. Drinking. Next to me Jack starts to get out of the car, but I grab his shoulder.

"Are you drunk?" I ask. Jack sits still.

"No," Ellen says after I hear her swallow. "I'm just having a couple of beers."

"Where are you?" I ask.

"In my hotel room," she says.

"You sound sort of drunk," I say. Jack looks at his watch. I look at the clock on the dash. It's 4:16.

"Don't tell Jason I even cared," Ellen goes.

"Were you drinking when you called him?"

"What's the difference, Anna?" Ellen goes. "My cell's dying. I have to find the charger."

"Wait," I say, but the phone's gone dead.

"She was drinking?" Jack asks.

"Do you think I should worry?"

"It's four in the afternoon," Jack says.

"Yeah."

"Huh." Jack's staring at me. "Your eye looks pretty cool. The pupil is vertical, you know. Sort of like a snake's eye."

"I prefer cat," I tell him.

The mudroom door opens again. It's my mom. She walks down the steps. I roll down my window, but instead of leaning in to say something, she gets into the backseat.

Jack and I look at each other.

"Um . . . ," I go. I've been reduced to *um* way too much lately.

"What are you doing?" Jack asks her.

"I have absolutely no idea," my mom says.

"Where's Dad?" I ask.

"Oh." She waves her hand, weary. "Ranting and raving somewhere on the second floor."

"He really needs some therapy," Jack mutters.

"Look who's talking," my mother says.

"What about you?" I ask her, and I sound mad. "You look who's talking."

"I am, Anna." She leans her head back on the fresh leather. And then she actually smiles at me.

"Oh," I go.

The mudroom door swings open a third time.

"What the hell are you all doing in there?" my father shouts.

We don't answer. He glares down at us. We look back. It feels like we're in one of those drive-through animal parks, and he's some strange monkey specimen. Usually the animals are in packs, though. Munching on something or rolling around or relaxed in a group squat, grooming one another. The thing is, my dad is just standing there. One person. All alone.

"Amanda?" he goes. "Jack?" He's squinting into the car at us, and for just a second I see something on his face. Worry or curiosity. "Anna?"

Maybe it's fear.

It was a striped-umbrella day, with slippery rafts and gentle undertow and the glinty sun reflecting off wet bathing suits. That morning there was a sandbar far out in the water, separated from the beach by green, lakelike ocean. So calm that my father said he'd swim Jack and me out there. Other parents were doing the same. Already the billowy swim trunks of fathers and the seal-slick backs of small kids decorated the water.

My father moved slowly between Jack and me, coaching Jack's seven-year-old crawl and my six-year-old breast stroke.

"Can I stand here, Dad?" I gurgled, halfway to the sandbar, arms and legs frogging madly.

"Not here," he said. "Too deep."

"Can you stand here, Dad?" Jack spluttered.

"Let me see." We stopped stroking and started treading while my dad went vertical and then sank straight down. I squealed, and my father's head popped up.

"Nope," he said. "Over my head here too. Swim."

So we kicked and paddled, the three of us side by side by side, until first my dad could stand on the sharp incline of sand, and then Jack and I could, and we were all on top of the bar.

"Neat," Jack said.

The water reached only to my knees, to my father's shins. It was like we were on an island. With our backs to shore, we could be smack in the middle of the sea.

"Look!" I pointed. Girls about my age had found a spot that seemed only top-of-the-feet deep. They were sitting on their behinds, making drip castles.

"Pretty unusual," another father said to mine.

"Anna," Jack went. "Let's find the edge."

"Never seen anything like this," my father answered. He caught a fugitive swim tube on his foot and held it there until a kid in a tie-dyed T-shirt and navy blue trunks plucked it off him.

Jack and I splashed farther toward the horizon, looking for the edge.

"It's there," some other kid said, pointing. She was older than we were. Ten or eleven maybe, and she was wearing a pretty yellow bikini.

"The edge?" Jack asked her. "Is that the edge?"

"I think," the girl said. She called over her shoulder. "Mom? Is that the edge?"

I looked where the girl was looking, to a woman who must have been her mother, standing not far from my dad. I saw the mother's mouth loosen and open, and then I saw my dad's eyes widen and his body straighten.

"Jack," he called. "Anna." His voice was sharp. "Come here."
Jack and I glanced at each other and then back at my father.
"Come here. Now." His face was pink. Was it the sun, or was
it him mad?

"Come on," Jack muttered.

We turned back. Then we heard a gasp. And another. The
father who had been talking to mine started running. It's hard
to run in shallow water. You have to sort of step high, and you
splash a lot. As he grabbed his son other parents began to step
high too.

"Matteo!" a woman yelled.

"Claire!"

"Lily! Catherine!"

My father grabbed my hand on one side and Jack's on the
other. He held on hard. It hurt. Why was he mad? What had I
done? My head began to fill with black fuzz.

"Now, listen." His voice was deep and like nothing I'd ever
heard. "There's a very, very big wave coming." Parents were
running and yelling and snatching up their kids. My father kept
us still. He was crushing my fingers. "It's going to break on us.
That means crash, Anna. It's going to crash on top of us. Hold
my wrist as tightly as you know how."

The steadiness of his voice helped the fuzz clear. My fingers
hurt, but he wasn't mad. I looked up and out. We were facing
the open ocean. And in the distance was a curl. It seemed small
to me. Long and low.

"Do not let go of me. Do. Not. Let. Go." My father's big
hand shifted to latch below my palm to my wrist. The way trapeze artists hold each other, flying through the air. I clutched

back. "Spread your feet apart and lean forward a little bit," my father said. I felt the sand suck at my ankles as I did what I was told. The curl was gliding closer and rising bigger.

Most of the other parents were clasping their kids to their chests and making for the shore. When I twisted to look, I could see frantic heads bobbing, arms reaching, legs kicking. "There may be more waves after this one that we can't see," my father said as it rushed toward us. His voice wasn't angry. It was patient. "I'm not going to let go of you." I heard more calls and screams and saw glimmers of color and flashes of bodies as parents lurched and kids scrambled. "You are not to let go of me. Hold on tight. Hold on. Hold on."

The wave was now directly in front of us, rearing and looming like some sort of sea monster with foam breath and a freezing roar. It was the biggest wave I'd ever seen. Bigger than five of my father stacked up. Louder than a thousand of him.

"Hold on!" my father shouted.

The weight of it blew my feet out from under me in an instant, the wet howling engulfed my head and body with weight, pressure. I held on as hard as I could. I held on and held on and held on, while the wave tried to rip us apart. My father gripped me so tightly that it felt as if my palm might tear off the stem of my wrist. So tightly that his hand and arm were shaking with the strain. Shaking and shaking and shaking against a wet force blasting down and around and through me.

And then the force was gone, and my father's shaking hand was yanking my wrist hard and high, and my body followed in a kind of jerk, sail, and drop, and I was on my feet, drenched and gasping for air, still gripping his wrist. I caught a glimpse of Jack, naked, and of my father's gray hair pasted sideways to his head as he spun us around, finally letting go of our hands, throwing us, hurling us in front of him, off the sandbar and into the water toward shore.

"Swim!" my father shouted.

There was yelling and a yellow bikini top floating quietly in my path. Adult bodies crashing through the water past me to the sounds of kids crying and lifeguard whistles.

"Keep swimming," I heard my father breathing from my left, my brother kicking hard on the other side of him. "Keep swimming."

My mother was at the shoreline, pushing aside another mother to get to us and with a towel to hide Jack's middle, and the edge of the ocean was filled with people hugging and scanning and crying and calling, while my mom hustled us to our spot, with our low-slung chairs and red-striped umbrella and sandy books, and Jack and I blew our noses into our towels, and so did my dad, and it made me and Jack giggle because it was gross to do that and we were never allowed, plus the commotion on the sand and in the water of all the people and lifeguards yelling and running, with the ocean so calm and peaceful now, seemed funny, like a sped-up cartoon, and then I stopped giggling, stopped short, because my father was huddled against my mother, and she was holding his big, wet head tightly against her neck with one hand and stroking his shuddering back with the other, crooning, "I know, I know," and I could see his entire body—legs, arms, back, bottom—shaking, shaking, shaking.

219

25

SETH AND JASON AND I GO TO THE MALL. IT'S THE DAY BEFORE
Christmas, and ridiculously, we all have a ton of presents to
buy. As we're walking past the insanely long Santa line I hear
someone calling my name.

"Anna!"

I look around. So do Seth and Jason.

"Anna." It's an Ashley. I don't think I've ever seen one without the other.

"Is she talking to me?" I whisper to Seth. He catches my
hand and slows down. So does Jason. So do I.

"Hi," I go to Ashley. She's standing next to this kid. He's not
little. He looks about twelve or thirteen. He's pudgy, with wide-
set eyes and a round mouth, and he's sort of drooling.

"How are you?" Ashley goes. She's wearing a down coat that

flares at the bottom and leather shoes with an amazing heel.

"Fine," I say, as if we actually know each other.

"How's Jack?"

"He's fine." Seth squeezes my hand. Little squeezes, one after the other, in a rhythm. Like a heartbeat.

"Hi, Jase," Ashley goes. "Thanks for sticking up for me in Gusty's class. What an asshole."

"Yeah," Jason says. "You're welcome."

Seth keeps squeezing.

"Listen—," Ashley goes, but then her brother interrupts her.

"Are you going to see Santa Claus?" He has a deep voice, sort of like Rob's.

"No interrupting," Ashley tells him. She puts her arm around his shoulders and looks back at me. "I've been wanting to tell you and Jack . . . and Ellen, too . . . that—"

"I'm going to see Santa Claus."

"Excuse me," Ashley reminds him. She sounds like a teacher. A nice teacher, but a teacher. Bizarre.

"Excuse me," he goes. "Now can I talk?"

Ashley sighs. "This is Matt," she tells me and Seth and Jason. Seth has stopped squeezing. His hand is still and warm in mine.

"Truck," Matt says. "My name is Truck."

We nod hello to him. The Santa line moves forward a little. We all move with it.

"Just . . ." Ashley wipes her perfectly polished index finger over Matt's drool. I could pass out from shock. "Ash and I have been saying for months how awful that whole thing was . . . and . . ."

"Ash!" It's Ashley Two. She's walking fast, dressed in cute boots with fur trim at the top edges and a pink-and-gray knit hat, completely model-like.

"Lee!" Matt yells, and he breaks away from Ashley One and nearly tackles Ashley Two.

"Truck!" She hugs him back.

My face is hot, and the place between my heart and my stomach feels all lit up. It's shame, I think. Because I'm sort of stunned to see them human, and really, that's so unfair.

"Hi," Ashley Two says to all of us. She throws Ashley One a look.

"I was in the middle of trying," Ashley One says.

Ashley Two turns to us. To me. "Mostly, we've been wanting to tell you and your brother and Ellen how much we . . ." She blushes. I've never seen an Ashley blush.

"We just felt so bad for you," Ashley One says.

Seth squeezes again. That's almost exactly what he said to me that day on the L of my couch.

"Thanks," I say. There's this awkward pause. "Nice to meet you, Truck," I tell Matt. Ashley One smiles at me. She has something that looks like a poppy seed stuck in her teeth.

"Nice to meet you, too," Matt says.

Jason and Seth and I are quiet for a long time after we leave the Ashleys. We walk by a bunch of stores on the second floor, spacing out from the quiet *sshuush* sound of the massive wall waterfall in front of the toy store. We end up at the courtyard with fake palm trees near the glass elevators.

"So that was weird," I finally say.

"I didn't know she had a retarded brother." Seth's trying to chew the head off a gummy bear.

"Down's syndrome," Jason goes.

"Ellen knew that," I tell them.

"Have you talked to her?" Jason asks.

"A few times. I need an earlobe massage." He moves around to the back of me and starts. It really does feel good. It probably looks weird, but it's incredibly relaxing. I have a flash of Cameron playing with her earlobe that day of the cake.

"Don't get too comfy there, tough guy," Seth tells Jason.

I take a deep breath. "Ellen doesn't sound very good."

"What do you mean?" Seth gives up on the head and pops the whole bear into his mouth.

"She's drunk a lot when we talk."

"Again?" Jason stops with my ears.

"Not drunk totally," I go. "Just . . . um . . . like she's been drinking."

"That sounds drunk to me," Seth says.

"Yeah."

"She seems pretty down a lot." Jason moves away. My whole neck is warm.

"I know," I say. "Her leg and ribs. And all."

"When does she get back?" Seth asks me.

"The twenty-eighth."

"There's your brother." Jason points. Jack's in the glass elevator with Rob, moving upward from the first floor. They've got a ton of bags.

"We just saw the Ashleys," I tell them when they step out.

Rob blushes and looks around.

"What are you getting Mom and Dad?" Jack asks.

I have no idea what to get them. "What are you?"

"I was thinking about a cat."

"A cat?" I say.

Jack nods. "Dogs are out, obviously, because of Dad."

"My father hates them," I tell everybody.

"Cats are pretty independent," Jason says. "You don't have to do a lot to take care of them."

"Mom's always wanted a cat," Jack says.

"Really?" I didn't know that. I make a mental note to ask her about it.

"I got my mother a gift certificate for a massage," Seth says.

"That's much better than a cat," I go.

Jack and I buy our mom a gift certificate for two massages. Jack finds four books on Texas Hold 'Em that we don't think my father owns.

Rob buys his mother a coffee mug with snowflakes all over it. He buys his father a mug with a bunch of cartoon bears. If you look really close, you can see the bears are in all these different sexual positions.

"What would your grandmother think of that?" I whisper to Jason. He raises his left eyebrow at me.

"You are so out there," Jack tells Rob, who just shrugs.

We end up in the food court, eating quesadillas.

"You know, you two look alike," Seth tells me and Jack.

"Shut up," we say.

Uncle Buck and Aunt Jerry come over Christmas Day. They leave their dogs at home. They give me a silver pendant with an opal stone. They give Jack a year's subscription to this Web site where you can mail-order DVDs for half price. They give my parents plane tickets and hotel reservations to go to Paris for a long weekend in the summer.

"We can't accept this," my mother goes.

"You have to," Aunt Jerry says. "They're nonrefundable."

"It's too much," Mom argues.

My father stays quiet. I know what he's thinking. He doesn't want to miss a Friday and Monday of work.

I give Jack these new headphones that shut out the sound of ambient noise. He seems to like them. He gives me a professionally framed photo. The colors are bright and clear: yellows and whites and blues and grays. It's of the ocean. Specifically, of a wave. Huge. Sparkling.

"How did you know?" I ask him, gaping.

Jack looks pleased but confused. "What do you mean?"

I stare, astonished.

Jack shrugs. "I just saw it in that gallery at the mall," he says. "I thought you'd like it."

Later, as I'm standing in the doorway of my room examining my walls to figure out where to hang it, I overhear my mom and Aunt Jerry walking up the stairs.

"I started last week," my mom is saying.

"Do you like him?" Aunt Jerry asks.

"We'll see," my mom says.

Normally I'd mind my own business.

"Started what?" I call. I step back out of my room and into the hall. My mom and Jerry are at the landing. "Like who?"

Jerry looks at my mom. My mother sighs and looks at me.

Normally she wouldn't really answer. "My new therapist," she says.

"Does Dad know?" I ask.

"Of course," Mom says.

"Oh."

Seth has to spend all of Christmas Day with his family.

"I only have a minute," he tells me at the edge of our lawn, by the street, next to his car.

"I know," I say. We're bundled up in hats and scarves and down and Gore-Tex.

"Merry Christmas." He hands me a long white box. "Don't open it out here," he says. "It's too cold."

"Is it roses?" I ask. My father is allergic to roses. Seth kisses the tip of my nose and then my mouth. His lips are freezing. So is his mint breath. "See you," he goes.

Inside I open the box, and my mom helps me find a vase and trim the stem bottoms underwater, on an angle.

"Oh my God." I'm reading the card.

"What?" my mother asks.

"I'm getting a dozen roses on the first of each month for the next year," I tell her.

"That's a lot of money," my mom says. "Where is Seth going to get all that money?"

"In the mail," I say. She frowns. "It's a long story."

"It would have to be." She sounds like Ellen's mom a little when she says that. I kind of like her sounding that way.

"All I got him was a stupid gift basket." With dozens of candy packages surrounding bubble bath, food coloring, and a sweater. Lame, lame, lame.

My mother hands me the vase. The roses smell sweet, and they're this deep red and a little over the top. "You never told me he was your boyfriend," she says. She glances at me and pulls a bottle of baby aspirin off the shelf next to the sink. She shakes out two pills and drops them into the vase. "It would be nice if you told me things every now and then." Her voice sounds careful.

Suddenly I wonder about how popular she is with her students. All those excellent evaluations. Does she hang out with them on campus? Do they tell her things? I wonder what she thinks about when she's in her office, up there on the third floor. Or reading her survival books.

"What?" she goes.

"Nothing," I say. "What about Dad's allergies?" 227

"We'll see if they kick in," my mom suggests. But then she doesn't have any other ideas.

"What are the aspirin for?"

"They make flowers last longer."

The carefulness of her voice, and the way she stepped between my father and me the other day, make me feel sort of formal for some reason. "Thank you."

"What if we break up before the year is over?" I ask Seth over the phone.

"Oh," he says. "Does that mean we're going out now?"

"Funny," I say.

"Don't worry so much, Anna," he goes.

"But that's what I do," I tell him.

"I know. But if we break up, I'll just change the address with the florist and have them sent to my mother."

"Seth!" I go.

"Okay. To your mother."

"Seth!"

"Come on," he goes. "Do you even like my present a little?"

"A lot," I say. Why can't I be nicer? "But that's so much money. Ellen wouldn't approve." I'm not telling him about my dad's allergies. I don't have the heart.

"Ask her," Seth says.

I hang up with him and dial Ellen. It's their last day in Florida. It's still early, and I'm hoping I won't hear the sound of beer in her voice. I don't, so I tell her about the roses.

"I think it's the most romantic present I ever heard of," Ellen says. "And it's a total waste of money, and you'll never get treated this well by anyone again, so you might as well enjoy it."

I hang up on Ellen and dial Seth.

"See?" he goes. "Told you so."

On top of the lemons and perfume, now Ellen's house smells like pine needles. Her mother puts their tree up the day after Thanksgiving each year and takes it down the day after they get back from wherever they've vacationed.

Ellen's moving a lot more smoothly with her crutches now. Her cast looks sort of beaten up, though. It's dingy and the edges are grayish. She's written stuff all over it. Not sentences. Just words. *Panacea. Absinthe. Mired. Avuncular. Thrice.*

"I think you should have a certain New Year's resolution," I tell her. We're back in her old room. She can do stairs. She's not nimble on them or anything. But she can do them.

"Like what?" she asks. She's hanging up a bunch of new clothes onto wooden hangers. I'm pulling them all out of shopping bags, cutting off tags, and handing items to her.

"Like no more drinking in the daytime."

She bangs a hanger onto her closet bar and then turns to frown at me. She has this way she can lean one armpit on a crutch and sort of balance like that.

"What's that supposed to mean?"

"That I think you have something weird going with alcohol."

"Oh, please." Ellen rolls her eyes. I try to hand her a pair of brown wool pants with cuffs at the bottom, but she won't take them from me.

"You can be mad," I say, and I feel strangely calm. "But that's still what I think."

"Right," Ellen snorts. "Because drinking and all that intimidates you. You're just scared of everything."

It's not only that I'm tired of hearing that. I mean, I consider it. I really do. But this time I know she's wrong. I can feel it. "A little scared," I admit. "About different things. But not the way I was before." Something about my voice or my face gets her attention. She drops her sneer and flops down on her bed. Then she winces, but her face doesn't grit itself the way it used to. Her chest tube sore is basically healed, and her ribs aren't far behind.

"You seem so different lately," she finally says.

"I am," I say. "We all are." She knows I mean her and me and Jack. "It's bad," I tell her. "Drinking a bunch of beers alone in the afternoon is bad." She massages her neck. "You don't have to be a rocket scientist to know that much."

"It's not a bunch of beers," she tries. "And you're no rocket scientist."

"Obviously."

"Wow," she says. "One meeting with the Ashleys, and you can be a better bitch than me."

"See?" I go. "You just called them the Ashleys."

Ellen rolls her eyes. "Okay," she says. "I won't drink in the afternoon."

"You better not," I tell her. "I mean it."

"I know."

Christina Noonan throws a New Year's party. We all go, which is different to begin with. Because, among other reasons, I've never once been to the same party as my brother. And the last party I made it to was Wayne's.

Ellen gets a little drunk, but I can't yell at her because it's New Year's and not in the afternoon.

"He'll be here," she keeps telling Jason every second. His boyfriend was supposed to show up. She's trying to be supportive.

"When we want something, we always have to reckon with probabilities," Jason goes.

"Absolutely." Ellen takes another swig from her beer and then gets up to go pee for the eightieth time.

Jason plays with his right earlobe, and Seth pulls my curls and feeds me chocolate-covered pretzels between sips of beer. The truth is, I hate the taste of beer.

Right before midnight Ashley One and these two guys and these three other girls grab me.

"It's your brother," they say. "Come on."

They lead me and everyone to Christina's parents' bedroom, which has an OFF-LIMITS—NO JOKE—STAY OUT OF THIS ROOM sign on it.

Jack's inside sitting on the edge of a canopy bed. His arms are crossed over his gut, and his head is slumped over his arms, and he's bawling.

"He's really drunk," Ashley One tells me. "Carl's been trying to get him to throw up."

"He never vomits," I say, the ink everywhere, heavy and ugly.

"Never?" somebody asks me.

"Not in his whole life," I say. Black and thick.

We hear people screaming outside the room. "Ten! Nine!"

"It's the countdown," I tell everyone.

"I'm finding Rob," Ellen goes, and she leaves the room.

Jack is trying to suck in air between sobs. Seth and Jason stand by the door, their feet wedged against the bottom, making sure nobody else walks in.

"Jack." I sit next to him, sinking with weight.

"Six! Five!"

Jack's body is heaving. He's moaning. My teeth start to chatter.

"Great party," somebody mutters.

"Get the fuck out of here," I hear Jason snarl, while Ashley's going, "You asshole!" and there's movement and the door is opening and closing, and I don't even know who's in this room anymore.

"Jack," I go. I ball my hands into fists to keep them from trembling.

He tries to say something to me, but he's crying so hard I can't understand him.

"What?" I ask. "What?"

"Want it . . . stop."

"What?" I say again. Sinking. Sinking.

"Make," Jack gasps. "Time . . . stop." Drowning. "Make . . . it stop."

"Two! One!"

"I can't," I say, helpless. Seth is here, next to me, leaning down toward us, swallowing and swallowing.

"Make it stop," Jack begs me.

"I can't."

Seth and Jason and Rob haul Jack into Rob's car. Rob's sober, thank you, God. He drives me and my brother home. We try to sneak Jack upstairs, but my parents are in the kitchen, just back from their own party, and they catch us.

"We're drunk," Jack tells them. And then he passes out.

26

MY FATHER DOESN'T TALK TO ANY OF US ALL THE NEXT DAY. HE can't really talk to Jack because my brother keeps his door locked. My dad doesn't even try to force him to open up.

I arrange myself on the L of the couch and watch TV and whisper on the phone to Ellen and to Seth.

My mother stays in her study in the corner of the third floor.

My father sits in the kitchen playing poker, swearing and humming, and getting up to pace the house every hour or so. I keep hearing him stand up, walk the stairs, creak around the third floor, then the second, then back down the steps, through the entryway and family room and living room, past me, and back to the kitchen.

"Dad," I say on his fifth tour.

He stops walking.

"Tuesday's my last therapy session, if we're still going by what you said when I started." He stays quiet, which, truthfully, makes me nervous. "But I want to keep seeing Frances." He touches his fingertips to his chin.

"Dad?"

"All right," he says. And he goes back to the kitchen.

Frances's freckled face looks windburned. I wonder if she went skiing over the holidays, but I don't ask.

"Everybody's had a pretty challenging time," she says after I'm done telling her what's been going on. It's such a therapist thing to say. Then she asks, "Do you have any ideas why you have so many mixed feelings about going out with Seth?"

I shake my head a little and feel tired. I wonder why, of all the things I've told her, that's the one she decides to ask me about. "It just seems hard." I don't even really know what I mean. "It's another person you have to . . ."

"You have to what?" Frances goes.

"You have to . . . I don't know. Take care of. Not piss off. Not disappoint."

"That's what a boyfriend is?" Frances asks.

"I guess that's not how other people see it," I go, feeling stupid.

"You like Seth, right?" Frances asks.

"A lot," I admit. "He's really funny and nice and sort of weird, but in a cool way."

"You like the fooling around?" Frances asks.

"Frances!"

"Well?" She smiles. A wide smile. That fang. "Fooling around is a big part of romantic relationships."

"Yes," I tell her. "I like it."

"You enjoy how you feel when you're with him?"

I nod.

"But not enough to want to take responsibility for his happiness?"

"I guess," I say.

"What if you were to consider the possibility that in relationships you're not responsible for the other person's happiness?"

"Huh?"

"That maybe we're responsible for our own," Frances says. "Other people can help or hinder, or sometimes both. But in the end it's up to each of us."

"It's hard for me to see it that way," I tell her. "I mean, if you mess up with someone, they can't handle it and they don't like you, and you feel awful and it's just not worth it."

"Is that right?" Frances asks.

"Plus, people leave."

"Leave?"

"You know. Break up with you or break your heart or . . ."

"Or?"

"I don't know. They just leave you. They . . . they . . ."

"Die?"

"Why are you being so mean?"

"I'm not trying to be mean," Frances says. "I just had a feeling that's what you were thinking, and so I said it for you."

"Well, what if I didn't want you to say it for me? What if that's not even what I was thinking?"

"Then, I made a mistake," Frances says. "And I'm sorry."

I stew on that for a while and stroke my suede pillow. Then

I say out loud what's in my head. "Why should I get to be happy with somebody as amazing as Seth when Jack will never be happy with someone again?"

She waits awhile, but I don't say anything else, and she doesn't speak for me this time.

"I think that question is one we should definitely talk about," she finally says. I don't say something back about it. I can't go there right now. That whole topic just makes me tired.

"Aren't we supposed to do EMDR today?"

"Nice dodge," Frances goes. She looks at me without moving for just long enough to let me know she's not going to forget to bring it up again. "But yes." She pulls out the gray box and starts to untangle the wires. "Let's start by checking what we did last session."

"It's hard to remember," I say, getting myself situated with legs up and crossed under my pillow.

"That's okay." Frances hands me the buzzers. "Just tell me, when you do think of the work we did last time, what comes up?"

There was the key chain. I can see it dangling from the steering wheel made of light on that bright day by the windy road. Also there was the thing about screaming. But what I remember more is wet grass.

"Sprinklers," I tell Frances. "Wet grass and little kids playing in the sprinklers."

Frances nods and turns on the buzzers.

The sprinklers make that *snickety, snickety* sound over and over, and all that black, wiry hair on Ellen's leg, with the razor going *snick, snick* over and over, repeating and repeating, and then the black hairs turn into green blades of grass strewn with brown leaves the size of barrettes, and I'm picking them up and saying, "In order to add fractions, you have to find a common numerator," and my father is standing over me, glaring and vein-popping, screaming, "Why are you always repeating the same wrong thing?" And there's dread and weight and blackness, and he's looming, like a monster, screaming and screaming, and I try to pick up the leaves, but they crumble or blow away under his monster breath, and it's my fault because I'm repeating the same wrong thing over and over, always wrong, always bad, and it's better to be still and calm, but I can't do it, it's never right, I'm bad, always so bad.

237

"Take a deep breath," Frances tells me as she turns off the buzzers. "And let it go." It's wild how you forget to breathe sometimes.

"It's my father," I tell her. "He's mad. He's yelling at me. I hate the way he always yells and makes up his stupid rules at the drop of a hat and won't let you even say anything."

"Go," Frances says.

My father's face bloats and then lengthens and gels into a brackish green wave, and my brother has his feet planted and his arms up and out, and he's going, "I can stop the wave, Anna! I can stop the wave!" Only, he can't, and the father face breaks hard on top of us, and Jack yells for me to help, only I'm no help, I'm no help at all, I can't help Jack, and Jack can't help me because it's too much, too fast, and another one rears above us, and the vein in the temple ripples and froth foams at the mouth, and it crashes, and there's nothing you can do because it's so much bigger and smarter and stronger than you and it knows what you deserve anyway.

"I have a sour taste in my mouth," I tell Frances, and she keeps the buzzers going. "Like I'm going to throw up, only I'm not, and it's this feeling of desperation and despair and dread, and I hate it. I so hate it."

"Just notice," Frances tells me in her steady voice.

Another father face looming and rearing and screaming and crashing black noise over and through us, and another and another and another, and our feet are planted wide and our heads are ducked low, bracing ourselves for wave after wave after wave after wave.

"I hate him," I tell Frances, clutching the buzzers. "I hate him. I hate how he can't stop. He never stops. He never stops and you can't breathe or move, there's never any room, and I can't stand it, I can't stand it."

He's crashing down on us, down on me and Jack, and we struggle to stay standing, to breathe, we struggle under that wave and then another and another, and then suddenly there's a pocket of air and we suck it in, gasping, just as another father face lifts and poises to strike, and Jack is clutching my hand, and the wave above is roaring, howling, only somehow it isn't angry anymore, it's afraid, it's a wave afraid to hurt us and afraid of us getting hurt, and the mouth in the wave is a circle of fear and the eyes are wide, and it's straining not to crash, shuddering and shaking with the effort because the gravity of the tides and of the moon and of everything is stronger than anything, and when it can't stop itself anymore, the father face cascades down on us, screaming, "Hold on! Hold on!" And Jack and I wind our arms together, clasping each other's wrists, like trapeze artists, gripping so hard we're shaking and trembling, but we still hold on, we hold on, even though we can't stop the waves, even though we can't stop anything, we hold on together, and it helps.

Frances turns off the buzzers and hands me a tissue. I see those stupid certificates and some fresh tulips in a vase, and inside I notice that I'm wondering where she got tulips from in the middle of the winter and if she put aspirin in them, but what I say is, "I don't know." Frances waits, and I blow my nose. "I just see me and Jack and my father, and it's just . . . I don't know. Emotional."

Jack and I are underneath rushing and blackness and weight and pressure, but we're holding on to each other, side by side, feet planted, heads down, hands gripping wrists, and we hold on and hold on and hold on, and it helps, it helps a lot, and then the wave has passed, and there's no more, there's really no more, and we squint out at the horizon to make sure, but the ocean has morphed into a magical Caribbean sea of dazzling turquoise, and we're standing next to each other in the warm, soft water. Calm and still and peaceful, with a barely moving ship on the horizon and a V of pelicans gliding above. We look behind us, and on the pink sand, by the red-striped umbrella and damp towels and low-slung chairs, my parents are lazing in the sun. The brim of my father's white hat is tilted low over his eyes, and the strap of my mother's straw one is tied firmly under her chin. We're looking over our shoulders, back at them, and they see us and wave, and in my father's hand is number 1,000 coconut sunblock, and Jack and I turn back to the ocean, side by side, palms cupping the surface of the beautiful, beautiful blue water.

"Look," Jack says. "Minnows."

27

"HERE," I SAY, SHOVING MY SIXTH BOUQUET AT JASON. WE'RE IN Ellen's room, upstairs. It's June, and I've had to give all my roses away because as it turns out, my dad started sneezing and swelling immediately with the first one.

"Thanks," Jason goes. But he doesn't take them from me. His eyes are puffy.

"I'm really sorry," I tell him. Sweatshirt cheated on him. With a girl.

Ellen takes the flowers and leaves the room, probably to find a vase. She barely has a limp anymore. At first when she got the short cast off, she walked sort of funny. Tippy-toed. She couldn't get her heel flat on the ground. But now she's moving pretty smoothly.

Jason flops onto Ellen's bed. He's half sitting on Whitey, but

I don't say anything. He leans back and stares at the upside-down dried roses hanging from Ellen's ceiling fixture. I gave her bouquet number four. My mother got number three for her office, and Seth got number two, just for kicks.

"He was so mad about prom. I should have taken him." Jason took Ellen to prom instead of Sweatshirt. As friends, obviously. None of us thought our school could handle two guys going together. Not yet, anyway. Maybe in a couple of years.

"For someone who wasn't even out until he met you, that seems totally unfair," I tell Jason.

The prom committee thing turned out to be not so bad. I ended up tagging along with Ellen and Jack to most of the meetings anyway, and nobody cared that I was an unofficial member. Jack wanted to DJ prom himself, but he got voted down because even though he's pretty popular, nobody much likes his music, and we hired a band instead. But Jack did manage to convince the band and the committee to let him set up movie clips on a big screen on one side of the gym, and everybody thought that was completely cool.

Seth and I spent so much time fooling around outside on the football field that a bunch of people said they thought we hadn't shown up at all. Lisa started liking Jack and wanted to go to prom with him, but he hasn't liked anyone since Cameron, and especially not Lisa. So she went with some guy she met at the mall who Ellen and Jason reported was cute, but who didn't say a word the whole time.

"Besides which," Ellen goes, walking back into the room with a vase full of water, "what's he fooling around with a girl for if he's gay?" She sits at her desk and starts arranging the roses. "He's confused, Jase."

Jason starts to cry again. Well, not cry exactly. It's more of a weep. Which makes me think about Seth. Which makes me think about sex. Which makes me internally slap myself so that I can focus on Jason, who needs his friends.

"You deserve better," I tell Jason. "A lot better than that guy."

"Yeah," Ellen says. "You need someone like Keith."

She's sort of dating some guy she met in physical therapy who smashed his arm in another car wreck. He looks a little bit like Bono, but he's not all that charismatic. I like him, though, and he likes Ellen, and that's good enough for me. She still drinks too much at parties, but she's stopped drinking during the day, and Keith is on my side about the whole thing, so that's good.

"If Seth cheated on me, I think I'd die," I tell Jason. He's stopped weeping.

"Especially if he cheated on you with a guy," he points out.

"Don't," I go. "Do you think he's gay?" Panicked, I'm remembering all those rumors about Jason and Seth after the accident.

Ellen snorts. "No way."

"You'd never fool around with him, would you?" I ask Jason. "That would be, like, insanely cruel."

Now Jason snorts. "No offense, Anna," he goes. "But no way."

"So have you guys done it yet?" Ellen asks. She's finished with the roses. She spins around on her desk stool to look at me. She means have we gone all the way, made it home, gotten busy, done the dirty. Had sex.

But she knows we haven't. She's just trying to distract Jason.

"Stop trying to distract me," Jason goes.

"Fine," Ellen goes. "You're sitting on Whitey." Jason lifts his butt, and Ellen gets off her stool to pull Whitey free. She starts rubbing him over her chin. "I know you know I made a pass at Jason," Ellen goes to me out of the blue. Then she blushes.

"You told her?" I ask Jason.

"No." Jason arches his left eyebrow and looks at Ellen. "How do you know?"

"Whitey told me."

"How would Whitey know?" I go.

Ellen shrugs. "Whitey knows everything."

When I get home, my parents are in the kitchen. The weird thing is, it's my mom yelling instead of my dad.

"Responsibility!" my mom's saying. My father's sitting at the table in front of a Texas Hold 'Em online game.

"What's happening?" I ask Jack, who's in the family room on the L-shaped couch with his DVD paused. Somehow I get the feeling this fight has been going on for a while.

"Mom's pissed," Jack says.

"Mom's pissed?" I can't remember the last time my mother was the one who was pissed.

"Bullshit," my father's saying, only kind of weak.

"You can't tell anything from two sessions!" my mom yells. "It takes time, Harvey. It takes time and effort!"

"The guy's an idiot," my dad says back. "I'm not going to sit in some room with an idiot for an hour a week and pay him for idiocy."

"This is not a debate," my mom goes. "This is an ultimatum!"

"Damn it," my father says. "I had three aces."

We hear a crash and then silence.

Jack and I look at each other and then race to the kitchen doorway. My father's laptop is on the floor. Someone knocked it off the table. He and my mother are staring at it.

"You can't really force someone into therapy," Jack says into the quiet room. He should know.

"This is none of your business," my mom answers.

"Bullshit," Jack goes.

"Yeah," I say. I feel strangely calm. "Bullshit."

"Go to your rooms," my father tells us, still staring at his laptop.

"You can't make someone go to therapy," I say. "But you can be really pissed at someone for a long time for not going." I look hard at Jack when I say that.

"I said," my dad repeats, "go to your rooms."

We ignore him. We go back to the L-shaped couch instead. Jack unpauses his DVD. It's footage of some god-awful band.

"What's this one called?" I ask him after about three seconds.

"Mystic Circles of the Young Girls. It's good, right?"

"Yeah," I say. "Right."

I hear him crying through the wall in the middle of the night. I kick off my sheet and pull on decent pajama bottoms and the TALK TO MY AGENT T-shirt and leave my room to go to his. In the hallway I stop short, surprised to see my mother, her ear an inch away from Jack's closed door. She straightens up in her slippers and looks sheepish for a minute. We watch each other listening to Jack for a while, and then my mom motions for me to follow her. She leads me to the kitchen and makes us peanut butter and jelly sandwiches.

"Are you taking Jack and me to Paris if dad won't go?" I ask her.

"We'll see," she says.

"Do you think Jack's going to pick NYU or UCLA?"

She chews her sandwich for a while without answering.

"Mom?" I say.

"NYU," she tells me. "Please pass the milk."

Jack won't do therapy.

"It really helps," I try to tell him one Sunday afternoon after Seth has left.

"Leave me alone, Anna," he goes.

"With EMDR, your brain makes these little movies in your head," I tell him for the tenth time. "I mean, some people's do. Mine does. Yours probably would. You'd like that."

"I know," he says. "You've told me about it ten times."

"Even Dad's in therapy," I argue.

"Twice. To some guy he thinks is a moron," Jack says. "That's not exactly therapy. And you don't see him going back, do you? Besides, it's not a competition."

"Ellen says it's totally ironic that out of the whole family you're the only one not even willing to give it a try."

"Ellen is too smart for her own good," Jack goes.

"I heard you crying a few nights ago," I tell him.

"Shut up."

"I just want to help," I say.

He throws his pillow at me. "Yeah," he goes. "I know."

• • •

I still haven't looked at the memorial Web site for Cameron. Frances and I talk some about it and do some EMDR, and it's not bad the way it used to be, but I don't want to click the final click. I don't want to read what everybody has to say about Cameron and how she's not here. The screaming, stopped, doesn't haunt me the way it used to. It doesn't haunt me at all, actually, but the sadness isn't something you can buzz away. It's just sad, and even though I know it's not my fault, it's still sad.

So it's not like you live happily ever after. It doesn't work that way. You still have bad dreams sometimes, only instead of waking up drenched and shouting, it's more like you wake up really tired in the morning, feeling that sadness and thinking, *That was so awful. That was such an awful thing that happened.* It's not like my mother doesn't still spend tons of time up in her study and my dad doesn't yell at all of us for little things. It's just more that none of it feels as terrifying and out of control. As lonely.

Mostly you realize you can handle it. You'd rather turn it all upside down and dump it out and watch it scatter and disappear. You'd rather do that, because you don't want to have to handle it. You really don't. It's too stupid and crazy and incredibly, incredibly unfair.

But you do handle it. Because the thing you learn is that you can.

ACKNOWLEDGMENTS

The author gratefully acknowledges and warmly thanks:

Dr. Bennett S. Burns, Dr. Steven Covici, Dr. Mark Klion, and Dr. Kevin J. Mickey for their speedy and thorough courses in ophthalmology and orthopedics;

Gina Colelli for accepting endless requests for information and assistance, and for her sensitive supervision of EMDR;

Ann Griffin for making AP biology a surprising pleasure;

Richard Jackson for encouraging without pushing, and then patiently waiting;

Stephen Lucas for his love, support, and band names;

Dr. Tanya Lucas for her medical expertise and for connecting me with Dr. Covici and Dr. Burns;

Amy Rosenblum for suggesting that Grandma be calmed down and Dad be kept on the beach;

Dr. William Rosenblum for catching blood-alcohol level inaccuracies;

Charlotte Sheedy for so readily supporting the path I requested; and

Mike and Anna Stewart for connecting me with Dr. Klion.

Love and
Responsibility

KAROL WOJTYLA
(POPE JOHN PAUL II)

Love and
Responsibility

TRANSLATED BY
H. T. WILLETTS

✤

FARRAR · STRAUS GIROUX
New York

Originally published in Polish as *Miłość I
Odpowiedzialność*, Krakow, Wydawnicto, Znak, 1960
Revised edition first published in English in
1981 by William Collins Sons & Co. Ltd., London
and Farrar, Straus and Giroux, Inc., New York

Library of Congress Cataloging in Publication Data
John Paul II, Pope.
Love and responsibility.
Translation of: Miłość i odpowiedzialność.
Includes bibliographical references and index.
1. Sex (Theology)   2. Sexual ethics.   I. Title.
BT708.J6313   1981   241'.66   81-2261
                                          AACR2

The publishers wish to make acknowledgment to Henry March

CONTENTS

CONTENTS

CHAPTER IV: JUSTICE TOWARDS THE CREATOR

CHAPTER V: SEXOLOGY AND ETHICS

INTRODUCTION TO
THE PRESENT EDITION

The book now in the reader's hands has a history. It first appeared 20 years ago. Books are written and published nowadays at such a rate, and there is as a result such a rapid turn-over of literature on the market, that 20 years is a long time even in such fields as philosophy, in which books age much less quickly than in some others. What is more, the book has a long pre-history. It originated in response not to a need of the moment, but to a demand which is always topical. In this sense it has a very long pre-history indeed. A pre-history written by the experience of many people, which has in a way become the experience of the Author himself, as their pastor and their confidant. Their experience converged with and so to speak supplemented his own personal experience of, and feelings about, these matters, prompted him to reflect and meditate on them, and as time went by made him feel the need to testify to his knowledge. *Love and Responsibility* was the work intended to give voice to this testimony. It first found expression in the form of a series of lectures given in the Catholic University of Lublin in 1958–9, and was finally published in book form by the TNKUL (Learned Society of the Catholic University of Lublin) in 1960.

From that moment the work began to live a life of its own. The author of a book retains his title to authorship of course, but even if he continues to develop its themes he is no longer writing it. Once he has finished it the book writes its own history, and in some measure that of the author too. *Habent sua fata libelli.*

It is largely the history of a confrontation: between the experience discussed, the testimony given in the book, and certain conceptions and propositions which invoke the same source, or at least look to it for legitimation and justification. How well has *Love and Responsibility* stood up to that confrontation? The question is natural and inevitable, since the problems which the book raised have loomed large in the two decades of its existence. The reader must obviously be asking the question at this moment. And expecting an answer here and now. But to try answering it now could only jeopardize the whole conception of the work. The intention of the book is to provide an opportunity for continuous, uninterrupted 'confrontation', a chance to 'test experience by experience'. As something that can be invoked at any moment, whenever the need to appeal to the experience as originally described arises or takes on a new urgency.

Tolle et lege – but above all *vide*! It is then in the nature of the book that – as the author himself acknowledges in the preface to the second edition – it envisages co-authorship; it envisages that those who think through its theories to their conclusion, or carry over its formulation into practice, will, so to speak, make a continuing creative contribution to it. This work is open to every echo of experience, from whatever quarter it comes, and it is at the same time a standing appeal to all to let experience, their own experience, make itself heard, to its full extent: in all its breadth, and all its depth. When we speak here of depth we have in mind all those things which do not always show themselves directly as part of the content of experience, but are none the less a component, a hidden dimension of it, so much so that it is impossible to omit them, if we want to identify fully the contents of experience. If we do omit them, we shall be detracting from and impoverishing experience, and so robbing it of validity, though it is the sole source of information and the basis of all reliable knowledge on whatever subject. *Love and Responsibility*, with this sort of methodological basis, fears nothing and need fear nothing which can be legitimized by experience. Experience does not have to be afraid of experience. Truth can only gain from such a confrontation.

Looked at from this angle, the history of *Love and Responsibility* reveals the quite extraordinary vitality of the book. It would obviously be a simplification, indeed a vulgarization, to speak of its 'victorious progress'. It is obvious however, that it did not have to await 'rediscovery' or 'resurrection' until its Author became Pope. If we really want to look for cause and effect perhaps it is exactly the other way round. Ought we not to speak rather of the work taking a peculiar revenge on its Creator? *Habent sua fata libelli* – yes indeed! But thanks to their books – *habent etiam sua fata eorundem auctores*. The authors of books find that their history is written in a certain sense by all who live by their inspiration. By the testimony which has begotten in others the need to testify in turn. Who knows whether only human voices make themselves heard in this testimony. *Vox populi.* . . .

In any case, *Love and Responsibility* has lived, and lives still, not only in its successive editions, three in Polish (two of these published in Poland, which given the situation which everyone knows to exist in the country is an event worthy of note), and several in foreign languages: French, Italian, Spanish. A no less clear testimony to its vitality – and paradoxical though it is this is something which cannot go unmentioned here – are the editions which were supposed to materialize but never did. Why not? Certainly not because *Love and Responsibility* feared confrontation with experience. . . . Great works have a great though not always an easy lot. Their destiny is great because even their misadventures reveal what they might have been expected or perhaps were intended to disguise: their true greatness. They are beyond the reach of defeat, 'too big' for it, although there is much which may seem to create an illusion of defeat.

Although almost twenty years after its first publication the work is sufficient recommendation for itself, and needs no other, it obviously needs to be seen in the setting which has grown up around it in the course of those years.

On the one hand, the context is set by the debate on the central problems raised by Pope Paul VI in his encyclical *Humanae Vitae*. As the reader will know, the debate in its first phase concentrated exclusively on the rather chaotic search for arguments and counter-arguments, as each side sought to win over supporters, but moved on later to the stage of self-examination of a methodologically profounder kind. It became a discussion on the means by which the correctness of moral norms might be established.

So that, without calling in question the fundamental correctness of the norms laid down in *Humanae Vitae*, the discussion thereafter concerned the limits within which they are binding, and made the decision on this particular question dependent on the resolution of the dispute between teleological and deontological theories on procedures for testing the correctness of moral norms. Deeper analysis of the subject of debate revealed, however, both that the problems themselves were more complicated than at first appeared, and also, to the great surprise of both sides – that an intermediate position was possible and indeed necessary. It revealed also that the only solutions which can expect to be fully accepted must be based both on honest anthropology and on a profound insight into the act itself, revealed in particular that it is impossible to isolate the question of the legitimacy of the act so completely as to separate it from its primary function in inter-personal relations; that of expressing love, or in other words affirming the person so as to enhance its dignity.

It is certainly interesting to look at the discussion, ten years after the appearance of the encyclical *Humanae Vitae*, from the vantage point of this other work, which appeared ten years before it. A work untouched by the atmosphere of animosity, of polemic and counter-polemic, a work the spirit of which is determined by its sole concern: to ensure a hearing for all the truths that experience can furnish on the subject of a love worthy of the human person. But for this very reason there is a need to put the present work in the same context, to exhibit it against this background. This it is that justifies the addition of notes, which are intended to provide a commentary linking the text of *Love and Responsibility* to the context mentioned above. Such a commentary, indeed, has become quite indispensable.

Nor must we overlook the fact that in the course of the same twenty years the Author of *Love and Responsibility* has published a large number of articles, written with direct reference to it, and further developed its themes in a number of directions, with particular attention to family ethics and to the philosophy and theology of the body. The need to take cognisance of this other, 'authorial' context seems perfectly obvious. So much so that there was at first some thought of publishing these works as appendixes to *Love and Responsibility*. Quite apart from the fact that such an annexe would dwarf the book itself, there was another and weightier consideration against amalgamation. One work by the Author of quite exceptional importance in this context would necessarily have remained outside the scope of the annexe. This is 'Person and Act', the work in which the Author has given the fullest account of his views on the subject of the human person.

There is probably no need to waste words showing how very closely the subject matter of that work is connected with the question of responsible love, which is the main theme of *Love and Responsibility*. The person, through its own action and the action of another person, becomes the object and subject of responsible love. The person is an actor in the drama – *dramatis persona* – in which it writes 'its truest history', the history of love or of its negation. The text of *Love and Responsibility* would be impoverished at its very core if some way were not found of making the necessary connections with 'Person and Act' and putting it in the context of K. Wojtyla's 'Treatise on Man'. This is the second reason for the decision that a commentary was necessary and that it should take this form.

In the notes to *Love and Responsibility* the reader will find, firstly, references to other works by the Author and, secondly, observations which bring out the significance of the work as a challenge to debate. To the confrontation of other people's views and concepts with – what? with the Author's work? Certainly, with that too, but still more important, confrontation through the medium of the work, with the exposition of an integrated experience, the testimony of this experience concerning the love of one human person for another. A love which – as experience again continually tells us – is itself real love only when it reaches the highest point of affirmation of the dignity both of its object and of the subject himself. The authors of this introduction cherish the hope that the reading of *Love and Responsibility* will, by opening up this debate, bring the reader much satisfaction – and not merely intellectual satisfaction.

AUTHOR'S INTRODUCTION TO THE FIRST EDITION (1960)

✤

It is sometimes said that only those who live a conjugal life can pronounce on the subject of marriage, and only those who have experienced it can pronounce on love between man and woman. In this view, all pronouncements on such matters must be based on personal experience, so that priests and persons living a celibate life can have nothing to say on questions of love and marriage. Nevertheless they often do speak and write on these subjects. Their lack of direct personal experience is no handicap because they possess a great deal of experience at second-hand, derived from their pastoral work. For in their pastoral work they encounter these particular problems so often, and in such a variety of circumstances and situations, that a different type of experience is created, which is certainly less immediate, and certainly 'second-hand', but at the same time very much wider. The very abundance of factual material on the subject stimulates both general reflection and the effort to synthesize what is known.

That indeed is how this book came about. It is not an exposition of doctrine. It is, rather, the result above all of an incessant confrontation of doctrine with life (which is just what the work of a spiritual adviser consists of). Doctrine – the teaching of the Church – in the sphere of 'sexual' morality is based upon the New Testament, the pronouncements of which on this subject are brief but also sufficient. It is a marvel that a system so complete can be based on such a small number of statements. Quite obviously, they touch the problem at its most sensitive points, the crucial points which determine all further principles and moral norms. You need only have these few texts to hand – Matthew 5:27, 28, Matthew 19:1–13, Mark 10:1–12, Luke 20:27–35, John 8:1–11, I Corinthians 7 (throughout), Ephesians 5:22–33, to form sufficiently clear views on the subject. In the present book (which is not meant as an exercise in exegetics), this handful of most important statements is our frame of reference throughout.

But although it is easy to draw up a set of rules for Catholics in the sector of 'sexual' morality the need to validate these rules makes itself felt at every step. For the rules often run up against greater difficulties in practice than in theory, and the spiritual adviser, who is concerned above all with the practical, must seek ways of justifying them. For his task is not only to command or forbid but to justify, to interpret, to explain. The present book was born principally of the need to put the norms of Catholic sexual morality on a firm basis, a basis as definitive as possible, relying on the most elementary and incontrovertible moral truths and the most fundamental values or goods. Such a good is the person, and the moral truth most closely bound up with the world of persons is 'the commandment to love' – for love is a good peculiar to the world of persons. And therefore the most fundamental way of looking at sexual morality is in the context of 'love and responsibility' – which is why the whole book bears that title.

This approach calls for a number of analytical exercises. Although the purpose of the book is to synthesize, it is at the same time extremely analytical. The subject of analysis is in the first place the person as affected by the sexual urge, then the love which grows up on this basis between man and woman, next the virtue of purity as an essential factor in that love, and finally the question of marriage and vocation. All these problems are the subject of analysis, not of mere description – for the aim is to elicit the basic principles in which the rules and norms of Catholic 'sexual' morality find their *raison d'être*. The book is, by and large, of a philosophical character – for ethics is (and can only be) part of philosophy.

Does it have a practical significance? Does it deal with real life? Basically very much so, although it never strains to give ready made prescriptions or detailed rules of behaviour. It is not casuistic. Its concern is rather to create a view of the problem in its entirety rather than solutions to particular instances of it – all of which are in some way accommodated within the general view. The title of the book indicates most accurately what that view is: for in the context of relationships between persons of different sexes, when we speak of 'sexual morality' we are really thinking of 'love and responsibility'.

The most important concept here is that of love, to which we therefore devote the greater part of our analytical exercises – and indeed in some sense all the analyses in this book. For there exists, especially if we start from the Christian ethics born of the New Testament, a problem which can be described as that of 'introducing love into love'. The word as first used in that phrase signifies the love which is the subject of the greatest commandment, while in its second use it means all that takes shape between a man and a woman on the basis of the sexual urge. We could look at it the other way round and say that there exists a problem of changing the second type of love (sexual love) into the first, the love of which the New Testament speaks.

The problem awaits discussion. Manuals of ethics and moral theology tend to deal with these two kinds of love separately: with the first in discussions of the theological virtues, since love is the greatest of these, and with the second primarily within the framework of discussion of the cardinal virtue of continence, since sexual purity is connected with this. The result may be a certain hiatus in our understanding, a feeling that the second kind of love cannot be reduced to the first, or at any rate ignorance of the ways in which this can be realized. At the same time, observation of life (and in particular pastoral experience) shows that there is an immense demand for knowledge of these ways. And the moral teaching of the Gospel seems to provide a clear inspiration for it. The Gospel is read both by believers and by unbelievers. Believers discover in the commandment to love one another the kingpin of the whole supernatural order, but believers and unbelievers alike are capable of discovering in it the affirmation of a great human good, which can and must be the portion of every person. In the present work, it is in fact on this second aspect that we lay the main emphasis.

In the commonest view it goes without saying that problems of sex are above all problems of the 'body'. Hence the tendency to allow physiology and medicine an almost exclusive right to speak on these matters – psychology is allotted only a secondary role. The same sciences are also supposed to be capable of generating ethical norms unaided. This book puts the problem in a fundamentally different perspective. Sexual morality is within the domain of the person. It is impossible to understand anything about it without understanding what the person is, its mode of existence, its functioning, its powers. The personal order is the only proper plane for all debate on matters of sexual morality. Physiology and medicine can only supplement discussion at this level. They do not in themselves provide a complete foundation for the understanding of love and responsibility: but this is just what matters most in the relations between persons of different sex.

For the same reason, the treatment of all matters to be discussed in this book has throughout a personalistic character. Physiological and medical details will have their place in the notes.* I take this opportunity to thank warmly those persons who have assisted me in assembling the data, and in supplementing my bibliography and revising some of the entries in it.

The Author

*In the present edition these matters are dealt with in Chapter V.

CHAPTER I

The Person and
the Sexual Urge

❧

ANALYSIS OF
THE VERB 'TO USE'

❧

The Person as the Subject and Object of Action

The world in which we live is composed of many objects. The word 'object' here means more or less the same as 'entity'. This is not the proper meaning of the word, since an 'object', strictly speaking, is something related to a 'subject'. A 'subject' is also an 'entity' – an entity which exists and acts in a certain way. It is then possible to say that the world in which we live is composed of many subjects. It would indeed be proper to speak of 'subjects' before 'objects'. If the order has been reversed here, the intention was to put the emphasis right at the beginning of this book on its objectivism, its realism. For if we begin with a 'subject', especially when that subject is man, it is easy to treat everything which is outside the subject, i.e. the whole world of objects, in a purely subjective way, to deal with it only as it enters into the consciousness of a subject, establishes itself and dwells in that consciousness. We must, then, be clear right from the start *that every subject also exists as an object, an objective 'something' or 'somebody'.*[1]

As an object, a man is 'somebody' – and this sets him apart from every other entity in the visible world, which as an object is always only 'something'. Implicit in this simple, elementary distinction is the great gulf which separates the world of persons from the world of things. The world of objects, to which we belong, consists of people and things. We usually regard as a thing an entity which is devoid not only of intelligence, but also of life; a *thing* is an inanimate object. We would hesitate to call an animal, or even a plant, a 'thing'. None the less, no-one can speak with any conviction about an animal as a person. We speak of individual animals, looking upon them simply as single specimens of a particular animal species. And this definition suffices. But it is not enough to define a man as an individual of the species *Homo* (or even *Homo sapiens*). The term 'person' has been coined to signify that a man cannot be wholly contained within the concept 'individual member of the species', but that there is something more to him, a particular richness and perfection in the manner of his being, which can only be brought out by the use of the word 'person'.

The most obvious and simplest reason for this is that man has the ability to reason, he is a rational being, which cannot be said of any other entity in the visible world, for in none of them do we find any trace of conceptual thinking. Hence Boethius's famous definition of a person as simply an individual being of a rational nature (*individua substantia rationalis naturae*). This differentiates a person from the whole world of objective entities, this determines the distinctive character of a person.

The fact that a person is an individual of a rational nature – or an individual of whose nature reason is a property – makes the person the only subject of its kind in the whole world of entities, a subject totally different from such other subjects as, for instance, the animals – though these, and some of them in particular, are relatively close to man in respect of bodily structure. Speaking figuratively, we can say that the person as a subject is distinguished from even the most advanced animals by a specific inner self, an inner life, characteristic only of persons. It is impossible to speak of the inner life of animals, although physiological processes more or less similar to those in man take place within their organisms. Because of this bodily structure they develop – again to a greater or lesser extent – a rich sensual life, ranging far beyond the simple, vegetative life of plants, and recalling at times to a quite deceptive degree the activities typical of human life: cognition and desire, or to give the second activity a somewhat broader name, striving.

In man cognition and desire acquire a spiritual character and therefore assist in the formation of a genuine interior life, which does not happen with animals. *Inner life means spiritual life. It revolves around truth and goodness.* And it includes a whole multitude of problems, of which two seem central: what is the ultimate cause of everything and – how to be good and possess goodness at its fullest. The first of these central problems of man's interior life engages cognition and the second desire or, rather, aspiration. Both of these functions, though, seem to be more than that, to be rather what might be called natural tendencies of the whole human entity. Significantly, it is just because of his inner being, his interior life, that man is a person, but it is also because of this that he is so much involved in the world of objects, the world 'outside', involved in a way which is proper to him and characteristic of him. *A person is an objective entity, which as a definite subject has the closest contacts with the whole (external) world and is most intimately involved with it precisely because of its inwardness, its interior life.* It must be added that it communicates thus not only with the visible, but also with the invisible world, and most importantly, with God. This is a further indication of the person's uniqueness in the visible world.

The person's contact with the objective world, with reality, is not merely 'natural', physical, as is the case with all other creations of nature, nor is it merely sensual as in the case of animals. A human person, as a distinctly defined subject, establishes contact with all other entities precisely through the inner self, and neither the 'natural' contacts which are also its prerogative, since it has a body and in a certain sense 'is a body', nor the sensual contacts in which it resembles the animals, constitute its characteristic way of communication with the world. It is true that a human person's contact with the world begins on the 'natural' and sensual plane, but it is given the form proper to man only in the sphere of his interior life. Here, too, a trait characteristic of the person becomes apparent: a man does not only intercept messages which reach him from the outside world and react to them in a spontaneous or even purely mechanical way, but in his whole relationship with this world, with reality, he strives to assert himself, his 'I', and he must act thus, since the nature of his being demands it. Man's nature differs fundamentally from that of the animals. It includes the power of self-determination, based on reflection, and manifested in the fact that a man acts from choice.[2] This power is called free will.

Because a human being – a person – possesses free will, he is his own master, *sui juris* as the Latin phrase has it. This characteristic feature of a person goes with another distinctive attribute. The Latin of the philosophers defined it in the assertion that personality is *alteri incommunicabilis* – not capable of transmission, not transferable. The point here is not that a person is a unique and unrepeatable entity, for this can be said just as well of any other entity – of an animal, a plant, a stone. The incommunicable, the *inalienable*, in a person is intrinsic to that person's inner self, to the power of self determination, free will. *No one else can want for me.* No one can substitute his act of will for mine. It does sometimes happen that someone very much wants me to want what he wants. This is the moment when the impassable frontier between him and me, which is drawn by free will, becomes most obvious. I may not want that which he wants me to want – and in this precisely I am *incommunicabilis*. I am, and I must be, independent in my actions. All human relationships are posited on this fact. All true conceptions about education and culture begin from and return to this point.

For a man is not only the subject, but can also be the object of an action. At every step acts occur which have, as their object, other human beings. Within the framework of this book, the subject of which is sexual morality, actions of precisely this sort will be our constant theme. In dealings between persons of different sexes, and especially in the sexual relationship, the woman is always the object of activity on the part of a man, and the man the object of activity on the part of the woman. That is why it is right to begin by enquiring, however, briefly, who it is that acts – who is the subject – and who is acted upon – who is the object of the action. We know already that the subject and the object of the action alike are persons. It is now necessary to consider carefully the principles to which a human being's actions must conform when their object is another human person.[3]

The First Meaning of the Verb 'to Use'

To this end we must analyse thoroughly the word 'to use'. It denotes a certain objective form of action. *To use means to employ some object of action as a means to an end* – the specific end which the subject has in view. The end is always that with a view to which we are acting. The end also implies the existence of means (our name for those objects upon which our action is focused with a view to an end which we intend to attain) so that in the nature of things the means is subordinated to the end, and at the same time *subordinated to some extent to the agent*. It cannot be otherwise, since the person who is acting employs the means to achieve his aim – the expression 'employs' itself suggests the subordinate and as it were 'subservient' position of the means in relation to the agent: the means serves both the end and the subject.

It seems, then, beyond doubt that the relationship between a human being, a person, and various things, or beings, which are only individuals or specimens of their species, is and must be of this kind. Man in his various activities makes use of the whole created universe, takes advantage of all its resources for ends which he sets himself, for he alone understands them. Such an attitude on the part of man towards inanimate nature whose riches are so important to economic life, or towards living nature, whose energies and riches man appropriates, does not in principle arouse any doubts. Intelligent human beings are only required not to destroy or squander these natural resources, but to use them with restraint, so as not to impede the development of man himself, and so as to ensure the coexistence of human societies in justice and harmony. In his treatment of animals in particular, since they are beings endowed with feeling and sensitive to pain, man is required to ensure that the use of these creatures is never attended by suffering or physical torture.[4]

All these are simple principles, easily understood by any normal man. A problem arises when we seek to apply them to relations with other human beings, other persons. Is it permissible to regard a person as a means to an end and to use a person in that capacity? The problem which this question raises is a far-reaching one, with implications for a number of aspects of human life and human relationships. Let us take as instances the organization of labour in a factory, or the relationship between a commanding officer and a ranker in an army, or even relations between parents and children in the family. Does not an employer use a worker, i.e. a human person, for ends which he himself has chosen? Does not an officer use the soldiers under his command to attain certain military ends, planned by himself and sometimes known only to himself? Do not parents, who alone know the ends for which they are rearing their children, regard them in a sense as a means to ends of their own, since the children themselves do not understand those ends, nor do they consciously aim at them? Yet both the worker and the soldier are adults and fully developed people, while a child, even an unborn child, cannot be denied personality in its most objective ontological sense, although it is true that it has yet to acquire, step by step, many of the traits which will make it psychologically and ethically a distinct personality.

The same problem will loom again when we come to analyse in depth the entire relationship between woman and man, which forms the background to our discussion on the subject of sexual ethics.[5] We shall uncover this problem in various strata, so to speak, of our analysis. Does not a woman constitute for a man, in the sexual relationship, something like a means to the various ends which he seeks to attain within that relationship? Equally, does not a man constitute for a woman the means towards the attainment of her own aims?

Let us content ourselves for the time being with asking these questions, which embody a very important ethical problem. Not primarily a psychological problem but one of ethics,[6] for a person must not be *merely* the means to an end for another person. This is precluded by the very nature of personhood, by what any person is. For a person is a thinking subject, and capable of taking decisions: these, most notably, are the attributes we find in the inner self of a person. This being so, every person is by nature capable of determining his or her aims. Anyone who treats a person as the means to an end does violence to the very essence of the other, to what consitutes its natural right. Obviously, we must demand from a person, as a thinking individual, that his or her ends should be genuinely good, since the pursuit of evil ends is contrary to the rational nature of the person. This is also the purpose of education, both the education of children, and the mutual education of adults; it is just that – a matter of seeking true ends, i.e. real goods as the ends of our actions, and of finding and showing to others the ways to realize them.

But in this educational activity, especially when we have to do with the upbringing of young children, we must never treat a person as the means to an end. This principle has a universal validity. Nobody can use a person as a means towards an end, no human being, nor yet God the Creator.[7] On the part of God, indeed, it is totally out of the question, since, by giving man an intelligent and free nature, he has thereby ordained that each man alone will decide for himself the ends of his activity, and not be a blind tool of someone else's ends. Therefore, if God intends to direct man towards certain goals, he allows him to begin with to know those goals, so that he may make them his own and strive towards them independently. In this amongst other things resides the most profound logic of revelation: God allows man to learn His supernatural ends, but the decision to strive towards an end, the choice of course, is left to man's free will. God does not redeem man against his will.

This elementary truth – that a person, unlike all other objects of action, which are not persons may not be an instrument of action, is therefore an inherent component of the natural moral order. Thanks to this, the natural order acquires personalistic attributes: the order of nature, since its framework accommodates personal entities as well as others, must possess such attributes. It may not be irrelevant to mention here that Immanuel Kant, at the end of the eighteenth century, formulated this elementary principle of the moral order in the following imperative: act always in such a way that the other person is the end and not merely the instrument of your action. In the light of the preceding argument this principle should be restated in a form rather different from that which Kant gave it, as follows: whenever a person is the object of your activity, remember that you may not treat that person as only the means to an end, as an instrument, but must allow for the fact that he or she, too, has, or at least should have, distinct personal ends. This principle, thus formulated, lies at the basis of all the human freedoms, properly understood, and especially freedom of conscience.[8]

'Love' as the Opposite of 'Using'

Our whole discussion of the first meaning of the word 'to use', has so far given us only a negative solution to the problem of the correct attitude to a person; a human being cannot be solely or mainly an object to be used, for this reason, that the role of a blind tool or the means to an end determined by a different subject is contrary to the nature of a person.

If we go on to seek a positive solution to this problem we begin to discern love, to catch a preliminary glimpse of it, so to speak, as the only clear alternative to using a person as the means to an end, or the instrument of one's own action. Obviously, I may want another person to desire the same good which I myself desire. Obviously, the other must know this end of mine, recognize it as a good, and adopt it. If this happens, a special bond is established between me and this other person: the bond of a *common good* and of a common aim. This special bond does not mean merely that we both seek a common good, it also unites the persons involved internally, and so constitutes the essential core round which any love must grow. In any case, love between two people is quite unthinkable without some common good to bind them together.[9] This good is the end which both these persons choose. *When two different people consciously choose a common aim* this puts them on a footing of equality, and precludes the possibility that one of them might be subordinated to the other. Both – (although there may be more than two people tied by a common end) – are as it were in the same measure and to the same extent subordinated to that good which constitutes their common end. When we look at man we discern in him an elemental need of the good, a natural drive and striving towards it. This does not necessarily mean that he is capable of loving. In animals we observe the manifestations of an instinct which is similarly directed. But instinct alone does not necessarily imply the ability to love. This capacity is, however, inherent in human beings and is bound up with their freedom of will. Man's capacity for love depends on his willingness consciously to seek a good together with others, and to subordinate himself to that good for the sake of others, or to others for the sake of that good. *Love is exclusively the portion of human persons.*

Love in human relationships is not something ready-made. It begins as a principle or idea which people must somehow live up to in their behaviour, which they must desire if they want – as they should – to free themselves from the utilitarian, the 'consumer' attitude (Latin *consumere* = 'use') towards other persons. Let us look back for a moment at the examples given above. Inherent in the 'employer-employee' relationship there is a serious danger that the employee may be treated as a mere instrument; various defective systems of organizing labour give evidence of this. If, however, the employer and the employee so arrange their association that the common good which both serve becomes clearly visible, then the danger of treating a person as someone less than he really is will be reduced almost to nothing. For love will gradually eliminate the purely utilitarian or consumer attitude to the person of the employee in the behaviour of both the interested parties. In this example much has been simplified, leaving only the gist of the problem. It is just the same in the second example, that of the attitude of an officer towards the soldier under his command. When they are both united by an attitude based on something like love (we are obviously not speaking here of emotional love itself) deriving from the joint pursuit of a common good, which in this case is the defence of the fatherland, or the belief that it is in danger, then just because they both desire the same thing it is impossible to say that the soldier's person is used merely as a blind tool, as a means to an end.

The whole discussion[10] must now move on to the relationship between 'woman and man', the background of sexual ethics. Even here, and indeed, especially here, only love can preclude the use of one person by another. Love, as we have said, is conditioned by the common attitude of people towards the same good, which they choose as their aim, and to which they subordinate themselves. *Marriage is one of the most important areas where this principle is put into practice.* For in marriage two people, a man and a woman, are united in such a way that they become in a sense 'one flesh' (to use the words of the Book of Genesis), i.e., one common subject, as it were, of sexual life. How is it possible to ensure that one person does not then become for the other – the woman for the man, or the man for the woman – nothing more than the means to an end – i.e. an object used exclusively for the attainment of a selfish end? To exclude this possibility they must share the same end. Such an end, where marriage is concerned, is procreation, the future generation, a family, and, at the same time, the continual ripening of the relationship between two people, in all the areas of activity which conjugal life includes.

These objective purposes of marriage create in principle the possibility of love and exclude the possibility of treating a person as means to an end and as an object for use. To see how the former possibility is to be realized within the framework of the objective purpose of marriage we must examine more closely the actual principle which precludes the possibility of one person being treated by another person as an object of use in the sexual context. The mere definition of the objective purpose of marriage does not completely solve this problem.

For it would seem that the sexual relationship presents more opportunities than most other activities for treating a person – sometimes even without realizing it[11] – as an object of use. We must also take account of the fact that the subject matter of sexual morality in its totality is wider than that of marital ethics alone, and that it embraces a large number of questions in the area of the relationship between, or perhaps we may even say the co-existence of man and woman. Within the framework of this relationship, or coexistence, everyone must always, with all possible conscientiousness and with a feeling of total responsibility, make his concern that basic good for each of us and for all of us together which is, quite simply, 'humanity', or if you like, the assertion of the value of the human person. If we take this basic relationship 'woman-man' in the broadest sense, and not merely within the limits of marriage, then the love of which we speak is identified with a particular readiness to subordinate oneself to that good, which 'humanity', or more precisely, the value of the person represents, regardless of difference of sex. This subordination is a particularly strict obligation in marriage, and the objective aims of that institution can be realized only if the partners adopt the broad principles which follow from acknowledgement of the value of the person in the context of a fully developed sexual relationship. This context creates a quite specific set of moral problems – and so, for the specialist, a specific set of problems in moral philosophy – whether we are dealing with marriage or with any of the many other forms of relationship or association between persons of different sex.

The Second Meaning of the Verb 'to Use'

If we are to obtain a comprehensive view of this subject we must also consider a second sense in which the verb 'to use' is quite frequently employed. Our thinking, and our acts of will – and it is these which determine the objective structure of human activity – are accompanied by various emotional overtones or states. They may precede the activity, coincide with it, or emerge into consciousness when the action is already complete.[12] These emotional-affective overtones or states are like a distinct thread which insinuates itself into and, at times importunately, forcibly encroaches upon the

fabric of human action. In itself, an objective act would sometimes be a dim event, barely perceptible to human consciousness, if it were not heightened and thrown into relief by the
varied and intense emotions (or sentimental states) experienced. What is more, these emotions or sentiments
usually have some influence in determining the objective
structure of people's actions.

We shall not analyse this problem in detail for the moment,
because we shall have to revert to it more than once in the
course of the book. Here, only one point need be noted: that
the emotional-affective overtones or states which are so important a part of man's entire inner life have as a rule either a
positive or a negative colouring, contain, so to speak, either a
positive or a negative charge. A positive charge is *pleasure*
and a negative charge is pain. Pleasure appears in different
guises or shades – depending on the emotional-affective experiences with which it is connected. It may be either sensual
satisfaction, or emotional contentment, or a profound, a total
joy. Pain also depends on the character of the emotional-
affective experiences which have caused it and appears in
many forms, varieties and nuances: as sensual disgust, or
emotional discontent, or a deep sadness.

It is necessary here to call attention to the particular richness, variety and intensity of those emotional-affective experiences and states which occur when the object of activity
is a person of the opposite sex. They then colour this activity
in a specific way and make it an extraordinarily vivid experience. This is true of certain activities in which the sexes
are normally associated and of the sexual relationship proper.
This is why the second meaning of the verb 'to use' looms
particularly large in this area of activity. 'To use' (= enjoy)
means to experience pleasure, the pleasure which in slightly
different senses is associated both with the activity itself and
with the object of the activity. In any association between a
man and a woman, and in the sexual relationship itself the
object of activity is of course always a person. And it is a
person who becomes the proper source of various forms of
pleasure, or even of delight.

The fact that a person is for another person the source of

experiences with a special emotional-affective charge is easily understood. For only a human being can be an object of equal status for another human being – a 'partner' in activity – this equality between the subject and the object of activity forms a special basis for emotional-affective experiences and for the positive or negative charges which they carry, in the shape of pleasure or pain. Nor should we suppose that the pleasure in question here is solely and exclusively sensual. To suppose this would be to undervalue the natural importance of a contact which in every case preserves its interpersonal, human character. Even purely 'bodily' love, because of the nature of the partners involved in it does not cease to be a fact of this order. For this reason we cannot really compare the sexual life of man with that of animals, although they also obviously have a sexual life which for them too is the basis of procreation, and of the maintenance and continuation of the species. However, the sex life of animals is on the natural and instinctive level, that of man on the personal and moral level. Sexual morality comes into being not only because persons are aware of the pupose of sexual life, but also because they are aware that they are persons. The whole moral problem of 'using' as the antithesis of love is connected with this knowledge of theirs.

The problem has already been touched upon in connection with the first meaning of the verb 'to use'. The second meaning of this verb is equally important for morality. For man, precisely because he has the power to reason, can, in his actions, not only clearly distinguish pleasure from its opposite, but can also isolate it, so to speak, and treat it as a distinct aim of his activity. His actions are then shaped only with a view to the pleasure he wishes to obtain, or the pain he wishes to avoid. If actions involving a person of the opposite sex are shaped exclusively or primarily with this in view, then that person will become only the means to an end – and 'use' in its second meaning (= enjoy) represents, as we see, a particular variant of 'use' in its first meaning. This variant, however, is a very common one, and can easily occur in a man's – a person's – behaviour. It does not arise in the sexual life of animals, which is conducted exclusively at the natural and instinctive level, and is therefore directed solely to the purpose which the sexual urge serves – i.e. procreation, the maintenance of the species. At this level sexual pleasure – purely animal sexual pleasure, of course – cannot constitute an end in itself. It is different with man. Here it is easy to see how the fact of being a person, and rational, begets morality. This morality is personalistic both in relation to its subject and in relation to its object – objectively because it is concerned with the proper treatment of a person in the context of sexual pleasure.

A person of the opposite sex cannot be for another person only the means to an end – in this case sexual pleasure or delight. The belief that a human being is a person leads to the acceptance of the postulate that enjoyment must be subordinated to love. 'Use', not only in the first, broader and more objective, meaning, but also in its second, narrower, more subjective meaning (for the experience of pleasure is by its nature subjective) can be raised to the level appropriate to an interpersonal relationship only by love. Only 'caring' precludes 'using' in the second sense, as well as in the first. This means that the science of ethics, if it is to fulfil its proper function in the field of sexual morality, must, in all the profusion and variety of human actions, and indeed of passive experiences too, whenever questions of sexual morality arise, distinguish very carefully between whatever shows 'loving kindness', and whatever shows not that but the intention to 'use' a person even when it disguises itself as love, and seeks to legitimate itself under that name. A more thorough examination of this question from the standpoint of ethical theory (which, however, finds confirmation in the relevant area of practical morality) requires at this point a critical analysis of what is called utilitarianism.

Critique of Utilitarianism[13]

Against the background of our discussion so far we see emerging a critique of utilitarianism both as a specific concept in ethical theory and as a practical programme of action. The present book will have to revert frequently to this critique, since utilitarianism is so characteristic of modern man's mentality and his attitude to life. Not that we could very easily claim that this outlook is peculiar to modern man. Utilitarianism is a channel, so to speak, along which the lives of individuals and of collectives have tended to flow throughout the ages. In modern times, however, what we have to deal with is a conscious utilitarianism, formulated from philosophical premises, and with scientific precision.

The word itself is derived from the Latin verb *uti* ('to use', 'to take advantage of'), and the adjective *utilis* ('useful'). True to its etymology, 'utilitarianism' puts the emphasis on the usefulness (or otherwise) of any and every human activity. The useful is whatever gives pleasure and excludes its opposite, for pleasure is the essential ingredient of human happiness. To be happy, according to the premises of utilitarianism, is to live pleasurably. Pleasure itself of course exists in different forms and degrees of intensity. But there is no need to pay too much heed to this, to commend some types of pleasure as being of a higher spiritual order and to deprecate others – the sensual, the carnal, the materialistic. The utilitarian considers pleasure important in itself, and, with his general view of man, fails to see that he is quite conspicuously an amalgam of matter and spirit, the two complementary factors which together create one personal existence, whose specific nature is due entirely to the soul. To a utilitarian a man is a subject endowed with the ability to think and to feel. His sensibility makes him desirous of pleasure and bids him shun its opposite. The ability to think, to reason, is given to man to enable him to direct his activities to the attainment of a maximum of pleasure with a minimum of discomfort. Utilitarians regard the principle of the maximization of pleasure accompanied by the minimization of pain as the primary rule of human morality, with the rider that it must be observed not only by individuals, egoistically, but also collectively, by society. Thus, in its definitive formulation the *principle of utility* (*principium utilitatis*) preaches the maximum of pleasure for the greatest possible number of people – obviously with a minimum of discomfort for the same number.

At first glance this principle seems both right and attractive – it is difficult indeed to imagine people behaving otherwise, to imagine them wanting to encounter more pain than pleasure in their lives, individual and collective. A rather more searching analysis, however, inevitably reveals the weaknesses and the superficiality of this way of thinking and of this principle for the regulation of human actions. The real mistake is the recognition of pleasure in itself as the sole or at any rate the greatest good, to which everything else in the activity of an individual or a society should be subordinated. Whereas pleasure in itself is not the sole good, nor is it the proper aim of a man's activity, as we shall have the opportunity to see later. Pleasure is essentially incidental, contingent, something which may occur in the course of action. Naturally, then, to organize your actions with pleasure itself as the exclusive or primary aim is in contradiction with the proper structure of human action. I may want or do that which is accompanied by pleasure and I may not want or not do that which is accompanied by pain. I may even want or not want, do or not do, this or that because of the pleasure or pain entailed. All this is true. But pleasure (as opposed to pain) cannot be the only factor affecting my decision to act or not to act, still less the criterion by which I pronounce judgement on what is good and what is bad in my own or another person's actions. Quite obviously, that which is truly good, that which morality and conscience bid me do, often involves some measure of pain and requires the renunciation of some pleasure. The pain involved, or the pleasure which I must forego, is not the decisive consideration if I am to act rationally. What is more, it is not fully identifiable beforehand. Pleasure and pain are always connected with a concrete action, so that it is not possible to anticipate them precisely, let alone to plan for them or, as the utilitarians would have us do, even compute them in advance. Pleasure is, after all, a somewhat elusive thing.

We could point to many difficulties and confusion inherent

in utilitarianism, whether as a theory or in practice. But let us ignore the rest, and concentrate on just one of them, the one in fact which was also noticed by that resolute opponent of utilitarianism, Immanuel Kant. His name has already been mentioned in connection with the moral imperative which demands that a person should never be the means to an end, but always the end, in our activities. This demand reveals one of the weakest points of utilitarianism: if the only or the main good, the only or the main aim, of man is pleasure, if it is also the whole basis of moral norms in human behaviour, then everything we do must perforce be looked at as a means towards this one good, this single end. Hence the human person – my own or any other, every person – must figure in this role: as a means to an end. If I accept the utilitarian premise I must see myself as a subject desirous of as many experiences with a positive affective charge as possible, and at the same time as an object which may be called upon to provide such experiences for others. I must then look at every person other than myself from the same point of view: as a possible means of obtaining the maximum pleasure.

In this form the utilitarian mentality and attitude must be a heavy liability in various areas of human existence and co-existence, but they would seem to be a particular threat in the sphere of sexual relations. The great danger lies in the fact that starting from utilitarian premises it is not clear how the cohabitation or association of people of different sex can be put on a plane of real love, and so freed from the dangers of 'using' a person (whether in the first or in the second meaning of that word) and of treating a person as the means to an end. Utilitarianism seems to be a programme of thoroughgoing egoism quite incapable of evolving into authentic altruism. Although in the declarations of its adherents the rule we come across is that of 'the *maximum* pleasure ("greatest happiness") for the greatest number', there is an internal contradiction at the heart of this principle. Pleasure is, of its nature, a good for the moment and only for a particular subject, it is not a super-subjective or trans-subjective good. And so, as long as that good is recognized as the entire basis of the moral norm, there can be no possibility of my transcending the bounds of that which is good for me alone.

We can only close this gap by a fiction, a semblance of altruism. If, while regarding pleasure as the only good, I also try to obtain the *maximum* pleasure for someone else – and not just for myself, which would be blatant egoism – then I put a value on the pleasure of this other person only in so far as it gives pleasure to me: it gives me pleasure, that someone else is experiencing pleasure. If, however, I cease to experience pleasure, or it does not tally with my 'calculus of happiness' – (a term often used by utilitarians) then the pleasure of the other person ceases to be my obligation, a good for me, and may even become something positively bad. I shall then – true to the principles of utilitarianism – seek to eliminate the other person's pleasure because no pleasure for me is any longer bound up with it – or at any rate the other person's pleasure will become a matter of indifference to me, and I shall not concern myself with it. It is crystal clear that if utilitarian principles are followed, a subjective understanding of the good (equating the good with the pleasurable) leads directly, though there may be no conscious intention of this, to egoism. The only escape from this otherwise inevitable egoism is by recognizing beyond any purely subjective good, i.e. beyond pleasure, an objective good, which can also unite persons – and thereby acquire the characteristics of a common good. Such an objective common good is the foundation of love, and individual persons, who jointly choose a common good, in doing so subject themselves to it. Thanks to it they are united by a true, objective bond of love which enables them to liberate themselves from subjectivism and from the egoism which it inevitably conceals.[14] *Love is the unification of persons.*

In reply to this reproach consistent utilitarians can (must, indeed) invoke something called the harmonization of egoisms, and a dubious idea it is too, since, as we have seen, on utilitarian premises there is no escape from egoism. Is it possible to harmonize different egoisms? Is it possible, for instance, to achieve harmony, in the sexual context, between the egoism of a man and that of a woman? This certainly can be done according to the principle 'greatest possible pleasure for each of the two persons' – but the practical application of this principle can never deliver us from egoism. Egoism will remain egoism in this type of harmony, the only difference being that these two egoisms, the man's and the woman's, will match each other and be mutually advantageous. The moment they cease to match and to be of advantage to each other, nothing at all is left of the harmony. Love will be no more, in either of the persons or between them, it will not be an objective reality, for there is no objective good to ensure its existence. 'Love' in this utilitarian conception is a union of egoisms, which can hold together only on condition that they confront each other with nothing unpleasant, nothing to conflict with their mutual pleasure. Therefore love so under-stood is self-evidently merely a pretence which has to be carefully cultivated to keep the underlying reality hidden: the reality of egoism, and the greediest kind of egoism at that, exploiting another person to obtain for itself its own 'maxi-mum pleasure'. In such circumstances the other person is and remains only a means to an end, as Kant rightly observed in his critique of utilitarianism.

Thus, instead of love, which as a reality present in different persons, a particular man 'x' and a particular woman 'y' let us say, enables them to escape from the situation in which each uses the other as a means to a subjective end, utilitarianism introduces into their relationship a paradoxical pattern: each of the persons is mainly concerned with gratifying his or her own egoism, but at the same time consents to serve someone else's egoism, because this can provide the opportunity for such gratification – and just as long as it does so. This para-doxical pattern, which is not just one of many to which their relationship might conform, but the only possible one when utilitarian thinking and attitudes are acted upon, means that the person – and not only 'the other person', but the first person too – sinks to the level of a means, a tool. There is an ineluctable, an overwhelming necessity in this: if I treat someone else as a means and a tool in relation to myself I cannot help regarding myself in the same light. We have here something like the opposite of the commandment to love.

The Commandment to Love, and the Personalistic Norm

The commandment laid down in the New Testament demands from man love for others, for his neighbours – in the fullest sense, then, love for persons. For God, whom the commandment to love names first, is the most perfect personal Being. The whole world of created persons derives its distinctness from and its natural superiority over the world of things (non-persons) from a very particular resemblance to God. The commandment formulated in the New Testament, demanding love towards persons, is implicitly opposed to the principle of utilitarianism, which – as we have shown in the previous analysis – is unable to guarantee the love of one human being, one person for another. The opposition between the commandment in the Gospels and the principle of utilitarianism is *implicit* only in that the commandment does not put in so many words the principle on the basis of which love between persons is to be practised. Christ's commandment, however, and the utilitarian principle, seem to be on different levels, to be norms of a different order. They do not deal directly with the same thing: the commandment speaks of love for others, while the utilitarian principle points to pleasure not only as the basis on which we act but as the basis for rules of human behaviour. We have seen in our critique of utilitarianism that if we start from what utilitarians accept as the basis for the regulation of human behaviour we shall never arrive at love. The principle of 'utility' itself, of treating a person as a means to an end, and an end moreover which in this case is pleasure, the maximization of pleasure, will always stand in the way of love.

The incompatibility of the utilitarian principle with the commandment to love is then clear: if the utilitarian principle is accepted the commandment simply becomes meaningless. There is also an obvious connection between the utilitarian principle and a particular scale of values: that according to which pleasure is not only the sole, but also the highest, value. This we need not analyse here any further. But it becomes obvious that if the commandment to love, and the love which is the object of this commandment, are to have any meaning, we must find a basis for them other than the utilitarian premise and the utilitarian system of values. This can only be the personalistic principle and the personalistic norm. This norm, in its negative aspect, states that the person is the kind of good which does not admit of use and cannot be treated as an object of use and as such the means to an end. In its positive form the personalistic norm confirms this: the person is a good towards which the only proper and adequate attitude is love. This positive content of the personalistic norm is precisely what the commandment to love teaches.

In view of this can it be said that the commandment to love is the personalistic norm? Strictly speaking the commandment to love is only based on the personalistic norm, as a principle with a negative and a positive content, and is not itself the personalistic norm. It only derives from this norm which, unlike the utilitarian principle, *does* provide an appropriate foundation for the commandment to love. This foundation for the commandment to love should also be sought in a system of values other than the utilitarian system – it must be a personalistic axiology, within whose framework the value of the person is always greater than the value of pleasure (which is why a person cannot be subordinated to this lesser end, cannot be the means to an end, in this case to pleasure). So, while the commandment to love is not, strictly speaking, identical with the personalistic norm but only presupposes it, as it implies also a personalistic system of values, we can, taking a broader view, say that the commandment to love *is* the personalistic norm. Strictly speaking the commandment says: 'Love persons', and the personalistic norm says: 'A person is an entity of a sort to which the only proper and adequate way to relate is love.' The personalistic norm does, as we have seen, provide a justification for the New Testament commandment. And so, if we take the commandment together with this justification, we can say that it is the same as the personalistic norm.

This norm, as a commandment, defines and recommends a certain way of relating to God and to people, a certain attitude towards them. This way of relating, this attitude is in agreement with what the person is, with the value which the person represents, and therefore it is fair. Fairness takes precedence of mere utility (which is all the utilitarian principle has eyes for) – although it does not cancel it but only subordinates it: in dealings with another person everything that is at once of use to oneself and fair to that person falls within the limits set by the commandment to love.

In defining and recommending a particular way of relating to the particular beings called persons, a particular attitude to them, the personalistic norm in the form of the commandment to Love assumes that this relation, this attitude, will be not only fair but just. For to be just always means giving others what is rightly due to them. A person's rightful due is to be treated as an object of love, not as an object for use. In a sense it can be said that love is a requirement of justice, just as using a person as a means to an end would conflict with justice. In fact the order of justice is more fundamental than the order of love – and in a sense the first embraces the second inasmuch as love can be a requirement of justice. Surely it is just to love a human being or to love God, to hold a person dear. At the same time love – if we are to consider its very essence – is something beyond and above justice; the essence of love is simply different from the essence of justice. Justice concerns itself with things (material goods or moral goods, as for instance one's good name) in relation to persons, and hence with persons rather indirectly, whereas love is concerned with persons directly and immediately: affirmation of the value of the person as such is of its essence. Although we can correctly say that whoever loves a person is for that very reason just to that person, it would be quite untrue to assert that love for a person consists merely in being just. Later in the book we shall try to analyse separately and more fully what it is that constitutes love for a person. So far, we have elicited one fact – namely that love for a person must consist in affirmation that the person has a value higher than that of an object for consumption or use. He who loves will endeavour to declare this by his whole behaviour. And there can be no doubt that he will, *ipso facto*, be just towards the other person as a person.[15]

This aspect of the question, this interpenetration of love and justice in the personalistic norm is very important to the whole complex of our enquiries into sexual morality. It is precisely here that the main task is the elaboration of a concept of love which is just to the person, or if you like a love prepared to concede to each human being that which he or she can rightfully claim by virtue of being a person. For in the sexual context what is sometimes characterized as love may very easily be quite unjust to a person. This occurs not because sensuality and sentimentality play a special part in forming this love between persons of different sex (a fact which we shall also analyse separately), but rather because love in the sexual context lends itself to interpretation, sometimes conscious, sometimes unconscious, along utilitarian lines.

In a sense this kind of love is wide open to such an interpretation, which turns to account the natural gravitation of its sensual and sentimental ingredients in the direction of pleasure. It is easy to go on from the experience of pleasure not merely to the quest for pleasure, but to the quest of pleasure for its own sake, to accepting it as a superlative value and the proper basis for a norm of behaviour. This is the very essence of the distortions which occur in the love between man and woman.

Since, then, sexuality is so easily connected with the concept of 'love', and is at the same time the arena of constant conflict between two fundamentally different value systems, two fundamentally different ways of determining norms of behaviour, the personalistic and the utilitarian — we must, if the subject is to be fully clarified, distinctly state that the love which is the content of the commandment in the Gospels, can be combined only with the personalistic, not with the utilitarian norm. It is therefore within the compass of the personalistic norm that proper solutions to problems of sexual morality must be sought, if they are to be Christian solutions. They must be based upon the commandment to love. For although man can fully and completely realize the commandment to love in the full sense which the New Testament gives to it through supernatural love for God and his neighbours, this love nevertheless is not a contradiction of personalistic love, and indeed cannot be practised without it.

To conclude this discussion it may be worth recalling the distinction drawn by St Augustine between *uti* and *frui*. St Augustine differentiated in this way between two attitudes. One of them is intent on pleasure for its own sake, with no concern for the object of pleasure, and that is what he calls *uti*. The other finds joy in a totally committed relationship with the object precisely because this is what the nature of the object demands, and this he called *frui*. The commandment to love shows the way to enjoyment in this sense – *frui* – in the association of persons of different sex both within and outside marriage.

INTERPRETATION
OF THE SEXUAL URGE

❧

Instinct or Urge?

In our discussion so far we have tried to define the position of
the person as the subject and object of actions keeping in
mind the specific context of those actions – viz. the sexual
context. The fact that a man and a woman are persons in no
way alters the fact that those persons are also man and
woman. The sexual context, however, implies not only a
'static' difference of sex, but the effective participation in
human actions of a dynamic element intimately connected
with difference of sex in human persons. Ought we to call it
an instinct or an urge?

The question concerns two words which etymologically
have, strictly speaking, the same meaning. For 'instinct' comes
from the Latin *instinguere*, which means more or less the same
as 'to urge'. Hence instinct means the same as 'urge'. If
we ask about the emotional associations which are usually
attached to this particular expression, the associations of
the word 'urge' used with reference to a human being are on
the whole negative. The word 'urge' suggests the action of
urging, or instigation, and this is an action which if performed with a human being as its object arouses in him or her
instinctive resistance. A human being is conscious of his free
will, his ability to decide for himself, and so by reflex action
resists everything that does violence in any way to that freedom. The urge, then, is always felt to be to some extent
in conflict with freedom.

By *instinct*, the etymological meaning of which is identical
with that of 'urge', we mean a certain mode of action which
automatically declares its origin. This is *the reflex mode of
action, which is not dependent on conscious thought.* It is

45

characteristic of reflex action that the means are adopted without any conscious thought about (deliberation on) their relation to the end in view. Such a mode of action is not typical of man, who possesses the ability to reflect on the relation between means and ends. He selects the means in accordance with the end at which he aims. As a result man, acting in the way proper to him, consciously selects means and consciously adapts them to an end of which he is also conscious. Since the mode of action throws light on the origin of the action we must acknowledge that there is in man an innate principle which makes him capable of considered behaviour, of self-determination. *Man is by nature capable of rising above instinct in his actions.* And he is capable of such action in the sexual sphere as elsewhere. If it were otherwise, morality would have no meaning in this context, would simply not exist, but sexual morality as everyone knows is a universal phenomenon, something common to all humanity. It is, then, difficult to speak of the sexual instinct in man as though it meant the same as it does in animals, difficult to accept it as the sole and ultimate source of actions in the sexual sphere.

Though the word 'urge' means etymologically much the same as 'instinct', its emotional overtones are if anything even more negative. It can, however, be given another meaning, one more suitable to man's real nature. When we speak of the sexual urge in man we have in mind not an interior source of specific actions somehow 'imposed in advance', but a certain orientation, a certain direction in man's life implicit in his very nature. The sexual *urge* in this conception is a *natural drive born in all human beings, a vector of aspiration* along which their whole existence develops and perfects itself from within.

The sexual urge in man is not a source of self-contained actions but it is a particular property of human existence which is reflected and finds its expression in action. That property is something natural and hence something fully developed in man. The consequence of that property is not so much that man behaves in a particular way as that something happens to man, something begins to take place without any initiative on his part, and this internal 'happening' creates as it were a base for definite actions, for considered actions, in which man exercises self-determination, decides for himself about his own actions and takes responsibility for them. This is the point at which human freedom and the sex urge meet.[16]

Man is not responsible for what *happens* to him in the sphere of sex since he is obviously not himself the cause of it, but he is entirely responsible for what he *does* in this sphere. The fact that the sexual urge is the source of what happens in a man, of the various events which occur in his sensual and emotional life independently of his will, shows that this urge is a property of the *whole* of human existence and not just of one of its spheres or functions. This property permeating the whole existence of man is a force which manifests itself not only in what 'happens' involuntarily in the human body, the senses and the emotions, but also in that which takes shape with the aid of the will.

The Sexual Urge as an Attribute of the Individual

Every human being is by nature a sexual being, and belongs from birth to one of the two sexes. This fact is not contradicted by the phenomenon of so-called hermaphroditism – any more than any other sickness or deformity militates against the fact that there is such a thing as human nature and that every human being, even the deformed or sick human being, has the same nature and is a human being precisely because of it. In the same way every human being is a sexual being, and membership of one of the two sexes means that a person's whole existence has a particular orientation which shows itself in his or her actual internal development This development, more easily observable in the organism than in the psyche, will be dealt with in greater detail in the final section of this book, which will include a certain amount of data from the field of sexology.

The orientation given to a person's existence by membership of one of the sexes does not only make itself felt

47

internally, but at the same time turns outwards, and in the normal course of things (once again, we are not speaking of sicknesses or of perversions) manifests itself in a certain natural predilection for, a tendency to seek, the other sex. What is the goal of this orientation? Let us answer this question in stages. Looked at superficially, this sexual orientation has as its object 'the other sex' as a complex of certain distinctive properties in the general psychological and physiological structure of human beings.

Looking at sex exclusively from outside, with some sort of scientific detachment, we can define it as a specific synthesis of attributes which manifest themselves clearly in the psychological and physiological structure of man. Sexual attraction makes obvious the fact that the attributes of the two sexes are complementary, so that a man and a woman can complete each other. The properties which the woman possesses are not possessed by the man, and vice versa. Consequently, there exists for each of them not only the possibility of supplementing his or her own attributes with those of a person of the other sex, but at times a keenly felt need to do so. If man would look deeply enough into his own nature through the prism of that need it might help him to understand his own limitation and inadequacy, and even, indirectly, what philosophy calls the contingent character of existence (*contingentia*). But people in general do not get so far in their reflexions on the fact of sex. For in themselves sexual differences in people seem to indicate only a division in terms of psychological and physiological attributes within the boundaries of the species 'man', analogous to the division within animal species. The urge to mutual completion which accompanies this division indicates that the attributes of each sex possess some specific value for the other. We may therefore speak of sexual values which are connected with the psychological and physiological structure of man and woman. Is it that the attributes of each sex possess a value for the other, and that what we call the sexual urge comes into being because of this, or do these attributes, on the contrary, possess a value for them because of the existence of the sexual urge? We must declare ourselves for the second alternative. The sexual urge is something even more basic than the psychological and physiological attributes of man and woman in themselves, though it does not manifest itself or function without them.

Moreover, the sexual urge in man and woman is not fully defined as an orientation towards the psychological and physiological attributes of the other sex as such. These do not and cannot exist in the abstract, but only in a concrete human being, a concrete man or woman. Inevitably, then, the sexual urge in a human being is always in the natural course of things directed towards another human being – this is the normal form which it takes. If it is directed towards the sexual attributes as such this must be recognized as an impoverishment or even a perversion of the urge. If it is directed towards the sexual attributes of a person of the same sex we speak of a homosexual deviation. Still more emphatically do we speak of sexual deviation if the urge is directed not towards the sexual attributes of a human being but towards those of an animal. The natural direction of the sexual urge is towards a human being of the other sex and not merely towards 'the other sex' as such. It is just because it is directed towards a particular human being that the sexual urge can provide the framework within which, and the basis on which, the possibility of love arises.

The sexual urge in man has a natural tendency to develop into love simply because the two objects affected, with their different sexual attributes, physical and psychological, are both people. Love is a phenomenon peculiar to the world of human beings. In the animal world only the sexual instinct is at work.

Love is not, however, merely a biological or even a psychophysiological crystallization of the sexual urge, but is something fundamentally different from it. For although love grows out of the sexual urge and develops on that basis and in the conditions which the sexual urge creates in the psychophysiological lives of concrete people, it is none the less given its definitive shape by *acts of will at the level of the person*.

The sexual urge does not itself produce complete, finished

49

actions, it only furnishes, so to speak, in the form of all that 'happens' in man's inner being under its influence, what might be called the stuff from which action is made. Since there is nothing in all this to deprive man of his power of self-determination, the sexual urge is by its nature dependent on the person. It is in the control of the person, and the person can use it, can turn it to such purposes as he or she thinks fit. It must be added that this in no way lessens the force of the sexual urge – quite the contrary; though it does not have the power to determine acts of will in man, it may have the assistance of the will. The sexual urge in man functions differently from the urge in animals, where it is the source of instinctive actions governed by nature alone. In man it is naturally subordinate to the will, and *ipso facto* subject to the specific dynamics of that freedom which the will possesses. The sexual urge can transcend the determinism of the natural order by an act of love. For this very reason manifestations of the sexual urge in man must be evaluated on the plane of love, and any act which originates from it forms a link in the chain of responsibility, responsibility for love. All this is possible because, psychologically, the sexual urge does not fully determine human behaviour but leaves room for the free exercise of the will.

Here it should also be said that the sexual urge is an attribute and a force common to humanity at large, at work in every human being, although it is a force which manifests itself in different ways and indeed with different degrees of psychological and physiological intensity in different people. The urge, however, cannot be identified with the ways in which it shows itself. Since the urge itself is a universal human attribute we have to reckon with its effects at every turn in all relationships between the sexes and indeed wherever they exist side by side. They coexist within the framework of social life. Man is at once a social being and a sexual being. It follows that the rules governing the coexistence and association of persons of opposite sex are part of the general code regulating the life of human beings in society. The social aspect of sexual ethics must be given no less weight than the individual aspect. Living in a society we are continually concerned with the various forms of coexistence of the two sexes and for this reason ethics must put these relationships on a level consonant both with the dignity of human persons and with the common good of society. Human life is in fact 'co-educational' in many of its sectors.

The Sexual Urge and Existence

The concept of determination is indissociable from that of necessity. What is determined cannot be otherwise – it must be just as it is. If we are thinking of the human species as a whole we can speak of necessity, and hence of a measure of determinacy, in connection with the sexual urge. The existence of the whole species *Homo* depends directly on it. The species could not exist if it were not for the sexual urge and its natural results. So that a sort of necessity is clearly discernible. Human kind can be maintained in being only so long as individual people, individual men and women, human couples, obey the sexual urge. It furnishes, as we have seen, what we may call material for love between persons, between man and woman, but this seems to happen (if we focus our attention strictly on the final purpose of the urge) only incidentally, *per accidens*, since love between persons is essentially a creation of human free will. There may be affection between people who are not sexually attracted to each other. Obviously then it is not the love of man and woman that determines the proper purpose of the sexual urge. The proper end of the urge, the end *per se*, is something supra-personal, the existence of the species *Homo*, the constant prolongation of its existence.

There is here a marked similarity to the animal world, to the diverse species which nature produces. The species *Homo* is a part of nature, and the sexual urge operating within the species ensures its existence. Now, existence is the first and basic good for every creature. The existence of the species *Homo* is the first and basic good for that species. All other goods derive from this basic good. I can only act while I am.

Man's multifarious works, the creations of his genius, the fruits of his holiness are only possible if the man – the genius, the saint – comes into existence. To be he had to begin to exist. The natural route by which human beings begin to exist passes through the sexual urge.

We are entitled to think and to assert that the sexual urge is a specific force of nature, but not that it has a purely biological significance. That would be untrue. It has an existential significance, for it is closely bound up with the whole existence of the species *Homo*, and not just with the physiology or even the psycho-physiology of man as studied by the natural sciences. Unlike these, existence is not the proper and entire subject of any of the natural sciences, each of which merely takes existence for granted as a concrete fact inherent in the object which it studies. Existence itself is a subject for philosophy, which alone concerns itself with the problem of existence as such. An overall view of the sexual urge, which is so closely bound up with the existence of the species *Homo* and possesses, as has been said, an existential and not merely a biological character, is therefore the prerogative of philosophy. This is very important when we are trying to determine the true importance of the sexual urge, which has obvious implications in the realm of sexual morality. If the sexual urge has a merely biological significance it can be regarded as something to be used. We can agree that it is an object for man to enjoy just like any other object of nature, animate or inanimate. But if the sexual urge has an existential character, if it is bound up with the very existence of the human person – that first and most basic good – then it must be subject to the principles which are binding in respect of the person. Hence, although the sexual urge is there for man to use, it must never be used in the absence of, or worse still, in a way which contradicts, love for the person.

On no account then is it to be supposed that the sexual urge, which has its own predetermined purpose in man independent of his will and self determination, is something inferior to the person and inferior to love. The proper end of the sexual urge is the existence of the species *Homo*, its continuation (*procreatio*), and love between persons, between man and woman, is shaped, channelled one might say, by that purpose and formed from the material it provides.[17] It can therefore take its correct shape only in so far as it develops in close harmony with the proper purpose of the sexual urge. An outright conflict with that purpose will also perturb and undermine love between persons. People sometimes find this purpose a nuisance and try to circumvent it by artificial means. Such means must however have a damaging effect on love between persons, which in this context is most intimately involved in the use of the sexual urge.[18]

There are a number of reasons for the fact that the purpose of sexual relations is sometimes a nuisance; something will be said about them at a suitable point in the discussion. One of these reasons is certainly the fact that in his mind, in his reason, man often accords the sexual urge a merely biological significance and does not fully realize its true, existential significance – its link with existence. It is this link with the very existence of man and of the species *Homo* that gives the sexual urge its objective importance and meaning. This importance only emerges into consciousness when man is moved by love to take on himself the natural purpose of the sexual urge. But does not the predetermined fact that the existence of man, of his species, necessarily depends on the utilization of the sexual urge, prevent him from doing this? The answer is that every person is able to recognize and to accept consciously the necessary and predetermined conditions on which man and the species exist. They do not represent a necessity in the psychological sense, and so do not preclude love, but only give it a specific character. This is in fact the character of true conjugal love between two persons, a man and a woman, who have consciously taken the decision to participate in the whole natural order of existence, to further the existence of the species *Homo*. Looked at more closely and concretely these two persons, the man and the woman, facilitate the existence of another concrete person, their own child, blood of their blood, and flesh of their flesh. This person is at once an affirmation and a continuation of their own love. The natural order of human existence is not in conflict with love between persons but in strict harmony with it.

The Religious Interpretation

The problem of the sexual urge is one of the crucial problems in ethics. In Catholic teaching it has a profoundly religious significance. The established order of human existence, as of existence in general, is the work of the Creator, and not a work completed once and for all at some moment in the dim past of the universe, but a work continually in progress. God creates continuously and it is only because He does so that the world continues (*conservatio est continua creatio*). For the world is made up of *creatures, or in other words entities which have no existence of and by themselves, since they do not themselves contain the final cause or source of existence.* This source, and so the final cause of the existence of all creatures, is always and invariably to be found in God. None the less these creatures participate in the general order of existence not only in that they themselves exist, but also because some of them at least help to transmit existence to new beings each within its own kind. So it is with human beings, with the man and the woman who use the sexual urge in sexual intercourse and enter as it were into the *cosmic stream by which existence is transmitted.* The distinctive characteristic of their position is that they themselves both consciously direct their own actions and also foresee the possible results, the fruits of those actions.

Their awareness, however, has a wider range, and may be further extended in the same direction by the religious truth contained in the Book of Genesis and in the Gospels. A man and a woman by means of procreation, by taking part in bringing a new human being into the world, at the same time participate in their own fashion in the work of creation. They can therefore look upon themselves as the rational co-creators of a new human being. That new human being is a person. The parents take part in the genesis of a person. A person is, of course, not merely an organism. A human body is the body of a person because it forms a unity of substance with the human spirit. The human spirit is not born merely in consequence of the physical union of man and woman in itself. The spirit can never originate from the body, nor be born and come into being in the same way as the body. The sexual relationship between man and woman is fundamentally a physical relationship, though it should also be the result of spiritual love. A relationship between spirits which begets a new embodied spirit is something unknown to the natural order. Nor yet can the love of man and woman, however powerful and profound in itself, do this. None the less, when a new human being is conceived a new spirit is conceived simultaneously, united in substance with the body, which begins to exist in embryo in the mother's womb. If it were not so it would be impossible to understand how the embryo could subsequently develop into a human being, a person.

The essence of the human person is therefore – in the Church's teaching – the work of God himself. It is He who creates the spiritual and immortal soul of that being, the organism of which begins to exist as a consequence of physical relations between man and woman.[19] The physical relationship ought to be the result of love between persons and should find its full justification in love. Although this love does not by itself give existence to a new spirit – the soul of the child – it must be fully prepared to accept that new person which has come into existence because of a physical relationship, it is true, but is also the expression of the spiritual love of persons – and to ensure the full development not just physical but spiritual, of that new being. Full spiritual development of a human person is the result of education. Procreation is the proper end of the sexual urge which – as was said before – simultaneously furnishes material for love between persons, male and female. Love owes its fertility in the biological sense to the sexual urge but it must also possess a fertility of its own in the spiritual, moral and personal sphere. It is here that the full productive power of love between two persons, man and woman, is concentrated, in the work of rearing new persons. This is its proper end, its natural orientation. Education is a creative activity with persons as its only possible object – only a person can be educated, an animal can only be trained – and also one which uses entirely human material; all that is by nature present in the human being to be educated is material for the educators, material which their love must find and mould. This material includes also that which God gives, by supernatural dispensation of His Grace. For He does not leave the work of education, which may in a certain sense be called the continuous creation of personality, wholly and entirely to the parents but Himself takes part in it, in His own person. For something more than the love of parents was present at the origin of a new person – they were only co-creators; the love of the Creator decided that a new person would come into existence in the mother's womb. Grace is, so to speak, the continuation of this work. God Himself takes the supreme part in the creation of a human person in the spiritual, moral, strictly supernatural sphere. The parents, though, if they are not to fail in their proper role, that of co-creators, must make their contribution here too.

As you see, this aspect of reality, which we call the sexual urge, is not a fundamentally obscure and incomprehensible matter. It is in principle accessible to, penetrable by the light of human thought – especially when thought is supported by Revelation, and this is a condition of any love in which the freedom of the person expresses itself. The sexual urge is connected in a special way with the natural order of existence, which is the divine order inasmuch as it is realized under the continuous influence of God the Creator. A man and a woman, through their conjugal life and a full sexual relationship, link themselves with that order, agree to take a special part in the work of creation. The order of existence is the Divine Order, although existence is not in itself something supernatural. But then the Divine Order includes not only the supernatural order but the order of nature too, which also stands in a permanent relationship to God and the Creator. The expressions 'the order of nature' and 'the biological order' must not be confused or regarded as identical, the 'biological order' does indeed mean the same as the order of nature but only in so far as this is accessible to the methods of empirical and descriptive natural science, and not as a specific order of existence with an obvious relationship to the First Cause, to God the Creator.

This habit of confusing the order of existence with the biological order, or rather of allowing the second to obscure the first, is part of that generalized empiricism which seems to weigh so heavily on the mind of modern man, and particularly on modern intellectuals, and makes it particularly difficult for them to understand the principles on which Catholic sexual morality is based. According to those principles sex and the sexual urge are not solely and exclusively a specific part of the psycho-physiological make-up of man. The sexual urge owes its objective importance to its connection with the divine work of creation of which we have been speaking, and this importance vanishes almost completely if our way of thinking is inspired only by the biological order of nature. Seen in this perspective the sexual urge is only the sum of functions undoubtedly directed, from the biological point of view, towards a biological end, that of reproduction. Now, if man is the master of nature, should he not mould those functions – if necessary artificially, with the help of the appropriate techniques – in whatever way he considers expedient and agreeable? The 'biological order', as a product of the human intellect which abstracts its elements from a larger reality, has man for its immediate author. The claim to autonomy in one's ethical views is a short jump from this. It is otherwise with the 'order of nature', which means the totality of the cosmic relationships that arise among really existing entities. It is therefore the order of existence, and the laws which govern it have their foundation in Him, Who is the unfailing source of that existence, in God the Creator.[20]

The Rigorist Interpretation

The understanding of the sexual urge, its correct interpretation, has a no less fundamental importance for sexual ethics than the proper understanding of the principles governing interpersonal relations. We have, however, devoted the first part of this chapter ('Analysis of the verb "to use"') to the latter question, because it seems to have intellectual precedence over the interpretation of the sexual urge. The urge in the world of persons is not the same, nor does it have the same significance as elsewhere in the world of nature. Therefore the interpretation of the urge must be correlated at each stage with our understanding of the person and its elementary rights in relation to other persons, for which the first part of the chapter has been our preparation.

With the principles formulated there (the personalistic norm) in mind, we can now exclude erroneous, because one-sided and onesidedly exaggerated, interpretations of the sexual urge. One such is the *libido* interpretation (I am thinking particularly of Freud and the Freudian concept) which we shall look at later. Another such is the rigorist or puritanical interpretation, and this we shall try to set out and evaluate at once. It is all the more important to do so because this interpretation may impress people as a view of sexual problems based on Christian beliefs deriving from the Gospels, whereas in reality it is built around naturalistic or empirico-sensualist principles. It probably arose when it did to oppose in practice the premises which it accepts itself in theory (puritanism and sensualist empiricism are very close to each other historically and geographically: both grew up largely in England in the XVII century). But this fundamental contradiction between theoretical premises and practical aims made it possible for the rigorist and puritanical concept to take another path and lapse into utilitarianism, which is so fundamentally opposed to the value judgements and norms based on the Gospels. Let us now try to demonstrate this by bringing out the special features of this form of utilitarianism.

This view, in its developed form, holds that in using man and woman and their sexual intercourse to assure the existence of the species *Homo*, the Creator Himself uses persons as the means to His end. It follows that conjugal life and sexual intercourse are good only because they serve the purpose of procreation. A man therefore does well when he uses a woman as the indispensable means of obtaining posterity. The use of a person for the objective end of procreation is the very essence of marriage. To use in this way is a good thing (we have in mind here the first meaning of the verb to use – and refer the reader to the analysis carried out in the preceding section of this chapter). Using in the second sense, on the other hand – seeking pleasure and enjoyment in intercourse – is wrong. Although it is indissociable from use in the first sense it is an intrinsically impure element, a sort of necessary evil. That evil must, however, be tolerated since there is no way of eliminating it.

This view is a reversion to the Manichean tradition, which was condemned by the Church in the earliest centuries of its existence. True, it does not reject marriage as something evil and unclean in itself, because it is 'carnal' – this was a Manichean tenet – but stops short at the affirmation that marriage is permissible for the good of the species. Nevertheless, the interpretation of the sexual urge implicit in this view can be held only by very one-sided spiritualists. Because of their one-sidedness and their lack of balance they fall into the very error which the teaching of the Gospels and of the Church, properly understood, seeks to exclude. At the basis of this erroneous view lies a false understanding of the relation between God – the First Cause – and the persons who are here secondary causes. A man and a woman, uniting in sexual intercourse, do so as free and rational persons, and their union has a moral value, if it is justified by true love between persons. If then it can be said that the Creator 'makes use of' the sexual union of persons to realize the order of existence which he intends for the species *Homo*, we can still certainly not maintain that the Creator uses persons solely as means to an end determined by Himself.[21]

For the Creator, in giving men and women a rational nature and the capacity consciously to decide upon their own actions, thereby made it possible for them to choose freely the end to which sexual intercourse naturally leads. And where two persons can join in choosing a certain good as their end there exists also the possibility of love. The Creator, then, does not utilize persons merely as the means or instruments of his creative power but offers them the possibility of a special realization of love. It is for them to put their sexual relations on the plane of love, the appropriate plane for human persons, or on a lower plane. The Creator's will is not only the preservation of the species by way of sexual intercourse but also its preservation on the basis of a love worthy of human persons. We are compelled to understand the will of the Creator in this way by the implications of the commandment to love in the Gospels.

Contrary to the suggestion of puritanical rigorists with their one sided spiritualism, there is nothing inimical to the objective dignity of persons in the fact that sexual use is an element in married love. We are concerned here with all the things which we have subsumed under the second meaning of the verb 'to use'. This is what the rigorist interpretation wants to exclude or to limit by artificial means. And for this reason 'use' in the sense of enjoyment is all the more prominent in this interpretation, becomes as it were an end in itself, separable on the one hand from the operation of the sexual urge and on the other from love between persons. This is also, as we have seen previously, the fundamental thesis of utilitarianism: we see how rigorism strives to overcome in practice what it has completely accepted on theoretical grounds. But the many forms of pleasure connected with difference of sex, and even the sexual enjoyment connected with conjugal intercourse, cannot be understood as a separate end of action, for if they were we should, if only inadvertently, begin treating the person as a means to that end, and so as an object of use.

The problem for ethics is how to use sex without treating the person as an object for use. Rigorism, which is so one-sidedly intent on overcoming the element of *uti* in sex, unavoidably leads to precisely that, at least in the sphere of intention. The only way to surmount the element of 'uti' is to embrace simultaneously the alternative, fundamentally different, defined by St Augustine as *frui*. There exists a *joy* which is consonant both with the nature of the sexual urge and with the dignity of human persons, a joy which results from collaboration, *from mutual understanding and the harmonious realization of jointly chosen aims*, in the broad field of action which is love between man and woman. This joy, this *frui* may be bestowed either by the great variety of pleasures connected with differences of sex, or by the sexual enjoyment which conjugal relations can bring. The Creator designed this joy, and linked it with love between man and woman in so far as that love develops on the basis of the sexual urge in a normal manner, in other words in a manner worthy of human persons.

The 'Libidinistic' Interpretation

This deviation in the direction of exaggerated rigorism – in which we have none the less discovered a peculiar manifestation of utilitarian thinking (*extrema se tangunt!*) – is however not so common as its antithesis, which we shall call here the 'libidinistic' distortion. This term derives from the Latin word *libido* (enjoyment resulting from use), which Sigmund Freud used in his interpretation of the sexual urge. Let us refrain here from any broader discussion of Freud's psychoanalysis, and of his theory of the sub-conscious. Freud is thought of as a representative of pansexualism because he tends to interpret all the phenomena of human life from earliest infancy onward as manifestations of the sexual urge. True, only some of these phenomena have a direct and express reference to sexual objects and values, but all of them, if only indirectly and vaguely have enjoyment, *libido*, as their aim, and this always has a sexual significance. Hence Freud speaks above all of the pleasure principle (*libido, triob*) and not of the sexual urge. What matters here is that the sexual urge as he conceives it is fundamentally an urge to enjoy. This way of putting it is a consequence of a narrow and purely subjective view of man. In Freud's conception we must look for the essence of the sexual urge in the most intense and strongly felt element in human sexual experience. This, in Freud's opinion, is enjoyment or the *libido*. Man immerses himself in it when it comes his way, and longs for it when he is not actually experiencing it. He is then internally conditioned to seek it. He seeks it continually and in practically everything he does. Pleasure, it would appear, is the primary aim of the sexual urge, and indeed of the whole of man's instinctual life, an end in itself. The transmission of life, procreation, is in this conception only a secondary end, an end *per accidens*. Thus, the objective end of the sexual urge is in this view not the immediate or most important end. Man is depicted by psycho-analysis only as a subject, not as an object, one of the objects of the objective world. This object is at the same time a subject, as we said at the beginning of this chapter, and this subject possesses an inner self and an inner life peculiar to itself. A characteristic of this inner self is the ability to know, to comprehend the truth objectively and in its entirety. Thanks to this, man – the human person – is aware also of the objective end of the sexual urge, for he recognizes his place *in the order of existence, and at the same time discovers the part which the sexual urge plays in that order. He is even capable of understanding his role in relation to the Creator, as a form of participation in the work of creation.*

But if instead the sexual urge is understood as fundamentally a drive for enjoyment this inner life of the person is almost totally negated. In this conception the person is reduced to a subject 'externally' sensitized to enjoyable sensory stimuli of a sexual nature. This conception puts human psychology – perhaps without realizing it – on the same level as the psychology of animals. An animal may be conditioned to seek sensory pleasure and to avoid unpleasant experience of the same sort, since it normally behaves instinctively to achieve the ends of its existence.

With man, however, it is not so: the correct way to achieve the ends of his existence is a problem within the power of his reason, which governs his will so that the solution acquires a moral value, is morally good or evil. A human being who uses the sexual urge in one way or another, in doing so solves – correctly or incorrectly – the problem of how to achieve those objective ends of his existence which are specifically connected with the sexual urge. *The sexual urge, then, is not purely*

'libidinistic' but existential in character. Man cannot look for
libido alone in it, for that is contrary to his nature, simply
incompatible with what man is. A subject endowed with an
'inner self' as man is, a subject who is a person, cannot
abandon to instinct the whole responsibility for the use of the
sexual urge, and make enjoyment his sole aim – but must
assume full responsibility for the way in which the sexual
urge is used. This responsibility is the fundamental, the vital
component in the sexual morality of man.

It should be added that the 'libidinistic' interpretation of
the sexual urge is very closely related to the utilitarian standpoint in ethics. We have to do here with the second meaning
of the word 'use', which as we have said before, has a distinctly subjective colouring. This is why it is inescapably bound
up with the treatment of persons exclusively as the means to
an end, as objects for use. The 'libidinistic' distortion is a
frank form of utilitarianism, whereas of exaggerated rigorism
we can only say that certain symptoms of utilitarian thought
are inherent in it. Rigorism exhibits these symptoms only
indirectly so to speak, whereas the *'libido'* theory is a frank
and straightforward expression of them.

This whole problem must, however, also be seen against
another – the socio-economic – background. Procreation is a
function of the collective life of mankind: the very existence
of the species *Homo* is after all at stake. It is also a function of
social life in particular societies, social orders, states, families. The socio-economic problem of procreation is encountered at many levels. It is, quite simply, not enough merely to
bring children into the world: they must also be maintained
and educated. Humanity in our time is in the grip of acute
anxiety that it will not be able economically to keep up with
the natural increase of population. The sexual urge appears to
be a more potent force than human providence in the economic field. For some two hundred years mankind, expecially
in white, civilized societies, has been nagged by the need to
resist the sexual urge and its potential productivity. This
need found expression in the teaching of Thomas Malthus,
known after him as Malthusianism or in its later versions
as Neo-Malthusianism. We shall return to the question of

Neo-Malthusianism in Chapters III and IV. Malthusianism itself is a special problem, which we shall not discuss in detail in this book, since it belongs to the field of demography, which concerns itself with the problem of the actual or potential number of people on the terrestrial globe and in its particular parts. It is, however, pertinent to point out that Malthusianism has amalgamated with the purely 'libinistic' interpretation of the sexual urge. For if the earth is threatened with overpopulation, if the economists complain of the 'overproduction of people' to the point that production of the means of subsistence cannot keep up with it, we ought to aim at limiting the use of the sexual urge, having in mind its objective purpose. But those who like Freud have eyes merely for the subjective purpose of the urge, which is connected with the *libido* and puts the main emphasis on it, will also logically aim at the preservation in full of that subjective purpose, which is connected with the pleasure of sexual intercourse, while at the same time curbing or even suppressing the objective purpose, which has to do with procreation. A problem arises which adherents of the utilitarian way of thinking prefer to regard as one of a purely *technical* nature, but which in Catholic moral teaching is first and last an *ethical* problem. Utilitarian thinking here remains true to its premises: what matters is to *maximize* the pleasure which sex affords in such large measure in the form of the *libido*. Whereas Catholic ethics protest in the name of its own, personalistic premises: no-one must take the 'calculus of pleasure,' as his sole guide where a relationship with another person is concerned – a person can never be an object of use. That is the nub of the conflict.

Catholic ethics is very far from onesidedly prejudging the demographic problems raised by Malthusianism, the seriousness of which is confirmed by contemporary economists. The question of natural growth, the question of the number of people on the earth, or in its particular regions, is one of those which looks to human prudence for an answer, to the quasi providential role which man as a reasonable being must perform for himself, both as an individual and collectively. However correct or incorrect the demographic difficulties raised by economists may be the general problem of sexual relationships between man and woman cannot be solved in a way which contradicts the personalistic norm. We have to do here with the value of the person, which is for all humanity the most precious of goods – more immediate and greater than any economic good. It is therefore impossible to subordinate the person as such to economics, since its proper sphere is that of moral values, and they are intimately bound up with love for the person. The conflict between the sexual urge and economics must of necessity be considered from this angle too, and indeed from this angle above all.

I must conclude this chapter with another reflexion of relevance to any discussion of the sexual urge. In the basic structure of human existence – and the same is true throughout the whole animal world – we see two basic instincts: the instinct of self-preservation and the sexual instinct. The instinct of self-preservation, as its name indicates, has as its purpose the preservation and maintenance of a particular being, man or beast. We know of a number of manifestations of that instinct which we shall not examine in detail here. In characterizing it we can say that it is egocentric in so far as it is centred on the existence of the 'I' itself (the human 'I', of course, since we can scarcely speak of the 'I' of an animal: the 'I' is inseparable from individuality). This is what makes the instinct of self-preservation fundamentally different from the sexual urge. For if it follows its natural course the sexual urge always transcends the limits of the 'I', and has as its immediate object some being of the other sex within the same species and for its final end the existence of the whole species. Such is the objective purpose of the sexual urge, in the nature of which there is – and this is where it differs from the instinct of self-preservation – something that might be called 'altero-centrism'. This it is that creates the basis for love.

Now, the 'libidinistic' interpretation of the sexual urge utterly confuses these two concepts. It endows the sexual urge with a purely egocentric significance, of the sort which naturally belongs to the instinct of self-preservation. For the same reason the utilitarianism in sexual morality which goes with this interpretation involves a danger perhaps greater than is generally realized: the danger of confusing the basic and fundamental human tendencies, the main paths of human existence. Such confusion must, clearly, affect the whole spiritual position of man. After all the human spirit here on earth forms a unity of substance with the body, so that spiritual life cannot develop correctly if the elementary lines of human existence are hopelessly tangled in contexts where the body is immediately involved. Discussions and conclusions in the field of sexual ethics must go deep, especially when they take as their fixed point of reference the commandment to love.

Final Observations

As we come to the end of this part of the discussion, which was intended to give a correct interpretation of the sexual urge, in part by eliminating incorrect interpretations, some conclusions connected with the traditional teaching on the ends of marriage ask to be drawn. The Church, as has been mentioned previously, teaches, and has always taught, that the primary end of marriage is *procreatio*, but that it has a secondary end, defined in Latin terminology as *mutuum adiutorium*. Apart from these a tertiary aim is mentioned – *remedium concupiscentiae*. Marriage, objectively considered, must provide first of all the means of continuing existence, secondly a conjugal life for man and woman, and thirdly a legitimate orientation for desire. The ends of marriage, in the order mentioned, are incompatible with any subjectivist interpretation of the sexual urge, and therefore demand from man, as a person, objectivity in his thinking on sexual matters, and above all in his behaviour. This objectivity is the foundation of conjugal morality.

In the light of all the arguments contained in this chapter and particularly in its first part ('Analysis of the verb "to use"') it must be stated that in marriage the ends mentioned above are to be realized on the basis of the personalistic norm. By reason of the fact that they are persons a man and a woman must consciously seek to realize the aims of marriage according to the order of priority given above, because this order is objective, accessible to reason, and therefore binding on human persons. At the same time the personalistic norm contained in the Gospel commandment to love points to the fundamental way to realize the ends, which in themselves are also natural to man, and to which – as the preceding analysis has shown – he is oriented by the sexual urge. Sexual morality and therefore conjugal morality consists of a stable and mature *synthesis of nature's purpose with the personalistic norm*[22]. If any one of the above-mentioned purposes of marriage is considered without reference to the personalistic norm – that is to say, without taking account of the fact that man and woman are persons – this is bound to lead to some form of utilitarianism in the first or second meaning of the word 'use'. To regard procreation in this way leads to the rigorist distortion, while the 'libidinistic' distortion is rooted in a similar attitude to the tertiary end of marriage – *remedium concupiscentiae*.

The personalistic norm itself is not, of course, to be identified with any one of the aims of marriage: a norm is never an end, nor is an end a norm. It is, however, a principle on which the proper realization of each of the aims mentioned, and of all of them together, depends – and by proper I mean in a manner befitting man as a person. The same principle also guarantees that the ends will be achieved in the order of importance accorded to them here, for any deviation from this is incompatible with the objective dignity of the person. The practical realization of all the purposes of marriage must then also mean the successful practice of love as a virtue – for only as a virtue does love satisfy the commandment of the Gospel and the demands of the personalistic norm embodied in that commandment. The idea that the purposes of marriage could be realized on some basis other than the personalistic norm would be utterly un-Christian, because it would not conform to the fundamental ethical postulate of the Gospels. For this reason too we must be very much on guard against trivialization of the teaching of the purposes of marriage.

With this in mind, it seems equally clearly indicated that the *mutuum adiutorium* mentioned in the teaching of the Church on the purposes of marriage as second in importance after procreation must not be interpreted – as it often is – to mean 'mutual love'. Those who do this may mistakenly come to believe that procreation as the primary end is something distinct from 'love', as also is the tertiary end, *remedium concupiscentiae*, whereas both procreation and *remedium concupiscentiae* as purposes of marriage must result from love as a virtue, and so fit in with the personalistic norm. *Mutuum adiutorium* as a purpose of marriage is likewise only a result of love as a virtue. There are no grounds for interpreting the phrase *mutuum adiutorium* to mean 'love'. For the Church, in arranging the objective purposes of love in a particular order, seeks to emphasize that procreation is objectively, ontologically, a more important purpose than that man and woman should live together, complement each other and support each other (*mutuum adiutorium*), just as this second purpose is in turn more important than the appeasement of natural desire. But there is no question of opposing love to procreation nor yet of suggesting that procreation takes precedence over love.

These aims can, moreover, only be realized in practice as a single complex aim. To rule out, totally and positively, the possibility of procreation undoubtedly reduces or even destroys the possibility of an enduring marital relationship of mutual education. Procreation unaccompanied by this process of reciprocal education, and common striving for the highest good would also be in some sense incomplete and incompatible with love between persons. It is, after all, not only and exclusively a matter of the numerical increase of the human species, but also of education, the natural foundation for which is the family based on a marriage cemented by *mutuum adiutorium*. If there is intimate co-operation between the man and the woman in a marriage, and if they are able to educate and complement each other, their love matures to the point at which it is the proper basis for a family.

However, marriage is not identical with the family, and always remains above all an intimate bond between two people.

The third purpose, *remedium concupiscentiae*, in its turn, depends on the two others for its practical realization by human beings. We must recognize once again that those who cut themselves off absolutely from the natural results of conjugal intercourse ruin the spontaneity and depth of their experiences, especially if artificial means are used to this end. Lack of mutual understanding, and of rational concern for the full well-being of a partner, leads if anything still more certainly to the same result. We shall come back to these questions again in Chapter V.

CHAPTER II

The Person and Love

❧

METAPHYSICAL
ANALYSIS OF LOVE

*

The Word 'Love'

The word 'love' has more than one meaning. In this book we are deliberately narrowing down the range of its meanings, since we are only concerned with love between two persons who differ in respect of sex. But of course even in this narrower sense the word still has various meanings, and there can be no thought of using it as though it had only one. A detailed analysis is necessary to bring out, as best we can, the richness of the reality denoted by the word 'love'. It is a complex reality with many aspects. Let us take as our starting point the fact that *love is always a mutual relationship between persons.* This relationship in turn is based on particular attitudes to the good, adopted by each of them individually and by both jointly. This is the point of departure for the first part of our analysis of love, the general analysis. This part also attempts a general characterization of love between man and woman. To carry this out we must distinguish its basic elements, both the substantial elements connected with attitudes to the good, and the structural elements connected with the reciprocal relationship between persons. These elements are found in any love. There is, for instance, in every love attraction and goodwill. Love between man and woman is one particular form of love, in which elements common to all of its forms are embodied in a specific way. That is why we have called our general analysis metaphysical. Metaphysical analysis will clear the way for psychological analysis. The love of man and woman takes shape deep down in the psyche of the two persons, and is bound up with the high sexual vitality of human beings, so that what is really needed is a psycho-physiological or bio-psychological analysis. The bio-physiological aspects will be discussed in the final part of the book ('Ethics and Sexology'). Human love, love between persons, cannot be reduced to or fully identified with these factors. If it could, it would not be love except perhaps in the very broad sense in which we speak of *amor naturalis* or of cosmic love, which we see in all the teleological tendencies at work in nature.

The love of man and woman is a mutual relationship between persons and possesses a personal character. Its profound ethical significance is intimately bound up with this – in this ethical sense it constitutes the content of the greatest commandment in the Gospel. And it is to this significance that our analysis must eventually address itself. Its object at that point will be love as a virtue, and the greatest of virtues, which one might say embraces all the others and raises them all to its own level, imprinting its own distinctive features on them.

This tripartite analysis of the bond between man and woman is indispensable, if we wish step by step to disentangle the meaning which concerns us from the multitude of meanings which cling to the word 'love'.

Love as Attraction

The first element in the general analysis of love is the element of attraction. Love – as has been said – signifies a mutual relationship between two people, a man and a woman, based on a particular attitude to the good. This attitude to the good originates in their liking for, their attraction to each other. To attract some-one means more or less the same as to be regarded as 'a good'. A woman is readily seen by a man, and a man by a woman, as 'a good'. That the two parties so easily attract each other is the result of the sexual urge, understood as an attribute and a force of human nature, but a force which operates in persons and insists on being raised to the personal level. Liking for a person of the other sex raises that natural force, the sexual urge, to the level of the lives of human persons.

74

For liking is very closely connected with knowledge, and intellectual knowledge at that, although the object of knowledge, the woman or man, is concrete and so comes within the purview of the senses. At the base of attraction is a sense impression, but this is not decisive in itself. For we discover in an attraction a certain cognitive commitment of the subject, a man, let us say, towards the object, in this case a woman. Knowledge, even the most thorough knowledge, and thought about a given person do not themselves amount to attraction, which often develops without thorough knowledge or long thought about a person. Attraction does not possess a *purely* cognitive structure. On the contrary, we must recognize that not only extra-intellectual but extra-cognitive factors, namely the emotions and the will, are involved in that cognitive commitment which has the character of an attraction.

To be attracted does not mean just thinking about some person as a good, it means a commitment to think of that person as a certain good, and such a commitment can in the last resort be effected only by the will. 'I want' is always implicit in 'I like', although it does not make itself directly felt to begin with, so that attraction has at first a primarily cognitive character. It is, so to speak, a form of cognition which commits the will, but commits it because it is committed by it. It is difficult to explain attraction unless we accept the mutual interpenetration of reason and will. The emotions, which play a great part in attraction, will be the subject of a rather more searching analysis in the next section of this chapter. It must, however, be said at once that the emotions are present at the birth of love because they favour the development of a mutual attraction between man and woman. Man's emotions are in general not oriented towards intellectual knowledge but towards experience in a broader sense. This natural tendency expresses itself in an emotional-affective reaction to a good. Emotional-affective reactions to the good obviously contribute greatly to the development of an attraction, in which one person is perceived by another as a good.

Sensibility is the ability to react to a perceived good of a

75

particular kind, the capacity to be moved by contact with the good (we shall deal with the more detailed meanings of sensibility in our psychological analysis, where we contrast it with sensuality). The kind of good to which any given man or woman is capable of reacting to a special degree depends partly on congenital and hereditary factors, partly on characteristics acquired either under extraneous influences or as a result of conscious effort on the part of the particular person, of work by the person on himself or herself. This is what gives a person's emotional life the specific complexion which shows itself in particular emotional-affective reactions, and is of great importance in determining what will attract that person. It largely determines to whom a given person is attracted, what in that particular person exercises a particular attraction.

For every human person is an indescribably complex and, so to speak, uneven good. Man and woman alike are by nature corporeal and spiritual beings. And such a being is also at once a corporeal and spiritual good. This is how one person is seen by another, and the guise in which one attracts another. If we examine the image, so to speak, which an attraction to another imprints on the mind of the subject we can, without doing violence to or destroying its fundamental unity, discover that it consists of responses to a number of distinct values. All these values to which a person responds derive from the object of the attraction. The subject of the attraction finds them in its object. It is because of this that the object is seen by the subject as a good which has attracted him.

In spite of this, however, there is more to an attraction than the sensations awakened by the contact between two persons. It is something more than the state of mind of a person experiencing particular values. It has as its object a person, and its source is the whole person. Such an attitude to a person is nothing other than love, although it may be only in embryo. *Attraction is of the essence of love and in some sense is indeed love, although love is not merely attraction.* This was what medieval thinkers meant when they spoke of *amor complacentia*: attraction is not just one of the elements of love, one of its components so to speak, but is one of the essential aspects of love as a whole. Analogically we can use the word 'love' of an attraction. Hence *amor complacentia*. The experience of various values which can be more or less discerned in the mind is symptomatic of attraction in that it gives one or several main emphases to it. Thus, in y's attraction to person x the value most strongly in evidence is one which y finds in x and to which y reacts strongly.

'Y's reaction to a particular value depends however not only on the fact that it is really present in person 'x', but also on the fact that 'y' is particularly sensitive to it, particularly quick to perceive and respond to it. This is very important in love between man and woman. For although the object of an attraction is always a person, there can be no doubt that the attraction itself may take a variety of forms. For instance, in some-one capable of reacting solely or mainly to sensual and sexual values, attraction to and hence love for another person is bound to develop otherwise than it would in one more capable of responding eagerly to spiritual and moral values, intelligence, virtue, etc. We would expect these two to react in different ways to any particular person, and to be attracted to different persons.

The emotional-affective reaction plays a prominent part in attraction, and leaves a specific imprint on it. The sentiments in themselves have no cognitive power, but they have the power to guide and orient cognitive acts – and this is very strikingly evident in attraction. But this very fact creates a certain internal difficulty in the sexual lives of persons. This difficulty is inherent in the relationship of experience to truth. Feelings arise spontaneously – the attraction which one person feels towards another often begins suddenly and unexpectedly – but this reaction is in effect 'blind'. Where the feelings are functioning naturally they are not concerned with the truth about their object. Truth is for man a function and a task for his reason. And although there have been thinkers (Pascal and Scheler) who have strongly emphasized the distinctive logic of the emotions (*logique du coeur*) emotional-affective reactions may equally well further or hinder an attraction to a true good. This is extremely important to the value of any attraction, which often depends on whether the good to which it is directed is really what it is thought to be. So, in the attraction of 'y' to 'x' and 'x' to 'y', the truth about the value of the person to whom another person is attracted is a basic and decisive factor. And this is just where emotional-affective reactions often tend to distort or falsify attractions: through their prism values which are not really present at all may be discerned in a person. This can be very dangerous to love. For when emotional reactions are spent – and they are naturally fleeting – the subject, whose whole attitude was based on such reaction, and not on the truth about the other person, is left as it were in a void, bereft of that good which he or she appeared to have found. This emptiness and the feeling of disappointment which goes with it often produce an emotional reaction in the opposite direction: a purely emotional love often becomes an equally emotional hatred for the same person.

This is why in any attraction – and, indeed, here above all – the question of the truth about the person towards whom it is felt is so important. We must reckon with the tendency, produced by the whole dynamic of emotional life, for the subject to divert the question 'is it really so?' from the object of attraction to himself or herself, to his or her emotions. In these circumstances the subject does not enquire whether the other person really possesses the values visible to partial eyes, but mainly whether the newborn feeling for that person is a true emotion. Here we have one at least of the sources of that subjectivism which is so common in love (we shall revert to this later).

People generally believe that love can be reduced largely to a question of the genuineness of feelings. Although it is impossible to deny this altogether, if only because it follows from our analysis of attraction, we must still insist, if we are concerned with the quality of the attraction and the love of which it is part, that the truth about the person who is its object must play a part at least as important as the truth of the sentiments. These two truths, properly integrated, give to an attraction that perfection which is one of the elements of a genuinely good and genuinely 'cultivated' love.

Attraction goes very closely together with awareness of values. A person of the other sex may cause some-one to experience a number of different values. They all help to create the attraction, the dominant emphasis in which, as we have said, is determined by one particular value – that which has elicited the strongest response. When we speak of truth in an attraction (and by implication of truth in love) it is essential to stress that the attraction must never be limited to partial values, to something which is inherent in the person but is not the person as a whole. There must be a direct attraction to the person: in other words, response to particular qualities inherent in a person must go with a simultaneous response to the qualities of the person as such, an awareness that a person as such is a value, and not merely attractive because of certain qualities which he or she possesses. This is not the time to explain why this point is so very important in an attraction: the reasons will emerge mainly in the section devoted to the ethical analysis of love. In any case, an attraction which from amongst the various values belonging to a person fastens first and foremost upon the value of the person as such has the value of complete truth: the good to which it addresses itself is precisely the person, and not something else. And the person, as an entity, and hence as a good, is different from all that is not a person.

For something 'to please' means that it is apprehended as a good, or – we should say in the name of the truth which is so important a component of attraction – apprehended as that good which it in fact is. The object of attraction which is seen by the subject as a good is also seen as a thing of beauty. This is very important in the attraction on which love between man and woman is based. Beauty, feminine and masculine, is of course a subject, and a large one, in itself. The appreciation of beauty goes together with the appreciation of values, as though there was in each of them a 'supplementary' aesthetic value. 'Fascination', 'charm', 'glamour' – these and other similar words serve to describe this important aspect of love between persons. A human being is beautiful and may be revealed as beautiful to another human being. Woman is beautiful in a way of her own, and may attract the attention of a man by her beauty. A man is also beautiful in his own particular way, and because of his beauty may attract the attention of a woman. Beauty finds its proper place in the context of attraction.

This is not the place for a deeper analysis of this question. We should, however, recall here that a human being is a person, a being whose nature is determined by his or her 'inwardness'. It is therefore necessary to discover and to be attracted by the inner as well as the outer beauty, and perhaps indeed to be more attracted by the former than by the latter. This truth has a very special importance to the love of man and woman, which is, or at any rate ought to be, love between persons. The attraction on which this love is based must originate not just in a reaction to visible and physical beauty, but also in a full and deep appreciation of the beauty of the person.

Love as Desire

Following the principle established in our definition of attraction we can speak of desire also as one of the aspects of love. The word is translated by the Latin phrase *amor concupiscentia*, which indicates not so much that desire is one of the elements of love as that love is also found in desire. Like attraction, desire is of the essence of love, and is sometimes the most powerful element so that those medieval thinkers who spoke of 'love as desire' (*amor concupiscentia*) and of 'love as attraction' (*amor complacentia*), were entirely right to do so. Desire too belongs to the very essence of the love which springs up between man and woman. This results from the fact that the human person is a limited being, not self sufficient and therefore – putting it in the most objective way – needs other beings. Realization of the limitation and insufficiency of the human being is the starting point for an understanding of man's relation to God. Man needs God, as does every other creature simply in order to be.

What concerns us for the present is, however, something

different. A human being, a human person, is either man or woman. Sex is also a limitation, an imbalance. A man therefore needs a woman, so to say, to complete his own being, and woman needs man in the same way. This objective, ontological need makes itself felt through the sexual urge. The love of one person for another, of 'x' for 'y', grows up on the basis of that urge. This is 'love as desire', for it originates in a need and aims at finding a good which it lacks. For a man, that good is a woman, for a woman it is a man. Looked at objectively, then, their love is love as desire. There is, however, a profound difference between love as desire (*amor concupiscentia*) and desire itself (*concupiscentia*), especially sensual desire. Desire presupposes awareness of some lack, an unpleasant sensation which can be eliminated by means of a particular good. A man may, for instance, desire a woman in this way: a human person then becomes a means for the satisfaction of desire, just as nutriment serves to satisfy hunger. This is a very lame comparison, but nevertheless the implications of the word 'desire' suggest a utilitarian attitude – the object of which in this context would be a person of the other sex. This is precisely what Christ had in mind when He said (Matthew 5:28): 'Whosoever looketh upon a woman to lust after her hath committed adultery with her already in his heart.' This sentence throws a great deal of light on the nature of love and on sexual morality. This is a question which will need fuller treatment in the analysis of sensuality.

Love as desire cannot then be reduced to desire itself. It is simply the crystallization of the objective need of one being directed towards another being which is for it a good and an object of longing. In the mind of the subject love-as-desire is not felt as mere desire. It is felt as a longing for some good for its own sake: 'I want you because you are a good for me'. The object of love or desire is a good for the subject – the woman for the man, the man for the woman. And love is therefore apprehended as a longing for the person, and not as mere sensual desire, *concupiscentia*. Desire goes together with this longing, but is so to speak overshadowed by it. The subject in love is conscious of its presence, knows that it is there at his or her disposal so to speak, but working to perfect

81

this love, will see to it that desire does not dominate, does not overwhelm all else that love comprises. For even those that are not intellectually aware of it may sense that if desire is predominant it can deform love between man and woman and rob them both of it.

Although love as desire is not identical with the sensual desires as such it is that aspect of love in which attitudes close to the utilitarian can most easily find a home. For love as desire implies – as we have said – a real need, because of which, to repeat words used above 'You are a good for me'. The good which satisfies the need is in one sense useful. But to be useful is not the same as being an object for use. We can only say that it is in this aspect – 'love as desire' – that love comes closest to the region of utility, but that it nonetheless infuses desire with its own essence. Thus, true 'love as desire' never becomes utilitarian in its attitude, for (even when desire is aroused) it has its roots in the personalistic principle. Let us add that *amor concupiscentia* is present even in man's love of God, whom man may and does desire as a good for himself. And it is the same, if we may draw a remote but suggestive analogy, in the love between two persons. The analysis of their relationship demands particular precision at this point, or we may find ourselves fully equating the sensual desires themselves with love as desire, and supposing that this is the whole content of the love which one human being can feel for another (or indeed for God), the love of person for person.

Love as Goodwill

It should be emphasized here that love is the fullest realization of the possibilities inherent in man. The potential inherent in the person is most fully actualized through love. The person finds in love the greatest possible fullness of being, of objective existence. Love is an activity, a deed which develops the existence of the person to its fullest. It must of course be genuine love. What does this mean? A genuine love is one in which the true essence of love is realized – a love which is directed to a genuine (not merely an apparent) good in the true way, or in other words the way appropriate to the nature of that good. This criterion should be applied also to the love of man and woman. Here too genuine love perfects the life and enlarges the existence of the person. False love has directly opposite consequences. A false love is one which is directed towards a specious good or, most often, to a genuine good in a way which does not correspond to but is contrary to its nature. Such, often enough, is the love of man and woman, false either in its premises or, in spite of (apparently) sound premises, in its manifestations, its realization. A false love is an evil love.

Love between man and woman would be evil, or at least incomplete, if it went no farther than love as desire. For love as desire is not the whole essence of love between persons. It is not enough to long for a person as a good for oneself, one must also, and above all, long for that person's good. This uncompromisingly altruistic orientation of the will and feelings is called in the language of St Thomas *amor benevolentiae* or *benevolentia* for short, which corresponds (though not with absolute precision) to our concept of *goodwill.* The love of person for person must be benevolent, or it will not be genuine. Indeed, it will not be love at all, but only egoism. It is in the nature of love that desire and goodwill are not incompatible but, on the contrary, closely connected. If one person wants another as a good for himself or herself, he or she must want that other person to be a real good. It is here that we see how closely desire and goodwill can go together.

Nevertheless, there is more to goodwill as such than this complex of desires: it is not just that 'y' wants 'x' to be a good, and as great a good as possible, so that 'x' will be a still greater good for 'y'. Goodwill is quite free of self-interest, the traces of which are conspicuous in love as desire. *Goodwill is the same as selflessness* in love: not 'I long for you as a good' but 'I long for your good', 'I long for that which is good for you'. The person of goodwill longs for this with no selfish ulterior motive, no personal consideration. Love as goodwill, *amor benevolentiae*, is therefore love in a more unconditional sense than love-desire. It is the purest form of love. Goodwill brings us as close to the 'pure essence' of love as it is possible to get. Such love does more than any other to perfect the person who experiences it, brings both the subject and the object of that love the greatest fulfilment.

The love of man for woman and woman for man cannot but be love as desire, but must as time goes by move more and more in the direction of unqualified goodwill, *benevolentia*. This should be the tendency of love in every phase and every aspect of a shared life or an association. But it should be so to a special degree in marriage, where not only is 'love as desire' most clearly in evidence but desire as such is most conspicuous. It is this that makes married life so extraordinarily rich, but it is also the source of its peculiar difficulty. These are facts which must not be concealed or ignored. Genuine love as goodwill can keep company with love as desire, and even with desire itself, provided that desire does not overwhelm all else in the love of man and woman, does not become its entire content and meaning.

The Problem of Reciprocity

We must turn now to the problem of reciprocity. This requires us to consider the love of man and woman not so much as the love of each for the other but rather as something which exists *between* them. It is worth calling attention to the preposition. It suggests that love is not just something *in* the man and something *in* the woman – for in that case there would properly speaking be two loves – but is something common to them and unique. Numerically and psychologically, there are two loves, but these two separate psychological facts combine to create a single objective whole – we might almost say a single entity in which two persons are joined.

This brings us to the problem of the 'I – we' relationship. Every person is an 'I' of some sort, unique and unreproducible. This 'I' possesses its own inner self, by virtue of which it is as it were a little world, which owes its existence to God, but is at the same time autonomous within its own proper limits.

The route from one 'I' to another leads through the free will, through a commitment of the will. This route may however be a one-way street, and the love of one person for the other will then be onesided. True, it has its distinctive and authentic psychological profile but not the objective fullness which reciprocity would give it. This is what is called unrequited love, which as everyone knows is fraught with pain and suffering. If a love of this kind persists, as it sometimes does, for a very long time, this is because of some inner obstinacy, which however tends to distort love and rob it of its proper character. Unrequited love is condemned first to stagnation in the person who feels it, then to gradual extinction. Sometimes, indeed, as it dies it causes the very capacity for love to die together with it. But its results are not always so drastic.

In any case, it is clear to see that love is by its very nature not unilateral but bilateral, something 'between' two persons, something shared. Fully realized, it is essentially an interpersonal, not an individual matter. It is a force which joins and unites, of its very nature inimical to division and isolation. For love to be complete the route from 'x' to 'y' and the route from 'y' to 'x' must converge. Bilateral love creates the immediate basis on which a single 'we' can arise from two 'I's. Such is its natural dynamic. For a 'we' to come into existence, bilateral love is not in itself enough, since it still in spite of everything involves two 'I's, though they may be fully predisposed to become a single 'we'. It is reciprocity which determines whether that 'we' comes into existence in love. Reciprocity is the proof that love has matured, that it has become something 'between' persons, has created a community of feeling and that its full nature has thereby been realized. Reciprocity is an essential part of this.

This throws new light on the whole problem. We have asserted above that goodwill is naturally part of love, just as much as attraction and yearning (desire). Love as desire and love as goodwill differ, but not so far as to be mutually exclusive – 'y' may desire 'x' as a good for himself/herself and at the same time disinterestedly desire what is good for 'x'. The truth about reciprocity provides us with another way of explaining this. The fact is that a person who desires another

85

as a good desires above all that person's love in return for his or her own love, desires that is to say another person above all as co-creator of love, and not merely as the object of appetite. The 'selfishness' of love would seem then to lie only in seeking a response, a response which is love reciprocated. But since reciprocity is in the very nature of love, since the interpersonal character of love depends on it, we can hardly speak of 'selfishness' in this context. The desire for reciprocity does not cancel out the disinterested character of love. Indeed, requited love can be thoroughly disinterested, although that element in the love between man and woman which we call love as desire finds full satisfaction in it. Reciprocity brings with it a synthesis, as it were, of love as desire and love as goodwill. Love as desire becomes more conspicuous especially when one of the persons begins to be jealous of the other, when one of them fears the other's unfaithfulness.

This is a separate problem – a very serious one in any love between man and woman, and a very serious one in marriage. It is worth recalling here what Aristotle said long ago on the subject of reciprocity in his treatise on friendship (*Nicomachean Ethics* Books VIII & IX). In Aristotle's view there are different kinds of reciprocity, and the character of the good on which reciprocity and hence the friendship as a whole is based determines its quality in each case. If it is a genuine good (an honest good) reciprocity is something deep, mature and virtually indestructible. On the other hand, if reciprocity is created only by self-interest, utility (a utilitarian good) or pleasure then it is superficial and impermanent. In fact, although reciprocity is always something 'between' two persons, it none the less depends to a decisive degree on that which both persons contribute to it. Hence too the fact that each of the persons thinks of reciprocity in love not as something supra-personal but as something utterly personal.

So then – it comes back to Aristotle's thought – if that which each of the two persons contributes to their reciprocal love is his or her personal love, but a love of the highest ethical value, virtuous love, then reciprocity assumes the characteristics of durability and reliability. This accounts for that trust in another person which brings freedom from suspicion and from jealousy – that trust which is so important a factor in making love a genuine good for two people. To be able to rely on another person, to think of that person as a friend who will never prove false, is for the person who loves a source of peace and joy. Peace and joy are fruits of love very closely bound up with its very essence.

If on the other hand what both persons bring to their mutual love is only or mainly desire, if their aim is merely to use each other, to seek pleasure, then reciprocity itself does not possess the characteristics of which we have just spoken. It is impossible to put your trust in another human being, knowing or feeling that his or her sole aim is utility or pleasure. It is equally impossible to put your trust in a person if you yourself have the same thing as your main object. This is where that particular property of love, by dint of which it creates an interpersonal union, 'takes its revenge'. It is enough for one of the persons to have utilitarian aims, and 'mutual love' will become a problem which begets many suspicions and jealousies. Suspicions and fits of jealousy, to be sure, often spring from human weakness. People who, for all their weakness, none the less bring genuine goodwill to their love try to base reciprocity on an 'honest good', on virtue which may still be imperfect but is none the less real. Sharing their lives gives them a continuous opportunity to test their good faith and to reinforce it by virtue. Life together becomes as it were a school for self-perfection.

It is difficult, however, when each or for that matter either of the persons brings to their 'mutual love' only a 'consumer' attitude, a utilitarian intent. A woman and a man can afford each other pleasure of a sexual nature, can be for each other the source of various enjoyments. However, mere pleasure, mere sensual enjoyment is not a good which binds and unites people for long, as Aristotle has most justly observed. A woman and a man, if their 'mutual love' depends merely on pleasure or self interest, will be tied to each other just as long as they remain a source of pleasure or profit for each other. The moment this comes to an end, the real reason for their

87

'love' will also end, the illusion of reciprocity will burst like a bubble. There can be no genuine reciprocity based only on desire or on a 'consumer' attitude. For such an attitude does not really seek a response to love in the form of reciprocity but only the appeasement, the full satisfaction of desire. It is at bottom the merest egoism, whereas reciprocity inevitably presupposes altruism in both persons. *Genuine reciprocity cannot arise from two egoisms*, their product can only be a momentary or at best fairly short-lived semblance of reciprocity.

Two conclusions follow from this, one of primarily theoretical, the other of more practical significance. The first conclusion is this: in the light of our reflections on the theme of reciprocity we can see how very necessary it is to analyse love not only from the psychological but above all from the ethical point of view. The second, the practical conclusion, is that people should always carefully 'verify' their love before exchanging declarations, and especially before acknowledging it as their vocation and beginning to build their lives upon it. More precisely, they should assay that which is in each of the two co-creators of this love and by extension what there is 'between' them. They must determine what their reciprocity relies on, and whether it is not apparent rather than real. For love can endure only as a unity in which a mature 'we' finds clear expression, and will not endure as a combination of two egoisms, at the base of the structure of which two 'I's are clearly visible. The structure of Love is that of an interpersonal communion.

From Sympathy to Friendship

We must now look at human love in yet another of its aspects. Although this problem could very well wait for our section on psychological analysis we shall none the less make room for it here and now in this first part of the chapter, which is devoted to the general analysis of love. The word 'sympathy' is of Greek origin, and is formed from the prefix 'syn' ('together with') and the root of the verb 'pathein' ('to experience'). Literally, then, sympathy means no more nor less than 'experiencing together'. The literal meaning of the expression points to two aspects of sympathy. A certain community expressed in the prefix, and a certain passivity ('to experience') expressed in the verb root. Sympathy then means above all that which 'happens' between people in the realm of their emotions – that by means of which emotional and affective experiences unite people. That this is something which 'happens' to them, that it is not their doing, not the result of acts of will must be particularly emphasized. Sympathy is a manifestation of experience rather than of activity: people succumb to it in ways which they sometimes find incomprehensible themselves, and the will is captured by the pull of emotions and sensations which bring two people closer together regardless of whether one of them has consciously chosen the other as the object of his or her love. Sympathy is love at a purely emotional stage, at which no decision of the will, no act of choice, as yet plays its proper part. At most the will merely consents to the existence of a sympathy and the direction it takes.

Although etymologically sympathy appears to refer to emotional love 'between' persons we none the less often think and speak of one person's sympathy for another. When I find some person 'sympathetic' that person is present within my emotional field as an 'object' which awakens a positive emotional response, and that response automatically enhances the value of the person. This 'plus' is born with my sympathy, and can also die with it, since it depends entirely upon my emotional attitude to the person who is the object of my sympathy. On the other hand, this 'plus' based only on sympathy for another person may change gradually into an unqualified belief in that person's worth. Within the limits of mere sympathy, however, the worth of the object does not seem to be directly felt: x is aware of the value of y through the medium of his sympathy, thanks to which y acquires a value for x. There is a hint of subjectivism here, and this together with the passivity noticed at the beginning helps to account for a certain weakness which we find in sympathy.

This is that sympathy which often takes possession of one's feelings and will, irrespective of the objective worth of the person for whom it is felt. The value of the emotion is what matters rather than the value of the person (the object of sympathy).

What makes sympathy so weak is, as we see, its lack of objectivity. Hand in hand with this, however, goes the great subjective force of sympathy, which also gives human loves their subjective intensity. Mere intellectual recognition of another person's worth, however whole hearted, is not love (any more than it is attraction, of which something was said at the beginning of the section). Only sympathy has the power to make people feel very close to each other. But then love is an emotional experience, not the result of reflection. Sympathy brings people close together, into the same orbit, so that each is aware of the other's whole personality, and continually discovers that person in his own orbit. Precisely for this reason sympathy is that very important thing, the empirical and palpable manifestation of love between man and woman. It is thanks to sympathy that they are aware of their mutual love, and without sympathy they somehow lose their love and are left feeling once more that they are in a vacuum. As soon as sympathy breaks down they usually feel that love has also come to an end.

Yet sympathy is not by any means the whole of love, any more than excitement and emotion are the whole of a human being's inner life – it is only one element among others. The most profound, by far the most important element is the will, in which the power to create love in a human being and between people is vested. It is important to realize this inasmuch as love between a woman and a man cannot remain on the level of mere sympathy but must become friendship. For in friendship – and here it is unlike mere sympathy – the decisive part is played by the will. I desire a good for you just as I desire it for myself, for my own 'I'. The content and structure of friendship can be summed up in this formula. It brings out the element of *benevolentia* or goodwill, ('I want what is good for you'), and also the characteristic 'doubling' of the subject, the doubling of the 'I': my 'I' and your 'I' form a moral unity, for the will is equally well inclined to both of them, so that *ipso facto* your 'I' necessarily becomes in some sense mine, lives within my 'I' as well as within itself. This is the meaning of the word 'friendship'. The doubling of the 'I' implicit in it emphasizes the unification of persons which friendship brings with it.

This unification is different in kind from that which goes with sympathy. There it depends solely on emotion or sentiment, and the will merely acquiesces. Whereas in friendship the will is actively involved itself. For this reason friendship truly takes possession of the whole human being, it is something which he chooses to do, it implies a decisive choice of another person, another 'I', as the object of affection, whereas none of this would have taken place within the confines of sympathy. It is from this that friendship derives its objective force. Friendship, however, needs to be thrown into relief in a subject, needs so to speak a subjective accent. And this too sympathy supplies. Sympathy is not in itself friendship, but it creates conditions for friendship between two persons to spring up, and, once it exists, to obtain vivid subjective expression, its proper climate and its proper emotional warmth. For a mere bilateral and reciprocal 'I want what is good for you', although it is the nucleus of friendship, remains so to speak suspended in a vacuum if it is deprived of the emotional warmth which sympathy supplies. Emotion by itself is no substitute for this 'I want what is good for you', but divorced from emotion that wish is cold and incommunicable.

If we now consider the implications of all this for the education of love, there is one crystal clear requirement: sympathy must be transformed into friendship, and friendship supplemented by sympathy. This requirement, as you see, looks both ways. In mere sympathy there is as yet no active goodwill, and without that there can be no true love. Although sympathy may pass for goodwill (if not for something more than goodwill), there is here a measure of illusion. We have already drawn attention in the analysis of attraction to a subjectivist feature of emotion – namely that it exhibits a tendency to divert the subject's attention from the object, and to concentrate it exclusively on himself. A further result of this tendency is that sympathy and emotional love are taken for friendship, or even for something more than friendship. For this reason relationships which objectively considered should be based on nothing less than friendship, marriage for instance, are often based on mere sympathy. Friendship, as has been said, consists in a full commitment of the will to another person with a view to that person's good. There is, therefore, a need for sympathy to ripen into friendship and this process normally demands time and reflection. While it remains within the limits of sympathy, the attitude to the other person and to his or her value rests on emotion: what is necessary is to supplement the value of that emotion with an objective knowledge of and belief in the value of that person. For only on this basis can the will actively commit itself. The emotions themselves can commit the will, but only in a passive and somewhat superficial fashion, with a certain admixture of subjectivism. Friendship, however, demands a sincere commitment of the will with the fullest possible objective justification.

On the other hand, it is also necessary to supplement friendship with sympathy, without which it will remain cold and incommunicable. This process is possible, for although sympathy is born in human beings spontaneously and persists irrationally, it gravitates in the direction of friendship, it has a tendency to become friendship. This is a direct consequence of the structure of the inner self of a person, in which only things fully justified by free will and belief acquire full value. No mere sense impression, and no emotion based on such an impression, can take the place of this justification. A dawning sympathy between two persons brings with it as a rule the possibility or even the modest beginnings of friendship. Sympathy, however, is often intense right from the start, whereas friendship is faint and frail at first. The next stage is to take advantage of the emotional situation created by sympathy to fashion a mutual friendship, thereby endowing sympathy with a solid and objective significance. A mistake often made in love between people, and especially between man and woman, is to leave it, so to speak, at the level of sympathy, with no conscious attempt to mould it into friendship. One consequence of this mistake is the belief that when sympathy breaks down love is also at an end. This belief is very dangerous to human love, and the mistake from which it arises indicates one of the main gaps in the education of love.

Love cannot be merely a matter of 'consuming' sympathy, or of finding an outlet for one's feelings in it (frequently accompanied in relations between man and woman by sexual relief). No, love consists in the thoroughgoing transformation of sympathy into friendship. It is of its very nature creative and constructive, and not merely bent on enjoyment. Sympathy is always only a signal, and decidedly not a fully formed personal relationship. It must first establish itself on a firm foundation of friendship, just as friendship must be reinforced by the climate and temperature of sympathy. Sympathy and friendship are two processes which must interpenetrate without hindering each other. This is where the 'art' of education in love, the true 'ars amandi' comes into its own. It is against the rules of this art to let sympathy (especially intense in the 'man-woman' relationship, where it is combined with a powerful sensual and physical attraction) obscure the need to create friendship and make it impossible practice. There, I think, is the reason for many of the failures and disasters to which human love is exposed.

What lies behind them is an incongruity between the feelings of the subject and objective reality: the subjective and the objective shapes of love do not exactly fit. Sympathy, in which the subjective shape of love is clearly discernible, falls one step short of friendship, in which love first ripens in its objective form. None the less, love itself must be subjective, must reside in two personal subjects, take shape and find expression in them. We must not, however, confuse the idea of subjective love with that of subjectivity. Love is always a subjective thing, in that it must reside in subjects, but at the same time it must be free of subjectivity. It must be something objective within the subject, have an objective as well as a subjective profile. For this very reason it cannot be mere sympathy, but must include friendship. You may test the

93

maturity of the friendship between two persons by asking whether it is accompanied by sympathy, and more important still whether it is totally dependent on sympathy (on sentimental impulses and transient emotions) or whether it possesses, apart from all this, a distinct objective existence in the person and between the persons. Only if it does is it a friendship on the basis of which two people can build a marriage, and share their lives.

It also appears that comradeship can play an important part in the development of love between a man and a woman. Comradeship is distinct from both sympathy and friendship. It differs from sympathy in that it is not confined mainly to the emotional-affective sphere of life, but rests on such objective foundations as joint work, common goals, shared concerns, etc. It differs from friendship in that it is not an expression of the principle 'I want your good as much as I want my own'. Sharing brought about by particular objective factors is, then, the distinctive feature of comradeship. People attend the same class, work in the same laboratory, are employed by the same company, have the same special interest (philately, say), and this makes them comrades. Comradeship may equally well come into being between a man and a woman, with or without a pre-existing emotional sympathy. If sympathy is present, the combination is a very promising one for comradeship may assist the development of pure sympathy into true friendship. The fact is that comradeship gives a man and a woman an objective common interest, whereas sympathy links them only in a subjective way. Comradeship favours the development of love's objective side, without which it is always incomplete. The emotions themselves are, as experience shows, rather fickle, and so cannot lastingly and exclusively determine the attitude of one human being to another. It is necessary to find means by which the emotions may not only merge with the will but – and this is more important – bring about that union of wills (*unum velle*) by virtue of which two 'I's become a single 'we'. It is in friendship that such unity is found.

Mutual friendship has an inter-personal character, expressed in this 'we'. The 'we' is found in comradeship too, although there it still lacks the cohesion and depth which belong to friendship. Besides, comradeship may bind many people together, whereas friendship tends to bind only a few. The social characteristic of comradeship is conspicous in the fact that people linked by it usually form a distinct circle. This is another reason why comradeship may be very important for the development of mutual love between a man and a woman, if their love is to ripen into marriage and become the cornerstone of a new family. People capable of creating and living in a milieu of their own are probably well prepared to impart the character of a closely knit community to the family, and to create a good atmosphere for family life.

Betrothed Love

The general analysis of love has a primarily metaphysical character, although we have to refer continually to its psychological and ethical aspects. These various aspects of love interpenetrate, so that we cannot examine any one of them without mentioning the others. In our analysis so far we have tried to clarify what is essential to all forms of love, and manifests itself in a specific way in the love of man and woman. Love in the individual develops by way of attraction, desire and goodwill. Love however finds its full realization not in an individual subject, but in a relationship between subjects, between persons. Hence the problem of friendship, which we have analysed here in our discussion of sympathy, hence too a problem connected with friendship, that of reciprocity. The transition from 'I' to 'we' is no less important for love than the escape from one's own 'I' by way of attraction, desire and goodwill. Love, especially of the kind which concerns us in the present book, is not just an aspiration, but rather a coming together, a unification of persons. This takes place, of course, on the basis of the attraction, desire and goodwill which develop in individual subjects. The individual aspect of love does not disappear from view in its interpersonal aspect – on the contrary, the latter is conditioned by the former. As a result love is always a sort of interpersonal synthesis and synchronization of attraction, desire and goodwill.

Betrothed love differs from all the aspects or forms of love analysed hitherto. Its decisive character is the giving of one's own person (to another). The essence of betrothed love is self-giving, the surrender of one's 'I'. This is something different from and more than attraction, desire or even goodwill. These are all ways by which one person goes out towards another, but none of them can take him as far in his quest for the good of the other as does betrothed love. 'To give oneself to another' is something more than merely 'desiring what is good' for another – even if as a result of this another 'I' becomes as it were my own, as it does in friendship. Betrothed love is something different from and more than all the forms of love so far analysed, both as it affects the individual subject, the person who loves, and as regards the interpersonal union which it creates. When betrothed love enters into this interpersonal relationship something more than friendship results: two people give themselves each to the other.

This matter demands more thorough consideration. First of all, the question arises whether any person can give himself or herself to another person. We said above that the person is always, of its very nature, untransferable, *alteri incommunicabilis*. This means not only that it is its own master (*sui juris*) but that it cannot give itself away, cannot surrender itself. The very nature of the person is incompatible with such a surrender. Indeed, in the natural order it makes no sense to speak of a person giving himself or herself to another, especially if this is meant in the physical sense. That which is personal is on a plane where there can be no giving of the self, and no appropriation in the physical sense. The person as such cannot be someone else's property, as though it were a thing. In consequence, the treatment of a person as an object for use is also excluded, as we have already seen in our closer examination of that subject. But what is impossible and illegitimate in the natural order and in a physical sense, can come about in the order of love and in a moral sense. In this sense, one person can give himself or herself, can surrender entirely to another, whether to a human person or to God, and such a giving of the self creates a special form of love which we define as betrothed love.[24] This fact goes to prove that the person has a dynamism of its own, and that specific laws govern its existence and evolution. Christ gave expression to this in a saying which is on the face of it profoundly paradoxical: 'He who would save his soul shall lose it, and he who would lose his soul for my sake shall find it again' (Matthew 10:39).

Indeed, the problem of betrothed love does contain a profound paradox, a very real, and not merely a verbal paradox: the words of the Gospel point to a concrete reality, and the truth which they contain is made manifest in the life of the person. Thus, of its very nature, no person can be transferred or ceded to another. In the natural order, it is oriented towards self perfection, towards the attainment of an ever greater fullness of existence – which is, of course, always the existence of some concrete 'I'. We have already stated that this self-perfection proceeds side by side and step by step with love. The fullest, the most uncompromising form of love consists precisely in selfgiving, in making one's inalienable and non-transferable 'I' someone else's property. This is doubly paradoxical: firstly in that it is possible to step outside one's own 'I' in this way, and secondly in that the 'I' far from being destroyed or impaired as a result is enlarged and enriched – of course in a super-physical, a moral sense. The Gospel stresses this very clearly and unambiguously – 'would lose – shall find again' 'would save – shall lose'. You will readily see that we have here not merely the personalistic norm but also bold and explicit words of advice, which make it possible for us to amplify and elaborate on that norm. The world of persons possesses its own laws of existence and of development.

Self surrender as a form of love is the result of a process within the person, and presupposes a mature vision of values, and a will ready and able to commit itself in this particular way. Bethrothed love can never be a fortuitous or imperfect event in the inner life of the person. It always constitutes a special crystallization of the whole human 'I', determined because of its love to dispose of itself in this particular way. In giving ourselves we find clear proof that we possess ourselves. As for the particular manifestations of this form of love, they can, I think, vary greatly. Leaving aside the devotion of a mother to her child, do we not find self-giving in, for instance, the relationship of a doctor with his patient, or in a teacher, who devotes himself with utter dedication to the education of his pupil, or a pastor who devotes himself with equal dedication to a soul entrusted to his care? In the same way great public figures or apostles can devote themselves to many people at once, people for the most part personally unkown to them, whom they serve by serving society as a whole. To determine in any of the cases mentioned, or in others like them, how far genuine dedicated love is involved is no easy matter. For in each of them no more than sincere goodwill and friendliness may be at work. In order, for instance, to 'give oneself entirely' to the vocation of the doctor, teacher, or pastor, it suffices simply to 'desire the good' of those for whom these duties are performed. And even if this form of behaviour comes to resemble a complete surrender of the self and so establishes its claim to be love, it would still be difficult to apply the name 'betrothed love' to it.

The concept of betrothed love implies the giving of the individual person to another chosen person. We speak therefore of love in certain cases when we seek to define the relationship between man and God. (This will be discussed separately in Chapter IV.) We have also the best possible grounds for speaking of betrothed love in connection with matrimony. The love of two persons, man and woman, leads in matrimony to their mutal dedication one to the other. From the point of view of each individual person this is a clear surrender of the self to another person, while in the interpersonal relationship it is surrender of each to the other. 'Self-giving', in the sense in which we are discussing it, should not be identified (confused) with 'giving oneself' in a merely psychological sense, with the sensation of self-surrender, still less with surrender in a merely physical sense. As far as surrender in the first (the psychological) sense is concerned, it is only the woman, or at any rate it is above all the woman, who feels that her role in marriage is to give herself; the man's experience of marriage is different, since, 'giving onself' has as its psychological correlative 'possession'. However, the psychological approach is insufficient here for if we think the problem through objectively, and that means ontologically, what happens in the marital relationship is that the man simultaneously gives himself, in return for the woman's gift of herself to him, and thus although his conscious experience of it differs from the woman's it must none the less be a real giving of himself to another person. If it is not there is a danger that the man may treat the woman as an object, and indeed an object to be used. If marriage is to satisfy the demands of the personalistic norm it must embody reciprocal self-giving, a mutual betrothed love. The acts of surrender reciprocate each other, that of the man and that of the woman, and though they are psychologically different in kind, ontologically they combine to produce a perfect whole, an act of mutual self-surrender. Hence a special duty devolves upon the man: he must give to 'conquest' or 'possession' its appropriate form and content – which means that he too must give himself, no less than she does.

It is all the more obvious that this giving of oneself of which we speak cannot, in marriage or indeed in any relationship between persons of opposite sex, have a merely sexual significance. Giving oneself only sexually, without the full gift of the person to validate it, must lead to those forms of utilitarianism which we have endeavoured to analyse as thoroughly as we could in Chapter I. We must stress this because there is a more or less pronounced tendency to interpret the 'gift of self' in a purely sexual, or sexual and psychological, sense. A personalistic interpretation is, however, absolutely necessary in this context. Thus, the moral code which has the commandment to love at its centre finds itself in perfect agreement with the identification of marriage with betrothed love, or rather – looking at it from the educational point of view – with the treatment of marriage as the result of this form of love.

There are further consequences of this, to which we shall

return in Chapter IV (Part I) where we show the necessity for monogamy. When a woman gives herself to a man as she does in matrimony this – morally speaking – precludes a simultaneous gift of herself to other persons in the same way. The sexual aspect plays a specific part in the development of betrothed love. Sexual intercourse has the effect of limiting that love to a single pair of persons, though at the same time it gains in intensity. Moreover, only when it is so limited can that love open itself fully to the new persons who are the natural result of marital love between man and woman.

The concept of goodwill is crucial to the establishment of norms of sexual morality generally. There certainly exists a very special connection between sex and the person in the objective order, which at the level of consciousness has its counterpart in a special awareness of the right of personal property in one's 'I'. This question will be analysed separately in Chapter III ('The Metaphysics of Shame'). Consequently, there can be no question of a sexual giving of oneself which does not mean a giving of the person – and does not come in one way or another within the orbit of those demands which we have a right to make of betrothed love. These demands derive from the personalistic norm. Betrothed love, though of its nature it differs from all the forms of love previously analysed, can nevertheless not develop in isolation from them. In particular, it is essential that betrothed love should ally itself closely with goodwill and friendship. Without these allies it may find itself in a very dangerous void, and the persons involved in it may feel helpless in face of conditions, internal and external, which they have inadvertently permitted to arise within themselves or between themselves.

PSYCHOLOGICAL
ANALYSIS OF LOVE

❦

Sense Impression and Emotion[25]

In this part of our analysis we must start from what constitutes, so to speak, the 'elementary particle' of man's psychological life, that is to say the sense impression and the motor
responses connected with it. 'Sense impression' is our general
term for the content of any sensory reaction to objective
stimuli. The senses are dependent on the structure of the
human organism, although they and the organs connected
with them are not the same thing. Sight, for instance, cannot
be fully understood in terms of a mechanism forming part of
the human anatomy: an external receptor (the optic nerves)
and the corresponding centres in the brain. The visual sense
includes something more – a specific psychic quality and a
power which the organs mentioned do not possess, either
taken together or individually. This psychic quality belongs
to the sphere of cognition. By sight, as by any other sense, we
obtain knowledge of particular objects or, it would be better
to say, we obtain knowledge of objects in a particular way. I
have in mind material objects, for only they are accessible to
the senses. It is sometimes said that the proper objects of the
senses are the so-called sensual qualities.

Sense impressions are very closely connected with that
specific property and power of the senses which is called
cognition. The senses react to the objects relevant to them
with the help of impressions. The object is reflected or mirrored, the senses seize and retain its image. An impression
presupposes immediate contact between one of the senses
and a given object – the length of its existence is also properly
speaking the duration of the immediate experience. But
although the immediate experience ends, the senses continue

to retain the image of the object, only sensual impression is gradually superseded by imagination. In connection with this we also speak of interior senses. Our external senses are those which establish immediate contact with the object while it is present to them. Our interior senses maintain that contact when the object is no longer within the immediate range of the external senses.

Thus an impression always contains in itself an image of the object, and it is a concrete and particular image. All the characteristics of 'that particular' object are reflected in it – obviously to the extent to which the impression itself is accurate. For an impression may be imprecise: this happens when we take in certain characteristics which help the mind to classify the object in a general way, but fail to take in many more individual characteristics. We know, however, that we can subject a material object to closer observation – and that if we do so these other characteristics will make themselves evident and establish themselves as part of the knowledge obtained through the senses.

A man receives an enormous quantity of sense impressions. His sensory receptors work without pause, and his whole nervous system becomes so tired and exhausted as a result that it requires rest and recuperation like other parts of the human organism. Because the quantity of impressions is so great not all of them register in the same way in the human consciousness. Some are imprinted more clearly and durably, others less clearly and only fleetingly. A sensory image is often connected with a particular feeling or reaction. When someone says that a certain thing or person has 'made an impression' on him, he means that together with the reflection of a certain sense content he has experienced a palpable stimulus thanks to which the impression has impinged heavily on his consciousness. This is where we move on to the sphere of emotions.

Emotions are separate and distinct from sense impressions. An emotion is also a sensory reaction to some object, but the content of the reaction differs from the content of an impression. In the content of an impression what is reflected is the image of an object, whereas in an emotion we are reacting to a value which we find in that object. For we must take into account the fact that the different objects which we encounter in our immediate sensory experience impinge on our attention not only as having content but as having value. A sense impression is a reaction to content, an emotion is a reaction to value. Emotion is itself sensory, and what is more even has its corporeal coefficient – but this does not at all mean that only material values can evoke it. We know very well that emotions can be equally well evoked by non-material, by spiritual values. It makes no difference that the value in question must somehow be 'materialized' in order to cause an emotion. We have to observe or hear or imagine or remember the value for the emotion to arise. But such an emotion possesses greater depth. When its object is a material value the emotion is shallower, more superficial. When however the object of an emotion is a supra-material, or spiritual value, it reaches more deeply into a man's psyche. This is understandable: after all, the human spirit and its powers have obviously had directly or indirectly a larger share in the emergence of such an emotion. The strength of an emotion is yet again a different matter. Thus, an emotion can be shallow yet powerful, and it may be deep in its content, yet weak. The ability to experience emotions which are at once profound and powerful seems to constitute a particularly important factor in the interior life.

When an impression is linked with an emotion their common object is as a result more distinctly stamped on a man's consciousness and stands out all the more clearly. For what stands out in the consciousness in these circumstances is not merely the image but the value of the object, and consequently cognition takes on as it were an emotional colouring. There occurs a more intense experience, thanks to which the object itself becomes something of greater importance to the subject. This is just as important where the establishment of contacts between persons of different sex is concerned. We all know the importance in this area of what are called first impressions. We know how full of hidden meaning is the simple sentence 'she made an impression on him' or 'he made an impression on her'. But if human love begins with an impression, if everything in it (even its spiritual content) depends upon that impression this is because the impression is accompanied by an emotion, which makes it possible to experience another person as a value, or putting it differently, enables two persons, a woman and a man, each to experience the other as a value. For this reason we must in our further psychological analysis of love constantly refer to values.

Analysis of Sensuality

Any immediate contact between a woman and a man is always the occasion of a sensory experience for both of them. Each of them is a 'body', is therefore exposed to the senses of the other and creates some impression. This impression is frequently accompanied by emotion. This is because by nature the woman represents for the man and the man for the woman a certain value. This value easily attaches itself to an impression received by the senses and having as its source a person of the opposite sex. The ease with which the value and the impression coalesce, the resulting ease with which emotions arise in contacts between persons of different sexes, is bound up with the sexual urge as a natural property and energy of human existence.

An emotion of this type is combined with an impression received by the senses, so that it is itself in some way sensual, from which however it by no means follows that the value in such an emotion to which we react is itself merely sensual, that it inheres merely in the body of the other person or can be identified with it. It has been mentioned previously that emotions offer an extensive terrain for the infiltration of spiritual life – and by the same token our emotions are often stirred by spiritual values. In the present case, however, where we are concerned with immediate contact between a woman and a man we must recognize that what first reveals itself in the impression is the content immediately available to the senses. Thus there arises a sort of 'external' image of the other person. Is this image merely a reflection of a 'body'?

No, it is a reflection of a 'human being', a human being of the other sex. That this is the content of the impression is shown by the intellectual reaction which arises simultaneously in the consciousness. But it is not this which accounts for the vividness of the impression and results in a particular female 'making an impression' on a particular male or vice versa. Each of these persons 'makes an impression' on the other thanks to the values experienced together with intellectual cognizance of a 'person of the other sex'. The values are the object of emotion – it is in fact they which coalesce with the impression and account for its vividness to the subject receiving it.

In analysing what is called sensuality in this light, we must state that it is something more than an ordinary reaction of the senses to an object, to a person of the other sex. Sensuality is not just a matter of male x becoming aware of female y through his senses, or vice versa. Sensuality always implies experiencing a particular value bound up with this sensory awareness. Specifically we are concerned with a sexual value, connected above all with the body of a person of the other sex (we ignore for the moment those perversions in the context of which a sexual value may be connected with a person of the same sex, or not with a person at all but with an animal or an inanimate object). In such cases the ordinary short way of putting it is: 'Y affects my senses.' This effect upon someone's senses is only incidentally connected with awareness of the beauty of a body, with aesthetic appreciation. Another consideration is of real importance to sensuality. Namely, that when it only stirs sensuality a body is commonly experienced as a 'potential object of enjoyment'. Sensuality in itself has a 'consumer orientation' – it is directed primarily and immediately towards a 'body'. It touches the person only indirectly, and tends to avoid direct contact. Even with bodily beauty it has, as we have already said, only an indirect connection. For beauty is essentially an object of contemplative cognition, and to experience aesthetic values is not to exploit: it gives joy, enjoyment as defined by St Augustine in the word *frui*. Thus, sensuality really interferes with apprehension of the beautiful, even of bodily, sensual beauty, for it introduces a consumer attitude to the object: 'the body' is then regarded as a potential object of exploitation.

This orientation of sensuality is a matter of spontaneous reflexes. In this form it is not primarily an evil thing but a natural thing. To justify this statement we must take account of the connections which exist between sense reactions and the sexual vitality of the human body. It is the task of the biologist, physiologist or physician to illuminate that question in detail. Obviously, everyone is from birth a creature belonging to one sex or the other. Only gradually, however, does he or she attain actual sexual maturity. This usually happens in the second decade of the person's life. As the organism reaches sexual maturity, its sexual vitality simultaneously develops. A number of vegetative physiological processes are involved in this, as for instance the activity of hormones, ovulation in the woman, spermatogenesis in the male organism, etc. These processes take place in the organism and remain outside the range of immediate consciousness, which however does not mean that a person may not obtain a more or less precise knowledge of their nature and progress. We shall devote the final chapter of our book to these matters.

Sensuality itself is on no account to be identified with the sexual vitality of a man's or a woman's body, for this has a purely unconscious and infrasensual physiological character. This is why we come across manifestations of sensuality with a sexual colouring in children who are physically not yet sexually mature. Although sensuality is not to be confused with the sexual vitality of the human body as such the first must be taken in conjunction with the second, with the sexual life processes as a whole. The sexual urge expresses itself in these life processes in such a way that the organism possessing male properties 'requires' an organism possessing female characteristics, in conjunction with which it can attain its proper end – that end in which the sexual vitality of the body finds its natural consummation. For the sexual life process is naturally directed towards procreation, and the other sex serves this end. This orientation is not in itself a consumer orientation – nature does not have enjoyment for its own sake as its aim. It is, then, simply a natural orientation in which an objective requirement of existence finds expression.

This natural orientation, which is inherent in the spontaneous physiological sexual processes is communicated to the senses. Hence sensuality expresses itself mainly in an appetitive form: a person of the other sex is seen as an 'object of desire' specifically because of the sexual value inherent in the body itself, for it is in the body that the senses discover that which determines sexual difference, sexual 'otherness'. This value reaches the consciousness by way of an impression where the impression is accompanied by an emotion experienced not only mentally but bodily. Sensuality is connected with the stirrings of the body, especially in its so-called erogenous zones. This shows its close connection with the inner sexual vitality of the organism itself. For a body possessing male characteristics needs a body possessing female characteristics for the objective ends served by the sexual urge. The promptings of sensuality would give man all the guidance he needs in his sexual life if, in the first place, his sexual reactions were infallibly guided by instinct, and if in the second place the object of those reactions – a person of the other sex – did not demand a different attitude from that which is proper to sensuality.

However, a human person, as we know, cannot be an object for use. Now, the body is an integral part of the person, and so must not be treated as though it were detached from the whole person: both the value of the body and the sexual value which finds expression in the body depend upon the value of the person. Given, then, interdependence, a sensual reaction in which the body and sex are a possible object for use, threatens to devalue the person. To react in this way to the body of a person means to see using that body as a possibility. It is, therefore, easy to understand the reaction of conscience to the stirrings of sensuality. For it reacts either to an attempt artificially to divorce body and sex from the person, so that they are left alone as a 'possible object of use' or else to a valuation of the person exclusively as 'body and sex', as an object for use. In either case, we have something completely incompatible with the value of the person as such. Let us add that in man there can be no such thing as 'pure' sensuality, such as exists in animals, nor of the infallible regulation of sensual reactions by instinct. What then is completely natural in animals becomes sub-natural in man. The content of a sensual reaction, in which the body and sex are experienced as objects of enjoyment, itself indicates that sensuality in man is not 'pure', but modified in one way or another by awareness of values. Pure, natural sensuality, governed in its reactions by instinct, is not oriented towards enjoyment divorced from the end of sexual life, whereas sensuality in man is so oriented.

This further means that sensuality by itself is not love, and may very easily become its opposite. At the same time, we must recognize that when man and woman come together, sensuality, as the natural reaction to a person of the other sex, is a sort of raw material for true, conjugal love. By itself, however, it most certainly does not play that role. The yearning for a sexual value connected with 'the body' as an object of use demands integration: it must become an integral part of a fully formed and mature attitude to the person, or else it is certainly not love. A current of love as desire does, it is true, run through sensuality, but if it is not supplemented by those other, nobler, elements of love of which we spoke in Part I of this chapter, if it remains desire and nothing more, then it is quite certainly not love. Sensuality must then be open to the other, nobler elements of love.

Sensuality in itself is quite blind to the person, and oriented only towards the sexual value connected with 'the body'. For this reason it is characteristically fickle, turning wherever it finds that value, wherever a 'possible object of enjoyment' appears. The various senses signal the presence of such an object, each in its own special way – touch, for instance, in a different way from the higher senses, sight and hearing. But it is not only the external senses that serve sensuality: the inner senses, such as imagination and memory, also do so. With their assistance one can make contact even with the 'body' of a person not physically present, experiencing the value of that body to the extent that it consti-

tutes a 'possible object of enjoyment.' The reactions symptomatic of sensuality may occur incidentally even when the
body of the other person is not regarded as an object of enjoyment. They may for instance manifest themselves when the
body is the object of some scientific investigation or study, or
an object of artistic interest. Sensuality often insinuates itself
into such situations 'uninvited', so to speak – sometimes it
endeavours to draw the whole attitude to the body and to the
person into its own orbit, and at other times it only sets up a
typical reflex in the mind: it shows that the existing attitude
to the body and the person 'might be' drawn into the orbit of
sensuality, which lurks as it were just beyond the threshold.

All this however most certainly does not go to show that
sensual excitability, as a natural and congenital characteristic of a concrete person, is in itself morally wrong. An
exuberant and readily roused sensuality is the stuff from
which a rich – if difficult – personal life may be made. It may
help the individual to respond more readily and completely
to the decisive elements in personal love. Primitive sensual
excitability (provided it is not of morbid origin) can become a
factor making for a fuller and more ardent love. Such a love
will obviously be the result of sublimation.

Sentiment and Love

Sentimentality must be clearly distinguished from sensuality. We have said earlier that a sense impression is usually
accompanied by an emotional response. Although the impression is sensory, the emotion may have reference to a
non-material value residing in the object of the impression.
Direct contact between man and woman always entails an
impression which may be accompanied by an emotion. When
this emotion has as its object a sexual value residing in the
'body' itself as a 'possible object of enjoyment' it is a manifestation of sensuality. However, a sexual value which is the
object of emotion is by no means necessarily connected with
the 'body' itself as a 'possible object of enjoyment'. It may be

connected with the whole 'person of the other sex'. In that case, the object of emotional experience for a woman will be the value 'masculinity', and for a man the value 'femininity'. The first may be connected with, for instance, an impression of 'strength', the second with an impression of 'charm', but both are connected with a whole person of the other sex, not only with that person's 'body'. This susceptibility (which is different from sensual excitability) to the sexual value residing in 'a whole person of the other sex', to 'femininity' or 'masculinity', should be called sentiment.

Sentimental susceptibility is the source of affection. It differs greatly from sensuality, not so much in its basis as in its inner content. The basis of both alike is the same sensory intuition. The content of the sense impression is the whole 'person of the other sex', the whole 'woman' or 'man'. For sensuality, one part of this integral sense impression 'the body' immediately stands out from and is as it were dissociated from the rest, whereas sentiment remains attached to a whole individual of the other sex. Sexual value therefore continues to reside in the whole person, and is not confined only to that person's 'body'. Also, because of this, in sentiment we do not see that conspicuous drive for enjoyment which is so characteristic of sensuality. Affection is not an urge to consume. It is, therefore, compatible with the contemplative moods which go with a sense of beauty and responsiveness to aesthetic values. In the male, affection is permeated with a strong feeling for and admiration of 'femininity', and in the woman with a similar feeling and admiration for 'masculinity'. No desire to use the other is discernible within the limits of affection as such.

Affection appears to be free from that concupiscence of which sensuality is full. In such an emotional state, though, a different sort of desire is discernible and a different need makes itself felt. This is the desire for nearness, for proximity, and simultaneously for exclusivity or intimacy, a longing to be always alone together. Sentimental love keeps two people close together, binds them – even if they are physically far apart – to move in each other's orbit. This love embraces memory and imagination, and also communicates itself to the will. It does not arouse the will, but charms and disarms it. A person in this state of mind remains mentally always close to the other person with whom he or she has ties of affection. When a woman and a man tied together by a love of this sort are physically near to each other they seek external means of expressing what it is that binds them. They have many different ways of showing tenderness – in looks, words, gestures, in the way the presence of each draws closer to and merges with that of the other. I am deliberately not speaking in this context of 'bodily proximity' because to both of them, and to the woman in particular, their sentiments seem incorporeal. Affectionate love is not indeed focused on the body as is sensuality. For that reason it is so frequently identified with spiritual love.

Obviously, this closeness, although it expresses the tenderness which two persons feel for each other, and springs directly from affection, can very easily shift onto the territory of sensuality. It will not to begin with be frank sensuality, with a sharply defined focus on physical enjoyment, but a sensuality concealed and disguised as sentiment. In this respect there seems as a rule to be a marked difference between woman and man. It is pretty generally recognized that woman is 'by nature' more sentimental, and man more sensual. We have indicated already one trait which is symptomatic of sensuality (apprehension of sexual value residing in the body as a 'possible object of enjoyment'). Now, this form of sensuality is more readily awakened in the man, more readily crystallizes in his consciousness and in his attitude. The very structure of the male psyche and personality is such that it is more readily 'compelled' to disclose and objectivize the hidden significance of love for a person of the other sex. This goes with the relatively more active role of the male in such love, and also imposes a responsibility on him. Whereas in the woman sensuality is as it were covert, and concealed by sentimentality. For this reason she is 'by nature' more inclined to go on seeing as a manifestation of affection what a man already clearly realizes to be the effect of sensuality and the desire for enjoyment. There exists then, as we see, a certain psychological divergence between man and woman in the manner of their participation in love. The woman appears more passive, although in a different way she is more active. In any case, her role and her responsibility will be different from the role and the responsibility of the male.

Let us go back again for a moment to the beginning of our reflections on the theme of sentiment and sentimental love. The emotional experience which accompanies an impression has as its object a sexual value connected with an entire 'person of the other sex', and that experience in itself is free from any focus on enjoyment. Thanks to the fact that the whole sentimental attitude of a man to a woman, which is concentrated on her 'femininity', or that of a woman to a man, which is concentrated on his 'masculinity', is free from any 'consumer orientation', certain distinctive processes may occur around the central value which is the object of the sentimental experience. Thus in the eyes of a person sentimentally committed to another person the value of the beloved object grows enormously – as a rule out of all proportion to his or her real value. Sentimental love influences imagination and memory and is influenced by them in turn. This perhaps explains the fact that a variety of values are bestowed upon the object of love which he or she does not necessarily possess in reality. These are ideal values, not real ones. They dwell in the mind of a sentimentally committed person, often after sentimental love has summoned them up from their hiding place in the unconscious into the field of consciousness. Sentiment is fruitful within the subject: since it is the subject's wish, desire, dream that these various values should be found in the object of his love, sentiment calls them all into being and endows that person with them, so as to make the emotional commitment still fuller.

Idealization of the object of love is a well-known phenomenon. It is particularly characteristic of young love. Here, the ideal is more powerful than the real, living human being, and the latter often becomes merely the occasion for an eruption in the subject's emotional consciousness of the values which he or she longs with all his heart to find in another person. It does not matter whether they are really values possessed by the particular person towards whom the subject feels a sentimental love. For that person, as we have said, is less the object of than the occasion for affection. Sentimentality is subjective and feeds, sometimes to excess, above all on values which the subject bears within himself or herself, and for which he or she consciously or unconsciously yearns, And this is yet another difference between sentiment and sensuality, which is in its own way objective and nurtured by a sexual value connected with the 'body' of the person who is the object of desire – though of course this is the objectivity of desire, not the objectivity of love.

None the less the salient feature of human sentiment noted a moment ago seems to be the main source of the weakness of affection. That form of love shows a character-istic ambivalence; it seeks to be near the beloved person, seeks proximity and expressions of tenderness, yet it is re-mote from the beloved in that it does not depend for its life on that person's true value, but on those values to which the subject clings as to its ideal. This is why sentimental love is very often a cause of disillusionment. Disillusionment where the woman is concerned may come with the discovery as time goes by that the man's sentiment is only a sort of screen for concupiscence or for the will to use another. Man and woman alike may be disillusioned to find that the values ascribed to the beloved person are fictitious. The discrepancy between the ideal and the reality often results in sentimental love fading or indeed changing into a feeling of hatred. Hatred in its turn is intrinsically ('by its very nature') unable to discern the values which really exist in the other person. So it is not obvious whether this inner exuberance of sentiment, and the tendency to idealize the object of love which goes with it, is a strength or a weakness in sentimental love. We do however know that by itself, as a form of reciprocal rela-tionship between a man and a woman, it is insufficient. It too needs to be integrated, as does sensual desire. If 'love' remains just sensuality, just a matter of 'sex-appeal', it will not be love at all, but only the utilization of one person by another, or of two persons by each other. While if love remains mere senti-ment it will equally be unlike love in the complete sense of the word. For both persons will remain in spite of everything divided from each other, though it may appear that they are very close just because they so eagerly seek proximity. Sentiment itself suffers from subjectivism, so that although objective love can begin to take shape on this ground, to ripen it must draw sustenance from other sources – sentiment alone will not mould such a love. Left to itself, it too may prove only a consumer phenomenon. But more will be said about this in Chapter III.

We must now turn to those forces which have the capacity to fashion an objective love. These are the forces of the human spirit: it is they which make the integration of love possible.

The Problem of Integrating Love

Looked at in terms of psychology, love can be seen as a specific situation. It is on the one hand an internal situation, existing in a particular subject, and it is simultaneously a situation between two persons, a woman and a man. But whether we think of its internal or its external aspect it is a concrete situation, and therefore unique and unreproducible. The external concreteness and uniqueness of the situation which we call love is closely connected with its internal aspect, with what is within each of the persons, who are as it were actors in the drama of their own love. Love is certainly a drama in the sense that it is made up of happenings and of action (to do, to act is the meaning of the Greek word 'drao', from which 'drama' comes). Thus, the *'dramatis personae'* discover the plot of this drama in themselves, perceive their love as a psychological situation unique of its kind, and one of great and absorbing importance in their inner lives. A person is, of course, among all the varied objects of the visible world, that unusual one which is endowed with an inner self of its own, and is capable of an inner life.

Psychology, which is, as its name indicates, the science of the soul, endeavours to lay bare the structure and the foundations of man's inner life. Its investigations serve to confirm that the most significant characteristics of that inner life are the sense of truth and the sense of freedom. Truth is directly connected with the sphere of cognition. Human cognition does not consist merely in reflecting or producing 'mirror images' of objects, but is inseparable from awareness of truth and falsehood. This it is that constitutes the innermost and most important nerve in the human cognitive process. If cognition consisted only in 'reflecting' objects one might suspect that it was material in character.[26] But awareness of truth and falsehood lies altogether outside the boundaries of that which matter can furnish. Truth is a condition of freedom, for if a man can preserve his freedom in relation to the objects which thrust themselves on him in the course of his activity as good and desirable, it is only because he is capable of viewing these goods in the light of truth and so adopting an independent attitude to them. Without this faculty man would inevitably be determined by them: these goods would take possession of him and determine totally the character of his actions and the whole direction of his activity. His ability to discover the truth gives man the possibility of self-determination, of deciding for himself the character and direction of his own actions, and that is what freedom means.

The psychological analysis of love between persons of different sex so far carried out has shown that it originates in the sexual instinct. This has its immediate consequences in an experience which, as we have already stated, in each of the two persons, the woman and the man, centres around a sexual value. This value is associated with a 'person of the other sex'. When it is connected primarily with the 'body' and exhibits a distinctive propensity to use the other person for enjoyment, the subject's feelings are dominated by sensual desire. When on the other hand a sexual value as the content of an experience is not primarily connected with the 'body', the emphasis shifts in the direction of sentiment and desire does not obtrude on the foreground. This experience may take any one of an enormous number of forms, according to the distribution of emphasis in the response to the sexual value. Each such form is strictly individual, because it takes shape in a specific interior, and also in specific external conditions. The dominant psychic energies will decide whether we have to do with a violent affection or with passionate desire.

This play of inner forces is fully mirrored in the consciousness. A salient feature of sexual love is its great intensity – which indirectly testifies to the force of the sexual instinct and its importance in human life. This intense concentration of vital and psychic forces so powerfully absorbs the consciousness that other experiences sometimes seem to pale and to lose their importance in comparison with sexual love. You only have to look closely at people under the spell of sexual love to convince yourself of this. Plato's thinking on the power of Eros is for ever being confirmed. If sexual love can be thought of as a situation internal to a person it is psychologically an intensely pleasurable situation. A man finds in it a concentration of energies which he did not know that he possessed before this experience. For this reason the experience is, for him, associated with pleasure, with the joy of existing, of living and acting – even if, from time to time, discomfort, sadness or depression break in on it.

These are the salient characteristics of love in its subjective aspect and it is in this form that it always constitutes a concrete situation internal to a human being, unique and unrepeatable. At the same time, however, it aims not only at integration 'within' the person but at integration 'between' persons. The Latin word 'integer' means 'whole' – so that 'integration' means 'making whole', the endeavour to achieve wholeness and completeness. *The process of integrating love relies on the primary elements of the human spirit – freedom and truth.*

Freedom and truth, truth and freedom determine the spiritual imprint which marks the various manifestations of human life and human activity. They penetrate the remotest recesses of human action and experience, filling them with a content of which we never meet the slightest trace in the lives of animals. It is to this content that love between persons of different sexes owes its special consistency. However powerfully and explicitly it is dependent on the body and the senses it is not the body and not the senses alone that form its peculiar base and its peculiar character. Love is always an interior matter, a matter of the spirit. To the extent to which it ceases to be an interior matter and a matter of the spirit it also ceases to be love. What remains of it, in the senses and in the sexual vitality of the human body, does not constitute its essential nature. The will is so to say the final authority in ourselves, without whose participation no experience has full personal value or the gravity appropriate to the experiences of the human person. The value of the person is closely bound up with freedom, and freedom is a property of the will. It is love, especially, that 'demands' freedom – the commitment of freedom is, in a sense, its psychological essence. That which does not derive from freedom, that which bears the marks not of free commitment, but of determination and compulsion, cannot be acknowledged as love, lacks its essential character. Therefore, the process of psychological integration which accompanies sexual love within a person involves not only commitment of the will, but unconditional commitment of the will, demands that the will should commit itself in the fullest possible way, and in a way proper to itself.

A really free commitment of the will is possible only on the basis of truth. The experience of freedom goes hand in hand with the experience of truth.[27] Every situation has its own psychological truth: sensual desire has one truth, emotional commitment another. It is a subjective truth: a man truly desires x, since he discovers in his inner life an explicit feeling, directed specifically towards her, originating in the impression which she has made on him – just as a woman may be truly committed emotionally to a man because she finds in her inner life such emotions, such a disposition to emotion, such a desire to be near and to lean upon him, resulting from the impression made by his male strength, that she must recognize her interior state as love. Looking at the matter in its subjective aspects, we have to do in both cases with true love.

Love, however, also insists on objective truth. Only thanks to this, only on this basis, can the integration of love take place. As long as we consider it only in the light of its subjective truth, we can obtain no full picture of it and can say nothing of its objective value. But this last is, after all, what matters most. It is this that we shall try to bring out by means of the ethical analysis of love.

THE ETHICAL
ANALYSIS OF LOVE

❦

Experience and Virtue

There exists in contemporary ethics a characteristic tendency which we call *situationism*. It is closely connected with existentialism in philosophy.[28] Human existence is made up of a whole series of situations each of which is supposed to furnish of itself a norm of action. Each concrete situation must be accepted and experienced in its totality, with no concern for anything outside it. Whatever is 'outside the situation' cannot, for that very reason, be introduced into it and applied to it. Human life admits of no general and abstract norms 'outside the situation' – these are too inflexible and 'essential', whereas life is always thoroughly concrete and existential. Applying these assumptions to our own problem, the love of man and woman, as a specific fragment of their existence (or co-existence), would be seen to be composed of a number of situations which in themselves decide its value. These psychological situations would fully determine the structure and content of sexual love. Every situation in the development of that love would be at the same time a norm beyond which nothing more and nothing deeper should be sought. This view proclaims the primacy of experience over virtue.

At the same time, however, the view described above contains a false conception of freedom. It has already been said that freedom of the will is possible only if it rests on truth in cognition. This is where the concept of duty comes in. For it is a man's duty to choose the true good. It is, indeed, duty that most fully displays the freedom of the human will. The will 'ought to' follow the true good, but this 'ought to' implies that it 'may' equally well not do so. Situationism and existentialism, which reject duty allegedly in the name of freedom, thereby deny themselves any real understanding of free will, or at any rate of that which most fully reveals it. For the freedom of the human will is most fully displayed in morality through duty. But duty always grows out of the contact of the will with some norm. Hence one should look for the complete integration of human love not on the terrain of psychology itself but in ethics.

Where love between man and woman is concerned we must admit two meanings of the word: love can be understood as a certain situation with a psychological significance, but it also has an ethical significance, and so is connected with a norm. The norm in question here is the personalistic norm: it finds expression in the commandment to love. Situationism, which recognizes no norm, falls into vulgar psychologism in its understanding of love. For love in the psychological sense must be subordinated in man to love in the ethical sense – otherwise there can be no question of integration properly so called. As a result *there is no possibility of psychological completeness in love unless ethical completeness is attained.* Whether we look at love as a concrete situation or as a whole series, a continuum of such situations, all of them separately and together are psychologically complete and 'integrated' to the extent that the ethical value of love is present in them. In other words, *love as experience should be subordinated to love as virtue,* – so much so that without love as virtue there can be no fullness in the experience of love.

It will then be as well for us to take a look at love as a virtue in the relationship between man and woman. We must here note at once that Christian morality, basing itself on the Gospels, knows love as a supernatural, a divine virtue. Let us take this as our starting point, and proceed to analyse primarily the way in which on the human level this virtue is formed and manifests itself in the woman:man relationship. For every supernatural virtue takes root in nature and assumes a human form as a result of man's own actions, both in his interior and in his external behaviour. We can therefore study and analyse it as an aspect of human nature, and bring out its moral value from that angle. This is the way in which we now intend to look at the love of man and woman. The fact that it is, that it must be, a virtue may be taken as established, as firmly as it can be, by all that the general and psychological analysis of love has previously shown. We must refer back to various elements of those two forms of analysis. We shall in particular try to bear in mind that love between woman and man can take the form here called 'betrothed love', since it leads to marriage. Taking all this into account, we shall try to discover in what way this love can realize itself as a virtue. It is difficult to show this in full for the virtue of love, which is a spiritual reality, is not open to observation – hence we shall try to identify those elements which are most important, and which also stand out most clearly in experience. The first and most basic of them appears to be affirmation of the value of the person.

Affirmation of the Value of the Person

The commandment to love is, as has been said, a form of the personalistic norm. We start from the existence of the person, and go on to acknowledge the peculiar value of the person. The world of existences is the world of objects: amongst them we distinguish between persons and things. *A person differs from a thing in structure and in degree of perfection.* To the structure of the person belongs an 'interior', in which we find the elements of spiritual life, and it is this that compels us to acknowledge the spiritual nature of the human soul, and the peculiar perfectibility of the human person. This determines the value of the person. A person must not be put on the same level as a thing (or for that matter as an individual animal): the person possesses spiritual perfectibility, and is by way of being an (embodied) spirit, not merely a 'body' magnificently endowed with life. Between the psyche of an animal and the spirituality of a man there is an enormous distance, an uncrossable gulf.

The value of the person as such must be clearly distinguished from the particular values present in a person.[29] These are either inborn or acquired, and are linked to the whole complex structure of human existence. These values, as we have seen, find expression in love between man and woman – the psychological analysis of love has already shown this. The love of man and woman is based on an impression accompanied by an emotion and always having as its object a value. In the given case we have to do with a 'sexual' value, since the love of man and woman originates in the sexual instinct. This 'sexual' value may be attached to a 'whole person of the other sex', or it may be more especially identified with that person's 'body' as a 'possible object of use'. The value of a person is bound up with the whole being of the person and not with his or her sex: sex is only an attribute of that being.

That being so, every person of the opposite sex possesses value in the first place as a person, and only secondarily possesses a sexual value. Psychologically, the love of woman and man is an experience at the core of which is a reaction to a sexual value. In the context of that experience the person is apprehended primarily as a human being of the other sex – even where there is no special emphasis on 'the body as a possible object of enjoyment'. But the mind is simultaneously aware of this 'human being of the other sex' as a person. This knowledge is of an intellectual, conceptual kind – the person as such is not the content of an impression, for no essence can be so contained. Since the 'person' is not the content of an impression, but only the object of conceptual knowledge, it follows that a reaction to the value of a person cannot be as immediate as a reaction to the sexual value connected with the 'body' of the specific person, or – looked at more broadly – with the total phenomenon constituted by a 'human being of the other sex' (man or woman). What is immediately contained in an impression, and what the mind subsequently discovers in it, affect the emotions differently. None the less, the truth that a 'human being of the other sex' is a person, 'some-one', as distinct from any 'thing', is ever present in the consciousness. This it is that awakens the need for the integration of sexual love, and demands that the *sensual and emotional reaction* to a 'human being of the other sex' be somehow adjusted to the knowledge that the human being concerned is a person.

So in every situation in which we experience the 'sexual' value of a person, love demands integration, meaning the incorporation of that value in the value of the person, or indeed its subordination to the value of the person. This is where we see clearly expressed the fundamental ethical characteristic of love: it is an affirmation of the person or else it is not love at all. If it is informed with a proper attitude to the value of the person – this attitude we have called here 'affirmation' – it is love in all its fullness, 'integral' love. Whereas if love is not instinct with this affirmation of the value of the person it is an unintegrated love, and properly speaking not love at all, although the reactions or experiences concerned may have the most 'amorous' (erotic) character possible.

This is particularly true of love between man and woman. Love in the full sense of the word is a virtue, not just an emotion, and still less a mere excitement of the senses. This virtue is produced in the will and has at its disposal the resources of the will's spiritual potential: in other words, it is an authentic commitment of the free will of one person (the subject), resulting from the truth about another person (the object).

Love as a virtue is oriented by the will towards the value of the person. The will, then, is the source of that affirmation of the person which permeates all the reactions, all the feelings, the whole behaviour of the subject.

Love as a virtue is connected with emotional love, and with the love contained in sensual desire. In the moral order there can be no question of slurring over or neglecting the 'sexual' values to which the senses and emotions react. Our concern is simply to bind these values tightly to the value of the person, since love is directed not towards 'the body' alone, nor yet towards 'a human being of the other sex', but precisely towards a person. What is more, it is only when it directs itself to the person that love is love. It cannot be called love when it directs itself merely to the 'body' of a person, for we see here only too clearly the desire to use another person, which is fundamentally incompatible with love. Nor yet is love really love when it is merely an emotional attitude to a human being of the other sex. As we know, this feeling, which relies heavily on an emotional response to 'femininity' or 'masculinity', may in time fade in the emotional consciousness of a man or a woman if it is not firmly tied to affirmation of the person – that specific person to whom the man owes his experience of 'femininity' or the woman her experience of 'masculinity'.[30]

Sexual sentiment is a continually shifting response to many experiences, to impressions obtained from many persons. In the same way, sensuality is a shifting response to many 'bodies' in the presence of which awareness of 'a potential object of enjoyment' is aroused. For this very reason love cannot be founded on sensuality alone or on sentiment alone. Each of these bypasses, so to speak, the real person, prevents, or at any rate is not conducive to, the affirmation of the person. This in spite of the fact that emotional love appears to bring one so close to another human being, and that human being so close to oneself. But even emotional love while bringing the 'human being' closer can easily miss the 'person'. We shall have to return to this in the present chapter, and also in Chapter III. For observation of life leads us to think that emotional love is kindled, particularly in people of a certain psychological make-up, by the phenomenon 'human being' itself, if it carries an adequate charge of 'feminity' or 'masculinity' – but such love does not in itself have the mature interior cohesion which knowledge of the full truth about the person, the object of love, necessarily brings.

Affirmation of the value of a person, in which the full truth about the object of love is reflected, must be allowed to take its place among the erotic experiences which originate in man's sensuality or his sensibility. Affirmation of the value of a person generally leads in two directions, thus indicating in a general way two main areas of sexual morality. It may point the way to control over those experiences whose immediate source is man's sensuality and emotionalism. This matter will be thoroughly discussed in Chapter III, 'The Person and Chastity'.

The other direction in which affirmation of the value of the person may lead is towards the choice of one's principal vocation in life. A person's vocation as a general rule involves another person or persons in his or her life. Obviously, when a man chooses a woman to be the companion of his whole life, he designates the person who will play a bigger part in his life than any other, and indicates the direction which his life vocation will take. There is the closest possible link between the two choices, so that the direction in which he feels himself called can only be an affirmation of that person's value. This too will be dealt with more particularly in Chapter IV, and especially in its second part.

Membership of One Another

In the metaphysical analysis of love it was stated that its true nature is most fully revealed in the gift of self by the person who loves to the beloved person. What we have called betrothed love has a specific quality of its own, which differentiates it from other forms and manifestations of love. We realize this just as soon as we understand what is meant by the value of the person. The value of a person, as was said above, is inseparable from the essential being of that person. By its nature, because it is what it is, the person is its own master (*sui juris*), and cannot be ceded to another or supplanted by another in another in any context where it must exercise its will or make a commitment affecting its freedom. (It is *alteri incommunicabilis*.) But love forcibly detaches the person, so to speak, from this natural inviolability and inalienability. It makes the person want to do just that – surrender itself to another, to the one it loves. The person no longer wishes to be its own exclusive property, but instead to become the property of that other. This means the renunciation of its autonomy and its inalienability. Love proceeds by way of this renunciation, guided by the profound conviction that it does not diminish and impoverish, but quite the contrary, enlarges and enriches the existence of the person. What might be called the law of *ekstasis* seems to operate here: the lover 'goes outside' the self to find a fuller existence in another. In no other form of love does this law operate so conspicuously as it does in betrothed love.

This is the direction which love between man and woman should take. We have drawn attention on a number of previous occasions to its psychological intensity. This intensity is explained not merely by the biological force of the sexual instinct, but also by the nature of that form of love which here shows itself. The sensual and emotional experiences which are so vividly present in the consciousness form only the outward expression and also the outward gauge of what is happening, or most certainly should be happening, deep inside the persons involved. Self-giving can have its full value only when it involves and is the work of the will. For it is free will that makes the person its own master (*sui juris*), an inalienable and untransferable 'some-one' (*alteri incommunicabilis*). Betrothed love, the love that is a gift of self, commits the will in a particularly profound way. As we know already, it means disposing of one's whole self, in the language of the Gospels, 'giving one's soul'.

For contrary to the superficial view of sex, according to which love (meaning here erotic love) culminates in a woman's surrender of her body to a man, we should rightly speak of the mutual surrender of both persons, of their belonging equally to each other. Not mutual sexual exploitation, with 'x' giving her body for 'y' to possess, so that each can obtain the maximum of sexual pleasure, but the reciprocated gift of self, so that two persons belong each to the other – this is the only full and satisfactory description of 'betrothed love', which finds its fulfilment in marriage. In the absence of these characteristics love is by definition impossible, and mere 'use' (in the first and second meanings of the word) takes its place. Love cannot take the form of mere use, even if enjoyment is mutual and simultaneous. Instead, it finds its proper expression in the union of persons. The result of unification is that each belongs to the other, a reality expressed in various ways, among them full sexual inter-course, which we shall call marital intercourse since, as we shall see, marriage is the only proper place for it.

From the ethical point of view the important thing here is not to invert the natural order of events, and not to deny any one of them its place in the sequence. The unification of the two persons must first be achieved by way of love, and sexual relations between them can only be the expression of a uni-fication already complete. It is worth recalling here what has already been said about the objective and the subjective aspects of love. Love in its subjective aspect is always a psychological situation, an experience caused by a 'sexual' value, and hinging on awareness of that value in the subject, or in two subjects experiencing love each for the other. Love in its objective aspect is an interpersonal fact, is reciprocity, and friendship based on a shared good – it is, then, always the unification of two persons, with the result that they belong to each other. We cannot substitute two subjective loves, or their sum, for this objective love – the subjective and objective aspects are distinct and not interchangeable.

The objective aspect is the decisive one. It takes shape in two subjects, obviously drawing upon the wealth of sensual and emotional experiences which belong to the subjective aspect of love – but it is not to be identified with them. Sensual experiences have their own dynamic of desire, which depends upon instinctive feeling and the sexual vitality of the body. Emotional experiences also have a rhythm of their own: they serve to create those positive moods in which a feeling of closeness to the beloved, of spontaneous under-standing, can flourish. Love, however, makes for unification through the reciprocal gift of self. This is a fact of great objective, indeed ontological, significance, and so belongs to the objective aspect of love. Sensual and emotional ex-periences are not to be identified with it, though they create the set of conditions in which it is realized in practice. Simul-taneously, however, there exists another problem, which is more or less the converse: how to maintain and consolidate this reciprocity between two persons, amidst so many

sensual and emotional reactions and experiences, characterized by great mobility and mutability.

At this point a problem on which some light has previously
been thrown arises yet again: sexual values, which in various
forms constitute the catalyst of sensual and emotional
eroticism, must be firmly welded in the consciousness and
the will to the value of the person – the person who provides
so to speak the material of those experiences. Only then
can we think of the unification of persons, and of their
belonging to each other. Without this, however, 'love' can
only have an erotic significance and not its true (personal)
significance: it can lead to sexual 'union' but with no war-
ranty in a true union of persons. Such a situation has a
utilitarian character; the decisive feature of the relationship
between the two persons is that they 'use' each other (with
particular reference to the second meaning of the word). One
person belongs to another as an object of use, and tries to
derive some pleasure from allowing that other to make use of
him or her. Such an attitude, on both sides, is utterly incompatible with love, and there can be here no question of the
unification of persons. Quite the contrary: all the conditions
exist for a conflict of interests between the two parties –
which is bound to break out sooner or later. Egoism – the
egoism of the senses or of the emotions – cannot forever be
concealed in the recesses of the fictitious structure which
with every appearance of good faith calls itself love. The
ricketyness of the structure must show itself in time. It is one
of the greatest of sorrows when love proves to be not what it
was thought to be, but its diagonal opposite.

Such disillusionments must be avoided. Betrothed love,
which carries within itself an inner need to make a gift of
one's own person to another human being (a need realized
between man and woman in surrender of the body and in a
full sexual relationship as well as in other ways) has a natural
grandeur of its own. The measure of this is the value of the
person who gives himself or herself, and not just the degree of
sensual and sexual enjoyment which accompanies the gift of
self. It is very easy, however, to confuse the essence of the
problem with what is really an indirect reflection of it. Take

away from love the fullness of self surrender, the completeness of personal commitment, and what remains will be a
total denial and negation of it. This subtraction, taken to its
conclusion, leads to what we call prostitution.

Betrothed love comprises on the one hand the gift of the
person, and on the other hand, acceptance of that gift. Implicit
in all this is the 'mystery' of reciprocity: acceptance must
also be giving, and giving receiving. Love is of its nature
reciprocal: *he who knows how to receive knows also how to
give* – I am, of course, speaking of a 'skill' which is characteristic of love, for there is also a 'skill' in giving and receiving
which is characteristic of egoism. The skill in giving and
receiving which is typical of love is exhibited by the man
whose attitude to a woman is informed by total affirmation of
her value as a person, and equally by the woman whose
attitude to a man is informed by affirmation of his value as a
person. This skill creates the specific climate of betrothed
love – the climate of surrender of the innermost self. Both
man and woman need this genuine capacity for affirmation of
the value of the person, if the gift of self is to be fully valid,
and equally if acceptance of the gift is to be valid. A woman is
capable of truly making a gift of herself only if she fully
believes in the value of her person and in the value as a person
of the man to whom she gives herself. And a man is capable of
fully accepting a woman's gift of herself only if he is fully
conscious of the magnitude of the gift – which he cannot be
unless he affirms the value of her person. Realization of the
value of the gift awakens the need to show gratitude and to
reciprocate in ways which would match its value. We can
also see here how essential it is for betrothed love, a love
which is a reciprocal giving of self, to contain the inner
structure of friendship.

At any rate it is only when we consider the question on the
plane of the person, and in the light of the essential value of
the person, that the full objective importance of betrothed
love, of the reciprocal gift of the self and of the membership of
man and woman in one another, becomes clear and comprehensible. We can go on discussing this theme from the
'position' of sexual values, and the play of emotions and

passions connected with them, for as long as we like, and we shall never see the problem in its correct perspective. Nor, if we proceed in that way, shall we ever understand those principles of sexual morality which are intimately linked with the commandment to love – an expression of the personalistic norm, as we have seen. The commandment itself and all its consequences stand out clearly only when we rise to the plane of the person, to the height of its true value.

Choice and Responsibility

Nowhere else in the whole book, perhaps, is its title, *Love and Responsibility*, more to the point than it is here. There exists in love a particular responsibility – the responsibility for a person who is drawn into the closest possible partnership in the life and activity of another, and becomes in a sense the property of whoever benefits from this gift of self. It follows that one also has a responsibility for one's own love: is it mature and complete enough to justify the enormous trust of another person, the hope that giving oneself will not mean losing one's own 'soul', but on the contrary enlarging one's existence – or will it all end in disillusionment? Responsibility for love clearly comes down to responsibility for the person, originates in it and returns to it. This is what makes it such an immense responsibility. But its immensity can only be understood by one who has a complete awareness of the value of the person. Anyone who is capable only of reacting to the sexual values connected with the person, and inherent in it, but cannot see the values of the person as such, will always go on confusing love and eros, will complicate his own life and that of others by letting the reality of love, its true 'relish' escape him. For this 'relish' as I have called it goes with a sense of responsibility for the person, a concern for the true good of the person – which is the quintessence of altruism in any form, and also an infallible sign of a broadening of one's own existence, in contact with that 'other I', that other existence, which are as near and dear as one's own. To feel responsibility for another person is to be full of concern, but it is never in itself an unpleasant or painful feeling. For it represents not a narrowing or an impoverishment but an enrichment and broadening of the human being. Love divorced from a feeling of responsibility for the person is a negation of itself, is always and necessarily egoism. *The greater the feeling of responsibility for the person the more true love there is.*

This truth throws a great deal of light on the problem of choice. We have not forgotten that when love between a man and a woman takes its natural course they give themselves each to the other, become each other's property. Before their love can take on its definitive form, become 'betrothed love', the man and the woman each face the choice of the person on whom to bestow the gift of self. Its consequence makes the choice a weighty matter. To choose a person is also to opt for 'betrothed' love, for the reciprocal gift of self. The object of choice is another person, but it is as though one were choosing another 'I', choosing oneself in another, and the other in oneself. Only if it is objectively good for two persons to be together can they belong to each other. For a human being is always first and foremost himself ('a person'), and in order not merely to live with another but to live by and for that other person he must continually discover himself in the other and the other in himself. Love is impossible for beings who are mutually impenetrable – only the spirituality and the 'inwardness' of persons create the conditions for mutual interpenetration, which enables each to live in and by the other.

In this connection a very interesting and complex subsidiary problem arises, which might be called the problem of the 'psychology of choice'. What psycho-physiological factors make two people feel that they are suited to one another, that it is right for them to be together and to belong to each other? Are there in all this any rules or regularities traceable to the psycho-physiological make-up of human beings? What part is played here by somatic and constitutional factors and what by temperament and character? These are fascinating questions, but it seems to us that though various attempts have been made to find an answer of more or less general applicability, the way in which such choices are made remains one of the secrets of human individuality. There are no rigid rules, and philosophy and ethics owe their authority as teachers of practical wisdom to their insistence on explaining the facts only to the extent that they can be explained. Such sciences as physiology, sexology, and medicine would do well to adopt the same rule, and thus help philosophy and ethics to carry out their practical tasks.

Starting from empirical premises we are bound to recognize that the choice of a person of the other sex as the object of betrothed love, and as the co-creator of that love by way of reciprocity, must depend to a certain extent on sexual values. This love must, of course, have a sexual aspect, must form the basis for the whole life together of two persons of different sex. Unless both parties respond to sexual values there is no possibility of all this. Sexual values, as we know, are connected not just with the impression made by 'the body as a possible object of enjoyment', but also with the total impression made by a 'human being of the other sex' – by the 'womanliness' or 'manliness' of that other person. This second impression is the more important, and also makes itself felt earlier in time: in a naturally healthy and unspoilt young person the first experiences relating to sexual values have to do with a 'human being of the other sex', and not primarily with a 'body as the possible object of enjoyment.' Where this latter interest is earlier and dominant, we have to do with a product of corruption – the breakdown of the natural sequence in the reaction to sexual values will make love, and especially the process of choosing a person to love, more difficult.

For the choice of a person is a process in which sexual values cannot function as the sole motive, or even – if we analyse this act of will thoroughly – as the primary motive. This would be at odds with the very concept of 'choosing a person'. If sexual values in themselves were the only or even the primary motive for choice, we could not speak of 'choosing a person', but only of choosing the opposite sex, as represented by a particular 'human being', or perhaps even by a 'particular body which is a potential object of enjoyment'.

Clearly, if we are to speak of choosing a person, the value of the person must itself be the primary reason for choice. Primary reason does not mean sole reason. A formulation in which it seemed to mean this would not satisfy the criteria of healthy empiricism, and would bear the imprint of an apriorism reminiscent of Kant's formalistic personalism. The person as such must be the real object of choice, not values associated with that person, irrelevant to his or her intrinsic value. To choose these would be the behaviour of, for instance, a man who has no thought for anything but the sexual values he finds in a woman. Such a choice is clearly utilitarian in character, and not on the level of love for a person. The sexual values which a man finds in a woman, or a woman in a man, must certainly help to determine the choice, but the person making it must in doing so be fully aware that what he or she is choosing is a person. So that although the sexual values in the object of choice may disappear, and however they may change, the fundamental value – that of the person – will remain. The choice is truly choice of a person when it treats that value as the most important and decisive one. So that if we consider the whole process by which a man chooses a woman or a woman a man, we can say that it is set in motion by recognition of and reaction to sexual values, but that in the last analysis each chooses the sexual values because they belong to a person, and not the person because of his or her sexual values.

Only such an act of choice can be considered fully valid. For only thus can proper integration of the object of choice take place: only then is the truth about the person fully apprehended. The truth about the object of choice is attainable when, for the chooser, the value of the person as such is that to which all others are secondary. Sexual values, which act upon the senses and the emotions, are assigned their proper place. Whereas if they were the sole or the main motive for choosing a person that choice would be faulty and invalid, since it would not conform to the full truth about the object of choice, the person. Such a choice is inevitably the starting point for a love incapable of integration, a love that is defective and invalid.

True love, a love that is internally complete, is one in which we choose the person for the sake of the person, – that in which a man chooses a woman or a woman chooses a man not just as a sexual 'partner' but as the person on whom to bestow the gift of his or her own life. 'Sexual' values, vibrantly present in their sensual and emotional reactions, contribute to the decision and make it a more intense psychological experience, but it is not they which determine its authenticity. The essential reason for choosing a person must be personal, not merely sexual. Life will determine the value of a choice and the value and true magnitude of love.

It is put to the test most severely when the sensual and emotional reactions themselves grow weaker, and sexual values as such lose their effect. Nothing then remains except the value of the person, and the inner truth about the love of those concerned comes to light. If their love is a true gift of self, so that they belong each to the other, it will not only survive but grow stronger, and sink deeper roots. Whereas if it was never more than a sort of synchronization of sensual and emotional experiences it will lose its *raison d'être* and the persons involved in it will suddenly find themselves in a vacuum. We must never forget that only when love between human beings is put to the test can its true value be seen.

When a person's choice is a mature and valid act and love is integrated as it should be in the inner life of the person it is transformed both in its psychological and in its emotional aspect. For while not only sensual but emotional experiences too are of their nature unstable and changeable – and this always causes a certain anxiety, even if it is not always conscious – a love which has matured within the subject frees itself from this anxiety by its choice of person. The emotion becomes serene and confident, for it ceases to be absorbed entirely in itself and attaches itself instead to its object, to the beloved person. The purely subjective truth of the emotion has given place to the objective truth about the person who is the object of choice and of love. As a result the emotion itself seems to acquire new properties. It becomes simpler and soberer. Whereas that idealization of which we spoke in our 'psychological analysis' is characteristic of purely emotional love – the emotions themselves tend to endow their object with various values of their own creation – the love for a person which results from a valid act of choice is concentrated on the value of the person as such and makes us feel emotional love for the person as he or she really is, not for the person of our imagination, but for the real person. We love the person complete with all his or her virtues and faults, and up to a point independently of those virtues and in spite of those faults. The strength of such a love emerges most clearly when the beloved person stumbles, when his or her weaknesses or even sins come into the open. One who truly loves does not then withdraw his love, but loves all the more, loves in full consciousness of the other's shortcomings and faults, and without in the least approving of them. For the person as such never loses its essential value. The emotion which attaches itself to the value of the person remains loyal to the human being.

The Commitment of Freedom

Only true knowledge of a person makes it possible to commit one's freedom to him or her. Love consists of a commitment which limits one's freedom – it is a giving of the self, and to give oneself means just that: to limit one's freedom on behalf of another. Limitation of one's freedom might seem to be something negative and unpleasant, but love makes it a positive, joyful and creative thing. *Freedom exists for the sake of love*. If freedom is not used, is not taken advantage of by love it becomes a negative thing and gives human beings a feeling of emptiness and unfulfilment. Love commits freedom and imbues it with that to which the will is naturally attracted – goodness. The will aspires to the good, and freedom belongs to the will, hence freedom exists for the sake of love, because it is by way of love that human beings share most fully in the good. This is what gives freedom its real entitlement to one of the highest places in the moral order, in the hierarchy of man's wholesome longings and desires. But man longs for love more than for freedom – freedom is the means and love the end. He longs however for true love, for only if it is based on truth is a genuine commitment of freedom possible. The will is free, but at the same time it 'is obliged to' seek the good which is congenial to it, it can seek and choose freely, but it is not free from the need to seek and to choose.

The will cannot, however, allow an object to be imposed upon it as a good. It wants to choose, and to affirm its choice, for itself, for choice is always the affirmation of the value of the object chosen. Thus, in choosing a woman a man affirms her value – and this means her value as a person, not merely her 'sexual' value. Sexual values, after all, tend to impose themselves, whereas the value of the person waits to be chosen and affirmed. For this reason the will of a man who has not yet succumbed to mere passion but has preserved his inner purity is usually the arena for a struggle between the sexual instinct and the need for freedom. The sexual instinct endeavours to impose its own object and its own aim, endeavours to create a fait accompli within the person. The term 'sexual instinct' is used here not in its proper and full sense, as it was understood in the preceding section, but in a more limited sense. I have in mind some of its manifestations as a result of which sexual values take possession of an individual's senses and emotions, and, so to speak, 'lay siege to' his will. When the will succumbs to sensual attraction it begins to feel desire for another person. Sentiment frees desire of its carnal, 'consumer' character, and gives it instead that of longing for 'a human being of the other sex.' Nevertheless, as long as the will merely capitulates to the object of sensual attraction and emotional yearning it cannot make its proper creative contribution to love.

The will loves only when a human being consciously commits his or her freedom in respect of another human being seen as a person, a person whose value is fully recognized and affirmed. This commitment does not consist primarily of desire for that human being. The will is a creative power capable of bestowing goods from within itself, and not only of appropriating goods which already exist. Willed love expresses itself above all in the desire of what is good for the beloved person. Desire for the person as such gives the will no opportunity to reveal its creative potential, it does not constitute love in the full positive meaning of the word. The will of its nature desires the good – the good without limits, which is happiness. In striving towards this it seeks out a person and desires that person as a concrete good which can bring happiness. Man desires woman, woman desires man: at this stage love is concupiscence. But the senses and the emotions come to its aid, and a love so assisted may easily be the occasion for the will, with its natural aspiration to the infinite good which is happiness, to start wanting this good for another person too, the person who is for the senses and the emotions an object of desire. And this is where the tension between the dynamic of the sexual urge and that of the will becomes evident. The sexual instinct makes the will desire and long for a person because of the person's sexual value. The will, however, does not stop at this. It is free, or in other words capable of desiring everything relating to the unqualified good, the unlimited good, that is happiness. And it commits this capacity, its natural and noble potentiality, to the other person concerned. It desires the absolute good, the unlimited good, happiness for that person, and in this way compensates and atones for the desire to have that other person, a person of the other sex, for itself.[31] We have here, of course, been speaking of the sexual urge only in one particular aspect. For the will does not merely combat the urge: it simultaneously assumes within the framework of betrothed love responsibility for the natural purpose of the instinct. This is of course the continuation of the human race, which concretely requires that a new person, a child, shall be the fruit of conjugal love between man and woman. The will makes this purpose its own, and in consciously working towards it seeks greater scope for its creative tendency.

In this way true love, profiting from the natural dynamic of the will, attempts to give the relationship between man and woman a thoroughly unselfish character, to free their love from utilitarian attitudes, whether we think of the first or the second meaning of the verb 'to use'. This is the significance of what we have called here the struggle between love and the sexual instinct. The sexual instinct wants above all to take over, to make use of another person, whereas love wants to give, to create a good, to bring happiness. We see yet again how important it is for betrothed love to be permeated with that which constitutes the essence of friendship. From the desire for the 'unlimited' good of another 'I' springs the whole creative drive of true love – the drive to endow beloved persons with the good, to make them happy.[32]

This is, so to speak, the divine aspect of love. In point of fact, to desire 'unlimited' good for another person is really to desire God for that person: He alone is the objective fullness of the good, and only His goodness can fill every man to overflowing. It is through its connection with happiness, with the fullness of the good, that human love comes closest to God. True, this 'fullness of good', this 'happiness', are not often expressly understood in this way. 'I want happiness for you' means 'I want that which makes you happy' – but I do not for the moment enquire what that may be. Only people of profound faith tell themselves quite clearly that 'this means God'. Others do not complete their thought, but leave a blank to be filled in as it were by the beloved person: happiness is whatever you yourself want, that in which you see the fullness of the good for yourself. The whole energy of love is then concentrated in the claim that 'it is I who truly desire this for you'.[33]

The great moral force of true love lies precisely in this desire for the happiness, for the true good, of another person. This is what makes it possible for a man to be reborn because of love, makes him aware of the riches within him, his spiritual fertility and creativity: I am capable of desiring the good for another person, therefore I am in general capable of desiring the good. True love compels me to believe in my own spiritual powers. Even when I am 'bad', if true love awakens in me it bids me seek the true good where the object of my love is concerned. In this way, affirmation of the worth of another person is echoed in affirmation of the worth of one's own person – for it is awareness of the value of the person, not of sexual values, that makes a man desire the happiness of another 'I'. When love attains its full dimensions, it introduces into a relationship not only a 'climate' of honesty between persons but a certain awareness of the 'absolute', a sense of contact with the unconditional and the ultimate. Love is indeed the highest of moral values. But one must know how to transfer it to the ordinary affairs of everyday life. This is where the problem of educating love arises.

The Education of Love

What does 'the education of love' mean? Can love be improved by education? Is not love something complete from the start, something given ready made to a human being or to two human beings, what might perhaps be called an adventure of the heart? This is a very common assumption, especially among young people, but it is one which tends to prevent what we have called here the integration of love. Love so conceived is merely a psychological situation, and it seems unnatural to subject it to the dictates of objective morality. This however is the opposite of the truth: love should be governed by a norm or principle from which the full value of every psychological situation must be deduced: only then will the situation attain its proper fullness, only then will it express a commitment of the person. For love is never something ready made, something merely 'given' to man and woman, it is always at the same time a 'task' which they are set. Love should be seen as something which in a sense never 'is' but is always only 'becoming', and what it becomes depends upon the contribution of both persons and the depth of their commitment. This commitment is based on what is 'given'. Experiences which have their roots in the sensuality or the natural sensibility of a woman or a man constitute only the 'raw material' of love. There exists a tendency to regard them as its finished form. This is a mistake, and at the bottom of it lies that utilitarian, 'consumer' outlook, which as we know is contrary to the very nature of love.

Man is a being condemned, so to speak, to create. Creativity is a duty in the sphere of love too. We find that what develops from 'promising' raw material in the form of emotions and desires is often not true love, and often indeed sharply opposed to it, whereas a truly great love sometimes develops from modest material. But such a great love can only be the work of persons and – let us add here to complete the picture – the work of Divine Grace. Their workings will be examined in this book. We shall examine love primarily as the work of man and try to trace the main directions which his efforts take. But the operation of Grace is implicit in these efforts, for they are the contribution of the invisible Creator who is Himself love, and has the power to fashion any love, including that which in its natural development is based on the values of sex and the body – provided that human beings are willing to be His conscious co-creators. There is no need to be dismayed if love sometimes follows tortuous ways. Grace has the power to make straight the paths of human love.

To answer our questions (what does 'educating love' mean and is it possible?) we must, I think, simply return to the arguments put forward in this chapter. We must also go into them more deeply in the light of the Gospel, interpreted more fully than it has been hitherto. But even at this point it is obvious that the education of love involves a variety of actions, which are for the most part interior though they find exterior expression, actions which are in any case profoundly personal. The purpose of these actions is what we have called here the integration of love 'within' the person and 'between' persons. These reflections on love have, however, repeatedly reminded us that there is an insidious possibility of disintegration in relationships between men and women. It is, therefore, essential to round off the discussion by showing clearly how the love of man and woman can guard against disintegration. This will be the purpose of our discussion of chastity.

CHAPTER III

The Person
and Chastity

✤

THE REHABILITATION
OF CHASTITY

*

Chastity and Resentment

The title of this paragraph is borrowed from M. Scheler, who has published a study called *The Rehabilitation of Virtue* (*Rehabilitierung der Tugend*). It may seem provocative. For we use the word rehabilitation with reference to someone or something which has lost his or its good name and become unacceptable. Rehabilitation restores that good name and right to respect. Has virtue, then, lost its good name? Has the virtue of chastity in particular ceased to be respectable? Or is chastity no longer recognized as a virtue? It is not just a question of reputation. The use of a noun, and lip service to it, are not decisive. What matters is whether virtue is made welcome in the human soul, the human will. If not it ceases to have any real existence. Mere respect for the words 'virtue' and 'chastity' has no great significance. Scheler saw a need for the rehabilitation of virtue because he discerned in modern man a characteristic spiritual attitude which is inimical to sincere respect for it. He has called this attitude 'resentment'.

Resentment arises from an erroneous and distorted sense of values. It is a lack of objectivity in judgement and evaluation, and it has its origin in weakness of will. The fact is that attaining or realizing a higher value demands a greater effort of will. So in order to spare ourselves the effort, to excuse our failure to obtain this value, we minimize its significance, deny it the respect which it deserves, even see it as in some way evil, although objectivity requires us to recognize that it is good. Resentment possesses as you see the distinctive characteristics of the cardinal sin called sloth. St Thomas defines sloth (*acedia*) as 'a sadness arising from the fact that the good is difficult'. This sadness, far from denying the good,

143

indirectly helps to keep respect for it alive in the soul. Resentment, however, does not stop at this: it not only distorts the features of the good but devalues that which rightly deserves respect, so that man need not struggle to raise himself to the level of the true good, but can 'light-heartedly' recognize as good only what suits him, what is convenient and comfortable for him. Resentment is a feature of the subjective mentality: pleasure takes the place of superior values.

Chastity, more than any other, seems to be the virtue which resentment has tended to outlaw from the soul, the will and the heart of man. A systematic case has been built up against it, which seeks to show that it is not beneficial but harmful to human beings. I need only recall in passing the various objections of an allegedly hygienic and medical nature made against chastity and sexual self control. The argument that 'exaggerated chastity' (it is difficult to determine what this means) is harmful to health – 'a young man must have sexual relief' – is always in fashion. But chastity and sexual continence are seen above all as dangerous enemies of love – and are for this reason denied respect and their rightful place in the human soul. Chastity, in this view, may have some point elsewhere, but not in the love of man and woman, where it must give way. It is arguments of this sort that particularly encourage the growth of resentment, which however is not something peculiar to our age – a tendency towards it is latent in the soul of every human being: Christianity regards this tendency as one of the results of original sin. If, therefore, we are to free ourselves from resentment, and in particular from its influence on our way of looking at this most important problem, we must find some way to rehabilitate chastity. To this end we must first of all eliminate the enormous accretion of subjectivity in our conception of love and of the happiness which it can bring to man and woman.

We know that love must be integrated, in each of the lovers independently and between them. This has been shown by the analysis carried out in the preceding chapter. By analysing love in three distinct aspects (the metaphysical, psychological and ethical) we succeeded in distinguishing a number of its elements. These elements must be correctly integrated both in each of the persons and between them so as to form a *personal and inter-personal whole.* This is why the function of integration is so important. Love cannot remain merely a subjective 'situation' in which sensual and emotional energies aroused by the sexual urge make themselves felt. If it does, it cannot rise to the level appropriate to persons, and cannot unite persons. For love to attain its full personal value, and truly to unite a man and a woman, it must be firmly based on the affirmation of the value of the person. From this, it is a simple progression to whole-hearted desire of the beloved person's good – a good worthy of the person. This it is that gives love its character of a 'bringer of happiness'. Men and women desire love in anticipation of the happiness which it can bring into their lives.

The longing for true happiness for another person, a sincere devotion to that person's good, puts the priceless imprint of altruism on love. But none of this will happen if the love between a man and a woman is dominated by an ambition to possess, or more specifically by concupiscence born of sensual reactions, even if these are accompanied by intense emotion. Such emotions give love a 'relish', but do not always contain its objective essence, which is inseparable from reciprocal affirmation of the value of the person. It is impossible to judge the value of a relationship between persons merely from the intensity of their emotions. The very exuberance of the emotions born of sensuality may conceal an absence of true love, or indeed outright egoism. Love is one thing, and erotic sensations are another. *Love develops on the basis of the totally committed and fully responsible attitude of a person to a person, erotic experiences are born spontaneously from sensual and emotional reactions.* A very rich and rapid growth of such sensations may conceal a love which has failed to develop. For this reason we have stressed the need to distinguish between its objective and subjective aspects in our analysis of love.

For the same reason we must consider very seriously the possible failure to integrate love. By this we mean that an erotic experience, or a complex of such experiences, originating in and maintained by the senses and the emotions, may fail to ripen into a feeling at the personal level. Non-integration means above all underdevelopment of the moral component of love.[37] Sensual or emotional reactions to a person of the other sex which arise before and develop more quickly than virtue are something less than love. They are however more often than not taken for love and given that name – and it is to love thus understood that chastity is hostile, and an obstacle.

We see then that this main argument against chastity – that it is a hindrance to love – takes insufficient account both of the principle of the integration of love, and also of the possibility of 'non- integration'.

Only the correct concentration of particular sensual and emotional elements around the value of the person entitles us to speak of love. We cannot give the name to that which is only a particular element or 'part' of it, for these components, if they are not held together by the correct gravitational pull, may add up not to love, but to its direct opposite. What is more, from the ethical point of view there is the following fundamental requirement: for the good of love, for the realization of its true nature in each of the persons and be-tween them, they must free themselves from those erotic sensations which have no legitimation in true love, that is in a relationship between a man and a woman based on a total affirmation of the value of the person. This demand takes us to the heart of the problem of chastity. The word 'chaste' ('clean') implies liberation from everything that 'makes dirty'. Love must be so to speak pellucid: through all the sensations, all the actions which originate in it we must always be able to discern an attitude to a person of the opposite sex which derives from sincere affirmation of the worth of that person. Since sensations and actions springing from sexual reactions and the emotions connected with them tend to deprive love of its crystal clarity – a special virtue is necessary to protect its true character and objective profile. This special virtue is chastity, which is intimately allied to love between man and woman. We shall try to demonstrate this by searching analysis, utilizing the results of our analysis of love itself in the preceding chapter. This will also help to make it clearer that the attempt to oppose chastity to love of which we so often hear is the fruit of resentment.

Carnal Concupiscence

It is worth recalling here the basic fact which we pointed out at the beginning of the book. Any association between the sexes, and especially cohabitation, comprises a whole series of 'actions', the subject of which is a person of one sex and the object a person of the other. Only love blurs this relationship – the subject-object relationship gives way to a unification of persons, in which the man and the woman feel themselves to be, as it were, the conjoint subject of action. This feeling expresses a subjective state of mind, which none the less reflects their objective unification: their wills are united in that they desire a single good as their aim, their emotions in that they react together and in the same way to the same values. The deeper and riper their union is, the more surely a man and a woman feel that they form a single subject of action. This feeling, however, does nothing to alter the objective fact that they are in reality two different beings and two different subjects of action – that in fact each of the two persons is the subject of a whole series of 'actions' the object of which is the other.

By 'actions' here we mean not only external acts (*actus externi*), i.e. those which can be perceived and identified by an outside observer, but also internal acts (*actus interni*), known only to their author, who alone can perceive and define them by introspection. Let us for our present purpose use the word 'actions', although it is as a rule applied only to external actions, in the broader sense of the Latin word *actus*.

The questions with which we are concerned in this book, and especially in this chapter, make necessary an examination both of external and of internal actions. The Decalogue addresses itself expressly to both types of action in two of the commandments: the sixth (Thou shalt not commit adultery) and the ninth (Thou shalt not covet thy neighbour's wife). These are actions which have as their object a person of the other sex – the person, and not merely the sex of the person, though it is the difference of sex which gives rise to this particular moral problem. For the person, being a person, must be the object of love. Whereas sex, which manifests itself above all in the body and impinges on the senses as a property of the body, may arouse concupiscence. Carnal concupiscence is closely linked with sensuality. The analysis of sensuality carried out in the preceding chapter showed that it typically reacts to 'the body as a possible source of enjoyment'. Sensuality reacts to sexual values connected specifically with 'the body' and this reaction has a 'directive' character. Nevertheless it is not to be identified with lust. It merely orients the whole psyche towards the sexual values, awakening an interest in or indeed an 'absorption' in them. It is a very easy transition from this first stage in a sensual reaction to the second, which is concupiscence. Concupiscence differs from mere sensual interest or even absorption in the sexual values connected 'with the body'. Where they are concerned, we may say that the values impinge upon the subject, while concupiscence implies that the subject actively seeks the value in question. Something in the subject begins to strive towards, to hanker after, that value. A spontaneous process is set up in the subject which culminates in the desire to possess the value. Sensual concupiscence is not yet the desire to possess, but has a marked tendency to develop into it. The obvious ease of transition from each stage to the next – from the arousal of interest to sensual concupiscence, from sensual concupiscence to carnal desire – is the source of great tensions in the inner life of the person: and it is in connection with them that the virtue of continence comes into action. The structure of that virtue, which we shall discuss separately later in this chapter, is closely related to the structure of carnal concupiscence, as we have just described it.

The term 'carnal concupiscence' is accurate because it has as its object the body and sex, and also because it arises in the subject from the body and seeks an outlet in 'carnal love'. It is perhaps worth noting here that there exists a difference between carnal love and 'love of the body' – for the body as a component of the person may also be an object of love and not merely of concupiscence.

The fact that the first, sensual reaction – interest in the sexual value connected with the body – so easily turns into the second reaction. i.e. into carnal desire – proves that desire exists as a force underlying sensuality, a force which quickly channels sensual reactions in the direction of concupiscence. This is how the matter was seen by St Thomas Aquinas, who clearly distinguishes two different forces: the *appetitus concupiscibilis* (desire) and *appetitus irascibilis* (the urge to act). These are, in his view, the two main powers of the sensual soul (*anima sensitiva*), most closely connected with sensual cognition. Around them cluster a whole constellation of 'feelings' (St Thomas's *passiones animae*). Thus, some human feelings are characterized rather by desire (thirst is an example), others by the impulse to act (anger, for example). By feelings, we mean here both the first stirrings of feeling and certain more sustained emotional states, within which we can discern different degrees of intensity (from a mere velleity to an insane passion, from for instance a gentle affection to a violent amorous rage, from a slight irritation to an ungovernable outburst of fury, etc.).

When carnal desire is not kept within the bounds of the *appetitus concupiscibilis* but communicates itself to the will, on which it tries to impose its own characteristic attitude to the object, it orients the subject first towards 'the body and sex' and secondly toward 'enjoyment'. These are the objectives of sensual concupiscence, and so of carnal love. It seeks satisfaction in 'the body and sex', by way of enjoyment. As soon as it achieves its ends, its attitude to the object changes completely, all 'interest' in it disappears until desire is aroused again. Sensuality is 'expended' in concupiscence. The word is appropriate here because carnal concupiscence is oriented towards finding an outlet. whereupon the attitude to the object of desire abruptly changes. In the animal world, where sexual life is governed by the procreative instinct, which is geared to the need to preserve the species, nothing is lost when a carnal reaction ends in this way. But in the world of persons a serious danger of a moral nature arises when this happens.

This danger is bound up with the problem of love, and so with the attitude to the person. 'Carnal love' born of carnal concupiscence alone lacks the value which love for the person must contain. It substitutes for what should be the object of love, the person, a different object, namely 'the body and sex' of a person. The sensual reaction, as we know, does not relate to the person qua person, but only to 'the body and sex' of a concrete person, and to these specfically as 'a possible object of enjoyment'. This means that a person of the other sex is discerned by active desire resulting from carnal concupiscence not as a person but as 'body and sex'. The sexual value as such usurps the place of the personal value which is essential to love, and becomes the core around which the whole experience crystallizes. But since this experience is accompanied by a sensual feeling of love, desire acquires the character of an amorous experience, and an intense and powerful one at that, since it is strongly rooted in the sexual reactions of the body and in the senses. When we speak of a 'sensual feeling of love' we are not thinking of an emotional reaction proper, since emotionally people react not to 'the body and sex' but to 'a human being of the other sex' – to 'masculinity' or 'femininity', as the analysis in Chapter II made clear. 'Feeling' means here the sensual state caused in the first place by desire for the body and sex as the appropriate objects of sensuality, and in the second place by satisfaction of that desire through 'bodily love'.

We can now see where the moral danger of carnal concupiscence lies. It leads to a 'love' which is not love, a love which provokes erotic feelings based on nothing but sensual desire and its satisfaction. These feelings have as their object a person of the other sex, yet do not rise to the level of the person, since they do not go beyond 'the body and sex', as their proper and sole content. The result is the 'non-integration' of love. Carnal concupiscence impels, very powerfully impels, people towards physical intimacy, towards sexual intercourse, but *if this grows out of nothing more than concupiscence it does not unite a man and a woman as persons*, it does not have the value of a personal union, and is not love in the true (i.e. the ethical) sense. On the contrary, physical intimacy (sexual intercourse) which grows out of concupiscence and nothing more is a negation of the love of persons, for it rests on the impulse to 'enjoy' which is characteristic of pure sensuality. That impulse must be tied into a correct and respectful attitude to the person – this is what we mean by integration. Carnal concupiscence left to itself is not a source of love for the person, although it evokes amorous (erotic) experiences which carry a powerful charge of sensual feeling.

There is here a serious possibility not only that love will be deformed, but also that its natural raw material will be squandered. For sensuality furnishes love with 'material', but material which can only be shaped by the appropriate creative activity on the part of the will. Without this there can be no love, there is only the raw material which is used up by carnal concupiscence as it seeks an 'outlet'. This results in actions, interior and exterior, which have as their sole object the sexual values connected with a person, and which take the direction typical of mere sensuality – 'the body as a possible object of enjoyment'. Their relation to the person is therefore a utilitarian, a 'consumer' approach. They make the person an object of enjoyment. Whether the acts are purely internal or partly external depends in large measure on the sensual make-up of the person concerned.

Emotion serves to some extent as a natural safeguard against carnal concupiscence. We know already from the analysis carried out in the previous chapter that emotion in this context is the capacity to react to a sexual value, but to that which goes with the 'human being of the other sex' as a whole, to femininity or masculinity, not to 'the body as a possible object of enjoyment'. Sentimental reactions also have a specific orientation, but it is different from that of sensual reactions. Sentiment is not, itself, oriented towards the enjoyment which has 'the body and sex' as its object, and seeks its outlet in 'carnal love'. We sometimes speak of the need for emotional outlets but there is no real analogy here with sensual or sexual release. We have in mind, rather, the satisfaction of a need to feel emotion for its own sake, a need to 'be in love' with someone, or to be the object of someone else's emotion ('to be loved'). Sentiment has a world of its own, a world of interior happenings, and happenings between people, which have nothing to do with carnal concupiscence. Sentimental love seems so pure that any comparison of it with sensual passion is thought of as degrading and brutalizing it.

Sentimental love is not, however, a full and positive solution to the problem of concupiscence. At most, it removes that problem from the field of consciousness, by introducing into the attitude of a woman to a man, or a man to a woman, that tendency to idealize of which we spoke in the previous chapter. But idealization is an evasion of the problem, not an attempt to face and solve it. Experience tells us that a one-sidedly 'idealistic' approach to love is often the source of bitter disappointments later on, and that it results in decidedly erratic behaviour, especially in conjugal life. What emotion brings into the relationship between man and woman is only the 'raw material' of love. Complete security against carnal concupiscence is something we find only in the profound realism of virtue, and specifically the virtue of chastity. But emotion, and the 'idealization' of man by woman and woman by man to which it gives rise, may help greatly in the formation of the virtue of chastity. However, even the most delicate natural reactions to 'femininity' or 'masculinity', of sentimental origin, do not of themselves create a sufficiently firm foundation for love of the person.

Indeed there is some danger that concupiscence will swallow up these reactions, appropriate them as a sort of 'accompaniment' to screen its own characteristic attitude to a person of the other sex. 'Love' in this version will be primarily a matter for the body, and governed by concupiscence, though it may be enriched by a 'lyricism' deriving from sentiment. It should be added that sentiment which is not reinforced by virtue but left to its own resources, with the mighty force of concupiscence behind it, is most often reduced to that role. It does of course add a certain novelty: it makes of love a sort of subjective 'taboo', in which sentiment is everything and decides everything.

Subjectivism and Egoism

This brings us to the problem of subjectivism, for emotion more than anything else introduces a subjective element into love between people. We must distinguish emotion from sensibility. By sensibility we mean the ability to react to specific values connected with a 'person of the other sex' (to 'femininity' or 'masculinity', 'charm' or 'strength'). Whereas emotion is a subjective psychological fact, connected with the reaction to different values – and so connected also with the actions performed as a consequence of that reaction, as, so to speak, an extension of it. So then sensual and carnal feelings are linked with sensual reactions and with actions, exterior or interior, which have their source in concupiscence. They are also linked with emotional reactions and the actions to which those reactions provide the stimulus. When we speak of the need for integration, or the need to establish correct connections between all that originates in sensuality or emotion, so that it is part of an ethically complete relationship between two persons, we take full account of the plasticity of human emotions. Emotion can develop and adapt itself to the shape which a man consciously wills. The integration of love requires the individual consciously and by acts of will to impose a shape on all the material that sensual and emotional reactions provide. He must by unqualified affirmation of the value of the person place all this on the level of an interpersonal relationship and keep it within the limits of a true union of persons.

Subjectivism is fundamentally different from subjectivity in love. Subjectivity is in the nature of love, which involves two subjects, man and woman. Subjectivism, on the other hand, is a distortion of the true nature of love, a hypertrophy of the subjective element such that the objective value of love is partially or wholly swallowed up and lost in it. The first form of subjectivism can be defined as emotional subjectivism. Emotions play an enormous part in the development of the subjective aspect of love – it is impossible to imagine the subjective aspect of love without emotion. It would be absurd to want love to be 'free of emotion', as the Stoics and Kant did. On the other hand, we must not overlook the possibility that emotion may be excessively subjective. We can indeed say that emotion has its dangers, that they may be a threat to love. We have already pointed out in our analysis of attraction (Section 2 of Chapter II) that emotion may affect our apprehension of the truth. Man – a reasonable being – has a natural need to know the truth and to obey it: I mean the objective truth of action, which is the core of human morality. Now, emotion as it were diverts 'the gaze of truth' from the objective elements of action, from the object of the act and the act itself, and deflects it towards what is subjective in it, towards our feelings as we act. The effect of emotion is that the consciousness is preoccupied above all with the subjective 'authenticity' of experience. It is supposed true or 'genuine' to the extent that it is imbued with genuine (sincere) emotion.[35]

This fact has two consequences:

i) a certain 'dis-integration' may take place, since the immediate emotion overshadows the totality of other, objective, factors, and the principles which govern them – it detaches itself from the rest;

ii) those objective principles by which the value of a given act is measured are replaced by the value of the emotion itself, and it becomes the main criterion by which an act is evaluated: an act is good because it is 'authentic' or in other words imbued with 'true' emotion. But emotion in itself has only a subjective truth; genuine emotion may inform an act which objectively is not good. This also means that emotional objectivism in the love of man and woman opens wide the way to acts, interior and exterior, which though as emotional experiences they have an 'amorous' (erotic) character are incompatible with the true nature of love. Their 'authenticity', in the sense defined above, is supposed to legitimate these experiences. But of course the emotions which accompany mere carnal desire are also 'true' feeings, subjectively just as authentic as any others.

The road from this form of subjectivism, subjectivism of emotions, to subjectivism of values, is a straight and easy one – so easy that once a man has set foot on the inclined plane of subjectivism it is hard to see how he can stop half way. Love itself is oriented towards *objective values*, first among them *the value of the person, which both partners in love affirm*, and the union of persons to which love leads. Those values to which the senses and the sentiments naturally react are also objective – the values associated with 'the body as a possible object of use', and with the 'masculinity' or 'femininity' of 'a human being of the other sex'. Subjectivism means regarding these objective values – the person *qua* 'body and sex', 'femininity/masculinity' – solely and exclusively as the source of pleasure and a varied range of enjoyments. Pleasure becomes the only value, and the only scale by which we measure values. The result is a confusion, a disorientation of feelings and actions so serious that it ends by destroying completely not only the essence of love, but even the erotic character of the experiences in question.[36] For love must be unambiguously directed to the person, and even sensuality and sentiment, which supply love with 'raw material', are natural reactions to the corresponding values connected with the person. Whereas *subjectivism of values means fixation on pleasure alone*: pleasure is the end, and all else – the 'person', that person's 'body', 'femininity' or 'masculinity' – is only a means to it.

This form of subjectivism, then, destroys the very essence of love, and finds the whole value of erotic experiences (and indeed of love in general) in pleasure. Amorous (erotic) experiences give men and women intense pleasure, and a varied range of enjoyments, which are the sole *raison d'etre* both of the particular experiences and – indirectly – of the love between man and woman itself. Hedonism, in theory and practice, is the end result of subjectivism in love. When this point is reached, it is no longer the real immediate experience itself but the pleasure accompanying it that dominates the whole situation, including the principles which determine whether love is authentic. Pleasure becomes the exclusive and unconditional value to which all else must be subordinated, for it is the interior criterion by which all human acts are valued. This recalls the utilitarianism which we examined critically in Chapter I. Here the 'dangers of emotion' are more obvious than ever, since emotion is of its very nature biased in the direction of pleasure: pleasure is to it a good, just as pain is an evil to be shunned. While emotion tends to assert itself as the exclusive and proper content of love (emotional subjectivism), it will, unless controlled, indirectly impel the subject to seek pleasure and enjoyment. But when that happens love itself is judged and valued according to whether it affords such pleasure.

Subjectivism in both forms, but especially in the second, is the soil in which egoism grows. Both subjectivism and egoism are inimical to love – in the first place because love has an objective orientation, towards the person and the good of the person, and in the second place because love is altruistic, it is directed towards another human being. Subjectivism, on the contrary, is exclusively concerned with the subject and the 'authenticity' of the subject's feelings, the affirmation of love through those feelings alone. *The egoist is preoccupied to the exclusion of all else with his own 'I', his ego, and so seeks the good of that 'I' alone, caring nothing for others*. Egoism precludes love, as it precludes any shared good, and hence also the possibility of reciprocity, which always presupposes the pursuit of a common good. Putting your own ego first, keeping your eyes fixed on it alone – and this is characteristic of egoism – always means an exaggerated concern with the subject.

One's own 'I', considered primarily as a subject, becomes egoistic when we cease to see correctly its objective position amongst other beings, its connections and its interdependence with them. The second form of subjectivism in particular, subjectivism of values, cannot in the nature of things be anything except egoism. If the only value involved in the attitude of a man and a woman to each other is pleasure there can be no question of reciprocity or of the union of persons. The fixation on pleasure as their purpose restricts each of them to the confines of his or her 'I'. There can therefore be no reciprocity, but only 'bilateralism': there exists a quantum of pleasure deriving from the association of two persons of different sex, which must be so skilfully shared between them that each obtains as much as possible. Egoism excludes love, but permits calculation and compromise – even though there is no love there can be a bilateral accommodation between egoisms.

In these circumstances there cannot, however be any question of a 'common I', of the sort which comes into being when one of the persons desires the good of the other as his own and finds his own good in that of the other person.[37] It is not possible to desire pleasure itself in this way, because it is a purely subjective good, not trans-subjective, nor even inter-subjective. At most we can want another's pleasure 'besides' and always 'on condition of' our own pleasure. So, then, the subjectivism of values, the fixation on pleasure for its own sake, as the exlcusive end of the association and cohabitation of man and woman, is necessarily egoistic. This results from the very nature of pleasure. But this does not at all mean that we must see pleasure itself as evil – pleasure in itself is a specific good – but only points to the moral evil involved in fixing the will on pleasure alone. For such a fixation is not only subjective but also egoistic.[38]

People sometimes talk about the 'egoism of the senses' and the 'egoism of the emotions'. This distinction rests on the differentiation between sensuality and sensibility as two distinct foci of reaction to sexual values. None the less, feeling is at the base of each of these egoisms, in the first case a physical, sensual feeling, connected with sensual satisfaction, in the second the more subtle psychological feeling which accompanies emotional reactions. Emotion, whether as a 'strong' sensation, or as a more durable state of feeling, favours concentration on one's own 'I', which means that pleasure makes its appearance as an emotionally charged good for that 'I'.

The egoism of the senses is more closely connected with subjectivism of values. The subject aims directly at the pleasure which erotic experiences connected with 'the body and sex' can provide – and the person is quite unambiguously treated as an 'object'. This form of egoism is easy to see through. The egoism of the emotions is not so transparent and it is therefore easier to be confused by it. It is linked above all with emotional subjectivism, in which emotion for its own sake, not pleasure, is the centre of attention. The authenticity of the experience is determined by the emotion. The egoism of the emotions is then in search of an 'ego' rather than of pleasure. Yet here too pleasure is the final end: the fixation on pleasure is in the last resort what makes it egoism. The pleasure involved here is inherent in the experience, the awareness of the emotion itself. When an emotion becomes an end in itself, merely for the sake of the pleasure it gives, the person who causes the emotion or to whom it is directed is once again a mere 'object' providing an opportunity to satisfy the emotional needs of ones own 'ego'. The egoism of emotion, which often comes close to being a sort of game (we 'play with someone else's feelings'), is a no less drastic distortion of love than the egoism of the senses, the only difference being that the latter is more obviously egoistic, while the former can more easily disguise itself as love. Let us add that emotional egoism can be the cause of unchastity in a relationship between the man and woman just as surely as sensual egoism, though in a different way.

We began this discussion by distinguishing between subjectivism and subjectivity. Love is always a subjective and inter-subjective fact, it has a subjectivity peculiar to itself. At the same time it must be protected from subjectivist distortion, or else the tendency to disintegrate will insinuate itself, and various forms of egoism supervene. Therefore both persons involved, while cultivating as intensively as they can the subjective aspect of their love, must also endeavour to achieve objectivity. Combining the one with the other requires a special effort, but this is unavoidable labour if the existence of love is to be assured.[39]

The Structure of Sin

The analysis of concupiscence, and perhaps even more that of the problems of subjectivism and egoism, will enable us to understand the concept of 'sinful love'. This expression is frequently encountered, and superficially seems to be apt. Yet it embodies a profound paradox. For love is a synonym of the good, while sin means moral evil. There can however be a 'love' which is not only not morally good, but is on the contrary 'sinful', contains within itself the seeds of moral evil. How then can it be love? We have said that sensuality and emotionalism furnish so to speak, 'raw material for love', i.e. they create states of feeling 'within' persons, and situations 'between' persons favourable to love. None the less, these 'situations' are not quite love. They become love only as a result of integration, or in other words by being raised to the personal level, by reciprocal affirmation of the value of the person. Without this, the psychological states born of sensuality alone (or for that matter emotion alone) may easily become the 'raw material' of sin. We must have a clear view of the way in which sin may be produced from this raw material. We must therefore now examine the structure of sin.

Concupiscence – as has already been shown – does not mean only the natural faculty of carnal desire, that is to say orientation towards those values to which, in the context of sex, the senses respond. Concupiscence is a consistent tendency to see persons of the other sex through the prism of sexuality alone, as 'objects of potential enjoyment'. Concupiscence, then, refers to a latent inclination of human beings to invert the objective order of values. For the correct way to see and 'desire' a person is through the medium of his or her value as a person. We should not think of this manner of seeing and desiring as 'a-sexual', as blind to the value of 'the body and sex'; it is simply that this value must be correctly integrated with love of the person – love in the proper and full sense of the word. Concupiscence, however, looks upon a person as 'a potential object for use' precisely because of this value of 'the body and sex' (whereas the body as a component of the person should itself be an object of love only because of the value of the person) – *hence the distinction between 'love of the body' and 'carnal love'.*

Concupiscence is then in every man the terrain on which two attitudes to a person of the other sex contend for mastery. The object of the struggle is 'the body', which because of its sexual value ('body and sex') arouses an appetite for enjoyment, whereas it should awaken love because of the value of the person, since it is after all the body of a person. Concupiscence itself means a constant tendency merely to 'enjoy', whereas man's duty is to 'love'. This is why the view formulated in our analysis of love – that sensuality and emotion furnish the 'raw material' of love – needs some qualification. This happens only to the extent that sensual and emotional reactions are not swallowed up by concupiscence but absorbed in true love. This is difficult, especially where sensual reactions are concerned, for as we have said these are spontaneous, and they urge us in the same direction as concupiscence – so much so that sensual reactions are in some measure the cause of concupiscence. Sensuality is the capacity to react to the sexual value connected with the body as a 'potential object of enjoyment', while concupiscence is a permanent tendency to experience desire caused by sensual reactions.

If we are considering the structure of sin (as part of our analysis of 'sinful love') it must however be emphasized that neither sensuality nor carnal desire is in itself a sin. Catholic theology sees in concupiscence only the 'germ of sin'. It is difficult to deny that the germ of sin is present in the constant tendency to lust after the body of a person of the other sex as 'an object of enjoyment', when our attitude to persons should be supra-utilitarian (this is implicit in the concept of 'love'). This is why theology, basing itself on Revelation, sees carnal desire as a consequence of original sin. This constant tendency to improper and incorrect attitudes to the person determined by the sexual values of the body, must have a cause. The absence of a cause would be grounds for pessimism, like any incomprehensible evil. The truth of original sin explains a very basic and very widespread evil – that a human being encountering a person of the other sex does not simply and spontaneously experience 'love', but a feeling muddied by the longing to enjoy, which often overshadows 'loving kindness' and robs love of its true nature, leaving only the outward appearance intact. So then it is not altogether safe to put one's trust in the reactions of the senses (or even those of emotions, which have more or less the same source in the psychological life of the human being), they cannot be acknowledged as love, but only as something from which love must be obtained. There is in this a certain hardship, since any human being would like simply to follow his spontaneous inclinations, to find love fully present in all of his reactions which have another human being as their object.

Neither sensuality nor even concupiscence is a sin in itself, since only that which derives from the will can be a sin – only an act of a conscious and voluntary nature (*voluntarium*). Although the act of will is always interior, both interior and exterior actions may be inherently sinful, since they all originate in and are sustained by the will. Further, a sensual reaction, or the 'stirring of' carnal desire which results from it, and which occurs irrespectively and independently of the will, cannot in themselves be sins. No, we must give proper weight to the fact that *in any normal man the lust of the body has its own dynamic*, of which his sensual reactions are a manifestation. We have drawn attention to their appetitive character. The sexual values connected with the body of the person become not only an object of interest but – quite easily – the object of sensual desire. The source of this desire is the power of concupiscence (*appetitus concupiscibilis* as St Thomas calls it), and so not the will. Concupiscence of the senses tends to become active 'wanting', which is an act of will.[40] The dividing line between the two is however clear. Concupiscence does not immediately aim at causing the will fully and actively to want the object of sensual desire: passive acquiescence suffices.

Here we stand on the threshold of sin, and we see that concupiscence, which seeks continually to induce the will to cross it, is rightly called the 'germ of sin'. As soon as the will consents it begins actively to want what is spontaneously 'happening' in the senses and the sensual appetites. From then onwards, this is not something merely 'happening' to a man, but something which he himself begins actively doing – at first only internally, for the will is in the first place the source of interior acts, of interior 'deeds'. These deeds have a moral value, are good or evil, and if they are evil we call them sins.

In practice there is here a problem which some people sometimes find quite dificult, *the problem of the boundaries of sin*. Objectively, the dividing line is drawn by acts of will, by conscious and voluntary assent of the will. But there are people who have difficulty in identifying the border line. Concupiscence in human beings has its own dynamic, by which it endeavours to become a conscious desire, an act of will, and hence anyone who lacks the proper power of discrimination may easily take as an act of will what is only the prompting of the senses and of carnal desire.[41] A sensual reaction follows its own course for a time, thanks to the dynamic inherent in concupiscence, even when the will not only does not assent but expressly opposes it. An act of will directed against a sensual impulse does not generally produce any immediate result. In its own (psychological) sphere a sensual reaction generally runs its full course even if it meets emphatic opposition in the sphere of the will. No-one can demand of himself either that he should experience no sensual reactions at all, or that they should immediately yield just because the will does not consent, or even because it declares itself definitely 'against'. This is a point of great importance to those who seek to practice continence. There is a difference between 'not wanting' and 'not feeling', 'not experiencing'.

It follows then that in analysing the structure of sin we must not attach too much importance to sensuality as such nor yet to concupiscence. A spontaneous sensual reaction, a carnal reflex, is not in itself a sin, nor will it become sin, unless the will leads the way. And if the will conduces to sin it is because it is wrongly oriented, and is guided by a false conception of love. Here lies the temptation which opens the way to 'sinful love'. Temptation is not just 'wrong thinking', for involuntary error does not give rise to sin. If I believe that A is good, and I do A, I act well even if A is really bad.[42] Temptation however presupposes an awareness that 'A is bad' which is somehow falsified so as to suggest that 'A is good after all'. Subjectivism in all its guises creates opportunities for such chicanery in relations between the sexes.

Emotional subjectivism makes us susceptible to the suggestion that whatever is connected with 'genuine emotion', whatever must be recognized as 'authentic' in its emotional content, is good. Hence the temptation to reduce love to nothing more than subjective emotional states. If we do this, love finds its whole content and sole criterion in emotion. The affirmation of the value of the person, the aspiration to the person's true good, to union in a common true good – none of these things exist for a will subjectivistically fixed upon emotion as such. In these circumstances sin arises from the fact that a human being does not wish to subordinate emotion to the person and to love, but on the contrary to subordinate the person and love to emotion. 'Sinful love' is often very emotional, saturated in emotion, which leaves no room for anything else. Its sinfulness is not of course due to the fact that it is saturated with emotion, nor to the emotion itself, but to the fact that the will puts emotion before the person, allowing it to annul all the objective laws and principles which must govern the unification of two persons, a man and a woman. *'Authenticity' of feeling is quite often inimical to truth in behaviour.*[43]

Subjectivism in values insinuates yet another false suggestion: that what is pleasant must be good. The temptations of pleasure, of enjoyment often replace the vision of true happiness. This happens when the will is intent on the quest for pleasure as such. Once again temptation is not merely an 'error in thinking' – ('I thought this would be lasting happiness but it was only a fleeting pleasure') – but results from a disposition of the will, which wants unconditionally the pleasure desired by the senses. It is in these circumstances that love is most likely to degenerate into the gratification of carnal desire. Concupiscence and the spontaneous 'stirrings' of lust are not in themselves sinful. What makes them sinful is the deliberate conscious self-commitment of the will to the promptings of the body, which conflicts with objective truth. The will may obviously succumb temporarily to concupiscence – we sometimes call this the sin of weakness. But it succumbs only as and when it sees its good in pleasure itself – and that to such an extent that pleasure overshadows all else: the value of the person, and the value of a genuine unification of two persons in love.

The suggestion that 'what is pleasant is good' if it comes to govern the whole activity of the will completely perverts it. It results in an habitual incapacity for 'loving kindness' towards a person – the will to love is lacking. Love as a virtue is ousted from the will and replaced by a preoccupation with sensual and sexual enjoyment. The will has no contact with the value of the person, it lives by the negation of love, putting up no resistance to concupiscence.

Where the will is so oriented, concupiscence, the 'germ of sin', flourishes quite freely, for it finds in the will no countervailing force in the affirmation of the value of the person and the pursuit of that person's true good. 'Sinful love' comes into being when affirmation of the value of the person, and intentness on the true good of the person, (which are at the core of true love), are absent, and instead a hankering after mere pleasure, mere sensual enjoyment connected with 'sexual experiences' invades the relationship between man and woman. 'Enjoying' then displaces 'loving'. The moral evil embodied in sin consists, of course, in the treatment of one person by another, or of each of the partners by the other, as an 'object of enjoyment'.

Erotic experiences as such do not, for a time at least, reveal this orientation towards 'enjoyment'. They endeavour as best they can to preserve the 'flavour of love'. Hence the avoidance of reflection: it often creates an irresistible need to objectivize – which would make the sinfulness of the love in question immediately evident. Here the evil of subjectivism in the attitude of the will makes itself felt: we see that it is not just an error of thinking but a distortion of the whole direction of action. If one of the parties achieves objectivity, and especially if both of them simultaneously do so, they must correctly define what exists between them. Whereas a subjective orientation of the will not only makes true love unrealizable, because of an exaggerated fixation upon the subject, but also suggests that the subjective state of being saturated in emotion is love at its fullest and most perfect, is 'everything' that love has to offer. An orientation towards the subject is usually accompanied by a preoccupation with one's own 'I'. Subjectivism is commonly the origin of egoism – though this egoism (egoism of the senses) – is experienced as 'love', and is often so called, just as what is only a particular form of 'enjoying' the person was called 'loving'.

The particular danger of 'sinful love' consists in a fiction: immediately, and before reflection, it is not felt to be 'sinful', but it is, above all, felt to be love. The direct effect of this circumstance, it is true, is to reduce the gravity of the sin, but indirectly it makes the sin more dangerous. The fact that very many 'acts' in the association and cohabitation of man and woman occur spontaneously, under the influence of emotion, does not in the least alter the fact that the personalistic norm exists and is also binding in relations between persons. Only on the basis of the principle embodied in it can we speak of the unification of two persons in love, and this is equally true of married love, in which the union of man and woman is complemented by sexual partnership.

Sin always flouts this principle, and this is no less true when it has its immediate origin in amorous sentiment (amor sensitivus) which develops around experiences brought to human beings by sensuality or by a sensibility responsive to and at the service of sensuality. Sin is violation of the true good. For the true good in the love of man and woman is first of all the person, and not emotion for its own sake, still less pleasure as such. These are secondary goods, and love – which is a durable union of persons – cannot be built of them alone, although they are so much in evidence in its subjective, psychological profile. The person must never be sacrificed to them, for to do so is to introduce the germ of sin into love. 'Sinful love' is simply a relationship between two persons so structured that emotion as such and more particularly plea-sure as such have assumed the dimensions of goods in their own right, and are the sole decisive consideration, while no account at all is taken of the objective value of the person, or of the objective laws and principles governing the cohabita-tion and association of persons of different sex.

We see then that the sin in 'sinful love' is essentially rooted in free will. Carnal desire is only its germ. For the will can and must prevent the 'dis-integration' of love – prevent pleasure, or indeed emotion from growing to the dimensions of goods in their own right, while all else in the relationship of two persons of different sexes is subordinate to them. The will can and must be guided by objective truth. It can, and therefore must, demand of the reason a correct vision of love and of the happiness which love can bring to a woman and a man. (Evil in this context is often the result of a false, purely subjective vision of happiness, in which the 'fullness of good' is replaced by the 'sum of pleasures'.) Of course, there are irrational forces in human beings which favour the whole process of 'subjectivization' not only of the theoretical view of happi-ness, but above all of the pursuit of happiness in practice. This opens the way to various forms of egoism which break down and destroy human love ('dis-integration'). The task of the will (to which true love ought to be particularly attrac-tive, because it creates a real opportunity for the will to immerse itself in the good), is to safeguard itself against the destructive influence of those forces, to safeguard the person against 'evil love'. (And since love always joins two persons, to protect one's own person is also to protect the other.)

The True Meaning of Chastity

We shall now examine the problem of chastity in detail. Analysis of the problems of concupiscence, subjectivism and egoism, and more particularly the enquiry we have just made into the structure of sin, and of sinful love, have equipped us to do so. The negative attitude to the virtue of chastity of which we spoke at the beginning of the present chapter is really the result of resentment. People are unwilling to acknowledge the enormous value of chastity to human love because they reject the full objective truth about the love of man and woman, and put a subjectivist fiction in its place. When the objective truth about love is fully accepted, chastity is also given its full value, and seen to be a great positive factor in human life, an essential element in the 'culture of the person', which is the true core of human culture as a whole.[44]

It is impossible to understand the full significance of the virtue of chastity unless love is understood as a function of the attitude of person to person, which makes for union between them. This is why it was necessary to separate discussion of the psychology of love as such from discussion of the virtue of love. For the same reason it was necessary to emphasize strongly the principle of integration: *love* in a world of persons must possess its peculiar ethical wholeness and fullness (*integritas*), its psychological manifestations are not sufficient in themselves, – indeed, *love is only psychologically complete when it possesses an ethical value*, when it is a virtue. Only in love as a virtue is it possible to satisfy the objective demands of the personalistic norm, which requires 'loving kindness' towards a person and rejects any form of 'utilization' of the person. But this principle is not always observed throughout the whole range of phenomena which mere psychology defines as manifestations of love between man and woman. Sometimes, what is called a 'manifestation of love', or simply 'love', if subjected to searching critical examination turns out to be, contrary to all appearances, only a form of 'utilization' of the person. This gives rise to a great problem of responsibility – responsibility for love and for the person. What should we understand by 'chastity' in the true sense? According to Aristotle if we observe the moral life of man, we can distinguish various virtues which can then be classified and arranged to form a system. St Thomas Aquinas takes up this idea in the *Summa Theologica* (IIa – IIae), and gives us a very broad, but at the same time penetrating and detailed treatise on the virtues. In the hierarchy of virtues there are certain main virtues which assist the functionings of the main faculties of the human psyche – both the mental faculties (reason and will) and the sensual faculties (*appetitus irascibilis* and *appetitus concupiscibilis*), which have been mentioned before in this chapter. These main virtues, sometimes called 'cardinal virtues' (from the latin *cardo*, a hinge, making them as it were the hinges of the whole of moral life), underpin many other virtues, each of which either contains something of a cardinal virtue, some distinctive trace of it, or else is necessary to a cardinal virtue in the sense that the latter would be incomplete without it.

Chastity in St Thomas's system is linked with the cardinal virtue of moderation – (*temperantia*) – and its subordinate virtues. The virtue of moderation, according to St Thomas, has its immediate subject in man's concupiscence (*appetitus concupiscibilis*), to which it attaches itself in order to restrain the instinctive appetites for various material and bodily goods which force themselves upon the senses. Sensual reactions (*erga bonum sensibile*) (with regard to a good apprehended by the senses) must be subordinated to reason: this is the function of the virtue of moderation. If man lacked it, the will might easily become subject to the senses, and select as a good only that which the senses perceived and desired as a good. The virtue of moderation strives to save a reasonable being from this perversion of his nature. It is natural, that is in accordance with nature, for a reasonable being such as man is to desire and strive for that which reason recognizes as good. It is only in this pursuit, and in such an attitude to the good, that the true perfection of a reasonable being, a person, can be expressed, and realized. The virtue of moderation helps reasonable beings to live reasonably, and so to attain the perfection proper to their nature. In all that they wrote on ethics the standpoint of Aristotle and St Thomas is one of unqualified perfectionism. In this they are at one with the fundamental trend of the Gospels, expressed in the well-known words: 'You therefore must be perfect. . . .' (Matthew 5:48).[45]

We are, however, concerned here with a specific question, that of the subordination of the virtue of chastity to the

168

cardinal virtue of moderation. This latter virtue enables the will, and above all the appetite itself (*appetitus concupiscibilis*), to subdue the sensual impulses, which in man accompany sensual (or emotional) reactions, richly diverse as they are, to the value 'sex'. The virtue of chastity, as understood above, is simply a matter of efficiency in controlling the concupiscent impulses set up by the reactions mentioned. 'Efficiency' in doing something means more than the 'ability' to do it. For virtue is effectiveness, and indeed 'constant' effectiveness. If it were only occasionally effective it would not be efficient, for we should only be able to say that a given man had succeeded in controlling an impulse, whereas virtue must guarantee that he will certainly control it. The ability merely to subdue the appetites originating in sensuality as they arise falls short of virtue, it is not chastity in the full sense of the word, even if the individual concerned nearly always succeeds in controlling himself. Fully formed virtue is an efficiently functioning control which permanently keeps the appetites in equilibrium by means of its habitual attitude to the true good (*bonum honestum*) determined by reason.[46] So then 'moderation' in the first and less complete sense is a capacity to 'moderate' the appetites on occasions, or even on each particular occasion, but in its second and fuller sense it is an efficient regulator which ensures consistent moderation and with it a natural equilibrium of the sensual appetites.

No-one is likely to deny that this theory of virtue is profoundly realistic. But should we look for the essence of chastity in moderation? Is this, in fact, the best way of bringing out the real value and significance of chastity in human life? Against the background of our discussion and analyses so far we must, I think, endeavour to bring out and emphasize much more forcefully the kinship between chastity and love.

Chastity can only be thought of in association with the virtue of love. Its function is to free love from the utilitarian attitude. This attitude, as is evident from the analysis previously carried out in this chapter, derives not only from sensuality or concupiscence as such, but as much, or more, from subjectivism of the emotions, and especially subjectivism of value judgements, which is rooted in the will and directly creates conditions favourable to egoism in various forms (emotional egoism, sensual egoism). From this it is an easy transition to 'sinful love', which comprises an orientation towards 'enjoyment' masked by the semblance of love. The virtue of chastity, whose function it is to free love from utilitarian attitudes, must control not only sensuality and carnal concupiscence, as such, but – perhaps more important – those centres deep within the human being in which the utilitarian attitude is hatched and grows. There can be no chastity unless the forms of volitional subjectivism of which I have spoken, and the varieties of egoism which they conceal, are overcome: *the more successfully the utilitarian attitude is camouflaged in the will the more dangerous it is;* 'sinful love' more often than not is not called 'sinful' but simply 'love', since those who experience it try to convince themselves and others that love is just this and cannot be otherwise. To be chaste means to have a 'transparent' attitude to a person of the other sex – *chastity means just that – the interior 'transparency'* without which love is not itself, for it cannot be itself until the desire to 'enjoy' is subordinated to a readiness to show loving kindness in every situation.

This 'transparency' in one's attitude to questions of the other sex does not mean artificially banishing the values of the 'body' or more generally the values of sex to the subconscious, of pretending that they do not exist or at any rate have no effect. Chastity is very often understood as a 'blind' inhibition of sensuality and of physical impulses such that the values of the 'body' and of sex are pushed down into the subconscious, where they await an opportunity to explode. This is an obviously erroneous conception of the virtue of chastity, which, if it is practised only in this way, does indeed create the danger of such 'explosions'. This (mistaken) view of chastity explains the common inference that it is a purely negative virtue. Chastity, in this view, is one long 'no'. Whereas it is above all the 'yes' of which certain 'no's' are the consequence. The virtue of chastity is underdeveloped in anyone who is slow to affirm the value of the person and allows the values of sex to reign supreme: these, once they take possession of the will distort one's whole attitude to a person of the other sex. The essence of chastity consists in quickness to affirm the value of the person in every situation, and in raising to the personal level all reactions to the value of 'the body and sex'. This requires a special interior, spiritual effort, for affirmation of the value of the person can only be the product of the spirit, but this effort is above all positive and creative 'from within', not negative and destructive. It is not a matter of summarily 'annihilating' the value 'body and sex' in the conscious mind by pushing reactions to them down into the subconscious, but of sustained long term integration; the value 'body and sex' must be grounded and implanted in the value of the person.

The objection that chastity is merely negative is then incorrect. The very fact that it is bound up with the virtue of moderation (*temperantia*) means that it cannot be so. For by 'moderating' the feelings and actions connected with the sexual values we serve the values of the person and of love. True chastity does not lead to disdain for the body or to disparagement of matrimony and the sexual life. That is the result of false chastity, chastity with a tinge of hypocrisy, or, still more frequently, of unchastity. This may be strange and startling – but it cannot be otherwise. For recognition and appreciation of the true value of 'the body and sex' is conditional on the 'revaluation' of which we have spoken: the raising of these values to the level of the value of the person is characteristic of and essential to chastity. Thus also only the chaste man and the chaste woman are capable of true love.[47] For chastity frees their association, including their marital intercourse, from that tendency to use a person which is objectively incompatible with 'loving kindness', and by so freeing it introduces into their life together and their sexual relationship a special disposition to 'loving kindness'. The connection between chastity and love results from the personalistic norm, which – as we said in Chapter I – has a dual content: a positive content ('thou shalt love!') and a negative content ('thou shalt not use!'). It is of course true that all

human beings have to mature internally and externally –
(men in one way, women in a rather different way) – before
they are capable of such chaste 'loving kindness', before they
can learn to 'savour' it, since every human being is by nature
burdened with concupiscence and apt to find the 'savour' of
love above all in the satisfaction of carnal desire. For this
reason, chastity is a difficult, long term matter; one must
wait patiently for it to bear fruit, for the happiness of loving
kindness which it must bring. But at the same time, chastity is
the sure way to happiness.

It does not lead to disdain of the body, but it does involve a
certain humility of the body.[48] Humility is the proper attitude towards all true greatness, including one's own greatness as a human being, but above all towards the greatness
which is not oneself, which is beyond one's self. The human
body must be 'humble' in face of the greatness represented by
the person: for in the person resides the true and definitive
greatness of man. Furthermore, the human body must
'humble itself' in face of the magnitude represented by love –
and here 'humble itself' means subordinate itself. Chastity is
conducive to this. In the absence of chastity 'the body' is not
subordinated to true love, but on the contrary strives to
impose its own 'laws' and to subjugate love to itself: mere
carnal enjoyment, on the basis of an intense shared experience of the value sex, then usurps the essential role in
love, which should be that of the person, and in this way
destroys love. Hence the need for the humbling of the body.

'The body' must also show humility in face of human happiness. How often does it insinuate that it alone possesses the
key to the secret of happiness. 'Happiness', if this were so,
would have to be identified with mere enjoyment, with the
sum of the pleasures which the 'body and sex' can bring to the
relationship between man and woman. But this superficial
view of happiness for one thing obscures the truth that man
and woman can and must seek their temporal, earthly happiness in a lasting union which has an interpersonal character,
since it is based in each of them on unreserved affirmation of
the value of the person. Still more certainly does the 'body' –
if it is not 'humble', not subordinate to the full truth about

the hapiness of man – obscure the vision of the ultimate happiness: the happiness of the human person in union with a personal God. This is the sense in which we should understand Christ's words in the Sermon on the Mount: 'Blessed are the pure in heart, for they shall see God.' It should be added that the truth about the union of the human person with a personal God, which will be fully accomplished within the dimensions of eternity, at the same time illuminates more fully and makes plainer the value of human love, the value of the union of man and woman as two persons. Significantly the Old and the New Testament both speak of the 'marriage' of God with mankind (in the chosen people, or in the Church), and the writings of mystics of the 'conjugal' union of the human soul with God.

Let us now examine the two components of the virtue of chastity: shame and continence.

THE METAPHYSICS
OF SHAME

✤

The Phenomenon of Sexual Shame and
its Interpretation

The phenomenon of shame, and of sexual shame in particular, has in recent times attracted the attention of the phenomenologists (M. Scheler, F. Sawicki). It is a theme which opens up a broad field of observation and which lends itself to analysis in depth. At a first superficial glance it may be said that what we always find in shame is a tendency to concealment, whether of certain external facts or of certain states of mind and emotions. We must not oversimplify the matter by maintaining that people endeavour to conceal only what is regarded as bad – for we often feel 'ashamed' of what is good, of a good deed, for instance. The shame in the case probably relates not to the good itself, but solely to the fact that something which in the intention of the agent should have remained hidden has been made public: when this happens it is the publicity itself which is felt to be bad. We can, then, say that *the phenomenon of shame arises when something which of its very nature or in view of its purpose ought to be private passes the bounds of a person's privacy and somehow becomes public.*

We see from all this that there is an unmistakable connection between shame and the person. We need not discuss at this point whether or not the phenomenon also occurs in the animal world. In my opinion, we should find there only various forms of fear. Fear is a negative emotion always caused by the threat of some evil. This evil must of course be perceived or imagined before fear is felt. Shame is distinct from fear, although externally they may look similar. If a man is ashamed, his shame is accompanied by the fear that what should in his belief remain hidden may come into the open. Fear, then, may be linked with shame, but only indirectly, and secondarily. The essence of shame goes beyond such fear. It can only be understood if we heavily emphasize the truth that the existence of the person is an interior one, i.e. that the person possesses an interior peculiarly its own, and that from this arises the need to conceal (that is, to retain internally) certain experiences or values, or else to withdraw with them into itself. Fear does not exhibit this inwardness, it is a simple reaction to an evil perceived, imagined or experienced. No interior is necessary to this reaction, whereas shame cannot be conceived of without it. The need for concealment, characteristic of shame, arises in man because it finds in him, if I may put it this way, a terrain – his inner life – which lends itself to concealment of facts or values. This is different from the concealment of fear itself, the dissimulation of a psychological reaction, something of which animals too may be capable, whereas shame is bound up with the person, and its development proceeds together with that of the personality.

We are specifically concerned with sexual shame. Its external manifestations are connected with the body – it is to some degree simply physical shame. Particular objects of shame are those parts and organs of the body which determine its sex. Human beings show an almost universal tendency to conceal them from the gaze of others, and particularly of persons of the other sex. This largely explains the need they feel to avoid nakedness. Obviously other motives are at work here, particularly the organism's need for protection against cold, which is more or less important in particular climates: in tropical conditions primitive peoples live in partial or total nakedness. Many details in their way of life indicate that nakedness cannot be simply and unambiguously identified with shamelessness. On the contrary, for some primitive peoples, the concealment of parts of the body previously exposed is a manifestation of shamelessness. We doubtless see here the effect of habit, of a collective custom which has evolved under the influence of the prevailing climate. Nakedness assists the adaptation of the organism to climatic conditions and no other intention can easily be found in it, whereas other motives can easily be assigned to concealment of those parts of the body which distinguish male and female. We find that dress may serve not only to conceal but in one way or another to draw attention to these parts of the body. Sexual modesty cannot then in any simple way be identified with the use of clothing, nor shamelessness with the absence of clothing and total or partial nakedness. This is a secondary and variable factor. The most we can say is that a tendency to cover the body and those parts of the body which declare it male or female goes together with sexual shame but is not an essential feature of it.

What *is* an essential feature is the tendency to conceal sexual values themselves, particularly in so far as they constitute in the mind of a particular person 'a potential object of enjoyment' for persons of the other sex. For this reason, we do not encounter sexual shame in children at an age when the sexual values do not exist for them because their minds are not yet receptive to those values. As they become conscious or are made conscious of the existence of this sphere of values they begin to experience sexual shame – not as something imposed on them from outside, by the milieu in which they live, but as an interior need of an evolving personality. The development of sexual modesty – as we call the constant capacity and readiness to feel shame – follows one course in girls and women and another in boys and men. This is connected with something which we have already stressed in the psychological analysis of love – the rather different structure of the psychological forces, and specifically the different relationship between sensuality and emotion in the two sexes. Since sensuality, which is oriented towards 'the body as an object of enjoyment' is in general stronger and more importunate in men, modesty and shame – the tendency to conceal sexual values specifically connected with the body – must be more pronounced in girls and women. At the same time they are less aware of sensuality and of its natural orientation in men, because in them emotion is usually stronger than sensuality, and sensuality tends to be latent in emotion. This is why woman is often said to be 'purer' than man. This tells us nothing about the virtue of chastity. Woman is purer in as much as she experiences more powerfully the value of 'a human being of the other sex', the value of a sort of psychological 'masculinity'. She is, it is true, greatly influenced by physical masculinity – although the feminine reaction to both forms of masculinity is primarily psychological. But this very trait in her mentality may in a certain sense make modesty more difficult for her. For since a woman does not find in herself the sensuality of which a man as a rule cannot but be aware in himself she does not feel so great a need to conceal 'the body as a potential object of enjoyment'. The evolution of modesty in woman requires some initial insight into the male psychology.

The natural development of modesty in boys and men generally follows a different course. A man does not have to fear female sensuality as much as a woman must fear the sensuality of the male. He is, however, very keenly aware of his own sensuality, and this for him is the source of shame. For him, sexual values are more closely bound up with the 'body and sex as potential objects of enjoyment', this is the form in which he becomes aware of them, and experienced in this way they become for him a cause of shame. He is, then, ashamed above all of the way in which he reacts to the sexual value of persons of the other sex. He is equally ashamed of sexual values connected with his own 'body'. Perhaps this second form of shame is a consequence of the first: he is ashamed of his body because he is ashamed of the reaction to the value 'body' which he encounters in himself. Quite independently of this he is obviously ashamed of his own body, and of sexual values connected with it, in what may be called an immanent way, as distinct from the form of shame previously defined, which we might call relative. Shame is not only a response to someone else's sensual and sexual reaction to the 'body as an object of use' – a reaction to a reaction – it is also, and above all, an immanent need to prevent such reactions to the body in oneself, because they are incompatible with the value of the person. This is the origin of modesty, which is a constant eagerness to avoid what is shameless.

We see clearly here the intimate connection between the

phenomenon of shame and the nature of the person. The person is its own master (*sui juris*); no-one else except God the Creator has or can have any proprietorial right in relation to it. It is its own property, it has the power of self-determination, and no-one can encroach upon its independence. No-one can take possession of the person unless the person permits this, makes a gift of itself from love. This objective inalienability (*alteri incommunicabilitas*) and inviolability of the person finds expression precisely in the experience of sexual shame. *The experience of shame is a natural reflection of the essential nature of the person.* And if on the one hand the experience of shame presupposes the inner life of the person as the only terrain on which it can exist, if we probe more deeply we see that this experience requires the existence of the person as its natural basis. Only the person can feel shame, because only it of its very nature cannot be an object of use (in either meaning of the verb to use). Sexual shame is to some extent a revelation of the supra-utilitarian character of the person, whether the person is ashamed of the sexual values connected with its own body or of its attitude to such values in persons of the other sex, its fixation on them as mere objects of enjoyment. In the first case, the feeling of shame goes with the realization that one's person must not be an object for use on account of the sexual values connected with it, whether in fact or only in intention. In the second case, the feeling of shame goes with the realization that a person of the other sex must not be regarded (even in one's private thoughts) as an object of use.

We see then that a proper understanding of sexual shame gives us certain guidelines for sexual morality generally. Mere description of the phenomenon, even if it is as perceptive as that of the phenomenologists, is not sufficient here – a metaphysical interpretation of it is also necessary. Sexual ethics may then find an experimental point of departure in the feeling of shame. The person is at the centre of this experience and is at the same time its basis. Although the sexual values are the direct object of shame, the immediate content of the feeling, the indirect object is the person, the attitude of one person to another. The function of shame is to exclude – (whether passively, as is usual is with women, or actively, as is more often the case with men) – an attitude to the person incompatible with its essential, supra-utilitarian nature. The danger of such an attitude arises precisely because of the sexual values inherent in the person, and so sexual shame takes the form of a tendency to conceal them. This is a natural and spontaneous tendency. We see clearly here how the moral order is bound up with the existential order, the order of nature. Sexual morality is deeply rooted in the laws of nature.[48]

This spontaneous urge to conceal sexual values, and the sexual character of certain feelings, which we encounter in men and women has, however, another and deeper meaning. It is not just a matter of hiding anything that might produce a sexual reaction in another person, nor yet of internally hiding from one's own reaction to a person of the other sex. For this shrinking from reactions to mere sexual values goes together with the longing to inspire love, to inspire a 'reaction' to the value of the person, and with the longing to experience love in the same sense – the first perhaps stronger in women, the second in men, but one should not suppose that either is exclusive to either of the sexes. A woman wants to be loved so that she can show love. A man wants to love so that he can be loved. In either case sexual modesty is not a flight from love, but on the contrary the opening of a way towards it. *The spontaneous need to conceal mere sexual values bound up with the person is the natural way to the discovery of the value of the person as such.* The value of the person is closely connected with its inviolability, its status as 'something more than an object of use'. Sexual modesty is as it were a defensive reflex, which protects that status and so protects the value of the person. But there is more to it than that. It is a matter not just of protecting but of revealing the value of the person, and of doing so in the context of the sexual values which are simultaneously present in a particular person. Shame does not reveal the value of the person in some abstract way, as a theoretical magnitude which only the intellect can appreciate, but in a live and concrete fashion, bound up with the sexual values and yet superior to them. Hence the feeling of inviolability. (In the woman, it expresses itself like this: 'You must not touch me, not even in your secret carnal thoughts' and in the man like this: 'I must not touch her, not even with a deeply hidden wish to enjoy her, for she cannot be an object for use'.) This 'fear of contact' which is so characteristic of persons who truly love each other is an indirect way of affirming the value of the person as such, and this as we know is a constituent part of love in the proper, that is the ethical, sense of the word.

There also exists a certain natural shame of love in its physical aspect. The experiences which go with it are rightly described as 'intimate'. Men and women avoid other people, avoid being seen, when they make love, and any morally sound human being would consider it extremely indecent not to do so. There is here a sort of discrepancy between the objective importance of the act, of which we have spoken before in Chapter I, and the shame which surrounds it in people's minds, and which has nothing to do with prudery, or false shame. It is a proper shame, since there are profound reasons for concealing manifestations of love between man and woman, and particularly marital intercourse, from the eyes of other people. Love is a union of persons, brought about in this instance by physical intimacy and intercourse. This last consists in a shared experience of sexual values which makes possible mutual sexual enjoyment for both man and woman. The shared experience of sexual values may be inseparably bound up with love, may find its objective justification and foundation in love (this in fact is the way towards overcoming shame in the persons taking part in the sexual act: we shall speak of this more particularly elsewhere).

Only they, however, are aware of this justification, and it is only for them that love is an 'interior' matter of the soul, not just a physical matter. Anyone else would find himself confronted simply by the external manifestations, by the shared response to sexual values, while the union of persons itself, the objective reality of love, remains inaccessible to outsiders. Obviously, if shame endeavours to conceal the sexual values so as to safeguard the value of the person, it must also endeavour to conceal a shared response to sexual values so as to protect the value of love itself – in the first place for the two people who are experiencing it together. It is then not merely relative but also immanent shame.

The shared experience of sexual values is always attended by circumstances which demand a measure of concealment. Human beings are in general ashamed of what merely 'happens' to them, and is not the result of a conscious act of will. They are ashamed, for instance, of passionate outbursts of rage or panic fear, and they are still more ashamed of certain physiological processes which occur independently of their will in specific circumstances – the activity of the will being limited only to creating those conditions or allowing them to arise. We find here confirmation of the spirituality and 'inwardness' of the human person, which detects some evil in all that is not sufficiently 'inwardly' felt, or spiritual, but only exterior, physical and irrational. Given, then, that when a man and a woman share an experience of sexual values all these external aspects are conspicuous, while their personal union is as it were hidden within each of them and invisible to anyone from outside, we can see why love, in so far as it is a matter of 'the body and sex', needs concealment.

Law of the Absorption of Shame by Love

Externally (i.e. as seen by anyone other than the partner in love) love in its physical aspect is naturally inseparable from shame, but within the relationship between the man and woman concerned, a characteristic phenomenon occurs which we shall call here 'the absorption of shame by love'. Shame is, as it were, swallowed up by love, dissolved in it, so that the man and the woman are no longer ashamed to be sharing their experience of sexual values. This process is enormously important to sexual morality, for we can derive useful ethical guidance from it. It is a natural process which cannot be understood until we have grasped the relative importance of the value of the person and of sexual values in human beings, and in the love of man and woman.

In our analysis of sexual shame we came to the conclusion that it is a phenomenon so profoundly personal that it can exist only in the world of persons. Shame has, however, a dual significance: it means flight, the endeavour to conceal sexual values so that they do not obscure the values of the person as such, but it also means the longing to inspire or experience love. (Love between man and woman develops, as we know, on the basis of sexual values, but in the last resort the attitudes of each of them to the value of the person are the decisive factor, since love is a union of persons). Thus, our analysis of sexual shame shows that it clears the way, so to speak, for love.

To say that shame is 'absorbed' by love does not mean that it is eliminated or destroyed. Quite the contrary – it is reinforced, in man and woman, for only where it is preserved intact can love be realized in full. 'Absorption' means only that love fully utilizes for its own purposes the characteristic effects of shame, and specifically that awareness of the proper relationship[49] between the value of the person and sexual values which shame introduces as a natural and spontaneous feeling into the mutual relationship of man and woman. However, this awareness, unless it is cultivated as it should be, may die away, to the detriment of the persons and their mutual love.

In what, then, does this absorption of shame by love consist, and how is it to be understood? Well, shame is a natural *form of self-defence for the person* against the danger of descending or being pushed into the position of an object for sexual use. That position – as we have said several times already – is incompatible with the very nature of the person. The person cannot (must not) voluntarily descend to the position of an object of use for another person or persons. Equally, a person must not push any person of the other sex into the position of an object of use. In both parties sexual shame – physical shame, and shame for their emotions – militates against this. Love, as we said right at the beginning of this book, is an attitude to another person which essentially precludes treatment of the person as an object for use; it most certainly does not allow a person to descend to that level, nor yet does it permit one person to reduce another to that status. This is why shame leads so naturally to love.

What is most essential to love is affirmation of the value of the person: this is the basis on' which the will of the loving subject strives for the true good of the beloved person, the entire and perfect good, the absolute good, which is identical with happiness. Such a disposition of the will in a loving person is totally incompatible with any utilitarian inclination. Love, and the tendency to regard a person as an object of use, are mutually exclusive. Where there is love, shame as the natural way of avoiding the utilitarian attitude loses its *raison d'être* and gives ground. But only to the extent that a person loved in this way – and this is most important – is equally ready to give himself or herself in love. Let us remember here the conclusions we reached in our analysis of betrothed love. The law of the absorption of shame by love helps us to understand the whole problem of chastity or rather of conjugal modesty at the level of psychology. The fact is, however, that sexual intercourse between spouses is not a form of shamelessness legalized by outside authority, but is felt to be in conformity with the demands of shame (unless the spouses themselves make it shameless by their way of performing it).

Looking at the problem in its entirety (as the integral analysis of love in the last chapter has equipped us to) we are bound to say that only true love, a love which possesses in full the ethical essence proper to it, is capable of absorbing shame. This is easily understandable in that shame represents a tendency to conceal sexual values so that the value of the person is not obscured by them, but on the contrary is enhanced. True love is a love in which sexual values are subordinate to the value of the person. The last is dominant and affirmation of it pervades all the experiences born of man's natural sensuality or sentiment. Of course, these experiences are connected in a natural way with sexual values (sensuality with the value 'body and sex', sentiment with the value 'femininity' or 'masculinity' in an individual of the other sex). True love ensures that these experiences are imbued with affirmation of the value of the person to such an extent

183

that it is impossible for the will to regard the other person as an object for use. In practice, this is where the real strength of love lies – mere theoretical affirmation of the value of the person is not enough.

Given such an attitude there is no reason for shame, or for concealment of the values of sex, since there is no danger that they might obscure the value of the person or destroy its inalienability (*alteri incommunicabilitas*) and inviolability, reducing it to the status of an object for use. There is no longer any reason to be ashamed of the body once the positive urge to inspire love which is part of that shame has met with an adequate response. Nor is there any reason to be ashamed of one's feelings, since there can be no question of regarding the other person as an object for use. Even if sensuality, in its characteristic way, reacts to 'the body' as a 'possible object of use', the will is fixed by love not on the exploitation but on the true good of the other person, which (in marriage) does not exlude physical intercourse, and hence shared sexual enjoyment. The need for shame has been absorbed by mature love for a person: it is no longer necessary for a lover to conceal from the beloved or from himself a disposition to enjoy, since this has been absorbed by true love ruled by the will. Affirmation of the value of the person so thoroughly permeates all the sensual and emotional reactions connected with the sexual values that the will is not threatened by a utilitarian outlook incompatible with the proper attitude to a person. On the contrary, affirmation of the person influences the emotions in such a way that the value of the person is not just abstractly understood but deeply felt. This is the point at which love is psychologically complete, and sexual shame can be thoroughly absorbed. A man and a woman can become 'one flesh' – in the familiar words of the Book of Genesis (2:24), with which the Creator defined the essence of marriage – and that oneness will not be a form of shamelessness, but only the full realization of the union of persons, which results from reciprocal conjugal love. This has a very direct relevance to the problem of procreation, which will however be discussed separately in Chapter IV.

We must also point to a danger connected with the phe-

184

nomenon of the absorption of sexual shame. Shame has its roots deep in the very being of the person, which is why we must look to the metaphysics of the person for a full explanation of it. There is a danger that shame, and its absorption in the regular way by love, may be treated too superficially. Subjectively, of course, shame is a negative feeling, somewhat akin to fear. The feeling of fear is associated in the consciousness with the sexual values, and it yields to the realization that those values are not merely a stimulus to 'sexual desire'. Fear gradually diminishes as love grows. The feeling of shame inspired in one person by sexual desire for another is, as it were, blurred in the consciousness, where it coexists with a growing emotional attachment which has the power of absorbing, of swallowing up the feeling of shame, the power to liberate the minds of man and woman alike from the feeling of shame. And this emotional-affective process explains the view, so very often expressed or implied, that 'the emotion (love) itself gives men and women the right to physical intimacy and to sexual intercourse'.

This is a mistaken view, for love as an emotional experience even if it is reciprocated, is very far from being the same as love completed by commitment of the will. This last requires that each of two persons chooses the other, on the basis of an unqualified affirmation of the value of the other person, with a view to a lasting union in matrimony, and with a clearly defined attitude to parenthood. Love between persons possesses – and must possess – a clear-cut objective purpose. Love as an emotional-affective experience often has a purely subjective character, and is from the ethical point of view immature. We have said several times that this is an area in which merely 'using the material' must not be confused with creativity, and that transient erotic experiences must not be confused with love.

It follows that the 'absorption of shame by love' of which we have spoken must have more than a merely emotional-affective significance. The mere elimination of the feeling of shame by some sort of amorous feeling is not enough, for this contradicts the essential nature of sexual shame properly understood – indeed, we have here a form of shamelessness

(shamelessness takes advantage of these transitory emotions to legitimate itself). If the feeling of shame readily yields to the first emotional-affective experience, we have to do with a negation of shame and of sexual modesty. True shame gives way reluctantly (and as a result it does not ultimately leave the person in a shameful situation). True shame can be absorbed only by true love, a love which affirms the value of the person and seeks the greatest good for that person with all its strength. In shame in this sense resides the genuine moral strength of the person. But since there exists a real danger of its impoverishment, for reasons interior (some people seem to be less modest 'by nature') or exterior (opinions, life styles, modes of behaviour between men and women vary from one milieu to another and from one period to another) there is a need to *develop sexual shame by education.* This is an inseparable part of the education of love – because, in accordance with the 'law of absorption', only true and genuine shame insists upon a true and fully valid love.

The Problem of Shamelessness

In the light of what has been said above on the themes of sexual shame and the absorption of shame by love let us now try to examine the problem of shamelessness. The word itself refers simply to the absence or negation of shame. In practice they come to the same thing. We encounter various modes of being and behaving in persons of both sexes, and various situations involving them, which we define as shameless, by which we mean that they fall short of the demands of shame, that they clash with the exigencies of sexual modesty. There is a certain relativism in the definition of what is shameless. This relativism may be due to differences in the make-up of particular persons – a greater or lesser sensual excitablity, a higher or lower level of moral culture – or to different 'world-views'. It may equally be due to differences in external conditions – in climate for instance, as we have said before, and also in prevailing customs, social habits, etc.

Nevertheless, this relativity in determining whether or not particular manifestations of relations between persons of opposite sex are shameless does not at all mean that shamelessness itself is relative, that there exist no factors in or aspects of human modes of being and behaviour which have a constant significance for its evaluation even though variable conditions, internal and external, make different people, or different social formations, vary in their ideas as to what is shameless, and what is consonant with the demands of sexual modesty. Our concern here is not to compare different views as to what is and what is not shameless but to identify the common element in them.

Shame is a tendency, uniquely characteristic of the human person, to conceal sexual values sufficiently to prevent them from obscuring the value of person as such. The purpose of this tendency is self-defence of the person, which does not wish to be an object to be used by another, whether in practice or merely in intention, but does wish to be an object of love. Since it is particularly likely to become an object of use because of its sexual values, the tendency to conceal them comes into being – but to conceal them only to a certain extent, so that in combination with the value of the person they can still be a point of origin for love. Besides what may be called 'physical shame', since the sexual values are externally connected above all with the body, there exists another form, which we have called 'emotional shame', since it endeavours to conceal reactions and feelings in which the habit of regarding 'the body and sex' as objects for use is in evidence, to conceal them because the body and sex are the property of a human person who cannot be an object for use. This form of shame, like the other, can be effectively absorbed only by love.

Shamelessness wrecks this whole order of things. By analogy with our distinction between 'physical shame' and 'shame of feelings' we can speak of two corresponding forms of shamelessness. We shall use the term physical shamelessness to describe any mode of being or behaviour on the part of a particular person in which the values of sex as such are given such prominence that they obscure the essential value of the person. The consequence is that the person is put in the position of an object of use, a being which can be treated as something merely to be used (especially in the second meaning of the word), not to be loved. 'Emotional shamelessness' consists in the rejection of that healthy tendency to be ashamed of reactions and feelings which make another person merely an object of use because of the sexual values belonging to him or her. Thus for instance a man is shameless in his feelings toward a woman when he feels no inner shame for his urge towards sensual and sexual exploitation, when he refuses to accept that any other attitude is possible, and makes no effort to subordinate this urge to true love for the person, or to make the proper connections between the two things.

This internal 'shame of feelings' has nothing in common with prudery. Prudery consists in concealing one's real intentions with regard to persons of the other sex, or with regard to sexual matters in general. A prudish person intent on exploitation tries to make it appear that he has no interest at all in such matters – indeed he is prepared to condemn all, even the most natural, manifestations of sex and sexuality. Such behaviour is, however, very often not to be explained as prudery – which is a particular form of hypocrisy, a way of disguising one's intentions – but by some prejudice or other, perhaps the belief that everything to do with sex can only be an object for use, that sex merely gives the opportunity for sexual release and does not open the way to love between people. This view smacks of Manicheanism, and is incompatible with the view of physical and sexual matters found in the Book of Genesis, and more particularly in the New Testament. True emotional shame cannot possibly be identified with prudishness. Emotional shame is a healthy reaction within a person against any attitude to another person which disregards that person's essential value, degrading him or her to the level of an object for sexual use. Christ protested against this attitude to the person in the well-known words already quoted above: 'Everyone who looks at a woman lustfully has already committed adultery with her in his heart' (Matthew 5:28). This refers, obviously, to an interior act. Prudery is often, perhaps generally, linked with shameless intentions. This is different from shamelessness of feelings. We have already mentioned relativism in the classification of phenomena, especially external phenomena, ways of living and behaving, as shameless. A special problem arises when we come to decide whether or not an interior act, a way of thinking of, or appreciating sexual values, a way of reacting to them – is shameless. In this matter there is no exact similarity in the behaviour of particular people, even if they live in the same age and the same society. There is, above all, no precise correspondence between the views and feelings of men and those of women. Very often, a woman does not regard a particular way of dressing as shameless (we are speaking here of 'physical shamelessness') although some man, or indeed many men, may find it so. Conversely, a particular man may internally have shameless feelings towards a woman, or towards several women (here we are speaking of emotional shamelessness), although they have done nothing to provoke him by shameless conduct – by dressing or dancing improperly, for instance.

All the same, there is here a certain correlation: 'physical shame' is necessary because it is possible to be ashamed of one's feelings – and particularly it would appear, for a woman to be ashamed of her feelings towards a man. Conversely, 'emotional shame' is necessary – and this applies particularly to the feelings of men towards women – because physical shame exists as a possibility. It is however difficult to discern the connection in any particular case. That is why we must accept that the possibilities of shamelessness on both sides are greater than at first appears. The development of healthy customs in the context of sexual relations, or rather in different sectors of the life of men and women together, depend on our doing so. 'Healthy customs', however, have nothing in common with puritanism in sexual matters. For exaggeration easily results in prudery.

We have already touched on the question of dress. It is one of the matters concerning which problems of modesty and shamelessness most frequently arise. It is difficult for us to go into details or to discuss the nuances of fashion in male and female dress. These matters certainly have a bearing on the problem of modesty and shamelessness, though the connection is perhaps not that which is commonly thought to exist. Dress can, of course, help to accentuate the sexual values in different ways – in different ways on different occasions, irrespective of the congenital or acquired dispositions of a particular individual. This accentuation of sexual values by dress is inevitable, and is not necessarily incompatible with sexual modesty. What is truly immodest in dress is that which frankly contributes to the deliberate displacement of the true value of the person by sexual values, that which is bound to elicit a reaction to the person as to a 'possible means of obtaining sexual enjoyment' and not 'a possible object of love by reason of his or her personal value'.

The principle is simple and obvious, but its application in specific cases depends upon the individual, the milieu, the society. Dress is always a social question, a function of (healthy or unhealthy) social customs. We must simply stress that although considerations of an aesthetic nature may seem to be decisive here they are not and cannot be the only ones: considerations of an ethical nature exist side by side with them. *Man, alas, is not such a perfect being that the sight of the body of another person, especially a person of the other sex, can arouse in him merely a disinterested liking which develops into an innocent affection.* In practice it also arouses concupiscence, or a wish to enjoy concentrated on sexual values with no regard for the value of the person. And this must be taken into account.

This does not, however, mean that physical shamelessness is to be simply and exclusively identified with complete or partial nakedness. There are circumstances in which nakedness is not immodest. If someone takes advantage of such an occasion to treat the person as an object of enjoyment, (even if his action is purely internal) it is only he who is guilty of shamelessness (immodesty of feeling), not the other. Nakedness as such is not to be equated with physical shamelessness. Immodesty is present only when nakedness plays a negative role with regard to the value of the person, when its aim is to arouse concupiscence, as a result of which the person is put in the position of an object for enjoyment. What happens then may be called *depersonalization by sexualiza-tion*. But this is not inevitable. Even when nakedness goes with mutual sexual enjoyment respect for the dignity of the person can be fully preserved. This is how it must be in marriage, where there exist the objective conditions for the genuine absorption of shame by love. We shall return to this in the next chapter. In any case, unless we take this view of the role of the body in love between persons, we cannot think or speak of modesty and purity in married life, though these are of permanent and fundamental importance in Catholic teaching.

Although physical immodesty cannot be identified in a simple way with nakedness as such, it none the less requires a real internal effort to refrain from reacting to the naked body in an immodest way. It should however be added that there is a difference between immodesty in feelings on the one hand and reflex sensual reactions to the body and sex as a 'possible object of enjoyment' on the other. The human body is not in itself shameful, nor for the same reasons are sensual reactions, and human sensuality in general. Shamelessness (just like shame and modesty) is a function of the interior of a person, and specifically of the will, which too easily accepts the sensual reaction and reduces another person, because of the person's 'body and sex', to the role of an object for enjoy-ment.

While we are on the subject of dress and its relevance to the problem of modesty and immodesty it is worth drawing attention to the functional significance of differences in attire. There are certain objective situations in which even total nudity of the body is not immodest, since the proper function of nakedness in this context is not to provoke a reaction to the person as an object for enjoyment, and in just the same way the functions of particular forms of attire may vary. Thus, the body may be partially bared for physical labour, for bathing, or for a medical examination. If then we wish to pass a moral judgement on particular forms of dress we have to start from the particular functions which they serve. When a person uses such a form of dress in accordance with its objective function we cannot claim to see anything immodest in it, even if it involves partial nudity. Whereas the use of such a costume outside its proper context is immodest, and is inevitably felt to be so. For example, there is nothing immodest about the use of a bathing costume at a bathing place, but to wear it in the street or while out for a walk is contrary to the dictates of modesty.

It would be wrong not to refer here, if only cursorily, to another particular problem, that of pornography (or shamelessness) in art. It is a very broad problem, and extremely complex on detailed examination, because of the diversity of the arts. I am concerned for the present only to define the gist of the problem. An artist communicates in his work his own thoughts, feelings, and attitudes, but his work does not only serve this purpose. It serves the truth, in that it must capture and transmit some fragment of reality in a beautiful way. Aesthetic beauty is the most distinctive characteristic of a work of art. A fragment of reality which artists very frequently try to capture is the love of man and woman, and in the plastic arts the human body. This incidentally shows how important and attractive this theme is in the totality of human life. Art has a right and a duty, for the sake of realism, to reproduce the human body, and the love of man and woman, as they are in reality, to speak the whole truth about them. The human body is an authentic part of the truth about man, just as its sensual and sexual aspects are an authentic part of the truth about human love. But it would be wrong to let this part obscure the whole – and this is what often happens in art.

However, the essence of what we call pornography in art is further to seek. Pornography is a marked tendency to accentuate the sexual element when reproducing the human body or human love in a work of art, with the object of inducing the reader or viewer to believe that sexual values are the only real values of the person, and that love is nothing more than the experience, individual or shared, of those values alone. This tendency is harmful, for it destroys the integral image of that important fragment of human reality which is love between man and woman. For the truth about human love consists always in reproducing the interpersonal relationship, however large sexual values may loom in that relatonship. Just as the truth about man is that he is a person, however conspicuous sexual values are in his or her physical appearance.

A work of art must get at this truth, no matter how deeply it has to go into sexual matters. If it shows a tendency to distort this it can only give a distorted picture of reality. But pornography is not just a lapse or an error. It is a deliberate trend. If a distorted image is endowed with the power and prestige of artistic beauty there is a still greater likelihood that it will take root and establish itself in the mind and the will of those who contemplate it. For the human will often shows a great susceptibility to deformed images of reality. But for this very reason, when we condemn pornography we should often put the blame on immaturity and impurity, the absence of 'emotional shame' in those responsible for it.

THE PROBLEMS
OF CONTINENCE

❦

Self Control and Objectivization

In the first part of this chapter we pointed out that the practice of the virtue of chastity is very closely connected with the cardinal virtue which St Thomas Aquinas, following Aristotle, called *temperantia*. The function of that virtue is to moderate the promptings of concupiscence – hence it may be called moderation. In sexual matters we must consider particularly the capacity for self-control, the form which moderation takes in this context. The chaste man is the 'self-controlled' man. Aristotle and Thomas of Aquinas were familiar with the concept of self-control (*continentia*). A man must control the concupiscence of the body, must endeavour to control it at the moment when it makes itself felt and demands satisfaction in defiance of reason, and what reason recognizes as right and truly good – for it is assumed that reason knows the objective order of nature, or at least can and should know it. Conformity with the dictates of reason is thus at the same time a condition of the observance of the natural order and a condition of probity in action. The criterion of probity is whether the action is in accordance with reason, and worthy of a reasonable being, a person.[50] The principle of probity in action is fundamentally incompatible with the principle of expediency, favoured by the utilitarians. The dignity of the person demands control of concupiscence. If the person does not exercise such control it jeopardizes its natural perfectibility, allows an inferior and dependent part of itself to enjoy freedom of action, and indeed subjects itself to this lesser self.

This way of looking at the question of self-control derives mainly from the perfectionist tendency in ethics. There is no

194

contradiction between this and the general drift of our argument, although we have put the main emphasis on love for the person, on which the whole analysis of chastity and its rehabilitation in this work has also been based. *Control of concupiscence has as its objective not only the perfection of the person who attempts to achieve it, but also the realization of love in the world of persons,* and especially in relations between persons of different sex. A man who seeks to control physical desire must restrain the stirrings of sensual appetite (*appetitus concupiscibilis*), and thus moderate the various feelings or emotions which accompany these sensual reactions. Obviously they are the origin of acts, events internal or external, which may easily conflict with the principles of love for the person, since they are only a utilization of the person governed by none but sexual values.

As far as sensuality and the natural dynamic of sensations and sentiments (St Thomas's *passiones animae*) are concerned, Aristotle most aptly observes that in this particular individuals differ: we must recognize the existence of extreme sensual excitability (*hyper-sensibilitas*) on the one hand, and inadequate, unnaturally weak responses to stimuli (*hypo-sensibilitas*) on the other. We have previously distinguished between the content of emotional and that of sensual reactions, and we must draw an analogous contrast between an excessive and an inadequate, unnaturally low impressionability.

We still have to discuss the problem of moderation. If we have a realistic conception of man we must acknowledge that both sensual excitability and sentimental susceptibility are natural to him, fundamentally consonant with his nature, and therefore do not fundamentally contradict the realization of love in the world of persons, especially the love which unites the man and the woman. It is in this light that we solve the problem of moderation, without which the virtue of chastity in the relationship between such persons does not exist. By moderation we mean the ability to find that 'mean' in the control of sensual excitability and sentimental impressionability which in each concrete case, in every interpersonal configuration or situation, will best facilitate the realization of love, and avoid the danger of exploitation, which as we have seen can very easily be the result not only of sensual but of emotional reactions too.

Moderation, however, is not the same thing as a 'medium' capacity for sensual or sentimental reactions. If it were, people who were naturally unresponsive to sensual or emotional stimuli, the 'hypo-sensitive', would automatically be moderate. *Moderation is not mediocrity but the ability to maintain one's equilibrium amid the stirrings of concupiscence.* This equilibrium must provide the inner gauge for one's feelings, sensual and emotional, for one's actions and up to a point for one's state of mind. Virtue depends very closely on and is in a sense a function of this sort of moderation: we do not attempt a rigid definition of it, for it develops in different ways in different people, depending on their natural tendencies. The essential nature of moderation is unambiguous: whoever has not attained it, whoever is not self-controlled and moderate is not chaste. Whereas the ways in which this moderation is practised vary according to different combinations of interior and exterior conditions, social situation, vocation, etc.

We cannot easily discuss all the various ways of achieving self-control in sexual matters without which chastity is impossible. We can, however, attempt to describe the main methods. The word 'continence' is often heard in this connection. It suggests that the basic method described by it has something to do with 'containing'. This gives us a perfect image of those well-known interior crises in which the person undergoes something like an invasion, with its main forces based on sensuality, on carnal concupiscence or (at one remove) on natural sensibility. The person feels the need, natural to a reasonable being, to defend itself against the forces of sensuality and concupiscence, above all because their invasion threatens its natural power of self-determination. The person cannot allow things to 'happen' to it which it has not willed. The indirect reason for the person's natural tendency to defend itself lies in its order of values. Continence is very closely tied up with the natural need of the person to be its own master.

We noted earlier that virtue means something more than merely curbing the promptings of bodily desire or sensual reactions by pushing their content down into the subconscious. Chastity does not consist in systematic depreciation of the value of 'the body and sex' any more than it can be identified with the morbid fear which they may inspire, sometimes as a reflex. Such reactions are symptoms not of inner strength but rather of weakness. *Virtue can only come from spiritual strength.*[51] This strength derives in the last instance from the reason, which 'sees' the real truth about the values and puts the value of the person, and love, *above* the values of sex and above the enjoyment associated with them. But for this very reason chastity cannot consist in 'blind' self-restraint. Continence, efficiency in curbing the lust of the body by the exercise of will, the capacity for successful moderation of the sensations connected with sensual and even with emotional reactions, is the indispensable method of self-mastery, but it does not in itself amount to a full achievement of virtue. Above all, *continence cannot be an end in itself.* This follows in any case from our general analysis of values and of man's attitude to them.

By a value in the objective sense we mean all that man seeks in his interior life, all that towards which he strives in his activity.[52] So that the mere fact of cutting oneself off from certain values, for instance from those to which sensuality and sentiment are naturally responsive, does nothing to develop the person unless it results from acknowledgement of the objective order based on experience of the truth about those values. The acknowledgement at least is necessary even where there can have been no 'experience of the truth' of the values. This is the method by which values are objectivized. 'Blind' self-restraint alone is not enough. There is no valid continence without recognition of the objective order of values: the value of the person is higher than the values of sex. Practical recognition, that is to say a recognition which influences action, is meant here. The basic condition of self-control in matters of sex is that the superiority of the value of the person to that of sex should be recognized whenever sensuality and (indirectly) sentiment react primarily to sexual values. We might speak here of a sort of grafting of the value of the person onto the sensations which fill the whole consciousness with an intense awareness of sexual values. This is the first step on the road to chastity: continence subordinated to the process of objectivization, as described above, is necessary if in the midst of the values which appeal to the senses, the value of the person, for which the reason can speak, is to enter consciousness.

Thereafter, the value of the person must 'take command', so to speak, of all that happens in a man. When it does, continence is no longer 'blind'. It goes beyond mere self-restraint and interdiction and permits the mind and the will to 'open up' to a value which is both genuine and superior. Thus, objectivization is closely connected with sublimation.

How does the method of objectivization relate to the need to contain the promptings of the senses, or of the senses and the emotions together? Objectivization does not release us from that need: if some-one contents himself with objectivizing, i.e. understanding objectively and correctly the value of the person in relation to the sexual values, without at the same time containing the promptings of carnal desire, he cannot be said to be self-controlled or chaste. His behaviour would be all theory and no practice. Mere objectivization without continence does not constitute virtue, though continence becomes virtue in the full sense only thanks to objectivization. For man is a being internally so constructed that the promptings of carnal desire do not disappear merely because they are contained by willpower, although superficially they appear to do so; for them to disappear completely a man must know 'why' he is containing them. It may be said that the prohibition is self-justifying: 'why not?' – 'because I must not' – but this does not solve the problem satisfactorily, and does not amount to genuine objectivization.[53] We can speak of objectivization only when the will is confronted by a value which fully explains the necessity for containing impulses aroused by carnal desire and sensuality.[54] Only as this value gradually takes possession of the mind and the will does the will become calm and free itself from a characteristic sense of loss. For it is a fact which we all know from our own inner life that the practice of self control and of virtue is accompanied, especially in the early stages, by a feeling of loss, of having renounced a value. This feeling is a natural phenomenon, it tells us how powerfully the reflex of carnal desire acts upon the conscious mind and the will. As true love of the person develops, this reflex will grow weaker, the values will return to their proper places. Thus *the virtue of chastity and love of the person are each conditional upon the other.*

The sublimation of the emotions plays an important part in this whole process. As we have just said, objectivization and sublimation go closely together. The fact that reactions to a person of the other sex may be grounded in sentiment and not only in sensuality in itself favours sublimation. Because of it sensual passion may yield to another form of emotional commitment, free from the preoccupation with 'the body as an object of enjoyment' characteristic of sensuality. But can sentiment by itself displace sensuality and fashion an attitude to another person solely from its own reactions and within the limits of its own orientation? We know already that this orientation is quite distinct from that which prevails in sensuality. Sentimental desire is not directed solely towards sensual and carnal enjoyment. It is to a much greater extent a desire to be close to 'a human being of the other sex'. But if we leave the spontaneous reactions to take their course we must reckon with the danger of a lapse (or relapse) from the plane of sentiment to that of sensuality. It is difficult to imagine a sublimation of the sentiments without the participation of reflection and of virtue.

Sentiment may, however, play an important auxiliary role in the whole process of sublimation. *For the value of the person must be not merely understood by the cold light of reason but felt.* An abstract understanding of the person does not necesarily beget a feeling for the value of the person. This, in its full metaphysical sense, seems to transcend the upper limit of our emotional life, and to develop in parallel with the spiritualization of our inner life. But we may make use of elements inherent in sentiment to help us towards this fuller appreciation. The ability to react spontaneously to the value 'human being of the other sex', to 'femininity' or 'masculinity', coupled with a tendency to idealize those values, combine fairly easily in one's reactions with the concept of the person, so that what was a spontaneous process of emotional idealization may cease to centre on the values 'femininity' and 'masculinity', and centre instead on the value of the person, awareness of which simultaneously ripens in the mind as the result of conscious thought. In this way, the virtue of chastity also finds some support in the emotional sphere.

The practice of that virtue, rightly understood, means just this, as Aristotle and St Thomas of Aquinas point out. They both emphasize that in relation to the sensual and emotional sphere of his inner life a man must employ appropriate tactics, and even a certain diplomacy (*principatus politicus*). The use of the imperative is of little avail here, and it may even produce results the very opposite of what was intended. Their way of looking at the matter is a proof of great experience and practical wisdom. Indeed, every man must effectively deploy the energies latent in his sensuality and his sentiments, so that they become allies in his striving for authentic love, for they may, as we know, also be its foes. This ability to make allies of potential foes is perhaps an even more decisive characteristic of self-mastery and the virtue of chastity than is 'pure' continence. This constitutes the first part of the specific problem of what (using the commonest term for it) we have called continence. It will be discussed further in the next chapter, which deals with marital ethics. We come now to the second part of the problem, which concerns the relationship between tenderness and sensuality. This part of our discussion runs in parallel with the first, and at times seems to draw very close to it, but in fact they remain separate.

Tenderness and Sensuality

We must give some thought to tenderness, because it too originates in sentiment and develops on the basis of those concupiscent sensations of which we have spoken several times before. But tenderness has a significance and performs a function peculiarly its own in human life, and especially in the relationship between man and woman, the sublimation of which relies in large part on tenderness. For this reason we must now explain its function.

We feel tenderness for a person (or for that matter towards some unreasoning being, such as an animal or plant) when we become conscious of the ties which unite us. Awareness of a tie, awareness of a share in the existence and activity, the joys and sufferings of another being bids us think tenderly not only of other people, but also for instance of the animals who share our lot. We are overcome by tenderness for those various beings with whom we feel so closely linked that we can, as it were, enter into their inner feelings, and experience their state of mind in our own 'interior'. Tenderness borders very closely on compassion in the etymological sense (not sympathy in the ordinary sense, which may be seen rather as a consequence of tenderness, although it sometimes arises in a human being independently of this). Often enough this empathy with another being is at least partly imaginary, as when for instance we attribute to an animal 'interior' experiences which are exclusively our own, human, prerogative, or when we think of the suffering inflicted on trampled or broken plants, etc. Man is rightly aware of his ties with the whole natural world, but his ties and his union with other people are naturally closer than any others – and so it is they in particular that give rise to tenderness. It is especially in relationships between two human beings that one of them is able to, and feels the need to, enter into the feelings, the inner state, the whole spiritual life of the other – and is able and needs to make the other aware of this. These are precisely the functions of tenderness.

Tenderness is more than just an inner capacity for compassion, for sensitive awareness of another person's feelings and state of mind. Tenderness includes all this, but its essence is elsewhere – in the tendency to make one's own the feelings and mental states of another person. This tendency seeks outward expression: I feel the need to let the other 'I' know that I take his feelings and his state of mind to heart, to make this other human being feel that I am sharing it all, that I am feeling what he feels. *Tenderness, then, springs from awareness of the inner state of another person* (and indirectly of that person's external situation, which conditions his inner state) *and whoever feels it actively seeks to communicate his feeling of close involvement* with the other person and his situation. This closeness is the result of an emotional commitment – the analysis carried out in the last chapter showed that sentiment enables us to feel close to another 'I': sentiment naturally brings people closer together. Hence also the need actively to communicate the feeling of closeness, so that tenderness shows itself in certain outward actions which of their very nature reflect this inner approximation to another 'I'. These actions all have the same inner significance, though outwardly they may look very different: pressing another person to one's breast, embracing him, putting one's arms round him (if this is only a way of physically assisting someone its meaning is quite different), certain forms of kissing. These are active displays of tenderness. Willingness to receive them does not in itself mean that the feeling is reciprocated, only that there is no emotional antipathy to the person manifesting tenderness in this particular way. Tenderness resides in an inner emotional attitude, not in its outward manifestations, for they can equally well be purely conventional and social. Whereas tenderness is always personal, interior, private, – to some extent at least it modestly shuns the gaze of others. It can display itself freely only to those who can understand it and respond to it properly.

A very clear distinction must be drawn between tenderness and the various ways in which it manifests itself on the one hand, and various means of satisfying the demands of sensuality on the other. Their origins and objectives are quite different. Sensuality is naturally oriented towards 'the body as a possible object of sexual enjoyment', and aims at satisfying this need for enjoyment in the natural way: this is called finding a sexual outlet. Tenderness, on the other hand, comes from sentiment and its characteristic reaction to 'a human being of the other sex'. It is not an expression of concupiscence but of benevolence and devotion. Of course, a need to satisfy the demands of sentiment makes itself felt, but it is fundamentally different from the need to appease sensuality. Sentiment concentrates more on 'the human being', not on 'the body and sex', and its immediate aim is not 'enjoyment', but the 'feeling of nearness'.

All this deserves to be emphasized. Tenderness, both in its inner orientation and in its external manifestations, differs so much from sensuality and sensual enjoyment that they must not be regarded as identical or even comparable. Actions, both exterior and interior, which have their origin in tenderness cannot be assessed from the ethical point of view in the same way as those which originate in sensuality and the will to sexual enjoyment. Unlike these, tenderness may be entirely disinterested – when it exhibits above all concern for the other person and his inner situation. This disinterestedness diminishes as and when manifestations of tenderness serve primarily the need to gratify one's own feelings. But even this may have its value, in that it brings with it a feeling of closeness in relation to another human being, and especially if both persons feel a need for nearness. (A certain 'self-interest' enters into human love, without in any way detracting from its proper character – as our metaphysical analysis has shown. Every human being is a limited good, and for that reason capable of disinterestedness only within limits.)[55]

There exists, then, a problem of educating tenderness, within the general problem of educating love 'in' man and woman, and consequently 'between' them. This problem is part of the general problem of continence. For tenderness demands vigilance against the danger that its manifestations may acquire a different significance and become merely forms of sensual and sexual gratification. Tenderness, therefore, cannot do without a perfected inner self-control, which here becomes the index of the inner refinement and delicacy of one's attitude to a person of the other sex. Whereas mere sensuality pushes us towards enjoyment, and the man exclusively under its sway cannot even see that the association between man and woman may have some other significance, that its 'style' can be quite different, tenderness reveals so to speak this other style, and takes care that it is not subsequently destroyed.

Can we speak of 'a right to tenderness'? The expression must be taken to mean, on the one hand, the right to receive tenderness, and on the other, the right to show it. We speak deliberately of a right rather than a duty, in the second as well as in the first case, although there undoubtedly also exists a duty in some circumstances to show tenderness towards another human being. Thus, tenderness is the right of all those who have a special need for it – the weak, the sick, those who are in any way afflicted physically or morally. It would seem that children, to whom it is the natural way of showing love (though this is true not only of them), have a special right to tenderness. We must therefore apply to all, and particularly the outward, manifestations of tenderness one single criterion, that of love and love of the person. For there also exists a danger of inflaming egoism by exaggerated tenderness, which serves above all to satisfy the sentimental needs of the person who shows it, and has no regard to the objective needs and the good of the other human being. For this reason genuine human love, love 'for' a person, and love 'between' persons, must combine two elements: tenderness and a certain firmness. Otherwise, it will lose its inner soundness and resilience, and turn into sterile sloppiness and mawkishness. We must not forget that love for a human being must also contain certain elements of struggle. Struggle for the beloved human being, and his or her true good.

Tenderness, then, will gain in value if it is combined with a certain firmness and intransigence of will. A too facile tenderness, and particularly what is called sickly sentimentality, does not inspire profound confidence, but on the contrary, arouses a suspicion that for this particular human being a display of tenderness is only a way of trying to satisfy his sentimental needs, or perhaps even his sensual needs, his desire to enjoy. This being so, the only morally justifiable forms of tenderness are those which are fully attributable to love of the person, to the real bonds between human beings. Clearly, tenderness has no *raison d'etre* outside love. Save in love, we have no 'right' to show or receive tenderness – its exterior manifestations are empty gestures.

These observations apply particularly to relations between man and woman. Here more than anywhere the various forms of tenderness must be fully warranted by true love of the person. For we have to reckon with the fact that the love of man and woman is powered to a very great extent by sensuality and sentiment, which themselves demand full and over-abundant satisfaction. Hence, various forms of tenderness can easily diverge from love of the person, and stray in the direction of sensual, or at any rate emotional, egoism. Apart from this, exterior manifestations of tenderness may create an illusion of love, a love which in reality does not exist. The seducer's methods usually include a display of tenderness, just as the coquette tries to play on the senses, though in both these cases genuine love of the person is absent. Leaving aside 'love-games' – flirtation, romancing, etc. – we must draw attention to the fact that the subjective elements in love between man and woman, even if both of them intend it to be honest and genuine, usually develop more quickly than its objective content. Various psychological elements germinate earlier, while its ethical essence necessarily matures slowly and gradually. A great deal also depends on age and temperament. In young people, the divergence between these two internal processes is normally greater than in older and generally mature people. In people endowed with a lively and ardent temperament (people of the 'sanguine' type, for instance), the emotion of love is a sudden and powerful explosion, and the cultivation and education of virtue requires an effort so much the greater for that.

Accordingly, if we are to grant a man or a woman the 'right to tenderness' – whether to show it, or to receive it – we must also demand an even greater sense of responsibility. There undoubtedly exists a tendency, more pronounced in some than in others, to enlarge those rights, to seek to enjoy them prematurely when both are only at the stage of the arousal of sentiment, and with it of sensuality, while the objective aspect of love, and the union of persons, are still missing. Such premature tenderness in the association of a man and a woman quite often even destroys love, or at least prevents it from developing fully, of ripening both internally and objectively into a genuine love. We are not for the moment thinking of the various forms of exessive familiarity which belong to a different order of facts affecting the association of man and woman – excessive familiarity is a form of irresponsible sexual enjoyment, and may also be a manifestation of boorishness, or simply tactlessness. We are only concerned here with tenderness. Without the virtue of moderation, without chastity and self-control it is impossible so to educate and develop tenderness that it does not harm love but serves it. For there is a serious danger that, while the feeling is only shallow and superficial, an attempt may be made to 'use' love, i.e. to use the 'raw material' from which it is formed in a man or a woman – and within the limits of such a feeling the two of them will not succeed in perfecting the objective profile, and the true good, of love, but will stop short at purely subjective manifestations, deriving only a fleeting pleasure from them. In that case love, instead of continually beginning again, and continually growing, will be forever breaking off and stopping short. Let us add that a great deal depends here on the correct education of tenderness, and on responsibility for the ways in which it is shown.

We must stress yet again that tenderness is an important factor in love. There is no denying that the love of man and woman is based to a very great extent on sentiment – this is the material which our natural sensibility must constantly supply if the objective and subjective aspects of love are to be firmly knit together. We have in mind here not so much the 'first' emotional transports, connected with the experience of 'femininity' or 'masculinity', which heighten, in a sense artificially, the value of the beloved person. It is much more a matter of the steady participation of emotion, of a durable commitment to love, for it is this that brings a man and a woman close together, creates an interior climate of 'communicativeness'. Tenderness, when it has a base of this kind, is natural and authentic. A great deal of tenderness of this kind is needed in marriage, in that life together in which it is not only a body that needs a body, but a human being that needs a human being. Tenderness has a very important role to play here. Organically combined with genuine love of the person and 'disinterested', it has the power to deliver love from the various dangers implicit in the egoism of the senses and the hedonistic attitude. *Tenderness is the ability to feel with and for the whole person*, to feel even the most deeply hidden spiritual tremors, and always to have in mind the true good of that person.

This is the sort of tenderness which a woman expects from a man, and she has a special right to it in marriage, in which she gives herself to a man, and goes through such extremely important periods in her life, such difficult experiences as pregnancy, childbirth, and all that goes with them. Moreover, her emotional life is generally richer than a man's, and so her need for tenderness is greater. A man also has need of it, but to a different degree, and in a different form. Both in the woman and in the man tenderness creates a feeling of not being alone, a feeling that her or his whole life is equally the content of another and very dear person's life. This conviction very greatly facilitates and reinforces their sense of unity.

It may nevertheless seem strange that our discussion of tenderness forms part of a chapter devoted to the problem of continence. But the connection is a close one, and the discussion is in its proper place. There can be no genuine tenderness without a perfected habit of continence, which has its origin in a will always ready to show loving kindness, and so overcome the temptation merely to enjoy put in its way by sensuality and carnal concupiscence. Without such continence, the natural energies of sensuality, and the energies of sentiment drawn into their orbit, will become merely the 'raw material' of sensual or at best emotional egoism. This must be very clearly and emphatically stated. Life teaches us this lesson at every step. For believers, what lies behind this fact is the mystery of original sin, the consequences of which are particularly grave in the sphere of sex, and are a threat to the person, the greatest good in the created universe. This danger is, so to speak, a very near neighbour of love: for true love, a union of persons, may develop from just the same raw material as the semblance of love which merely masks an inner attitude, an egoism which is the contrary of love. Continence plays here a very important and positive part, in that it liberates us from that attitude and from egoism, and so indirectly creates love. Love between man and woman cannot be built without sacrifices and self-denial. We find the formula for this renunciation in the Gospel, in the words of Christ: 'Whoever would follow me must first renounce his own self. . . .' The Gospel teaches continence as a way of showing love.

CHAPTER IV

Justice Towards The Creator

✣

MARRIAGE

❖

Monogamy and the Indissolubility of Marriage

The whole course of the discussion in previous chapters logically and inevitably leads to recognition of the principle of monogamy and the indissolubility of the marriage tie. The personalistic norm formulated and explained in the first chapter is the foundation and the source of this principle. If a person can never in any circumstances be a mere object of enjoyment for another person, but can only be the object (or rather the co-subject) of love, the union of man and woman needs a suitable framework, one which permits the full development of the sexual relationship while ensuring the durability of their union. Such a union is, of course, called a marriage. Attempts to solve the problem of marriage other than by monogamy (which implies indissolubility) are incompatible with the personalistic norm and fall short of its strict demands, in that they put one person in the position of an object to be enjoyed by another: the woman in particular is in danger of becoming a mere object of enjoyment for the man. This is what happens where polygyny (the union of a man with several women, which is what we usually mean by 'polygamy') is practised. The history of mankind also, of course, furnishes examples of 'polyandry', the converse of polygyny – the union of a woman with more than one man.

We shall consider marriage here mainly in the light of the personalistic norm, which bids us show 'loving kindness', and treat a person in a manner appropriate to his or her essential nature. This principle is fully compatible only with monogamy and the indissolubility of marriage. It is fundamentally opposed to all forms of polygamy, whether polygyny or polyandry. It is likewise opposed in principle to the dissolution of marriage. In effect, in all these cases a person is put in the position of an object for use by another person. Marriage itself is then only (or at any rate mainly) an institutional framework within which a man and a woman obtain sexual pleasure, and not a durable union of persons based on mutual affirmation of the value of the person. For such a union must be durable, must last until one of the parties to the relationship ceases to exist. I am speaking not of spiritual existence, which is above and outside of time, but of existence in the body, which ends with death. Why is this so important? Because marriage is not only a spiritual but also a physical and terrestrial union of persons.[56] According to the answer which Christ gave to the Sadducees (Matthew 22: 23–30) when they asked him what would become of marriage after the resurrection of the body – which is of course an article of faith – 'those who live anew in their bodies neither marry nor are given in marriage but are like angels in heaven'. Marriage is strictly a feature of man's physical and terrestrial existence, so that it is naturally dissolved by the death of one of the spouses. The other is then free to marry another person. In law this is called *bigamia successiva* (= re-marriage), which must be strictly distinguished from *bigamia simultanea* ('bigamy' for short in ordinary useage), which means marrying another partner while an earlier marriage is still in being. Although remarriage after the death of a spouse is justifiable and permitted, to remain a widow or widower is none the less altogether praiseworthy since (among other things) it emphasizes more fully the reality of the union with the person now deceased. The value of the person, after all, is not transient, and spiritual union can and should continue even when physical union is at an end. In the Gospels, and especially in the Epistle of St Paul, we find widowhood and strict monogamy praised in several places.

The question of monogamy and the indissolubility of marriage is dealt with decisively and conclusively in Christ's teachings. Christ had before his eyes the fact that marriage as instituted by the Creator was originally strictly monogamous (Genesis 1:27 and 2:24) and indissoluble ('what God hath joined together let no man put asunder'), and continually referred to it. For the memory of the polygamy of the patriarchs, the great leaders and the kings (David and Solomon for instance), was still alive in the traditions of his immediate audience, the Israelites, as was the Mosaic letter of repudiation authorizing the dissolution of a legally valid marriage in certain circumstances. Christ uncompromisingly opposed these traditional usages, stressing the character of marriage as originally instituted and the primordial intention of the Creator ('. . . in the beginning it was not so'). The idea of monogamous marriage which dwelt in the mind and will of the Creator was distorted by the 'chosen people' as well as by others. The excuse often made for the polygamy of the patriarchs is their desire for a numerous progeny. If we accept that procreation as the objective purpose of marriage justified polygamy in Old Testament times it must by analogy be an equally valid justification wherever the purpose of polygamy is the same. But at the same time the books of the Old Testament provide sufficient evidence that polygamy (polygyny) is in practice conducive to the treatment of women by men as objects of enjoyment and so at once degrades women and lowers the level of morality amongst men. We need only remember the story of King Solomon.

The abolition of polygamy and the re-establishment of monogamy and the indissolubility of marriage are a necessary consequence of the command to love, understood, as we have understood it all along, as an embodiment of the personalistic norm. If all relationships between men and women are to be on this high level they must develop in accordance with and embody the principle of monogamy and indissolubility, which also throws light on other aspects of the coexistence and association of man and woman. The commandment to love, as it occurs in the Gospels, is more than the 'personalistic norm', it also embodies the basic law of the whole supernatural order, of the supernatural relationship between God and man. Nevertheless, the personalistic norm is most certainly inherent in it – it is the 'natural' content of the commandment to love, that part of it which we can equally well understand without faith and by reason alone. Let us add that without it the essentially supernatural content of the commandment cannot fully be understood or put into practice.

Polygamy and the dissolution of lawful marriages ('divorce'), which in practice leads to polygamy, are incompatible with the demands of the personalistic norm. The two things go together: where a person of the other sex is regarded as 'an object representing only a sexual value' the institution of marriage will be treated as though it is based on and serves that value alone, not as a means of bringing two people together in a union of persons.

Man is a being endowed with a capacity for conceptual thought, and so capable of behaving in accordance with general principles. In the light of these principles, that is to say if we adhere consistently to the personalistic norm, we must admit that where there are serious reasons (marital infidelity is a particularly serious one) why husband and wife cannot go on living together there is only one possibility – separation, but without dissolution of the marriage itself. Obviously, even separation is an evil ('a necessary evil'), if we take the view that marriage is of its nature a lasting union of man and woman. However, this evil does not negate the personalistic norm: neither of the persons (and it is the woman who is more at risk) is put in the position of an object of use for the other. This would be the case if a person could abandon the person to whom he or she had legally belonged in marriage and marry again during the lifetime of this former spouse. But if the parties to a marriage merely withdraw from it, and from their conjugal and family life together, and do not conclude marriages with other persons, there is no breach of the personalistic order. The person is not degraded to the status of an object of use, and marriage preserves its character as an institution facilitating the personal union of man and woman, and not merely sexual relations between them.

We must accept that in their conjugal life a man and a woman unite as person and that their union therefore lasts as long as they live. We cannot accept that their union lasts only as long as the persons themselves wish it to last, for that would be a contradiction of the personalistic norm, which is based on the concept of the person as a primary being. From this point of view, a man and a woman who have lived as husband and wife within the framework of a valid marriage are joined in a union which only the death of one of them can dissolve. And the fact that one or even both of them may cease in course of time to want this does nothing to alter the situation: their change of mind cannot cancel the fact that they are objectively united as man and wife. One, or both of them, may cease to feel that there is any subjective justification for this union, and gradually fall into a state of mind which is psychologically or both psychologically and physiologically incompatible with it. Such a condition warrants separation 'from bed and table', but cannot annul the fact that they are objectively united, and united in wedlock. The personalistic norm, which takes precedence of the will and the decisions of either of the persons concerned, demands that their union be maintained until death. Any other view of the matter in effect puts the person in the position of an object 'for use', which amounts to the destruction of the objective order of love, in which the supra-utilitarian value of the person is affirmed.

Conversely, the objective order is preserved in the principle of strict monogamy, which is identical with the indissolubility of lawful marriages. It is a difficult principle to observe, but an indispensable one if the life together of persons of different sex (and ultimately human life at large, which is to such a great extent based on this relationship) are to be raised to the level of the person and accommodated within the bounds of love. We are of course concerned here with love in its full objective sense, love as a virtue – and not only in its subjective, psychological sense. The difficulty of applying the principle of monogamy and the indissolubility of marriage arises because 'love' is so often understood and practised exclusively in the second rather than the first sense. The principle of monogamy and the indissolubility of marriage make necessary the integration of love (see the chapter devoted to the analysis of love, and especially Part III of that chapter). Without integration marriage is an enormous risk. A man and a woman whose love has not begun to mature, has not established itself as a genuine union of persons, should not marry, for they are not ready to undergo the test to which married life will subject them. This does not, however, mean that their love must have reached full maturity at the moment of marriage, but only that it must be ripe enough for its continued ripening in and through marriage to be ensured.

Renunciation of the good which monogamy and indissolubility represent is impossible not only from the supernatural standpoint, the standpoint of faith, but equally for purely rational and human reasons. What is at stake is the superiority of the value of the person to the value of sex as such, and the application of the norm in a context in which it can easily be ousted by the utilitarian principle. Strict monogamy is a function of the personal order.

The Value of the Institution

These considerations make it easier for us to understand the value of marriage as an institution. For it must be seen as an institution, and not reduced merely to a *de facto* sexual relationship between a man and a woman. Although there can be no doubt that the physical relationship between two people is of decisive importance to the institution (hence the old Latin adage *matrimonium facit copula*), it is nonetheless true that outside the institutional framework such a relationship does not constitute a marriage. The word 'institution' denotes something 'instituted', 'established' in accordance with a concept of justice. Now, we know that the order of justice affects both inter-personal matters and social matters (commutative justice and social justice). Marriage is in fact both an inter-personal and a social concern.

A sexual relationship between a man and a woman necessarily has an intimate character, for reasons already mentioned in the preceding chapter (The Analysis of Shame). Nevertheless, the parties to it belong to society and for many reasons must justify their relationship in the eyes of society. That is precisely what the institution of marriage does. We are not speaking here solely of justification in the sense of legalization, of conforming to the law. 'Justify' here means 'make just'. Nor does this have anything to do with self-justification, pleading mitigating circumstances to excuse something intrinsically bad.

The need to justify sexual relations between man and woman in the eyes of society arises not only from the normal consequences of the relationship but also in consideration of the partners themselves, especially the woman. The normal consequence of a sexual relationship between man and woman is progeny. A child is a new member for society to adopt, and (where society is sufficiently highly organized) register. The birth of a child turns the union of a man and a woman based on the sexual relationship into a family. The family is in itself a small society, and the existence of all large societies – nation, state, Church – depends on it. Obviously any large society will keep a watchful eye on the process of its own ceaseless recruitment by way of the family. The family is the primary institution at the base of our existence as human beings.[57] It forms part of the large society which it constantly helps to create, but it also has its own distinct existence, its own character and ends. Both these characteristics – its immanence in society on the one hand, its peculiar autonomy and inviolability on the other, must find reflection in legislation. The point of departure must be the law of nature; legislation concerning the family must objectively express the order implicit in its nature.

The family is an institution based on marriage. It is impossible in a large society to legislate correctly for the family unless we define correctly the rights and duties which go with marriage. This, however, does not mean that marriage should be regarded as solely a means to an end – the end being the family. For although marriage in the natural course of things leads to the existence of a family, and although the possibility that it will do so must always be kept open, marriage itself is not as a result absorbed by and lost in the family. It retains its distinct existence as an institution whose inner structure is different from that of the family. The family has the structure of a society, in which the father, and the mother too – each in his or her own particular way – both exercise authority, while the children are subject to that authority. Marriage does not possess the structure of a society, but an inter-personal structure: it is a union and a community of two persons.

The distinctive character of the institution of matrimony is preserved when the community of husband and wife expands to become a family. However, for a variety of reasons this may not happen but lack of family in no way deprives marriage of its proper character. The inner and essential *raison d'être* of marriage is not simply eventual transformation into a family but above all the creation of a lasting personal union between a man and a woman based on love. Marriage serves above all to preserve the existence of the species – as the discussion in Chapter I showed – but it is based on love. A marriage which, through no fault of the spouses, is childless retains its full value as an institution. No doubt a marriage serves love more fully when it serves the cause of existence, and develops into a family. This is how we should understand the statement that 'procreation is the principal end of marriage'. But a marriage which cannot fulfil that purpose does not lose its significance as an institution of an interpersonal character. Moreover, realization of the principal purpose of marriage demands that its inter-personal character be realized to the full, so that the love of the spouses may be fully mature and creative. It should be added that if their love is already more or less ripe procreation will ripen it still further.

Marriage is, then, a separate institution with a distinctive inter-personal structure. This institution grows into and becomes a family, and can be identified up to a point with the family, though it would perhaps be better to say that just as the family makes its imprint on marriage so marriage makes its characteristic mark on the family, in which it finds its confirmation and the means of attaining fulfilment. Thus, for example, an elderly couple who live with not only their own children, but their children's families and perhaps even great-grandchildren around them still form a separate 'institution' among this family hierarchy; at once a unit and an integral whole, existing and living by its own laws in accordance with its fundamental interpersonal character. That is what makes it an institution. The laws on which its existence is based must derive from the principles of the personalistic norm, for only in this way can the genuinely personal character of a union of two persons be ensured. The social structure of the family is sound to the extent that it makes possible and maintains the interpersonal character of marriage. This is why a family originating in polygamy, though it may be a larger society, and in material terms a stronger one (as were for example the families of the Old Testament patriarchs), will none the less necessarily have a lower moral value than a family originating in a monogamous marriage. In the structure of this second type of marriage the value of the persons, and the value of their love as a lasting union, which in itself has a great educational significance, is much more conspicuous, whereas in the structure of the polygamous family there is much more emphasis on mere biological fertility and quantitative increase than on the value of the person and the personal value of love.

The importance of the institution of marriage lies in the fact that it provides a justification for the sexual relationship between a particular couple within the whole complex of society. This is important not only because of the consequences of the relationship – we have spoken of these above – but for the sake of the partners themselves. It is also important to the moral evaluation of their love, since their relationship must be fitted into the context both of their immediate social milieu and of society at large. Nowhere else, perhaps, is man so conspicuously a social being as in this relationship in which strictly speaking everything takes place between two people and is a function of their love. The 'love' which psychologically is for both of them the justification and legitimation of their relationship must also gain acceptance by other people.

They may at first suppose that this is not necessary, but as time goes by they are bound to realize that without this acceptance their love lacks something very important. They will begin to feel that it must ripen sufficiently to be revealed to society. On the one hand, there is a need to keep private the sexual relations deriving from love, and on the other a need for social recognition of this love as a union of persons. Love demands this recognition, without which it does not feel fully itself. There is more than a merely conventional difference of meaning between such words as 'mistress', 'concubine', and 'kept woman' on the one hand and 'wife', 'fiancee', on the other. (These are all words referring to women, but whenever we use one of them we also say something about a man.) No, it is rather the blurring of the distinctions which is artificial and an afterthought, whereas the distinctions themselves are primordial, natural and fundamental. For instance, the term 'mistress' in modern usage implies that some man regards the woman referred to solely as an 'object' to be used in the sexual relationship, whereas 'wife' and 'fiancee' suggest the co-subject of a love having full personal and hence also full social value.

This then is the meaning of marriage as an institution. In a society which accepts sound ethical principles and lives in accordance with them (without hypocrisy and prudery), this institution is necessary to signify the maturity of the union between a man and a woman, to testify that their is a love on which a lasting union and community can be based. The institution is needed for this purpose not only in the interests of society, of the 'other people' who belong to it, but also, and mainly, in the interests of the persons who enter into a marriage. Even if there were no other people around them they would need the institution of marriage (or at any rate some 'form' or rite, which would mean in effect that the parties concerned had created the institution). Thus, though the institution might arise directly in certain situations, and especially from an existing sexual relationship, it would certainly be distinguishable from the factors which produced it. An actual sexual relationship between a man and a woman demands the institution of marriage as its natural setting, for the institution legitimates the actuality above all in the minds of the partners to the sexual relationship themselves.

It may be helpful here to note that the Latin word for marriage, *matrimonium*, puts the emphasis on 'motherhood', as though to convey that a woman who lives a conjugal life with a man has a specific responsibility. Responsibility for maternity is a question to which we shall revert later in the chapter. For the present it suffices to say that a quasi-conjugal sexual relationship certainly demands the institutional framework of *matrimonium*, to ensure that the partners treat each other as persons. Sexual relations outside marriage automatically put one person in the position of an object to be used by another. Which is the user, which the used? It is not excluded that the man may also be an object to be enjoyed, but the woman is always in that position in relation to the man. This is a deduction easily made – by contrast – from analysis of the word *matrimonium* (*matris munia – maternal duties*). A 'marital' sexual relationship outside the framework of marriage is always objectively a wrong done to the woman. Always – even when the woman consents to it, and indeed even when she herself actively desires and seeks it.

For this reason, 'adultery' in the broadest sense of the word is morally wrong. And it is used in the broadest sense in the Holy Scriptures, in the Decalogue and the Gospels, where it refers to sexual relations not just with another man's wife, but with any woman who is not one's own wife, whether she has a husband or not. In the case of a woman, the word refers to relations with any man who is not her husband. As the analysis of chastity in the previous chapter has shown, certain elements of adultery understood in this definition are present in such 'interior' acts as lust (see Matthew 5:28, which we have already cited more than once). Obviously, such 'acts' are all the more gravely adulterous when they concern another person's wife or husband. In such cases the moral evil is all the greater because the requirements of justice are flouted and the boundary between 'one's own' and 'another's' violated. However, this boundary is illegally crossed not only by those who aspire to what expressly belongs to another, but just as surely by anyone who seeks what is not his own.[58] It is the institution of marriage – in which two people belong each to the other – which decides in such cases the question of 'ownership'. Let us add that the value of this institution – as we have demonstrated above – is fully preserved only on condition of monogamy and indissolubility.

All that has been said here to prove that 'adultery' is morally evil entitles us to state that sexual relations between a man and a woman outside the institution of *matrimonium* are always morally bad, and that this applies as much to pre-marital as to extra-marital relationships. Still worse is 'free love' on principle, for it implies a renunciation of the institution of marriage, or at least a reduction of its role in sexual relationships between man and woman. Where this principle of 'free love' is accepted, the institution of marriage plays a minor and inessential part. Our analysis above sought to demonstrate that the role of marriage is in fact supremely important, indeed essential. Without the institution of *matrimonium* the person is necessarily degraded in the sexual relationship to the status of an object of pleasure for another person, and this is totally incompatible with the demands of the personalistic norm, without which one cannot imagine a relationship remaining at the level proper to the person. Marriage as an institution is essential to justify the existence of 'conjugal' relations between a man and a woman – in their own eyes above all, but also in the eyes of society. The use of the word justification clearly implies that the institution of marriage derives from the objective order of justice.

There is also a need to justify sexual relations between a man and a woman in the eyes of God the Creator. This too is demanded by the objective order of justice. Indeed, thorough analysis leads to the conclusion that justification of 'marital' relations between a man and a woman in the eyes of the Creator is fundamental to their justification in general, whether 'internally' between the two persons concerned, or 'externally' – in the eyes of society. Admittedly, only a religious person, that is one who recognizes the existence of God the Creator and accepts that all the beings in the universe around us, amongst them the human person, are God's creatures, can carry out such an analysis and accept its results. The concept 'creature' denotes a special form of dependence on the Creator – dependence for one's existence ('to be created' means 'to depend for one's existence'). This dependence is in turn the basis of the Creator's proprietorial rights in all creatures (*dominium altum*). The Creator possesses each of them absolutely – for if each of them exists because of the Creator, originates in Him, there is a sense in which all things are His, for even that which the creature creates presupposes his own existence. The activity of creatures only develops further what is contained in each of them by virtue of their existence.

Man differs from other creatures of the visible world in that his reason is capable of understanding all these things. Reason is at the same time the foundation of personality, the necessary condition of the 'interiority' and spirituality of the being and life of a person. Thanks to his reasoning power man realizes that he is at once his own property (*sui juris*) and as a creature, the property of the Creator; he feels the effects of the Creator's proprietorial rights over himself. This state of mind necessarily develops in a man whose reason is illuminated by faith. Reason also permits him to observe, and teaches him to recognize, that every other person is also *sui juris*, and at the same time, as a creature, the property of the Creator. Hence the dual necessity to justify sexual relations between man and woman by means of the institution of marriage, for the effect of such a relationship is to make each person in some way the property of the other. If, then, there is a need to justify this fact in the relationship between them, there is also an objective need to justify it in the eyes of the Creator. True, only religious people realize this need. For 'a religious man' means not so much 'one who is capable of religious experiences' (as is generally supposed) as above all 'one who is just to God the Creator'.

We are now on the verge of understanding the 'sacramental' character of marriage. According to the teaching of the Church, it has been a sacrament from the beginning, that is to say ever since the creation of the first human couple. The 'sacrament of nature' was subsequently reinforced, in the Gospels, by the institution or rather the revelation of the 'Sacrament of Grace', which is connected with it. The Latin word *sacramentum* means 'mystery' – which, in the most general sense, is something not fully known, because it is not fully visible, it does not lie within the field of direct sensory experience. Now, both the proprietory right which each of the persons has in relation to himself or herself and still more the *dominium altum*, which the Creator enjoys in relation to each of them, lie outside the field of immediate experience and are accessible only to reason. But if a couple accept, as every religious human being must, this supreme proprietorial right they must seek justification above all in His eyes, must obtain His approval. It is not enough for a woman and a man to give themselves to each other in marriage. If each of these persons is simultaneously the property of the Creator, He also must give the man to the woman, and the woman to the man, or at any rate approve the reciprocal gift of self implicit in the institution of marriage.[59]

This approval cannot be received through the senses, but only by way of an understanding of the natural order. Marriage as a *sacramentum naturae* is simply the institution of *matrimonium* based on a partial understanding of the Creator's rights with regard to the persons entering into it. Marriage as a *sacramentum gratiae* presupposes above all a full realization of those rights. Apart from this, the sacrament of marriage is founded on the conviction, which we owe to the Gospels, that the justification of man in the eyes of God is accomplished essentially through Grace.[60] Man obtains Grace through the sacraments administered by the Church, which was endowed by Christ with supernatural authority for this purpose. Thus, only the sacrament of marriage fully satisfies the need to justify a marital relationship in the eyes of God the Creator. This also explains the fact that the introduction of marriage coincided with the definitive revelation of the supernatural order.

Procreation and Parenthood

The value of the institution of marriage is that it justifies the existence of sexual relations between a man and a woman. By sexual relations we mean here not an isolated act but a regular succession of acts. Marriage is therefore a 'state' ('the married state'), a durable institution which forms the framework for the lifelong coexistence of a man and a woman. This framework obviously contains more than just sexual acts. It includes a whole complex of acts in a variety of contexts, acts of an economic, cultural, or religious character for instance. They combine to create a rich and multifaceted communal life, first for the married couple and then for the whole family. Each factor has its own importance and makes its own specific contribution to the development of the love between the man and the woman. Amongst the other factors their sexual relations are specially important since they affect the development of love between the persons very directly. The institution of marriage, as we have said, justifies the sexual relationship between a man and a woman. It does so to the extent that it creates the objective framework for a lasting union of persons (the conditions of which are of course monogamy and indissolubility).

But the realization of this union in each particular sexual act between the parties presents a particular moral problem, the internal problem of every marriage. Every such act must have its own internal justification, for unless justice is done there can be no question of a union of persons. There is then a special problem here, one of enormous importance from the point of view of morality and the culture of the persons, the problem of adapting sexual relations to the objective demands of the personalistic norm. It is in this context that fulfilment of those demands is particularly important, and also – we must not disguise the fact – particularly difficult, since a whole complex of internal factors and external circumstances tend to degrade the act of mutual love between persons to the 'utilitarian' level. It is in this context more than in any other that people must show responsibility for their love. Let us add at once that this responsibility for love is complemented by responsibility for life and health: a combination of fundamental goods which together determine the moral value of every marital act. We can, therefore, form a view as to its value by referring to each of these goods in turn and to man's responsibility for them. In this book, in accordance with its premises and with the main line of our argu-

225

ment, we shall take as our point of departure the good re-presented by the person and by love in its true sense. For this appears to be the most fundamental in the whole complex of goods, and conditions our attitude to the others.[61]

A man and a woman who, as husband and wife, unite in a full sexual relationship thereby enter into the realm of what can properly be called the order of nature. We pointed out in Chapter I that the order of nature is not to be identified with the 'biological order'. The order of nature is above all that of existence and procreation. We intend the word to be taken in its fullest sense when we say that the order of nature aims at 'procreation' by means of the sexual act. Sexual intercourse, on all occasions, is in the nature of things affected in one way or another by its primary purpose, procreation. Looked at objectively the marital relationship is therefore not just a union of persons, a reciprocal relationship between a man and a woman, but is essentially a union of persons affected by the possibility of procreation. This term is more appropriate here than 'reproduction', which tends to have a purely bio-logical meaning.[62] We are speaking of course, not merely of the beginning of life in a purely biological sense but of the beginning of a person's existence, and so it is better to use the term 'procreation'.

Thus, in the sexual relationship between man and woman *two orders meet*: *the order of nature*, which has as its object reproduction, and *the personal order*, which finds its expression in the love of persons and aims at the fullest realization of that love.[63] We cannot separate the two orders, for each depends upon the other. In particular, the correct attitude to procreation is a condition of the realization of love. In the animal world there is only reproduction, which is achieved by way of instinct. In that world there are no persons, hence there is no personalistic norm to proclaim the principle of love. In the world of persons on the other hand instinct alone decides nothing, and the sexual urge passes, so to speak, through the gates of the consciousness and the will, thus furnishing not merely the conditions of fertility but also the raw material of love. At a truly human, truly personal level the problems of procreation and of love cannot be resolved separately. Both procreation and love are based on the conscious choice of persons. When a man and a woman consciously and of their own free will choose to marry and have sexual relations they choose at the same time the possibility of procreation, *choose to participate in creation* (for that is the proper meaning of the word procreation). And it is only when they do so that they put their sexual relationship within the framework of marriage on a truly personal level.[64]

It is here that the problem of parenthood arises. Nature's only aim is reproduction (let us add that the very word 'nature' comes from the verb *nascor*, to be born). Reproduction depends on biological fertility, which enables adult individuals to become parents by bringing progeny, new individuals of the same species, into the world. In this respect the species *Homo* is no different from others. But a human being is a person, so that the simple natural fact of becoming a father or a mother has a deeper significance, not merely a biological but also a personal significance. Inevitably, it has profound effects upon the 'interior' of a person, which are summarized in the concept of parenthood. For human parenthood implies the whole process of conscious and voluntary choice connected with marriage and with marital intercourse in particular. Since marital intercourse is, and must be, a manifestation of love, and what is more, at the personal level, we must find the proper place for parenthood too within the limits of love. Sexual relations between a man and a woman in marriage have their full value as a union of persons only when they go with conscious acceptance of the possibility of parenthood. This is a direct result of the synthesis of the natural and the personal order. The relationship between husband and wife is not limited to themselves, but necessarily extends to the new person, which their union may (pro-)create.[65]

The word 'may' must be specially emphasized in this context, since it indicates the *potential* character of the new relationship. Marital relations between two persons 'may' give life to a new person. Hence, when a man and woman capable of procreation have intercourse their union must be accompanied by awareness and willing acceptance of the possibility that 'I may become a father' or 'I may become a mother'. Without this the marital relationship will not be 'internally' justified – quite the contrary. Mutual betrothed love demands a union of persons. But the union of persons is not the same as sexual union. This latter is raised to the level of the person only when it is accompanied in the mind and the will by acceptance of the possibility of parenthood. This acceptance is so important, so decisive that without it marital intercourse cannot be said to be a realization of the personal order. Instead of a truly personal union all that is left is a sexual association without the full value of a personal relationship. If we examine this situation carefully and draw the logical conclusions we see that the association rests only on affirmation of the value 'sex', not on affirmation of the value of the person. Neither in the man nor in the woman can affirmation of the value of the person be divorced from awareness and willing acceptance that he may become a father and she may become a mother.

If this is lacking, sexual intercourse between them will have no full objective justification, not only from the point of view of third persons considering the situation in an abstract, theoretical way, but in the eyes of the spouses themselves. If the possibility of parenthood is deliberately excluded from marital relations, the character of the relationship between the partners automatically changes. The change is away from unification in love and in the direction of mutual, or rather, bilateral, 'enjoyment'.[66] This is an inevitable process, but one which takes a variety of forms. We shall try to look into them more deeply later in the chapter, since this is a matter which demands very precise analysis. We must in any case note that when a man and a woman rule out even the possibility of parenthood their relationship is transformed to the point at which it becomes incompatible with the personalistic norm. When a man and a woman entirely reject the idea that he may become a father and she a mother, when they deliberately exclude the possibility of parenthood from their relationship, the danger arises that objectively speaking there will be nothing left except 'utilisation for pleasure', of which the object will be a person.

Put like this, our view may provoke a great deal of resistance, in theory and in practice. We must therefore revert to matters which we have discussed previously, especially in Chapter I. The proper way for a person to deal with the sexual urge is, on the one hand, consciously to make use of it for its natural purposes, and on the other to resist it, when it threatens to degrade the relationship between two persons to a level lower than that of love, lower than the level on which the value of the person is affirmed in a union with a truly personal character. Sexual (marital) relations have the character of a true union of persons as long as a general disposition towards parenthood is not excluded from them. This implies a conscious attitude to the sexual instinct: to master the sexual urge means just this, to accept its purpose in marital relations. Some people might say that this ruling subordinates man, who is a person, to 'nature', whereas in so many fields he triumphs over nature, and dominates it. This however is a specious argument, for wherever man dominates 'nature' it is by adapting himself to its immanent dynamic. *Nature cannot be conquered by violating its laws.* Mastery over nature can only result from thorough knowledge of the purposes and regularities which govern it. Man masters 'nature' by exploiting more and more effectively the possibilities latent in it. The bearing of these principles on our problem seems fairly clear. We shall look at it more closely later in the chapter. Where the sexual urge is concerned, as in other matters, man cannot triumph over 'nature' by doing violence to it, but only by understanding the laws which govern it, adapting himself to its immanent purposes and making use of its latent possibilities. There is a direct connection between this and love. Since the sexual relationship is grounded in the sexual urge, and since it draws another person into a whole complex of acts and experiences, the attitude to that person and that person's moral value is indirectly determined by the way in which gratification of the sexual urge is geared into the relationship. In the order of love a man can remain true to the person only in so far as he is true to nature. If he does violence to 'nature' he also 'violates' the person by making it an object of enjoyment rather than an object of love. Acceptance of the possibility of procreation in the marital relationship safeguards love and is an indispensable condition of a truly personal union. The union of persons in love does not necessarily have to be realized by way of sexual relations. But when it does take this form the personalistic value of the sexual relationship cannot be assured without willingness for parenthood. Thanks to this, both persons in the union act *in accordance with the inner logic of love*, respect its inner dynamic and prepare themselves to accept a new good, an expression of the creative power of love. Willing acceptance of parenthood serves to break down the reciprocal egoism – (or the egoism of one party at which the other connives) – behind which lurks the will to exploit the person.

As we see, everything depends on the premise that there exists a close connection between the order of nature and the person, the realization of personhood. It must be acknowledged that people have difficulty in understanding and accepting the order of nature as an abstract value: it is generally confused with the 'biological order' and so deprived of all importance.[67] It is much easier to understand the power of the natural order (and its constitutive significance for morality, and for the development of the human personality) if we see behind it the personal authority of the Creator. Hence the whole argument in the present chapter bears the title 'Justice to the Creator'. This concept will be separately analysed later.

In practice, the problem is not an easy one to solve, in that love combined with a sexual relationship, or indeed with any association between people of different sexes, very readily lends itself to subjectivization. Where this happens the most ephemeral erotic sensation may be taken for love. After all, the argument runs, there is no love without erotic experiences. This argument is not altogether false, it is merely incomplete. For if we look at the problem in the round, we are bound to say that there is no love without reciprocal affirmation of the value of the person, for the union of man and woman as persons depends on this. Erotic experiences, then, favour this union (love) in so far as they do not negate the value of the person. Then again, not all erotic feelings truly facilitate the union of two persons in love. The union is certainly not helped by feelings which, looked at objectively, detract in some way from the value of the person. And that, precisely, is the effect of erotic experiences in the relationship between a man and a woman who deliberately rule out parenthood. For the value of the person is fully brought out by fully conscious activity which is completely in harmony with the objective purposes of the world ('the order of nature'), and by excluding all possibility of exploitation of the person. There is a fundamental contradiction between 'loving' and 'using' a person.

We can usefully recall here our analysis of shame in the previous chapter and the phenomenon, or law, of the absorption of sexual shame by love, which was discussed there. In marital intercourse both shame and the normal process of its absorption by love are connected with the conscious acceptance of the possibility of parenthood. – ('I may become a father', 'I may become a mother'). If there is a positive decision to preclude this eventuality sexual intercourse becomes shameless. The fact that it takes place witin the framework of a lawful marriage seldom wipes out all trace of shame in the feelings of persons who have artificially precluded the possibility of parenthood. True, this feeling does not always show itself in the same way. It may seem at times that it is more easily awakened in women than in men. It must, however, be emphasized that this conjugal shame (which is the basis of conjugal chastity) meets with powerful resistance in the consciousness of men and women alike. This resistance originates in the fear of maternity and paternity. A man and a woman may 'be afraid of a child': often a child is not only a joy but also – there is no denying it – a burden. But when fear of having a child goes too far it paralyses love. Its immediate effect is to deaden the feeling of shame. There is a solution to this problem, which conforms to the laws of which we know, and is worthy of human persons: continence, which however demands control over erotic experiences. It also demands a profound culture of the person and of love. Genuine continence in marriage grows out of shame, which reacts negatively to 'exploitation' of the person, in whatever form. Shame is, however, strongest where continence and hence the culture of the person and the 'culture' of love is most genuine.

It is a natural reaction, an elementary component of natural morality. The following sentences from Gandhi's autobiography bear witness to it:

> In my view to say that the sexual act is an instinctive activity, like sleep, or the appeasement of hunger, is the height of ignorance. The existence of the world depends upon the reproductive act, and since the world is God's domain, and a reflection of his power, this act must be subject to controls, the purpose of which is the continuation of life on earth. The man who understands this will strive at all costs to master his senses, arm himself with the knowledge that is necessary to the physical and spiritual welfare of his posterity, and transmit this knowledge to the future, for its benefit.

Elsewhere in his *Autobiography* Gandhi confesses that twice in his life he had succumbed to propaganda in favour of artificial contraceptives. He had, however, come to the conclusion that in one's actions one must be able to rely on one's own internal impulses, to control oneself. Let us add that this is the only solution of the problem of birth control at a level worthy of human persons. No attempt to solve it can ignore the fundamental fact that men and women are persons.

In the whole complex of arguments on procreation and parenthood two concepts demand special and detailed analysis. The first of these is parenthood *in potentia*, the second deliberate prevention of pregnancy. They are so closely connected that the second of them cannot be understood without a grasp of the first.

(1) When we write about morality in sexual relations and in marriage we always stress that it depends on conscious and willing acceptance by the man and the woman of the possibility of parenthood, without which a marital relationship between persons not afflicted with congenital or acquired infertility will lose the value of a union in love and become merely

a bilateral arrangement for sexual enjoyment. Sexual relations between a man and a woman entail the possibility of conception and procreation, which are the natural consequence of the marital relationship. It is not, however, an inevitable consequence. It depends on a combination of conditions which man can discover and to which he can adapt his behaviour. There is no reason to hold that sexual intercourse must necessarily have conception as its end. Even biological laws formulated with scientific precision rest on imperfect induction and do not exclude an element of uncertainty as to whether sexual intercourse between a particular couple on a particular occasion will or will not result in conception. We cannot therefore demand of the spouses that they must positively desire to procreate on every occasion when they have intercourse. To say that intercourse is permissible and justified only on condition that the partners hope to have a child as a result of it would be an exaggeratedly strict ethical position. It would be at odds with the order of nature, which characteristically leaves the connection between the sexual act and reproduction in particular marriages a matter of some uncertainty. Obviously, the endeavour to overcome this uncertainty to some extent, to establish as nearly as possible whether or not a particular occasion of sexual intercourse is likely to result in conception, is justified, and this is the essence of 'planned maternity' properly understood.

Returning to the view mentioned above, that sexual intercourse is permissible and just only when the immediate intention of the partners is to produce offspring, we must note that this attitude may be another disguise for utilitarianism (treating the person as a means to an end – see Chapter I) and so conflict with the personalistic norm. Marital intercourse is, and should be, the result of reciprocal betrothed love between spouses, of the gift of self made by one person to another. Intercourse is necessary to love, not just to procreation. Marriage is an institution which exists for the sake of love, not merely for the purpose of biological reproduction. Marital intercourse is in itself an interpersonal act, an act of betrothed love, so that the intentions and the attention of

233

each partner must be fixed upon the other, upon his or her true good. They must not be concentrated on the possible consequences of the act, especially if that would mean a diversion of attention from the partner. It is certainly not necessary always to resolve that 'we are performing this act in order to become parents'. It is sufficient to say that 'in performing this act we know that we may become parents and we are willing for that to happen'. That approach alone is compatible with love and makes it possible to share the experience of love. *A man and woman become father and mother only in consequence of the marital act: it must be an act of love, an act of unification of persons, and not merely the 'instrument' or 'means' of procreation.*

(2) If, however, excessive emphasis on the intention to beget a child seems incompatible with the true character of conjugal relations, the express exclusion of procreation (or to be more exact the possibility of procreation) is even more so. A certain tendency to over-emphasize the intention to procreate is perfectly understandable in married people who have been long childless: we see here not a perversion of the act of love but merely a heightened awareness of the natural connection between love and parenthood. On the other hand the positive exclusion of the possibility of conception deprives marital intercourse of its true character as potentially an act of procreation, which is what fully justifies the act, especially in the eyes of the persons taking part in it, since it enables them to see it as modest and chaste. When a man and a woman who have marital intercourse decisively preclude the possibility of paternity and maternity, their intentions are thereby diverted from the person and directed to mere enjoyment: 'the person as co-creator of love' disappears and there remains only the 'partner in an erotic experience'. Nothing could be more incompatible with the proper ends of the act of love. The intentions, and attention, of each party to the act should be directed to the other person, as a person, the will should be wholly concerned with that person's good, the heart filled with affirmation of that person's specific value. By definitively precluding the possibility of procreation in the marital act a man and a woman inevitably shift the

whole focus of the experience in the direction of sexual pleasure as such. The whole content of the experience is then 'enjoyment', whereas it should be an expression of love with pleasure as an incidental accompaniment of the sexual act.

The very fact of deliberately excluding the possibility of parenthood from marital intercourse makes 'enjoyment' the intention of the act. We need only remind ourselves that what we call here 'deliberate exclusion' means quite simply prevention by artificial means. Man, as an intelligent being, can arrange things so that sexual intercourse does not result in procreation. He can do this by adapting himself to the fertility cycle – having intercourse during infertile periods, and abstaining during fertile periods. If he does this procreation is excluded in the natural way. Neither the man nor the woman is using any 'artificial' method or means to prevent conception. They are merely adapting themselves to the laws of nature, to the order which reigns in nature. The fertility cycle in woman is part of that order. Nature makes procreation possible in the fertile period, and impossible in the infertile period. But deliberate prevention of procreation by human beings acting contrary to the order and the laws of nature is quite a different matter. By deliberate prevention of procreation we mean that the man and the woman use (or one of them uses with the approval of the other) 'artificial' methods or devices to make procreation impossible. Since these means are artificial they deprive conjugal relations of their 'naturalness', which cannot be said when procreation is avoided by adaptation to the fertility cycle. That is fundamentally 'in accordance with nature'. But is it not all the same a total avoidance of procreation, and by definition morally bad? To answer this question we must examine thoroughly the ethics of periodic continence. This we shall do in the next paragraph.

From all that has been said it follows that there is a close connection between the biology and the morality of reproduction in conjugal life. Since sexual intercourse implies the possibility of procreation, conjugal love demands that the possibility of paternity and maternity shall not be completely excluded when intercourse takes place. Deliberate exclusion of this possibility conflicts not only with the order of nature but with love itself, the union of a man and a woman on a truly personal level, in that it reduces the whole content of the marital act to sexual 'enjoyment'. It must be emphasized that it is only deliberate exclusion of the possibility that has this consequence. For as long as a husband and wife do not use artificial means and methods to prevent procreation *in potentia*, so long do they accept in their consciousness and their will the possibility of parenthood ('I may become a father', 'I may become a mother'). It is enough that they are willing to accept conception, although in the particular instance they do not 'desire' it. It is not necessary for them expressly to desire procreation. They may continue to have sexual relations even in spite of permanent or temporary infertility. For infertility in itself is not incompatible with inner willingness to accept conception, should it occur. It makes no difference that conception may not occur because it is precluded by nature. After all, elderly spouses, who are physically incapable of becoming parents, continue to have sexual relations. If we leave aside circumstances on which the will of man has no influence we must accept that the attitude described justifies ('makes just') sexual intercourse between a married couple in their own eyes and before God the Creator. The true greatness of the human person is manifested in the fact that sexual activity is felt to require such a profound justification. It cannot be otherwise. *Man must reconcile himself to his natural greatness.* It is especially when he enters so deeply into the natural order, immerses himself so to speak in its elemental processes, that *he must not forget that he is a person.* Instinct alone can resolve none of his problems, everything demands decisions from his 'interior self', his reason and his sense of responsibility. And this is particularly true of the love to which human kind owes its continual renewal. Responsibility for love, to which we are giving particular attention in this discussion, is very closely bound up with responsibility for procreation. Love and parenthood must not therefore be separated one from the other. Willingness for parenthood is an indispensable condition of love.

Periodic Continence: Method and Interpretation

From our discussion so far it follows that sexual intercourse between husband and wife has the value of love, that is to say of a true union of persons, only when neither of them deliberately excludes the possibility of procreation, only when in the mind and will of husband and wife respectively it is accompanied by acceptance of the possibility of paternity or maternity. In the absence of this the man and the woman should refrain from intercourse. They should refrain from it also when they 'are unwilling to' or 'must not' become father and mother. The words in inverted commas cover many different situations. But whenever a man and a woman ought to abstain from intercourse, and from the erotic experiences of a sensual and sexual character which accompany it, continence is the obvious course, for continence is a condition of love, the only attitude towards a partner in marriage, and particularly towards a wife, compatible with affirmation of the value of the person. Let us recall that the question of continence was discussed in the previous chapter in connection with the virtue of moderation (*temperantia*). This is a peculiarly difficult virtue to practice, for it is often necessary to master not only the promptings of sensuality, in which a powerful instinct makes itself felt, but also those emotional reactions which are such an intimate part of love between man and woman, as we saw in our analysis of marital love.

Marital continence is so much more difficult than continence outside marriage because the spouses grow accustomed to intercourse, as befits the state which they have both consciously chosen. Once they begin to have sexual intercourse as a habit, and a constant inclination is created, a mutual need for intercourse comes into being. This need is a normal manifestation of love, and not only in the sensual-sexual sense but in the personal sense too. In matrimony the man and the woman belong to each other in a special way, they are 'one flesh' (Genesis 2:24). The mutual need of the two persons for each other expresses itself also in the need for sexual intercourse. This being so, the idea of refraining from intercourse inevitably runs into certain difficulties and objections. On the other hand, a couple who do not some-times refrain from sexual intercourse may see their family increase excessively. This problem is an extremely impor-tant one in our time. In the conditions of modern life we find that the family in its old traditional form – the large family relying on the father as the breadwinner, and sustained internally by the mother, the heart of the family – has reached a state of crisis. The fact that married women must or at any rate are able to take up regular employment seems to be the main symptom of the crisis, but it is obviously not an isolated symptom: several distinct factors combine to create this situation.

To discuss this question at length would take us away from the main theme of our book, although it is undoubtedly relevant. Let us simply note here that the circumstances mentioned above are often put forward as strong arguments for the limitation of births. As was mentioned in Chapter I, such demands are linked with the name of Thomas Malthus, an Anglican clergyman, author of *Essay on the Principle of Population*. According to 'Malthusian' doctrine the limitation of births is an economic necessity, since the means of subsistence, which increase by arithmetic progression, cannot keep up with the population, which naturally increases by geometric progression.[68] This idea took root in intellectual ground culti-vated by sensualist empiricism and the utilitarianism which goes with it, and the fruit which it bore there was what is called 'neo-Malthusianism'. We met in Chapter I (section on the 'Critique of Utilitarianism') the view that reason's task is to help man to calculate how to combine throughout his life the maximum of pleasure with the minimum of pain – this combination being synonymous with 'happiness', superficially understood. Since sexual intercourse gives men and women so much pleasure, so much intense enjoyment, means must be found to spare them the need to refrain from it even when they do not want offspring, when they 'cannot' become father and mother ('cannot' in the sense defined above). We are here at the source of the various 'methods' recommended by neo-Malthusians. For human intelligence, since it is able to see the process of intercourse and the attendant possibility of procreation as a whole, can devise a variety of means for the deliberate avoidance of procreation. Neo-Malthusianism points particularly to those means which in one way or another interfere with the normal, 'natural' course of the whole process of the sexual act.

Obviously if we resort to such means we find ourselves in conflict with the principle formulated in the previous paragraph of this chapter ('Reproduction and Parenthood'). Sexual intercourse in marriage takes place at the level of a union of loving persons only if they do not deliberately exclude the possibility of procreation and parenthood. When the idea that 'I may become a father'/'I may become a mother' is totally rejected in the mind and will of husband and wife nothing is left of the marital relationship, objectively speaking, except mere sexual enjoyment. One person becomes an object of use for another person, which is incompatible with the personalistic norm. Man is endowed with reason not primarily to 'calculate' the maximum of pleasure obtainable in his life, but above all to seek knowledge of objective truth, as a basis for absolute principles (norms) to live by. This he must do if he is to live in a manner worthy of what he is, to live justly.[69] Human morality cannot be grounded in 'utility' alone, it must sink its roots in 'justice'. Justice demands recognition of the supra-utilitarian value of the person: and in this the contrast between 'justice' and mere 'utility' is most clearly evident. In sexual matters in particular it is not enough to affirm that a particular mode of behaviour is expedient. We must be able to say that it is 'just'. Now if we wish to take our stand firmly on the dictates of justice and the personalistic norm which goes with it, the only acceptable 'method' of regulating conception in marital relations is continence. Those who do not desire the consequence must avoid the cause. Since sexual intercourse is the biological cause of conception spouses who wish to avoid conception must abstain from intercourse. From the moral point of view the principle is absolutely clear. It remains for us to deal with the practice known as 'periodic continence'.

It is a matter of common knowledge that biological fertility in woman is cyclical. She has natural periods of infertility, and it is fairly easy to formulate general rules for determining them. Difficulties arise when the general rules are applied to a particular woman. This is a special question, to which we shall revert in the concluding chapter. For the moment we are concerned with the purely ethical problem: if a man and a woman time their periods of continence to coincide with the above-mentioned periods of fertility, and so have sexual intercourse only as and when they expect procreation to be biologically impossible, can it be said that they bring to the marital act that readiness for parenthood, that acceptance of the idea that 'I may become a father', 'I may become a mother', of which we have spoken? After all, they have intercourse in the expectation that they will not become parents: it is precisely for that reason that they have chosen the period during which the woman is supposed to be infertile. Are they, then, not deliberately excluding the possibility of procreation? Why should the natural method be morally superior to artificial methods, since the purpose is the same in each case – to eliminate the possibility of procreation from sexual intercourse?

To answer this we must rid ourselves of some of the associations of the word 'method'. We tend to approach 'the natural method' and 'artificial methods' from the same point of view, to derive them from the same utilitarian premises. Looked at like this, the natural method is just another means to ensure the maximum pleasure, differing from artificial methods only in the direction it takes. But this is where the fundamental error resides. It is clearly not enough to speak of a method without going on to interpret it correctly. Only then shall we be able to answer the question asked above. Periodic continence as a means of regulating conception is, then, (1) permissible because it does not conflict with the demands of the personalistic norm and (2) permissible only with certain qualifications.

To take (1) first, in marital relations, as we have said before, the demands of the personal norm and those of the natural order are in agreement. The natural method, unlike artificial methods, seeks to regulate conception by taking advantage of circumstances in which conception cannot occur for biological reasons. Because of this the 'naturalness' of sexual intercourse is not affected – whereas artificial methods do destroy the naturalness of intercourse. In the first case, infertility results from the natural operation of the laws of fertility, in the second it is imposed in defiance of nature.[70] Let us add that this problem is closely bound up with that of justice to the Creator – which we shall examine later in order to reveal its personalistic significance. The personalistic value of periodic continence as a method of regulating conception is evident not only in the fact that it preserves the 'naturalness' of intercourse, but even more in the fact that in the wills of the persons concerned it must be grounded in a sufficiently mature virtue. And this is where we see how important it is to interpret periodic continence correctly: the utilitarian interpretation distorts the true character of what we call the natural method, which is that it is based on continence as a virtue and this – as was shown in the previous chapter – is very closely connected with love of the person.

Inherent in the essential character of continence as a virtue is the conviction that *the love of man and woman loses nothing as a result of temporary abstention from erotic experiences, but on the contrary gains*: the personal union takes deeper root, grounded as it is above all in affirmation of the value of the person and not just in sexual attachment. *Continence as a virtue cannot be regarded as a 'contraceptive measure.'* The spouses who practice it are prepared to renounce sexual intercourse for other reasons (religious reasons for instance) and not only to avoid having children. Self-interested, calculating continence awakens doubts. Continence must, like all other virtues, be disinterested, and wholly concerned with 'justice', not with 'expediency'. Otherwise there will be no place for it in a genuine love of persons. Continence, unless it is a virtue, is alien to love. The love of man and woman must ripen to the point where continence is possible, and continence must acquire a constructive significance for them, become one of the factors which gives shape to their love. Only then is the 'natural method' congruent with the nature of the person: its secret lies in the practice of virtue – technique alone is no solution here.

We have noted above (point 2) that the natural method is permissible only with certain reservations. The most important concerns attitudes to procreation. If continence is to be a virtue and not just a 'method' in the utilitarian sense, it must not serve to destroy readiness for parenthood in a husband and wife, since acceptance that 'I may become a father'/'I may become a mother' is what justifies the marital relationship and puts it on the level of a true union of persons. We cannot therefore speak of continence as a virtue where the spouses take advantage of the periods of biological infertility exclusively for the purpose of avoiding parenthood altogether, and have intercourse only in those periods. To apply the 'natural method' in this way would be contrary to nature – both the objective order of nature and the essential character of love are hostile to such a policy.[71]

So, then, if periodic continence can be regarded as a 'method' at all, it is a method of regulating conception and not of avoiding a family. Until we realize the true significance of the family we shall not understand the relevant moral rules. The family is an institution created by procreation within the framework of marriage. It is a natural community, directly dependent on the parents for its existence and functioning. The parents create the family as a complement to and extension of their love. To create a family means to create a community, since the family is a social unit or else it is not a family. To be a community it must have a certain size. This is most obvious in the context of education. For the family is an educational institution within the framework of which the personality of a new human being is formed. If it is to be correctly formed it is very important that this human being should not be alone, but surrounded by a natural community. We are sometimes told that it is easier to bring up several children together than an only child, and also that two children are not a community – they are two only children. It is the role of the parents to direct their children's upbringing, but under their direction the children educate themselves, because they develop within the framework of a community of children, a collective of siblings.

Those who set about regulating conception must consider this aspect of the matter before all else. The larger social unit – the state or nation within which the family happens to live – must see to it that the family is a genuine social unit. At the same time, parents themselves must be careful, when they limit conception, not to harm their families or society at large, which has an interest of its own in the optimum size of the family. A determination on the part of husband and wife to have as few children as possible, to make their own lives easy, is bound to inflict moral damage both on their family and on society at large. Limitation of the number of concep-tions must in any case not be another name for renunciation of parenthood. From the point of view of the family, *periodic continence as a method of regulating conception is permis-sible in so far as it does not conflict with a sincere disposition to procreate.* There are, however, circumstances in which this disposition itself demands renunciation of procreation, and any further increase in the size of the family would be incompatible with parental duty. A man and a woman moved by true concern for the good of their family and a mature sense of responsibility for the birth, maintenance and upbringing of their children, will then limit intercourse, and abstain from it in periods in which this might result in another pregnancy undesirable in the particular conditions of their married and family life.[72]

Acceptance of parenthood also expresses itself in not en-deavouring to avoid pregnancy at all costs, readinesss to accept it if it should unexpectedly occur. This acceptance of the possibility of becoming a father or a mother must be present in the mind and the will even when the spouses do not want a pregnancy, and deliberately choose to have inter-course at a period when it may be expected not to occur. This acceptance, in the context of any particular occasion of inter-course, together with a general disposition to parenthood in the broader context of the marriage as a whole, determines the moral validity of periodic continence. There can be no question here of hypocrisy, of disguising one's true intentions – it cannot be said that the man and the woman, in defiance of the Creator, are unwilling to become father and mother, since they themselves do nothing definitively to preclude this possibility (though of course they obviously could). They do not apply all means to this end, and in particular not those which are incompatible with a disposition to parenthood, and therefore deprive marital intercourse of the value of love and leave it only the value of 'enjoyment'.

VOCATION

❖

The Concept of 'Justice Towards the Creator'

Our whole discussion so far has been conducted on the plane of the personalistic norm. In asserting that the person must not be an object to be used, but only an object of love (hence the commandment to love), the personalistic norm lays down the rights of the person. Thus love presupposes justice. There is a need to justify the whole behaviour of person to person in sexual matters, to justify the various manifestations of sexual life as they affect the person. This has been the central theme of our discussion so far – what might be called '*horizontal justice*'. There still remains the separate problem of '*vertical justice*': the justification of the whole sexual behaviour of man in the eyes of God. We have referred to this already in the first part of this chapter ('Value of the Institution'). We must now examine this aspect of the whole question more broadly and thoroughly.

Justice is universally recognized as a cardinal and fundamental virtue, since without it human beings can have no ordered communal life. When we speak of justice towards God we are saying that He too is a Personal Being, with whom man must have some sort of relationship. Obviously this position presupposes a knowledge and understanding of the rights of God on the one hand and the duties of man on the other. These rights and duties derive essentially from the fact that God is the Creator and man his creature. Faith founded on Revelation discloses other respects of man's dependence on God: God is the Redeemer, and God sanctifies man by Grace. Revelation enables us to understand God's work of redemption and sanctification, from which it is most apparent that God relates to man as a person to a person, that his attitude to man is one of 'love'. Thus, the 'personalistic norm' may be said to have its fullest justification and its ultimate

245

origin in the relationship between God and man. It is worth recalling the commandment to love in its full form: 'Thou shalt love the Lord thy God with all thy heart and all thy mind and all thy soul, and thy neighbour as thyself.'

We know, however, that the basis of this norm (which enjoins on us the love of the person) is justice. It follows that the more fully man is aware of God's love towards him the better he will understand God's claims on his person and on his love. He will see the extent of human obligations towards God and try to fulfil them. True religion consists in justice towards God so understood, or as St Thomas puts it, the virtue of religion constitutes *pars potentialis justitiae.*

Justice so understood has its origin in the fact of creation. God is the Creator, and so all beings in the universe, creatures in general and man in particular, owe their existence to Him. Not only is God the Creator, the constant renewer of existence, but the essences of all creatures derive from Him and reflect the eternal thoughts and plans of God. Thus, the whole order of nature has its origin in God, since it rests directly on the essences (or natures) of existing creatures, from which arise all dependencies, relationships and connections between them. In the world of creatures inferior to man, creatures without reason, the order of nature is realized through the workings of nature itself, by way of instinct and (in the animal world) with the help of sensory cognition. In the world of human beings the dictates of the natural order are realized in a different way – they must be understood and rationally accepted. *And this understanding and rational acceptance of the order of nature – is at the same time recognition of the rights of the Creator.* Elementary justice on the part of man towards God is founded on it. Man is just towards God the Creator when he recognizes the order of nature and conforms to it in his actions.

But it is not just a matter of respecting the objective order of nature. Man, by understanding the order of nature and conforming to it in his actions, participates in the thought of God, becomes *particeps Creatoris*, has a share in the law which God bestowed on the world when He created it at the beginning of time. This participation is an end in itself. The value of man, a reasonable being, is nowhere more obvious than in the fact that he is *particeps Creatoris*, that he shares in God's thoughts, and His laws. Justice towards the Creator, in its most fundamental sense, consists in precisely this. Man, being a reasonable creature, is just towards the Creator by striving in all his activities to achieve this specifically human value, by behaving as *particeps Creatoris*. The antithesis of this belief is autonomism, which holds that man most fully asserts his value when he is his own legislator, when he feels himself to be the source of all law and all justice (Kant). This is erroneous: man could only be his own ultimate lawgiver if, instead of being a creature, he were his own first cause. Since he is a creature, since his existence depends on God, to whom in the last analysis he also owes his nature, as do all other created things, his reason must assist him to read aright the laws of the Creator, which finds expression in the objective order of nature, and so to make human laws conform to the law of nature. But before and above all else man's conscience, his immediate guide in all his doings, must be in harmony with the law of nature. When it is, man is just towards the Creator.

Justice towards the Creator, on the part of man, comprises as we see two elements: obedience to the order of nature and emphasis on the value of the person. The value of the created person is most fully exhibited by participation in the thought of the Creator, by acting as *particeps Creatoris* in thought and in action. This makes possible a correct attitude to the whole of the real world, in all its component parts and elements. This attitude is a specific form of love and not merely love of the world, but also love of the Creator. True, the love of the Creator is only indirectly present in it, but it is none the less real. The man who has a correct attitude to the whole of created reality thereby adopts, if only indirectly, a correct attitude to the Creator, and is essentially just to Him. In any case there can be no justice towards the Creator where a correct attitude to his creatures, and in particular to other human beings, is lacking. This brings us back to the personalistic norm. *Man can only be just to God the Creator if he loves his fellows.*

This principle has a special relevance to the conjugal and sexual life of men and women. Our whole discussion so far, which has hinged on the problem of 'love and responsibility', has been at the same time an analysis of the obligations comprised in justice to the Creator. It is impossible for a man and a woman to behave justly towards God the Creator if their treatment of each other falls short of the demands of the personalistic norm. God is in a special sense the Creator of the person, since the person reflects to a special degree His nature. Being the Creator of the person God is therefore the source of the whole personal order, which transcends the order of nature precisely because of man's ability to understand the latter and consciously to define his position within it. Justice towards the Creator therefore demands above all respect on man's part for the personal order. And love is a very specific manifestation of that order, reflecting in a special way the essential nature of God, for as the Scriptures (1st Epistle of St John, 4:8) tells us 'God is Love'.

Sex, throughout the natural world, is connected with reproduction. The conjugal relationship makes a man and a woman intermediaries in the transmission of life to a new human being. Because they are persons, they take part consciously in the work of creation (*procreatio*), and from this point of view are *participes Creatoris*. It is, therefore, impossible to compare their marital life with the sexual life of animals, which is governed completely by instinct. But it is precisely for this reason that the question of justice towards the Creator arises both in married life and in any form of relationship or association between people of different sexes. It is inseparable from responsibility for love. This makes necessary the instituion of marriage, and a morally correct single solution to the problems of reproduction and parenthood within the framework of marriage. Man does not fully discharge his duties to the Creator simply by successfully reproducing his kind. The person transcends the world of nature. The personal order is not fully encompassed by the natural order. For this reason a man and a woman who have marital relations fulfil their obligations to God the Creator only when they raise their relationship to the level of love, to the level of a truly personal union. Only then are they *participes Creatoris* in the true sense of those words. It further follows that marital intercourse itself must be informed by a willingness for parenthood. Love itself, and not merely reproduction, demands this. Unwillingness for parenthood in a man and a woman deprives sexual relations of the value of love, which is a union on the truly personal level, and all that remains is the sexual act itself, or rather reciprocal sexual exploitation.

Mystical and Physical Virginity

Monogamous and indissoluble marriage solves the problem of sexual relations between men and women in a way that is just to the Creator. Within the framework of marriage justice to the Creator demands a correct combination of sexual relations with procreation, for without this the man and the woman will not be respecting either the order of nature or the personal order, which demands that they base their relationship on true love. Thus, justice to the Creator is done when reasonable creatures acknowledge His supreme rights both in the sphere of nature and in the sphere of the person and adapt their behaviour to them. But the very concept of 'justice' opens up further perspectives. To be just means rendering to another person all that rightly belongs to that person. God is the Creator, the unfailing source of the existence of every creature. And existence determines all that any being is and all that it possesses. All the qualities, characteristics, and perfections of the creature in question are what they are and have the value they have because the creature exists, and they exist in it. This being so, the rights of the Creator over the creature are very extensive: it is in its entirety the property of the Creator, for even beings who have themselves 'created' depend upon existence: if the creature did not exist its own creative activity would be impossible. If a man considers the implications of all this for justice to the Creator he must reach the following conclusion: if I want to be completely just to God the Creator, I must offer him all that is in me, my whole being, for he has first claim on all of it. Justice demands equality: justice is done when dues are paid *usque ad aequalitatem*. Perfect equality, however, is possible only where the two sides, the persons, are fundamentally equal. So from this point of view man cannot in practice do full justice to the Creator. The creature can never cancel his debt to his Creator, not being His equal, can never face Him as an equal 'partner' or 'contracting party'.[73]

A relationship with God, a religion, based on justice alone, is of necessity incomplete and flawed, since the relationship of man to God is in principle one in which justice cannot be done. Christ offered a different solution. Man's relations with God must not be based on justice alone. Man cannot surrender everything that is in him to God and become His 'partner', a 'contracting party' who has paid his debt in full. Instead, he must surrender himself to God, with no hope of the satisfaction of feeling, as he might if he stayed within the limits of pure justice, that 'I have given up everything', 'I owe nothing'. *Self-giving has other roots – not justice, but love.* Christ taught humanity a religion based on love, which makes straight the way from person to person, and from man to God (without evading the problem of the debtor's obligation to pay his debt). At the same time, love raises man's relations with God to a higher level than mere justice could. Justice is not at all concerened with the unification of persons, whereas love aims precisely at this.[74]

When the relationship of man to God is understood in this way the idea of virginity acquires its full significance. 'Virgin' means 'untouched' – we speak in this sense of virgin forest for instance. Applied to a man or a woman 'virgin' means untouched, intact from the sexual point of view. Virginity even finds expression in the physical make-up of a woman. Sexual intercourse destroys this physical virginity: as soon as a woman gives herself to a man she ceases to be a virgin. But since marital intercourse take place between persons virginity acquires a deeper signficance than the merely physiological. The person as such is inalienable (*alteri incommunicabilis*), is *sui juris*, belongs to itself – and apart from itself belongs only to the Creator, in as much as it is a creature. Physical virginity is an external expression of the fact that the person belongs only to itself and to the Creator. When a person gives himself or herself to another person – when for instance a woman gives herself to a man in marital intercourse, this gift must have the full value of betrothed love. The woman ceases to be a 'virgin' in the physical sense. Since the self-giving is mutual the man also ceases to be 'virgin'. It makes no difference here that giving is experienced as surrender only by the woman, whereas the man feels it to be rather 'possession' of another. In any case marriage rests on mutual betrothed love: without that the reciprocal physical surrender of man and woman would not be fully warranted by an interpersonal relationship.

Within man's relationship with God, understood as a relationship of love, man's posture can and must be one of surrender to God. This is perfectly comprehensible, especially as the religious man knows that God gives Himself to man, in a divine and supernatural fashion (a mystery of faith revealed to mankind by Christ). We see then the possibility of betrothed and requited love between God and man: the human soul, which is the betrothed of God, gives itself to Him alone. This total and exclusive gift of self to God is the result of a spiritual process which occurs within a person under the influence of Grace. This is the essence of mystical virginity – *conjugal love pledged to God Himself.* Its name indicates its close connection with physical virginity. Physical virginity in a man or a woman is the characteristic condition of one who abstains completely from marriage and from sexual intercourse. The person who chooses to give himself or herself wholly and exclusively to God combines this with physical virginity, which he or she decides to preserve. Physical virginity means that the person is his or her own master and belongs to no-one, except God the Creator. Virginity emphasizes still more that the person belongs to God: what was a natural condition becomes an object of will, of conscious choice and decision.

Spiritual virginity is closely connected with physical virginity. When a married person, or a person who has been married and is now widowed, gives himself or herself to God we do not speak of virginity, although giving oneself to God as an act of betrothed love may be analogous to that which constitutes the essence of virginity. We should not, however, suppose that physical virginity or celibacy is the essence of virginity. Physical virginity is a factor favouring spiritual virginity, and also the result of this. It is possible to remain physically virginal to the end of one's days without this physical virginity ever becoming spiritual virginity. Those who choose spiritual virginity, on the other hand, remain in that state as long as they preserve physical virginity.

Nor is celibacy the same thing as spiritual virginity. Celibacy is merely abstention from marriage, which may be dictated by a variety of considerations and motives. Thus, people who dedicate themselves to learning or to some form of creative or public activity may decide to abstain from marriage. Sick people unable to live a normal married life may also abstain from it. There are also a large number of persons, especially women, who, although they have no wish at all to renounce marriage, nonetheless remain unmarried. The celibacy of priests in the Catholic Church is a special phenomenon. It is, so to speak, on the border line between celibacy made necessary by the exigencies of social work (the priest has a care of souls, and must live and work for a number of people, a whole community, a parish, for instance), and the spiritual virginity which results from betrothal to God. Priestly celibacy, which goes so closely with dedication to the business of the kingdom of God on earth, asks to be reinforced by spiritual virginity, although the sacrament of Holy Orders can be taken by people who have previously been married.

There is here a general problem to be considered: the spiritual attitude which is the innermost essence of spiritual virginity, the will to give oneself entirely and without reservation to God – may develop late, that is to say in a person no longer physically virgin. This state of mind, moreover, is often the result of a spiritual quest amid life's uncertainties: a person at first looks towards marriage for a solution to the problem of his or her vocation in life, but failing to find the answer there abstains from it. Renunciation of marriage, however, is only a negative solution. Man has an inborn need of betrothed love, a need to give himself to another. The purely negative fact of not belonging to another can be taken as indicating at least the possibility of giving oneself to God. A not unimportant psychological difficulty arises here; can a man give to God what he has 'failed' to give to another person? It is a psychological difficulty in as much as marriage, and still more spiritual virginity combined with betrothed love, must in the general belief be the result of 'first love', that is to say of one's first choice. To realize the possibility of a 'secondary virginity' (one resulting from a second choice) we must remember that human life can be and should be a quest for a road to God, an ever better and ever shorter road.

According to the teaching of Christ and of the Church virginity is just such a road. The man who chooses virginity chooses God. This does not however, mean that in choosing marriage he renounces God for a human being. Marriage and the betrothed love for a human being which goes with it, the dedication of oneself to another person, solves the problem of the union of persons only on the terrestrial and temporal scale. The union of person with person here takes place in the physical and sexual sense, in accordance with man's physical nature and the natural effects of the sexual urge. Neverthe-less, the need to give oneself to another person has profoun-der origins than the sexual instinct, and is connected above all with the spiritual nature of the human person. It is not sexuality which creates in a man and a woman the need to give themselves to each other but, on the contrary, it is the need to give oneself, latent in every human person, which finds its outlet, in the conditions of existence in the body, and on the basis of the sexual urge, in physical and sexual union, in matrimony. But the need for betrothed love, the need to give oneself to and unite with another person, is deeper and connected with the spiritual existence of the person. It is not finally and completely satisfied simply by union with another human being. Considered in the perspective of the person's eternal existence, marriage is only a tentative solution of the problem of a union of persons through love. It is also a fact that most people opt for this solution.

Spiritual virginity, in the perspective of eternal life, is another attempt to solve the problem. The movement towards final union through love with a personal God is here more explicit than in marriage, and in a sense spiritual virginity anticipates that final union in conditions of the physical and temporal life of the human person. In this lies the great value of virginity. We should not look for it in the negative fact of renunciation of marriage and family life. The essential character of virginity is often wrongly thought of as the lot imposed by fate on deluded persons or people incapable of marriage and of family life. Nor is it, as people often suppose, the superiority of spiritual to physical values that determines the true value of virginity. If that were so conjugal life would amount to a choice of physical in preference to spiritual values, or at least the former would predominate, whereas virginity would emphatically proclaim the superiority of spirit over the body and matter. The element of truth in this is easily confused with the Manichean antithesis between spirit and matter. Marriage is by no means just a 'physical matter'. If it is to have its full value it must, just as much as virginity or celibacy, effectively mobilize all man's spiritual energies.

Which of the two is easier or more difficult is not the criterion by which the relative value of marriage and virginity should be judged. As a general rule, people find marriage 'easier' than virginity, because it seems to be a natural stage in the course of their development, whereas virginity is something of an exception. But there are some respects in which virginity is easier than married life. If we consider just the sexual side of life, virginity means complete aloofness from the sexual activity to which marriage introduces a person, making it a habit and a need. Thus, the difficulties of the person who must try to achieve continence (if only periodic continence) in his or her married life may be at times greater than those of one who has from the beginning held aloof from sexual life. There are some respects in which virginity may sometimes be an easier way of life than marriage. There are certainly some people who find virginity easier, and would find married life harder than others do, just as there are people with a preference for married life and a decided disinclination to remain virgin. These inclinations and disinclinations are, however, not exclusive. A human being profoundly influenced by an ideal may sometimes succeed in adopting a way of life to which he is not obviously predisposed by nature, and may even be naturally averse. (Think for instance of Charles de Foucauld or St Augustine.)

We see then that the primacy of the spiritual as against the physical and material is not the criterion by which we can judge the value of virginity. The value of virginity, and indeed its superiority to marriage, which is expressly emphasized in the Bible (1 Corinthians 7), and has always been maintained in the teaching of the Church, is to be found in the exceptionally important part which virginity plays in realizing the kingdom of God on earth. The kingdom of God on earth is realized in that particular people gradually prepare and perfect themselves for eternal union with God. In this union the objective development of the human person reaches its highest point. Spiritual virginity, the self-giving of a human person wedded to God Himself, expressly anticipates this eternal union with God and points the way towards it.

The Problem of Vocation

We must say something here, if only briefly, on the subject of vocation. This concept is confined to the world of persons and the order of love. In the world of things it is meaningless. It is impossible to speak of the vocation of a thing. We can only speak of the functions of particular things, the purposes which they serve. Nor are there any vocations in the order of nature itself, where all is pre-ordained, and the capacity for choice and self determination is lacking. It can hardly be said of animals, for instance, that they are fulfilling a 'vocation' in preserving their species by reproduction, since they do this instinctively. When we speak of someone having a vocation (being 'summoned' or 'called') we imply a personal commitment to a purpose such as only a rational being can make. Vocations, then, are peculiar to persons, and the very concept takes us into a very interesting and profound area of man's interior life. This may not always be immediately obvious, since we often speak of someone being 'called' in an administrative or legal sense – 'called' to the colours, or to a particular post, for instance. The 'call' or 'summons' issues from an institution of some kind, and the individual concerned, and especially his inner life, is its object, not its subject. Even when a vocation for the priesthood is in question the social-institutional factor plays a big part. Such a vocation is thought of as a summons from a particular religious community, a diocese for instance, to discharge priestly duties, and it finds expression in a decision by the head of that community, that is the bishop, to admit a particular candidate to holy orders.

But besides this external, social and institutional meaning the term has another, personal and psychological meaning, and it is this which we must examine here. In this other meaning the word 'vocation' indicates that *there is a proper course for every person's development to follow*, a specific way in which he commits his whole life to the service of certain values. Every individual must plot this course correctly by understanding on the one hand what he has in him and what he can offer to others, and on the other what is expected of him. To plot the course which best suits one's own capabilities, and commit one's self accordingly, is one of the decisive processes in the formation of the personality – and it is even more important to the inner life of the individual than to his or her position amongst other people. It is not enough merely to plot the course – active commitment of one's whole life to it is essential. That a particular person has a particular vocation always, then, means that his or her love is fixed on some particular goal. A person who has a vocation must not only love someone but be prepared to give himself or herself for love. We have said already in our analysis of love that this self-giving may have a very great creative effect on the person: the person fulfils itself most effectively when it gives itself most fully.

The process of self-giving is an essential aspect of wedded love. *Hence both virginity and marriage understood in an uncompromisingly personalistic way*, are vocations. As far as marriage is concerned, I must stress the importance of the philosophical position from which we approach it, because this determines whether we see it as a vocation or not. This, moreover, affects much more than our view of marriage, which if our premises are materialistic and purely biological, can be understood only as a necessity rooted in 'the body and sex'. Given this general view of reality, all other vocations also lose their *raison d'être*, since it leaves no room for the person. Virginity, if we start from non-personalistic premises, can only be seen as a mere consequence of conditions and inclinations (or rather disinclinations) physiological and psychological, and of a given objective social and economic situation. Vocations are meaningful only within the framework of a personalistic vision of human existence, in which conscious choice determines the direction which a person's life and actions will take.

In the vision of human existence put forward by the New Testament the interior life of the person is not the sole source of a vocation. An inner need to determine the main direction of one's development by love encounters an objective call from God. This is the fundamental appeal of the New Testament, embodied in the commandent to love and in the saying 'Be ye perfect', *a call to self-perfection through love*. This summons is addressed to everyone. It behooves every 'man of good will' to give it concrete meaning, in application to himself. by deciding what is the main direction of his life. 'What is my vocation' means 'in what direction should my personality develop, considering what I have in me, what I have to offer, and what others – other people and God – expect of me?' A believer who is unreservedly convinced of the truth and reality of the New Testament's vision of human existence is also aware that his own spiritual reserves alone are inadequate to the development of his personality through love. In calling upon us to seek perfection, the Gospel also requires us to believe in divine Grace. The operations of Grace take man beyond the confines of his personal life and bring him within the orbit of God's activity and His love. As he seeks to determine the particular lines along which his personality must develop, the main direction of his love, every man must learn to integrate himself into the activity of God and respond to His love. A fully valid solution of the problem of vocation depends on this.

The New Testament is quite explicit on the subject of pre-marital virginity (Matthew 19:8; 1 Corinthians 7). In accordance with the consistent teaching and practice of the Church, virginity as a deliberately chosen vocation, based on a vow of chastity, and in combination with vows of poverty and obedience, creates particularly favourable conditions for the attainment of perfection in the New Testament sense. The combination of conditions created by men who follow the Gospel's advice in their personal lives, and more particularly in their lives together, is called a state of perfection. This, however, is not to be identified with the perfection that every man attains by striving in the manner appropriate to his vocation to fulfil the commandment to love God and one's neighbour. It is possible for a man living outside the 'state of perfection', but observing that greatest of commandments, to be closer to perfection than one who has chosen that state. In the light of the Gospel it is obvious that every man solves the problem of his vocation in practice above all by adopting a conscious personal attitude towards the supreme demand made on us in the commandment to love. This attitude is primarily a function of the person: the condition of the person – whether the person is married, celibate, or even virgin (if virginity is thought of simply as a status or a factor in the status of the person) is here of secondary importance.

Paternity and Maternity

We have already said something on this theme in our discussion of the relation between reproduction and procreation.

Parenthood is something more than the external fact of bringing a child into the world and possessing it. More particularly it implies an internal attitude, which should characterize the love of a man and a woman living a conjugal life. Parenthood, considered on the personal and not merely the biological level, is so to say a new crystallization of the love between persons, the result of their perfect union. There is nothing surprising about this development: it is deeply rooted in the whole existence of man and woman. It is often said that woman's maternal inclinations are naturally so strong that what she seeks in marriage is a child rather than a husband. At any rate her longing for a child is a manifestation of potential maternity. Similarly, a man may desire fatherhood. But it appears that men in general are less subject than women to the desire for parenthood, which is readily explained by the fact that the female organism from the start develops with a view to maternity. Physically, a woman becomes a mother thanks to a man, while paternity in its psychological and spiritual aspects is the effect on a man's interior life of a woman's maternity. The physical implications of paternity have a smaller place in the life of a man, and especially the life of his organism, than those of maternity in the life and the organism of a woman. For this reason paternal feelings must be specially cultivated and trained, so that they may become as important in the inner life of the man as is maternity in that of the woman, for whom the biological facts alone suffice to make it important. We are speaking for the present of paternity and maternity primarily in a physical and biological sense: possession of a child to whom one has given life, transmitted existence (*procreatio*). A certain natural perfection of man's being finds expression in this fact. That man can give life to a being in his own likeness makes plain his intrinsic value: in the well-known Latin saw which St Thomas and other Christian thinkers often quote, *bonum est diffusivum sui*. This makes the desire for a child perfectly comprehensible in a man as well as a woman. The man expects a child from the woman, and for this reason takes her into his care (*matris munus*) by marrying her. Both find in parenthood confirmation not merely of their physical but of their spiritual maturity, and a promise of the prolongation of their own existence. When their lives in the body cease, their child will continue to live – the child who is 'flesh of their flesh', and above all a human person whose inner self they have both helped to form, in whom they have fashioned that which above all determines personhood. For the person is much more an 'interior' than a 'body'.

We come here to the nub of another question. Paternity and maternity in the world of persons are certainly not limited to the biological function of transmitting life. Their significance is much deeper, and must be so in as much as the transmitter of life, father or mother, is a person. Paternity and maternity in the world of persons are the mark of a certain spiritual perfection, the capacity for 'procreation' in the spiritual sense, the forming of souls. So that spiritual paternity and maternity have a much wider significance than physical parenthood. A father and mother who have given their children life in the merely biological sense must then supplement physical parenthood by spiritual parenthood, taking whatever pains are necessary for their education. This, however, is something in which others too have a part. The parents must share their role with others, or skilfully incorporate in their own educational activity whatever benefits, spiritual and physical, moral and intellectual, their children can obtain from others.

Spiritual paternity and maternity are characteristics indicative of mature parenthood in man and woman. And spiritual paternity has much more in common with spiritual maternity than does physical paternity with physical maternity. The realm of the spirit is unaffected by sexual differences. The Apostle Paul, referring to his spiritual paternity, did not hesitate to call the Galatians 'My little children, with whom I am again in labour . . .' (Galatians 4:19). Spiritual parturition is a symptom of the maturity of the person and of a certain fullness which the person wishes to share with others (*bonum est diffusivum sui*). It therefore seeks 'children', that is to say other people, particularly young people, who will take what it offers. And those who do take it become the object of a special love, resembling the love of parents for their children, and like that explained partly by the fact that what has ripened in the spiritual father or mother will live on in the children. We may, then, observe various manifestations of spiritual paternity and various crystallizations of the love that goes with it: for instance the priest's love of souls, the teacher's love for his pupils, etc. Spiritual kinship based on the union of souls is often stronger than the kinship created by the blood tie. Spiritual paternity and maternity involve a certain transmission of personality.

Spiritual parenthood as a sign of the inner maturity of the person is the goal which in diverse ways all human beings, men and women alike, are called to seek, within or outside matrimony. This call fits into the Gospel's summons to perfection of which the 'Father' is the supreme model. So then, human beings will come particularly close to God when the *spiritual parenthood of which God is the prototype* takes shape in them. We shall have to speak of this at the end of a work which is so closely concerned with the problems of procreation and parenthood. In the natural world, 'father' and 'mother' are individuals to whom a new individual of the same species owes its life. 'Father' and 'mother' in the world of persons are, so to speak, embodied ideals, models for others, and specifically for those whose personality must take shape and evolve within their sphere of influence. In this way, the order of nature goes no further than the biological facts which, within limits, are complete in themselves and final, but which in the world of persons acquire a new content of a kind which they cannot find in the natural order. The New Testament teaches us that they can only derive this content from God himself.

Any attempt to diminish human beings by depriving them of spiritual paternity and maternity, or to deny the central social importance of maternity and paternity, is incompatible with the natural development of man.

CHAPTER V

Sexology and Ethics

�֒

A SUPPLEMENTARY
SURVEY

Introductory Remarks

This chapter forms not so much an appendix to the four preceding chapters as a 'supplementary survey' of the whole range of questions with which we are concerned in this book.

These questions, as we know, affect persons: *the love of man and woman is above all inter-personal.* We have tried in preceding chapters to bring out the fundamental importance of this truth, which explains why we approach, and must approach, sexual morality from a personalistic point of view. The proper subject matter of sexual morality is by no means exclusively 'the body and sex': it also includes the personal problems, the problems of love between man and woman, which are inseparable from the theme of 'the body and sex'. Love in the sense in which we understand it can only be experienced by persons. The proper concerns of sexual morality are not 'the body and sex' but the personal relationships and the interpersonal love between man and woman inseparable from them. Love in the sense in which we are using it here can only be the lot of particular persons. Questions of 'the body and sex' play a part in it in that they are subject to the principles which determine the order which should prevail in the world of persons.

This means too that sexual morality cannot be the same thing as sexology, i.e. a view of man and woman and of love which approaches the whole problem solely or mainly from the point of view of 'the body and sex'. This approach is characteristic of 'pure sexology', which deals with problems of sexual life from the medical or physiological point of view. The biologist studying sex is also well aware that the man and the woman are 'persons', but this fact is not the starting point of his enquiries, or of his general way of looking at the problem of their love. As a result, his view is correct as far as it goes, but it is only part of the truth. The only fully correct view must be one that starts from thorough analysis of the fact that a man and a woman are persons, and that their love is a mutual relationship between persons. If, and only if, he accepts this, the knowledge of the sexologist can make a very great contribution to the detailed understanding of the principles of sexual ethics. If we do not recognize the primary importance of the person, if we do not make the necessary connection between love and the person we deny ourselves the necessary basis for judgements in this difficult sphere of human morality. The right standpoint, then, must be personalistic, and not sexological. Sexology can only furnish a supplementary view.

Scientific sexology is normally connected with medicine, and so becomes clinical sexology. The viewpoint of medicine, which is not only a science but also an art (the art of healing, based on the scientific observation of the human body) is not identical with the viewpoint of ethics. Medicine is concerned with the health of the body – physical health is its proper object and aim. Whereas ethics finds its proper object and aim in the moral good of the person. Physical health itself cannot be identified with the moral good of the whole person – in relation to moral welfare it is only a partial good. There are, of course, healthy people who are evil, just as there are sick and physically feeble people of exceptional moral worth. Of course, care for one's health, and the preservation of biological life, are amongst the concerns of morality (the commandment 'thou shalt not kill') but they are not the only ones. Fundamentally, the proper concern of medicine ('take care of your health, avoid sickness') is only marginally connected with sexual ethics, in which the personalistic standpoint is dominant. *What matters is the man's duty to the woman, and the woman's duty to the man by virtue of the fact that they are both persons, and not merely what is beneficial to their health.* The standpoint of clinical sexology gives, then, only a partial view – hence sexology must be subordinated to ethics, and specifically to the de-

mands of the personalistic norm. Since that excludes treatment of a person as an object of use, and insists on seeking out
the true good of the person, it obviously demands amongst
other things care for the physical life and health of the person
as one of its goods. But this is not the sole good envisaged by
the norm, nor even a higher, let alone the 'ultimate' good.

Our 'pre-scientific' assertion that sex is an attribute of the
human individual opens up wide horizons. For the human
individual is a person, and the person is the subject and object
of love, which is born between persons. A man and a woman
come to love each other not because they are two sexually
differentiated organisms, but because they are two persons.
Looking at it from the biological point of view, sexual differences are significant only for one purpose – reproduction:
sexual differentiation exists solely and simply for the purpose
of reproduction. The idea that procreation must base itself on
love is not derivable from a biological analysis of sex, but only
from the metaphysical (i.e. ultra- and supernatural) fact of
being a person. Sex as the attribute of a person has a role in the
origin and development of love, but does not itself provide an
adequate base for love.

In our analysis of love in its psychological aspect in Section
2 of Chapter I we defined the value of 'body and sex' as the
proper object of sensual reactions, while pointing out that
these reactions furnish as it were the material of love between man and woman. Our analysis above of particular
factors of sex and sexual life does not, however, tell us anything about the nature of this value and the way in which it is
experienced. Somatic events and physiological processes
which belong to the vegetative system affect man's experience of the value 'body and sex' only externally. This
experience is by no means identical with the biological
events, although it has its origin in them and is conditioned
by them. If this experience can have the sort of importance to
love which we indicated in earlier parts of the book (particularly Chapter II), this is because sex is an attribute of the
human person as a whole.

The Sexual Urge

In section 2 of Chapter I we defined the sexual urge as a specific orientation of the whole human being resulting from the division of the species *Homo* into two sexes. It is directed not towards sex as an attribute of man, but towards a human being of the other sex, since its final end is the preservation of the human species. We can now supplement this knowledge of the sexual urge with the biological data, keeping in mind all that was said about sex, and particularly its somatic and physiological aspects, in the preceding section. The existence of somatic differences and the activity of the sexual hormones release and direct the sexual urge, which however cannot be completely reduced to a combination of anatomical and somatic or physiological factors. The sexual urge is a special force of nature for which those factors are only a basis. Let us look briefly at the stages in its development.

The majority of physiologists and sexologists hold that the sexual urge is first fully awakened only at the age of puberty. This stage occurs in girls between the ages of 12 and 13, and in boys somewhat later. It is preceded by the pre-pubertal stage. Sexual maturity in the physiological sense is identified in girls with the beginning of menstruation and the ability to conceive, and in boys with the ability to produce sperm. This is accompanied by characteristic psychological phenomena: a period of animation and heightened reactions is followed by one in which reactions are slower and more sluggish (this is particularly noticeable in girls, who are usually more deeply affected).

Before the age of puberty the sexual instinct exists in a child in the form of a vague and indeed unconscious interest which only gradually becomes conscious. Puberty brings a rapid, indeed one might say an explosive, intensification of the urge. In the subsequent period of physical and psychological maturity the urge becomes stable. Finally, it passes through a stage of heightened activity in middle age (the climacteric), after which it gradually declines in old age.

When we speak of the sexual urge, its awakening, growth or decline, we have in mind a number of different reactions. The same is true when we point to variations in the intensity of the reactions as between individuals, or at different ages, or in different circumstances. Sexology here supplements the analysis of sensuality in section 2 of Chapter III. The fact that we find different 'thresholds of sexual arousal' in different people means that they react differently to stimuli which cause sexual excitement. The root causes for this are to be found partly in man's somatic and physiological make-up. As a physical phenomenon sexual arousal is easy to describe. It happens as the result of a nervous reflex. It is a state of tension caused by stimulation of the nerve ends of the sensory organs, either directly or else psychologically through associations in the imagination. Sexual stimuli may act upon any of the senses, more particularly touch or sight, but also hearing, taste, or even smell, and they produce a peculiar state of tension (tumescence) not only in the genital organs but in the organism as a whole. This finds expression in vegetative reactions and characteristically both systems, the sympathetic and the cerebro-spinal, exhibit a state of tension.

Sexual stimuli take effect by means of automatic and involuntary nervous reflexes (the reflex arc on the $S2$–$S3$ level). On the physiological and somatic side we must take note of the fact that there are places in the human body which conduct sexual stimuli with especial ease – the so-called erogenous zones, which are considerably more numerous in women than in men. The degree of excitement depends immediately on the quality of the stimulus and on the receiving organ. Various physiological factors can increase or diminish sexual excitability: thus, fatigue reduces it, yet excessive fatigue, and insomnia, may have precisely the opposite effect. A state of sexual excitement precedes intercourse but may occur independently of it.

Sexology introduces us, in a much more detailed fashion than has been done here, to the complex of somatic and physiological factors conditioning the sensual reactions in which the sexual urge manifests itself in human beings. It is, however, worth referring to Chapter II and remembering that things which in themselves must be recognized as manifestations of the sexual urge can be converted in the interior of a person into the real ingredients of love.

Marriage and Marital Intercourse

In the two preceding sections of this chapter our supplementary survey of questions raised in earlier chapters has merely provided a certain amount of data from the field of biological sexology. In the sections which follow we shall be concerned rather with medical sexology. Like every other branch of medicine, it has a normative character, in that it seeks to regulate man's actions in the interests of his health. Health, as was said previously, is a good for man as a psychophysical being. In our further discussion we shall be concerned to indicate the main areas in which that particular good, which is the object of the prescriptions of medical sexology, and which provides the basis for its pronouncements and its rulings, coincides with the moral good as defined by sexual ethics. Sexual ethics, as we have seen, takes as its starting point not the biological facts as such, but the concepts of the person and of love as a reciprocal relationship between persons. Can ethics be inimical to hygiene and to the health of man and woman? Can a thorough and final analysis leave any conflict between concern for the physical health of persons on the one hand and concern for their moral good, which means with the objective demands of sexual ethics, on the other? We frequently encounter the view that there is such a conflict. This then is another subject which requires some attention. We must look again at the matters dealt with in Chapters III and IV (Chastity and Marriage).

The proper foundation for a monogamous and indissoluble marriage is, as was stated in section 1 of Chapter IV, the personalistic norm together with recognition of the objective aims of marriage. From this norm also derives the prohibition of adultery in the broad sense of the word, and hence the prohibition of pre-marital relations. Only a profound conviction of the non-utilitarian value of the person (of the woman for the man, of the man for the woman) enables us to justify fully, fundamentally and irrefutably, this ethical standpoint and to try to observe it in practice. Can sexology give it any support, and so provide additional justification? To answer this question we must turn our attention to certain very important aspects of the sexual relationship (which, as has already been said in Part IV, preserves its personal dimension only in marriage, since outside the institution of marriage it puts one person – and this is particularly true of the woman in relation to the man – entirely and exclusively in the position of an object of use for another person).

Sexual relations (the sexual act) are not just a simple consequence of sexual arousal, which generally occurs without any act of will, spontaneously, and is only subsequently welcomed or resisted. As we know, sexual excitement may reach its climax, to which sexology gives the name 'orgasm', yet this climactic excitement is not one and the same thing as the sexual act (although as a rule it is not reached without some 'activity'). We have said already, in analysing concupiscence (Section I of Chapter II) that sensual reactions have their own dynamic in human beings – which is very closely associated not only with the value 'body and sex' but also with the instinctive dynamics of the sexual zones of the human body, i.e. with the physiology of sex. But sexual intercourse, the sexual act between a woman and a man, is unthinkable without an act of will, especially on the part of the man. It is not just a question of the actual decision but also of the physiological possibility of carrying out the act, of which a man is incapable in states in which he is unable to exercise his will, for instance while he is asleep, or unconscious for some other reason. It is in the very nature of the act that the man plays the active role and takes the initiative, while the woman is a comparatively passive partner, whose function it is to accept and to experience. For the purposes of the sexual act it is enough for her to be passive and unresisting, so much so that it may even take place without her volition while she is in a state in which she has no awareness at all of what is happening – for instance while she is asleep, or unconscious.

In this sense intercourse depends on the man's decision. Now, the fact that this decision is the result of sexual arousal in the man, which may take place without the woman experiencing anything similar, raises a problem of great practical importance both from the medical and from the ethical point of view. Sexual ethics, the ethics of marriage, must examine closely certain facts on which clinical sexology can provide precise information. We have defined love as an ambition to ensure the true good of another person, and consequently as the antithesis of egoism. Since in marriage a man and a woman are associated sexually as well as in other respects the good must be sought in this area too. From the point of view of another person, from the altruistic standpoint, it is necessary to insist that intercourse must not serve merely as a means of allowing sexual excitement to reach its climax in one of the partners, i.e. the man alone, but that climax must be reached in harmony, not at the expense of one partner, but with both partners fully involved. This is implicit in the principle which we have already so thoroughly analysed, and which excludes exploitation of the person, and insists on love. In the present case love demands that the reactions of the other person, the sexual 'partner' be fully taken into account.

Sexologists state that the curve of arousal in woman is different from that in man – it rises more slowly and falls more slowly. Anatomically, arousal occurs in the same way in women and in men (the locus of excitement is in the cerebro-spinal system at S2–S3). The female organism, as was mentioned above, reacts more easily to excitation in various parts of the body, which to some extent compensates for the fact that the woman's excitement grows more slowly than that of the man. The man must take this difference between male and female reactions into account, not for hedonistic, but for altruistic reasons. There exists a rhythm dictated by nature itself which both spouses must discover so that climax may be reached both by the man and by the woman, and as far as possible occur in both simultaneously. The subjective happiness which they then share has the clear characteristic of the enjoyment which we have called 'frui', of the joy which flows from harmony between one's own actions and the objective order of nature. Egoism on the other hand – and in this context it is obviously more likely to be egoism on the part of the man – is inseparable from the 'uti' in which one party seeks only his own pleasure at the expense of the other. Evidently, the elementary teachings of sexology cannot be applied without reference to ethics.

Non-observance of these teachings of sexology in the marital relationship is contrary to the good of the other partner to the marriage and the durability and cohesion of the marriage itself. It must be taken into account that it is naturally difficult for the woman to adapt herself to the man in the sexual relationship, that there is a natural unevenness of physical and psychological rhythms, so that there is a need for harmonization, which is impossible without good will, especially on the part of the man, who must carefully observe the reactions of the woman. If a woman does not obtain natural gratification from the sexual act there is a danger that her experience of it will be qualitatively inferior, will not involve her fully as a person. This sort of experience makes nervous reactions only too likely, and may for instance cause secondary sexual frigidity. Frigidity is sometimes the result of an inhibition on the part of the woman herself, or of a lack of involvement which may even at times be her own fault. But it is usually the result of egoism in the man, who failing to recognize the subjective desires of the woman in intercourse, and the objective laws of the sexual process taking place in her, seeks merely his own satisfaction, sometimes quite brutally.

In the woman this produces an aversion to intercourse, and a disgust with sex which is just as difficult or even more difficult to control than the sexual urge. It can also cause neuroses and sometimes organic disorders (which come from the fact that the engorgement of the genital organs at the time of sexual arousal results in inflammation in the region of the so-called little pelvis, if sexual arousal is not terminated by detumescence, which in the woman is closely connected with orgasm). Psychologically, such a situation causes not just indifference but outright hostility. A woman finds it very difficult to forgive a man if she derives no satisfaction from intercourse. It becomes difficult for her to endure this, and as the years go her resentment may grow out of all proportion to its cause. This may lead to the collapse of the marriage. It can be prevented by sexual education – and by this I mean more than merely instruction in sexual matters. For it must be emphasized yet again that physical disgust does not exist in marriage as a primary phenomenon, but is as a rule a secondary reaction: in women it is the response to egoism and brutality, in men to frigidity and indifference. But the woman's frigidity and indifference is often the fault of the man, when he seeks his own satisfaction while leaving the woman unsatisfied, something which masculine pride should in any case forbid. But in some particularly difficult situations natural pride may not be enough in the long run – everyone knows that egoism may either blind a man and rob him of his pride or, on the contrary, result in a morbid hypertrophy of pride, which causes him to lose sight of the other human being. Similarly, the natural kindness of a woman, who (so the sexologists tell us) sometimes 'shams orgasm' to satisfy a man's pride, may also be unhelpful in the long run. These are mere palliatives, and cannot in the end give satisfactory solutions to the difficulties experienced in intercourse. There is here a real need for sexual education, and it must be a continuous process. The main objective of this education is to create the conviction that 'the other person is more important than I'. Such conviction will not arise suddenly and from nothing, merely on the basis of physical intercourse. It can only be, must be, the result of an integral education in love. Sexual intercourse itself does not teach love, but love, if it is a genuine virtue, will show itself to be so in sexual relations between married people as elsewhere. Only then can 'sexual instruction' bestow its full benefits: without education in our sense it may even do harm.

This is where the 'culture of marital relations' comes in and what it means. Not the 'technique' but the 'culture'. Sexologists (e.g. van de Velde) often put the main emphasis on technique, whereas this should rather be thought of as something secondary, and often perhaps even inimical to the purpose which it is supposed to serve. The urge is so strong that it creates in the normal man and the normal woman a sort of instinctive knowledge 'how to make love' whereas artificial analysis (and the concept of 'technique' implies this) is more likely to spoil the whole thing, for what is wanted here is a certain spontaneity and naturalness (subordinated of course to morality). This instinctive knowledge must subsequently mature into a 'culture of marital relations'. I must refer here to the analysis of 'tenderness' and especially of 'disinterested tenderness' to be found in section 3 of Chapter II. This ability to enter readily into another person's emotions and experiences can play a big part in harmonization of marital intercourse. It has its origin in 'sentiment', which is directed primarily towards the 'human being' and so can temper and tone down the violent reactions of sensuality, which is oriented only towards the 'body' and the uninhibited impulses of concupiscence. Precisely because a slower and more gradual rise in the curve of sexual arousal is characteristic of the female organism the need for tenderness during physical intercourse, and also before it begins and after its conclusion, is explicable in purely biological terms. If we take into account the shorter and more violent curve of arousal in the man, an act of tenderness on his part in the context of marital intercourse acquires the significance of an act of virtue – specifically, the virtue of continence, and so indirectly the virtue of love (see the analysis in Section 3 of Chapter III). Marriage cannot be reduced to the physical relationship, it needs an emotional climate without which the virtues – whether that of love or that of chastity – become difficult to realize in practice.

What is needed, however, is not shallow sentimentality, or superficial love, which have little to do with virtue. Love should help one to understand and to feel for a human being, for this makes it possible to educate him, and in married life for husband and wife to educate each other. The man must reckon with the fact that the woman is in a sense in another world, unlike himself not only in the physiological but also in the psychological sense. Since he has to play the active role in the marital relationship, he must get to know that other world, and indeed as far as possible project himself into it emotionally. This indeed is the positive function of tenderness. Without it the man will only attempt to subject the woman to the demands of his own body, and his own psyche, frequently harming her in the process. Of course, the woman too must try to understand the man, and simultaneously to educate him to understand her. Each of those things is equally important. Neglect of education and the failure to understand may both be the result of egoism. Sexology itself provides support for this formulation of the principles of morality, and of education for marriage.

Does the total contribution of clinical sexology to our understanding of sexual relations between man and woman also directly support the principle of monogamy and the indissolubility of marriage? Is it opposed to adultery and pre-marital or extra-marital relations? Not perhaps directly, but then we cannot demand so much of sexology, since its immediate concern is with the sexual act as a limited physiological or at most psycho-physical process, and the way in which it is affected by particular conditions in the organism and in the psyche. Indirectly, however, sexology itself consistently favours natural sexual and marital morality, because it attaches so much importance to the psychological and physical health of man and woman , understood in the most fundamental sense. Thus, harmonious sexual intercourse is possible only where it involves no conflict of consciences, and is not troubled by fears. A woman can, for instance, obviously obtain complete sexual satisfaction in an extra-marital relationship, but the conflict of conscience may have the effect of disturbing the natural biological rhythm. Peace of mind and an untroubled conscience have a decided effect upon the organism too. Needless to say, this in itself is not an argument for monogamy and marital fidelity, and against adultery – it only indicates certain consequences of the natural laws of morality. Sexology does not have to furnish arguments from which we can deduce these rules – it is enough if it incidentally confirms rules already known from elsewhere and established by other means. It is, then, quite certain that marriage, as a stable institution which protects her in the event of maternity (*matris munus*), to a considerable extent liberates a woman from those reactions of fear which not only play havoc with her psyche, but may also disturb her natural biological rhythm. Not the least of these is the fear of having a child – the main source of female neuroses (to be discussed under the next heading).

A harmonious marriage can deal with these difficulties – but we have shown that this harmony cannot be the result of a 'technique' but only of 'marital culture', or in the last analysis of the virtue of love. In its very nature such a marriage is the result not just of sexual 'selection', but of an ethically valid choice.

Biology and physiology in themselves do not enable us to discover and to formulate any laws to explain why a man and a woman decide to marry. It appears that 'purely' biological attraction does not exist, though on the other hand persons who unite in marriage are certainly interested in each other sexually as well as in other ways – people who from the start feel physical disgust for each other do not enter into marriage. The laws of mutual attraction can only occasionally be defined in terms of the psychological principle of attraction of like by like, or conversely attraction of opposites: the matter is usually more complicated. The fact is that sensual and sentimental factors have a powerful effect at the moment of choice, but that rational analysis must nevertheless have the decisive significance.

It must also be stated that the much-recommended 'trial' periods of cohabitation before marriage give no guidance in selecting a spouse, for the specific features of cohabitation in marriage are one thing, and those of pre-marital cohabitation another. A mismatch is not merely a matter of physical incompatibility, and it is certain that one cannot test for compatibility 'in advance' by pre-marital cohabitation. Couples who subsequently consider themselves ill-matched very often have a perfect sexual relationship in the initial stage. The collapse of their marriage evidently has some other cause. This view of the matter is in close accord with the ethical principle which rules out pre-marital relations – it does not, to be sure, directly confirm it, but at all events it points towards the rejection of the opposite principle which permits and indeed recommends sexual intercourse before marriage. Where the choice of a spouse is concerned, concern for the possible offspring bids us observe the rules of healthy eugenics. Medicine advises people suffering from certain diseases not to marry – but this is a distinct problem, which we shall not deal with here, since it concerns the moral obligation to protect life and health rather than sexual morality, or in other words is covered by the Fifth, not the Sixth, commandment. At no point do the conclusions reached by clinical sexology conflict with the main principles of sexual ethics: monogamy, marital fidelity, the mature choice of the person, etc. The principle of marital modesty analysed in Section 2 of Chapter III also finds confirmation in the existence of neuroses, well known to sexologists and psychiatrists, which are the result of sexual intercourse accompanied by fear – fear of being taken by surprise by some unwelcome intrusion. Hence the need for a suitable place, one's own home or apartment, in which married life can take its course 'in safety', i.e. in accordance with the demands of modesty, and where both the man and the woman feel that they 'have the right' to live in total intimacy.

The Problem of Birth Control

Any discussion of sexual intercourse from the sexological point of view (in order to supplement what has been said from the viewpoint of ethics) necessarily confronts us with the problem of birth control. This is a matter so closely connected with that which we have just been discussing that it may almost be considered a corollary extension of it. The concept of 'planned motherhood' itself can be understood in a variety of ways. It can imply awareness of what motherhood (and by analogy, fatherhood) means – a matter to which we have already devoted quite a lot of space in Chapters I and IV. Usually, however, 'planned motherhood' means something different. It can be summed up briefly in the following sentences: 'know how, in the marital relationship, a woman becomes a mother and act so as to become a mother only when that is what you want.' This statement, although it sounds as though it were addressed to the woman, really concerns the man as her 'partner' in the sexual (marital) relationship, for in the majority of cases it is he who makes the decision.

This precept or programme – for planned parenthood is nowadays a clearly defined programme – if formulated as above may not seem to call for any qualifications. After all, man is a rational being, and to aspire to the fullest possible participation of his consciousness in all that he does is consonant with his nature. This applies equally to the aspiration to become a mother or father (no distinctions must be made here) with conscious intent. A man and a woman who have marital relations must know when and how they may become parents and regulate their sexual life accordingly. They have a responsibility for every conception, not only to themselves but also to the family which they are founding or increasing by that conception. Something has already been said about this in Chapter IV ('Procreation and Parenthood', 'Periodic Continence: Method and Interpretation'). Our present discussion plainly harks back to these sections. A programme of planned motherhood may easily ground itself on utilitarian assumptions – which will involve it in conflict with the idea to which more space has probably been devoted in this book than to any other: that the value of the person is distinct from and higher than any utilitarian value. The only way to avoid this conflict which accords with the character of the person, and so the only honourable way, is the virtue of continence, the pattern of which is more or less indicated by nature itself. To obtain a clearer understanding of this, however, we must examine it more fully in the light of sexology.

Woman's nature, as everyone knows, regulates the number of conceptions in a precise and so to speak 'economical' way, in that only one mature ovum capable of fertilization appears in the course of the monthly cycle. By contrast, as far as the man is concerned, intercourse may result in fertilization on every occasion. Thus, the determinant of the number of offspring is the female organism, and fertilization can only occur at the moment when the female organism permits it, which means when it has been prepared to do so by a whole series of preliminary biochemical reactions. The period of fertility can be determined, individually, for any particular woman, though there are no general and invariable rules. Every woman can observe in herself the changes which occur in the relevant phase of the cycle. Apart from this there exist objective scientific methods known to biology and medicine, which help us to determine the moment of ovulation, i.e. the beginning of the fertile period.

Let us begin, however, by examining the positive side of the question. Sexology speaks of the 'maternal instinct' and the 'paternal instinct'. Whereas the first usually awakens in a woman before the birth of the child, and frequently even before its conception, paternal feelings usually develop more slowly, sometimes only towards children who are already a few years old. The maternal instinct may develop in girls at the age of puberty, since it is biologically dependent on the action of the hormones, and the woman's sexual rhythm prepares her every month to conceive a child and adjusts her whole organism to this very purpose. This is the origin of that feeling for the child which sexology calls the maternal instinct, in recognition of the fact that it is largely the result of changes which recur monthly in the female organism. In the sexual act this feeling does not dominate the consciousness of the woman, still less does paternal feeling preoccupy the man, and there is no need for it to do so (in view of the conclusions drawn from our discussion of procreation and parenthood in Chapter IV). It will, however, easily be seen that the desire to have a child is naturally awakened by marriage and marital intercourse, whereas resistance to this desire in the mind and the will is unnatural. Fear of conception, fear of having a child, is a factor of great importance to the problem of planned motherhood. It is by way of being a paradoxical factor. For on the one hand, it is this that gives rise to the whole question of 'planned motherhood' in the form 'what must I do so as to have a child only when I wish to do so', and on the other hand, this same fear of the child makes it immensely more difficult to take advantage of opportunities in this context supplied by nature itself.

Here indeed lies the fundamental obstacle to a solution of the problem of birth control equally correct from the biological or medical and from the ethical point of view. The difficulty lies not in nature itself, which regulates the number of conceptions in a way which is clear to see and relatively easy to calculate. The factors which disturb the regularity of the biological cycle in women are above all of psychological origin. These are much commoner than disturbances of an organic nature. Of the psychological causes, fear of conception, of becoming pregnant, is the commonest. We know that fatigue, change of climate, stress, and especially fear, can delay or precipitate menstruation. Fear then is a powerful negative stimulus that can destroy the natural regularity of the female sexual cycle. Clinical experience also confirms the thesis that fear of pregnancy also deprives a woman of that 'joy in the spontaneous experience of love' which acting in accordance with nature brings. This fear, as a dominant emotion, prevails over all other feelings and leads to incalculable reactions.

All this implicitly shows the decisive importance in this matter of the moral stance analysed in Chapter IV. This can be reduced to two elements: readiness during intercourse to accept parenthood ('I may become a mother', 'I may become a father'), and that readiness to practise continence which derives from virtue, from love for the closest of persons. This is the only way in which a woman can achieve the biological equilibrium without which the natural regulation of conception is unthinkable and unrealizable. 'Nature' in human beings is subordinated to ethics, and the correct biological rhythm in women, and the possibility of natural regulation of conception which this gives, are inseparably connected with the love which shows itself on the one hand in willing acceptance of parenthood, and on the other in the virtue of continence, the ability to deny and to sacrifice the 'I'. Egoism is the negation of love, it shows itself in attitudes opposite to those described and is the most dangerous source of that overriding fear which paralyses the healthy processes of nature.

Practically nothing is said about this: people reduce the whole problem to the technical level, ruling out completely the possibility of pregnancy and failing to see the need to control fertility by natural means in accordance with the dictates of morality. It must be clearly stated that one basic method underlies all natural methods of regulating fertility: the 'method' of virtue (love and continence). Only when this method is accepted in principle and applied in practice will our knowledge of sexual and reproductive processes be effective. For if a human being realizes that fertilization is not a matter of 'chance', of a fortuitous combination of circumstances but a biological event carefully prepared by nature, and that the preparatory stages can be fully monitored, the possibility of regulating conception rationally and in a natural way will become so much the greater.

Methods of birth control are of two general types, already examined from the ethical point of view in Chapter IV. On the one hand, there are what are called natural methods, on the other artificial methods requiring the use of contraceptives. Contraceptives are of their very nature harmful to health. Biological methods besides causing temporary barrenness, may bring about serious and irreversible changes in the organism. Chemical means are in their very nature cellular poisons, otherwise they would not have the power to kill genital cells, and so they must be physically harmful. Mechanical means cause local injuries in the woman's reproductive tract, and what is more interfere with the spontaneity of the sexual act, which is something that women in particular find intolerable. Perhaps the most frequent method used by married couples is *coitus interruptus*, which they resort to thoughtlessly, without realizing at the time that it must inevitably have undesirable consequences. Ignoring for the moment the fallibility of this method of preventing fertilization, let us ask ourselves why people resort to it. At first glance it may seem that the egoism of the male is the sole cause of this behaviour. Deeper analysis, however, reveals that in interrupting the sexual act the male often supposes that he is doing so to 'protect' the woman. It is indeed true that when a man does this the woman is robbed of various goods – she is denied orgasm, her nervous equilibrium is upset, but her basic biological capacity, her fertility, is un-affected. For this reason women themselves are often con-vinced that 'it doesn't do any harm'. For his part, the man feels that he is in control of the situation, that he is making the decision. While the woman maintains the attitude of sexual passivity which is proper to her and leaves the responsibility to the man. In this situation, both of them may attain a certain good. But they do so by following an incorrect course. For if a couple have reached the legitimate conclusion that conception must be postponed, instead of interrupting the act once begun the man should refrain from it for the time being, and wait for the period of biological infertility in his wife. To this end both should get to know about the female organism and make their decision dependent on a precise knowledge of its functioning. But this brings us back to the subject of periodic continence.

The only natural method of regulating conception is that which relies upon periodic continence. It demands precise knowledge of the organism of the woman concerned and of her biological rhythm, and also the peace of mind and the biological equilibrium of which a great deal has already been said. But above all it demands a certain self-denial and self-restraint – which must be exercised instantly, especially on the part of the woman. For normally her sexual urge makes itself felt most insistently at the moment of ovulation, and during the fertile period (– the intensification of the urge is one of the symptoms of the so-called ovulatory syndrome –) and this is just the time at which she must refuse intercourse. Periodic continence presents the man with no such diffi-culty, since his sexual drive is not subject to such fluctuations as that of the woman. Male continence must therefore adapt itself to the indications which the woman's organism pro-vides. A more important task for the man than adapting himself to the biological cycle of the woman is the creation of a favourable psychological climate for their relationship without which the successful application of natural methods is out of the question. This demands the regular practice of continence on the part of the man, so that birth control by natural means depends in the last analysis on the moral attitude of the male. The marital relationship demands on his part tenderness, an understanding for the feelings of the woman. In this sense responsibility for planned motherhood rests mainly on the man, for only continence on his part makes it possible to capture the correct biological rhythm in marriage.

This rhythm is nature's rhythm, so that marital intercourse in accordance with it is also hygienic, healthy and free from all those neuroses which are caused by the artificial methods of preventing pregnancy mentioned above. It is, however, impossible to apply natural methods on the spur of the moment, and mechanically, without mastering the whole biological rhythm. Any attempt to do so will result in disappointment. It could hardly be otherwise in view of the facts presented above. Whereas if a man and a woman use these methods with full understanding of the facts and recognizing the objective purpose of marriage, natural methods leave them with a sense of choice and of spontaneity ('naturalness') in their experience, and – most important of all – the possibility of deliberate regulation of procreation. The effort put into the application of these 'methods' is essentially a moral effort, as was shown in Chapter IV. Unless the virtue of continence is properly understood, and its practice perfected there can be no thought of birth control and planned parenthood by natural methods.

The question of artificial termination of pregnancy could be fully treated only in a special study. All that we can do here is to touch on the subject in a few words. Leaving aside its moral aspect, the act of artificially terminating pregnancy is in itself highly 'traumatic', and in every respect comparable with those experiments which are designed to produce neuroses. It is indeed an artificial interruption of the natural biological rhythm with very far-reaching consequences. There is no analogy for the enormous feeling of resentment which it leaves in the mind of a woman. She cannot forget that it has happened and cannot get rid of her grudge against the man who has brought her to it. Apart from its physical effects artificial abortion causes an anxiety neurosis with guilt feelings at its core, and sometimes even a profound psychotic reaction. In this context we may note the significance of statements by women suffering from depression during the climacteric, who sometimes a decade or so after the event remember a terminated pregnancy with regret and feel a belated sense of guilt on this account. There is no need to add that morally termination of pregnancy is a very grave offence. There are no grounds for discussing abortion in conjunction with birth control. To do so would be quite improper.

Sexual Psychopathology and Ethics

There is a widely held view that to go without sexual intercourse is harmful to the life of human beings in general and of men in particular. No-one, however, has given the description of any set of morbid symptoms which might confirm this thesis. Our previous discussion showed that sexual neuroses are mainly the consequence of abuses in sexual life and that they result from failure to adapt to nature and to its processes. So that it is not continence, as such, that produces real diseases, but the lack of it. The lack of a sex life may also be the result of misguided repression of the sexual urge and its manifestations, which is wrongly identified with continence but which, as was shown in Chapter III, has little in common with the real virtue of continence and chastity. The sexual urge in man is a fact which he must recognize and welcome as a source of natural energy otherwise it may cause psychological disturbances. The instinctive reaction in itself, which is called sexual arousal, is to a large extent a vegetative reaction independent of the will, and failure to understand this simple fact often becomes a cause of serious sexual neuroses. The person involved in such a conflict is torn by two contrary tendencies which he cannot reconcile – hence the neurotic reactions. A considerable proportion of sexual neuroses are linked with irregularities in the marital relationship of which we have already spoken in the previous paragraph.

The neuroses which are described as 'sexual' have a clinical pattern similar to that of other neuroses but usually manifest themselves only in the sexual context. It can also happen that a neurosis with a quite different cause can result in anxiety and disorders in the sphere of sexual life, because any neurosis makes it more difficult for a man to control his actions. This is not the place for a detailed list of illnesses. Our concern is to give an overall view of the sexual life of human beings. The indispensable requirement of correct behaviour and health is training from childhood upwards in truth and in reverence for sex, which must be seen as intimately connected with the highest values of human life and human love. Sexual reactions can be provoked at any age, from early childhood on. A sexual urge prematurely awakened, at the wrong time of life, can become the source of neurotic disturbances if it is repressed in the wrong way. This is why sex education based on honest biological information is so important. Lack of information, and especially lack of training in the correct attitudes, may cause a variety of aberrations (such as infantile and adolescent masturbation). This is an educational rather than a medical problem, although as a rule when a person's attitudes are incorrect neuroses will be the response of the organism and of the nervous system to continual stress.

Therapy

Without at this point analysing the clinical symptoms of various aberrations which may occur I should like to suggest some ways of preventing such reactions. These suggestions can be reduced to a few basic points:

(a) It is often necessary to relieve people of the widespread conviction that the sexual drive is something naturally bad which must be resisted in the name of the good. It is necessary to inculcate a conviction, in accordance with the proper conception of man, that sexual reactions are on the contrary perfectly natural, and have no intrinsic moral value. Morally they are neither good nor bad, but morally good or morally bad uses may be made of them.

(b) If a man is to acquire the conviction that he is capable of controlling his reactions he must first be set free from the opinion that sexual reactions are determined by necessity and entirely independent of the will. He must be persuaded that his body can be made to 'obey' him if he trains it to do so.

(c) People, and particularly young people, must be set free from the belief that sexual matters are an area of incomprehensible, well-nigh calamitous phenomena, in which they find themselves mysteriously implicated and which threaten their equilibrium: instead we must reduce sex to a set of phenomena which though of great moment and great beauty are totally comprehensible and, so to speak, 'ordinary'. This demands the timely provision of correct biological information.

(d) The most important thing is to transmit the right hierarchy of values, and to show the position occupied by the sexual urge in that hierarchy. Its use will then be subordinated to the end which it exists to serve. People must be further persuaded of the possibility and necessity of conscious choice. We must, as it were, 'give back' to people their consciousness of the freedom of the will and of the fact that the area of sexual experience is completely subject to the will.

(e) There are obviously illnesses in which the help of a specialist – sexologist or psychiatrist – is necessary, but the advice given by such specialists must take into account the totality of human aims, and above all the integral, personalistic concept of man. For there are times when the doctor's advice is just what turns the patient into a neurotic, in that it blatantly contradicts the real nature of man. Some doctors have a narrowly biological view of things formed under the influence of the 'myth of orgasm' which causes them to give advice completely at variance with ordinary human knowledge and experience of sexual matters.

The psychotherapy of sexual neuroses is distinct from sex

education in that it deals not with people whose sexual inclinations are normal and healthy but with those afflicted by some sexual deviation or illness. The methods of treatment must therefore be more specific than those which we use in ordinary sex education. Such persons are less capable of 'love and responsibility' and psychotherapy aims at restoring the capacity to them. If we analyse thoroughly the guide lines which it follows, we arrive at the conclusion that it aims above all at delivering the patients from the oppressive notion that the sex urge is overwhelmingly strong, and inculcating in them the realization that every man is capable of self-determination with regard to the sexual urge and the impulses born of it. This in fact is the starting point of sexual ethics at large. Thus, psychotherapy, and through it clinical sexology, are connected with the super-material energies in man, and endeavour to cultivate appropriate beliefs, and patterns of behaviour based on them, try as it were to recapture man's 'interior' and only through its agency to obtain control of his 'outward' behaviour. In the formation of that 'inner self' a fundamental part is played by the truth about the sex instinct. This method is based on the conviction that only the man who has a correct conception of the object of his action can act correctly (that is to say at once both truthfully and well).

That object, as we know from the whole book, is not merely the sex instinct but the whole person connected with that force of nature which is the sex instinct – and that is why all correct sex education, including that which must take the form of therapy, cannot take as its starting point only the 'natural' plane of the sex instinct, but must proceed from the plane of the person, with which the whole subject of 'love and responsibility' is bound up. And it appears in the last analysis that there is no other cure and no other pedagogic remedy. A thorough knowledge of biological and physiological sexual processes is very important, very fitting, very valuable, but it cannot, either in education or in sexual therapy, achieve its proper end unless it is honestly grounded in an objective view of the person and the natural (and supernatural) vocation of the person, which is love.

NOTES

✤

1 'In the field of experience man appears both as a specific *suppositum* and as a concrete "I", unique and unrepeatable in each case. It is "the experience of a man" in two senses at once, since he who experiences is a man and he who is experienced by the subject of the experience is also a man. Man is subject and object simultaneously. One of the essential characteristics of experience is its objectiveness, it is always experience of 'something' or of 'somebody'. Hence man as subject is also experienced in the same way as an object. Experience pushes out of man's cognition the conception of pure subjectivity (pure consciousness), but welcomes all that this conception has done to deepen our knowledge of man to the dimensions of objective reality' ('The Person: Subject and Community' in *Roczniki Filozoficzne* 24.1976, p. 2 and p. 7.) In 'Person and Act' the author analyses a number of facts bearing on the dynamic integrality of the concept 'a man acts', which preserves its real objectivity solely in the subjectivity of man. On the strength of these facts we can correctly set limits to the fear of falling into subjectivism.

2 The author has made a detailed analysis of the faculty of self-determination in his study 'Person and Act', Cracow 1969, Part II of which is called 'The Transcendence of the Person in the Act' (pp. 107–196).

3 The term 'object' in the phrase 'human person as the object of another human being's action' is used in the broad sense implicit in the objectivist philosophical perspective adopted by the author from the outset of his enquiry (cf Footnote 1). This sense of the word must not be confused with the other, narrower sense in which the author will use it when he discusses the possibility of treating a human person as 'an object of use' (v.p. 25 seq.) To treat someone as an object of use is the same as treating him or her as a means to an end, as a thing, with no respect for the independent purposiveness which belongs to the person.

4 Thus, moral obligations are imposed on the person as subject of action not only by other persons by virtue of the intrinsic value called 'dignity', but also by non-personal beings by reason of

their specific value, and in particular by living creatures especially those capable of suffering. These beings, however, not only can but must be treated instrumentally (become objects of use and exploitation), whenever treating them so is the only way of affectively affirming a person or persons. Whereas to treat one person purely as an instrument 'for the good of' another or even of all other persons is impermissible. This fundamental difference permits us to adapt a definition of the basic ethical principle which is relatively narrow, seen in the context of man's general moral obligations, and to express it in the form of the 'personalistic norm', or in other words the demand for the affirmation of the person. Narrowing down the scope of the principle in this way is justified by the quite exceptional importance of the dignity of the person, a value not to be compared with anything in the world outside the world of persons.

5 The author has defined and developed the personalistic formulation of Catholic sexual morality in a separate article 'The Problem of Catholic Sexual Morality: Reflections and Postulates', in *Roczniki Filozoficzne* 13.1965 (2), pp. 5–25.

6 (i) The author has dealt with the distinction between psychological and ethical analyses in several places.

His broadest treatment of the subject will be found in the article 'The Problem of Will in the Analysis of Ethical Acts', in *Roczniki Filozoficzne* 5.1955–7 (I) pp. III–35. Psychology and ethics have the same point of departure, which is in this case the human being's actual inner awareness of his responsibility as agent (cf. also 'Person Act', Chapter I, 'Consciousness and Agency', pp. 27–106). The way in which human awareness of responsibility for action is understood by modern psychology shows the importance of St Thomas's analyses in this area, and certain shortcomings in the analyses of Kant and Scheler. Psychology and ethics see awareness of responsibility as an important element in the experience of the will and see the will at the core of the experience of responsibility. But at this juncture the two disciplines diverge, though in the course of further analysis there are other points at which they coincide. Psychology aims at disclosing by the empirical inductive method the specific mechanism by which the will operates, and identifying the concrete motive forces which make for the realization of a chosen end. Ethical analysis on the other hand aims at fully explaining the sense of rightness by identifying and characterizing the chosen end – its moral value. The feeling of being right is here seen as the source of an ethical value or of that through which a man becomes morally good or evil, which can be understood either in the broad sense (good or evil internally, as a human being), or in a precise personalistic sense (true in attitude and behaviour to the value represented by the person).

(ii) Kant meant the words 'merely the means to an end' in this context to signify that the person, as possessor of its own nature (understood substantially), can without harming itself assume the role, or even inadvertently perform the role of 'means to an end', on condition that the end which is someone else's is a lawful one, and that whoever 'uses' another's physical or psychic forces in this way is ready to put that person's inalienable value before the end immediately in view should an axiological conflict of that kind arise. In later pages of this study the author omits the word 'merely' (from the phrase 'merely a means to an end') when he has in mind not the substantial but merely the personal subjectiveness of human beings. Thus on p. 27 he states that '(Kant ... demands that the person should never be a means to an end, but always and exclusively an end ...'.

7 The author discusses the correct interpretation of the rights of God the Creator with regard to the human person more particularly in his article 'On the Meaning of Betrothed Love – Contribution to a Discussion', in *Roczniki Filozoficzne* 22.1974 (2), (v. especially pp. 166–72).

8 Because it reveals the essential truth about man as a person, the attitude to truth in particular is in the author's opinion of the essence of freedom and the conscience which binds freedom: 'Freedom is an attribute of the human person, not in the form of absolute independence, but as self-dependence comprising dependence on the truth . . . which finds its most striking expression in conscience . . . The proper and entire function of conscience consists in making action dependent on truth' ('Person and Act', pp. 162–3).

9 Common good is understood here in a radically personalistic way. 'What we are concerned with is the truly personalistic structure of human life in the community to which a human being belongs. Common good is the good of the community in that it creates in an axiological sense the conditions of communal being; action follows the course thus set for it.

It may be that the common good defines, in the axiological order, the community, association or society. We delimit each of these on the basis of the common good peculiar to it. In doing so, we take action (*operari*) together with existence (*esse*). Common good, however, touches above all on the sphere of existence 'in common with others'. Mere action 'together with others' does not reveal the reality of 'common good' so fully although it must be present here too. Ch. 'Person and Act', pp. 308–9. Also 'The Person: Subject and Community', in *Roczniki Filozoficzne* 24. 1976 (2), p. 23.

10 The author has devoted the last section of his 'Person and Act' (pp. 285–326), and an article called 'The Person: Subject and Community' (*Roczniki Filozoficzne* 24.1976 (2), pp. 5–28,) to the question, dealt with cursorily here, of the specific structure of an interpersonal community.

11 It is, of course, not enough just to *want* to affirm the other person for the consequent act (of goodwill) to become also an act of love. It is necessary in addition for the action undertaken with the intention of affirming another person to be objectively suited to the role which the agent's intention assigns to it. Whether it is or is not suitable is decided by the objective structure of the person affected by the action. Only success in understanding the other person and allowing when acting for that person's specific traits ensures that the act will be recognizable as a genuine act of love. An imperfect understanding of the structure of the object person must, in consequence become the source of (inadvertent and hence involuntary) action to the detriment of that person. The danger is all the greater in that utilization of the other takes place in the name of love. The agent is unaware of his delusion, and so immune from blame. None the less, the agent is responsible for an act of 'anti-love'. . . . because he loves. Only constant awareness of the danger of disintegration of love in this way (emotionalization) can help us to avoid it. Cf. Introduction to the first edition (Lublin 1960), p. 6, where the author postulates the need for 'the introduction of love into love'.

12 Further to the relationships between consciousness and emotion see 'Person and Act', pp. 51–6 and 258–75.

13 Utilitarianism has undergone a complicated evolution since the days of its founders. J. Bentham and J. S. Mill are best known as the propounders of the 'calculus of goods' as the only proper method of determining the moral value of actions. Different utilitarians, however, give different answers to the question which goods ought to be maximized. Many of them do not share Bentham's hedonistic identification of the highest good (which constitutes the ethically determined end of human aims) with pleasure (*bonum delectabile*). Such people accept as the good a more broadly and objectively conceived usefulness (*bonum utile*). Nor is there nowadays any lack of people who regard themselves as utilitarians while understanding the good which is the highest goal in a personalistic way, and subordinating the calculus of goods to the good (the perfection, the happiness) of

the person, always regarded as ethically the proper end of action (*bonum honestum*). Similarly, particular utilitarians given different answers when asked whose good we should be considering when we apply the calculus of goods; some prefer the private advantage of the subject of the action (variously defined, according to the answer given to the first question), others the advantage of a chosen social group (perhaps even a future generation of humanity, for which people now living are requested to sacrifice their happiness or to be sacrificed themselves), whilst others still prefer the greatest good of the greatest number.

The critique which follows here applies equally to the hedonistic variant of utilitarianism and to all others, to the extent that they represent an instrumentalist and reductionist attitude to the human person (I mean the tendency to reduce the person as a value to the value of that persons's function, or in other words to the value of its 'usefulness' not necessarily in a hedonistic sense). It is not, however, relevant to the 'personalistic' variety of utilitarianism mentioned above.

The calculus of goods (the basic idea of which is, incidentally, not unknown to the Thomist tradition – think of the complex of problems known as '*ordo bonorum et caritatis*') is all the more difficult to apply in practice when the highest good which is the measure of all particular goods is understood in any but a straightforwardly sensual way. There is, then, nothing surprising in the fact that hedonism was the first and so to speak the classical variant of utilitarianism.

The author gave an extended critical exposition of utilitarianism in his lectures in the Catholic University of Lublin in the Academic year 1956–57. Cf 'Problems of the Norm and of Happiness' (Typescript, Institute of Ethics, CUL).

14 A fuller definition of the difference between subjectivism and subjectivity is given below, and in 'Person and Act', pp. 56–60. See also 'Subjectivity and the Irreducible in Man'. In [*Analecta Husserliana*, Vol. VII, pp. 107–14 (in English)].

15 Justice, here, is used in what may be called the strict sense (for in the broad, biblical sense a 'just' man is the same as the 'man of good will'). Justice in the strict sense signifies satisfaction of someone's minimum entitlement to personal or material services. But since love is just only when it is not minimalistic the services which justice in this narrow sense demands can only be the basis and condition of a full interpersonal affirmation. Cf. Aristotle, *Nicomachean Ethics* VII 1–1955a 26, and St Thomas *Contra Gentiles* III, 130.

16 Cf. 'Person and Act' pp. 230–5.

17 The sexual urge – in the broad sense – is valuable to man not only

'procreationally' but as one of the ways in which a man and a woman complement each other in the course of their lives, in a number of reciprocal interactions which have nothing to do – concretely or generally – with the begetting and upbringing of children. If the spouses are to take legitimate advantage of the energy which the urge releases, and of its natural promptings, they must before all else take into account its basic meaning and rationale. If this condition (that nothing shall be done to negate the proper purpose of the urge) is fulfilled, then even when a new human being cannot be born from the union of a man and woman, or from a particular occasion of sexual intercourse, the spouses are none the less reborn in love, and so to speak give birth to each other in their interpersonal communion (*communio personarum*) Cf. 'The Problem of Catholic Sexual Morality' [*Roczniki Filozoficzne* 13.1965 (2), p. 16] and 'On the Meaning of Betrothed Love', [*Rocziniki Filozoficzne* 22.1971 (2), p. 169].

18 Cf. 'Person and Act', pp. 78–94, and pp. 197–235.

19 God – as the only Being existing of Himself and entirely perfect – creates man, whose person the Divine Persons summon to communion with other persons, and above all with themselves. It is this summons which permits the constitution in man of a subjectivity strictly personal in the natural and the supernatural order. Thus, the dignity of being a 'person' is bestowed on every man by God Himself. The share of the parents in the 'genesis of a person' acquires a new content when they take the child into the family as a community of persons, and accept it as an independent subject relating not only to them and to other people but also to God.

20 This special connection between the sexual urge and the value of existence, which shows itself in the part which the urge plays in the origin of a new personal life, gives it its very special position and status in the real structure of the human being. This is easy enough to see, but becomes especially evident if we look at the existence of the human person in the metaphysical perspective, as a work requiring incessant creative initiative on the part of the Divine Love. This view is sometimes objected to on the grounds that it endows facts and processes which are entirely natural with a normative significance (i.e. that it converts what is to what should be), and that this leads to the 'biologization of ethics'. As far as the author is concerned this objection is based on a failure to understand the views set out above (*ignorantia elenchi*), since there can be no need to *convert* a purely natural fact, the sexual urge, into a normative fact, inasmuch as the urge cannot be adequately identified and exhaustively described without its existential-axiological dimension. The accusation of

'biologism' can only be made if we asume in advace that the sexual urge in man has only a biological sense, that it is a purely natural fact. This assumption, however, made in a purely dogmatic way, begins by depriving the sexual urge of its existential-axiological dimension, reducing it to its biological significance, so as to make possible the accusation mentioned above. It is really this reductionism which deserves to be called 'biologism', since it allows the biological aspect (which is of course important) to obscure the phenomenon as a whole (*pars pro toto*), and absolutize it. The further stages in the logic of this reductionism, and the accusation of 'biologism' from this quarter, are easy to understand. The reductionists might, nevertheless, be expected to state candidly that they begin by denying the validity of any experience other than that obtained by external and internal observation, which obviously involves rejection of the validity of metaphysical cognition. They owe it to the reader to be honest about this. Less easily understood, if not altogether astonishing, are the arguments of some moral *theologians* who reduce the sexual urge in man to a biological fact so that they can then – quite logically, so that many people may be taken in – allow man that degree of freedom in his use of the sexual urge which he enjoys in relation to the growth of his nails or his hair.

These writers seem to be open to a charge of reductionism for another reason, besides that already mentioned. They do not take sufficiently into account the connection between the objective structure of the sexual urge and the Christian sense of betrothed love. For since, in accordance with the First commandment, the commandment to love, man may surrender himself completely in love to God alone, so that giving himself to another human being must be simultaneously a way of giving himself completely to God; since, moreover, in accordance with Catholic belief, a newly conceived human being is not only the fruit of intercourse between a man and a woman but above all the work and gift of God, the Giver of all existence, – justice towards the Creator demands particular respect for the procedure which he has established for the initiation of a new human life. These theological reasons for obedience to the law of nature – which are too often ignored by some Catholic theologians – are further developed in Chapter IV of this book.

21 'The Creator has written into the nature of personal being the possibility and power of giving oneself, and that possibility is closely associated with the structure of self-possession and self-mastery characteristic of the person, with the fact that the person is *'sui juris et alteri incommunicabilis'*. The ability to give oneself, to become a gift for others is rooted in this

ontological inalienability: ('On Betrothed Love', *Roczniki Filozo-ficzne* 22.1974 (2), p. 466 (166)2. 'The fact that the human person belongs to God as Creator and Redeemer does not take away (i.e. does not invalidate) man's right to give himself, which God Himself has written into the personal being of man ... The 'right to give oneself', which God as Creator has written into the being of the human person, of man and woman, is the specific basis of the *communio personarum* ... The Creator from the very start wants marriage to be a *communio personarum* in which a man and woman, each making and receiving a gift of self, realize from day to day and throughout their lives the ideal of personal union. Betrothed love can be thought of as precisely the realization of this ideal.' (ibid pp. 169–70.)

22 The synthesis in question can be described in a succinct formula: 'the fact that I must love has its objective foundation in the personal dignity of the object of my action (personalistic norm), but the way in which I must love has its objective founda-tion in human nature'. It must always be kept in mind that 'nature' here does not mean 'biological nature'. The author is thinking of the nature of man in the deeper sense, which takes account of and indeed gives pride of place to, those elements which are not and cannot be embraced by physical and still less by physicalist conceptions of man. These theoretic-descriptive elements, though they are ethically normative in their own way, do not generate moral duties of themselves, but only in their axiologized form, thanks to the synthesis with the personalistic norm mentioned above.

23 The capacity for participation in the love of mankind is at the core of all participation, and a condition of the personalistic value of all activity and all being 'together with others'. This commandment [to love – Ed.] confirms in a particularly empha-tic and logical way that the ability to relate to another as to one's 'neighbour' (in the biblical sense) has a fundamental importance in all activity and all being 'together with others' ('Person and Act', p. 322–23). 'The "I-Thou" relationship opens one human being to another. . . . Humanity is present in the "I-Thou" rela-tionship not as an abstract idea of man. . . . but as a "Thou" for the "I". Participation in this relationship is equivalent to realiza-tion of an interpersonal communion in which the "Thou" man-ifests itself through the "I" – and this reciprocally, – and above all the personal subjectiveness of both persons is grounded in, is assured by, and grows from this communion ('The Person: Sub-ject and Community', in *Roczniki Filozoficzne* 24.1976 (2), p. 36. Cf. also "Subjectivity and the Irreducible in Man", in *Analecta Husserliana* Vol. VII, pp. 107–14.)

24 'It' [betrothed love – Ed.] 'is realized according to Christ's teaching – in one way if a person gives himself or herself exclusively to God, in another in marriage where two human persons give themselves to each other. . . . At the same time it must be emphasized that although God as Creator possesses the *dominium altum*, the supreme right, in relation to all creatures, and hence also over man, who is a person, this decision to give oneself completely, become "the property of a beloved God" (KK 44), is, according to the will of Christ himself, left to the free choice of man under the influence of Grace.' ('On the Meaning of Betrothed Love', *Roczniki Filozoficzne* 22.1974 (2), p. 171.)

25 The paragraph which follows shows how in a personal act of love there takes place a harmonious unification of the various 'strata' of man's being, and how the structures and dynamisms proper to those 'strata' manifest their full meaning precisely in the act of love. This paragraph exemplifies, then, the theory of integration of the person in the act, which was later expounded fully and systematically in the study 'Person and Act' (pp. 199–82).

26 For a closer examination of consciousness and its reflexive function see 'Person and Act', pp. 44–51 (44–51).

27 'Freedom in the basic sense is the same as self-dependence. Freedom in the developed sense is independence in the sphere of intention. Which of various possible objects of desire one makes one's goal is not determined either by the objects themselves or by the way in which they present themselves. Independence in the sphere of intentions, understood in this way, is explained by that interior attitude to the truth, and dependence on it, which is in the nature of the will itself. *It is this dependence that makes the will independent of objects and of their appearance as such.*' ('Person and Act', p. 145. Author's underlining.)

28 Readers of the author's critique of situationism should keep two points in mind:

(1) It is not the author's intention to examine situationism from every angle, but only to indicate the danger of the one-sided interpretation of love, the subjectivization of that phenomenon, which can be observed, as the author cautiously puts it, in views characterized by a marked situationist tendency. This tendency initially showed itself above all in excessive emphasis on the role of the mood of the subject at the expense of proper attention to the objective structure of the person to whom his action is directed, a structure which remains fundamentally the same in spite of its changeable elements.

(2) Situationism was theoretically elaborated and became

particularly popular (with some theologians too) only in the sixties, some years after the publication of 'Love and Responsibility'. At this stage its ties with existentialism became considerably looser, as is obvious especially in the ultra-theological arguments concerning correct norms of behaviour which go by the name of act-utilitarianism.

This does not, however, mean that the author's warnings concerning situationism have lost their relevance. The author's critical attitude towards it is based on a conception of the human person (the subject and the object of moral action) fundamentally different from the conception implicit in both the form of situationism mentioned here.

29 'Value of the person as such' – i.e. of the person as person, and not of a distinct nature individualized in a way all its own, independent, then, of particular physical or psychic characteristics. The person in this sense is the subject of possible initiatives and commitments, constitutionally *sui juris*, unique and indivisible, so that it cannot belong even 'the least little bit' to anything or anyone else, but can without prejudice to its own, or anyone else's, identity, 'give hospitality' itself to other persons, and 'sojourn' in them as a gift validated by mutual affirmation within a communion of persons. Acts of 'self-determination' – when a given person enters into possession of his nature are not only actions but also the adoption of cognitive and appetitive positions, through which the person makes contact with the world of persons and the world of things.

30 For this reason, the declaration of a Philo – 'I love you madly, Laura, and all those like you!' cannot be accepted as an expression of love as it is meant here.

31 The will 'compensates' and 'atones for' means that it 'subordinates the desire of a person for oneself to the desire for the unconditional good of that person'. This 'equilibrium' would be upset if the second desire were outweighed by the first. That would be egoism: desiring another person for oneself at the expense of that person's good. Love, however, the essence of which is expressed by the act of affirming the person for its own sake, does not preclude the combination of this affirmation with a desire for the profoundest possible union with the person thus affirmed.

32 In this way love as an attitude of goodwill (*bene-volentia*) finds its objectivized expression and legitimation in a good deed on behalf of the beloved person, or in a 'will to do good' which is effectively of advantage to the existence and development of the person.

33 We often find in the love of one person for another a discrepancy

between the good desired for the beloved and the possibility of realizing it. The lover is not able to bestow immortality on the beloved person – although he desires to and undoubtedly would do so if he were omnipotent. This is the reason why 'what he really wants for the beloved is God'. The empirically inescapable connection between love and the affirmation of life compels us to recognize (as a result of metaphysical interpretation) that in the perspective of the Creative Love the death of personal existences can only be a transition to a higher form of life. *Morte fortius caritas.*

34 Man as a complex, 'many-layered' being manifests himself in many different dynamisms, each with its own specific interior ends.

The physical, psychic and personal levels (instinct, emotion and recognition of the value of the person) all have a part in the experience of love. Integration of these three kinds of dynamism takes place in human action, and in this particular case in the act of loving. They become part of the human act, which means that its integral character manifests itself in each part in a way appropriate to that part. Integration is not something arbitrary but constitutes a programme of 'making oneself whole', fulfilling oneself, which is characteristic of man as a person. Therefore failure to integrate these factors in actions is more than 'lack of integration'; it is 'counter-integration'. *Non-integration signifies a (more or less deepseated) incapacity for self-possession and self-mastery by way of self-determination* ('Person and Act', p. 205. [Author's underlining.])

35 It is not the strength or the genuineness of the conviction with which a subject delivers a judgement that determines whether or not it is true, but consonance with the facts about the thing or person judged. The subject is the sole author of his judgement, but not the author of its truth. People often fail to remember this distinction, especially when a judgement or assessment is accompanied by strong emotions. For this reason, it is as well to treat 'the evidence of one's own feelings' with a certain distrust. Nor should one overestimate the importance of the testimony which husbands and wives themselves are sometimes ready to give on this subject. To be realistic we must not forget that initial declarations of eternal love are always genuine, even from those who later – once more for the sake of 'being true to their feelings' – are unfaithful, sometimes repeatedly, to the object of their love. 'Being true to one's feelings' is no hindrance at all.

36 The author is analysing here the phenomenon of 'divorce between feeling and act', which is encountered in practice. Cases of such divergence may occasionally inspire attempts to absolutize

NOTES

sensations, emotions, etc., in theory as well as in practice. The author has given some attention to this problem, particularly in his study 'Assessment of the Possibility of Constructing a Christian Ethic on the Premises of Max Scheler's System' (Lublin 1959). See also 'The Problem of Divergence of Feeling and Act in Ethics, with special reference to the views of Kant and Scheler' in *Roczniki Filozoficzne* 5.1955–7 (3), 2 pp. 113–40; 'In Quest of Foundations for Perfectionism in Ethics', in *Roczniki Filozoficzne* 5.1955–7 (4), pp. 303–17; 'On the Leading or Subsidiary Role of Reason in Ethics. With special reference to the views of St Thomas Aquinas, Hume and Kant' in *Roczniki Filozoficzne* 6.1958 (2), pp. 13–31.

37 Love is the realization of a certain kind of communion based on a common good. The communion has two aspects: objective and subjective. Objectively, the communion is defined by the aim of the shared aspiration. This is the less complete definition of the communion. It is more precisely defined by its subjective aspect – sharing or participation . . . 'a man chooses something also chosen by others, perhaps even because it is chosen by others, but at the same time chooses it as a good for himself and the goal of his own aspiration. What he then chooses is his own good in the sense that he fulfils himself in it as a person'. 'Person and Act', p. 306. Cf. also 'Person, Subject, Communion' in *Roczniki Filozoficzne* 24.1976 (2), pp. 6–39.

38 In married love pleasure may be, and often is, the result of an endeavour to affirm the other person. It must not be the basic aim of that endeavour; promotion of the result to the rank of primary aim is simply an act of egoism. This egoism, however, not only injures the person who is the object of love by reducing him or her to the role of means to an end, but also makes it difficult for the subject to attain full happiness. For man attains happiness in love by giving himself in the way characteristic of the person, giving to the point of losing himself. ('If the seed does not die, it remains a seed, if it dies, it brings a great crop'). For this reason it is morally reprehensible not only to subordinate other persons to the quest for one's own pleasure, but also to strive on another's behalf for a good which takes no account of the nature of the person.

It is worth remembering that a man's true good is not only not to be identified with the pleasure he experiences, but is always difficult to calculate.

For even the non-eudaemonistic variant of utilitarianism (see note 15) involves a danger that 'calculable' goods will be preferred to those whose realization sometimes takes a long time and a considerable dedication, and which are themselves not measurable. One such good is surely the complete self-realization of the person obtained through mutual love in marriage. This is responsible love, since its aim is the profound happiness of another person, and not simply an increase of pleasure and the avoidance of discomfort.

39 Man 'makes himself whole', 'fulfils himself' always and only if he loves, i.e. if he affirms the worth of the object to the full extent of the objectively given truth which it is the task of the subject to affirm given to that particular subject to affirm it (Cf. 'Person and Act' pp. 182–7).

40 In the terminology adopted by the author 'wanting' is an act of will. Two observations are in order here:
   (1) Whenever we say 'I want' something we refer not to the person as such but to our concupiscence and its 'own dynamic'.
   (2) Although this dynamic exists and manifests itself in us of necessity, man is to some extent responsible for violent and disorderly manifestations of it.

41 An act of will ('wanting' or 'not wanting' something) implies intellectual knowledge of that something, and hence rational judgement. Hence the behaviour of a man experiencing 'morally suspect' emotions in a situation permitting only 'imaginary judgements' which are not actually delivered cannot be the object of moral assessment. Judgements on one's moral duty can be founded only on the basis of conscious activity of the intellect, and not just the imagination. To imagine that one has a duty to do something is not sufficient to create an actual obligation, just as to imagine oneself wanting something – as one might if one were acting in a play – and really to want it are two different things. One's actions may sometimes be 'unconsciously' guided by 'the truth about what is morally good', but only in the sense that the results of previous reasoning have firmly established themselves in a disposition to act in a certain way, and now make reasonable a particular action which is outside the range of the subject's immediate awareness. The moral value of human actions – given the frequency with which objects and circumstances of action change – cannot be incessantly controlled and verified within the immediate field of attention, in which room must be found for assessments of other kinds. So the "man of goodwill" rightly trusts – for he can do no other – in the "acquired spontaneity" which he owes to normally sound dispositions'. [In a self-respecting society people are given the benefit of the doubt 'donec contrarium probetur'.]

42 In this connection there is still an important distinction to be made between the morally good and the morally correct act, and

between the functions of conscience as source of information on these two aspects of an act. My judgement that 'I must perform action A in relation to person P' has two structurally distinct though closely connected aspects. The first is expressed in the judgement 'I must affirm P'. This aspect may be called that of 'protoconscience'. The other aspect is expressed in the judgement A is the appropriate (or even the only) way to affirm person P. Only in its first aspect is my judgement a reliable informant. Hence, a subject choosing to act according to his conscience can be sure only that he *wanted* to affirm P but not that he has chosen an act which is really suitable to the affirmation of P. In other words, it is possible to act according to one's conscience and with good intentions, and yet to the detriment of P. In such cases, we say that an action is morally positive only in intention, or that it is *morally good* but not morally positive in its actual effect on the object of the action. In other words it is *morally incorrect*. To act in accordance with one's conscience is always morally good, but not for that reason always morally correct. But conscience always obliges us to act in accordance with its dictates, even when they are erroneous, since if we err we shall do so inadvertently. The possibility of making a mistake in such an important matter must incline us to take special care for the accuracy of our moral diagnoses. The only way to guarantee this is to acquire an ever deeper knowledge of the objective structure of man. To show this structure in the general context of man's vocation to love – as commanded by the Creative Love itself – is the main object of this book.

43 It is not the strength of an experience of the authenticity of the conviction with which a particular subject forms a judgement that determines its truth, but the consonance of the judgement with that which it concerns. The subject is the sole author of the judgement, but he is not the author of its truth. This difference is commonly not remembered, especially when the judgements or the evaluations concerned are accompanied by strong emotional reactions. For this reason it is a good rule to treat 'the evidence of one's own feelings' with a certain distrust. Nor must we give too much value to the evidence which spouses themselves are often ready to offer in this context. For the sake of realism we must not forget that vows of 'eternal true love' are to begin with always sincerely made by those who afterwards – and again for the sake of 'being true to their feelings' – change the object of their affections, sometimes time and time again. 'Being true to their feelings' is no hindrance at all to this.

44 Although culture in general differs from nature in that it is the work of persons, the cultivation of the inner life – what the

author calls here 'cultivation of the person' – determines for any society both the 'points of departure' and the 'terminal points' of all creative cultural activities, and likewise their historical importance to humanity at large.

45 For a fuller treatment of perfectionism see the author's article 'Quest for Foundations of Perfectionism in Ethics' in *Roczniki Filozoficzne* 5.1955–57 (4), pp. 303–17.

46 Reason defines the true good in the sense that it is the authority which delivers judgements on values and duties. But although it creates these judgements it does not create their truth, it merely interprets it. It is only on the presupposition that there is a consonance between the judgement it gives and the matter which that judgement concerns that the reason is prepared to pass judgement and does so. Hence 'the experience of duty is very closely associated with the experience of truth'. ('Person and Act', p. 172.) 'Conscience is not such a subjective thing as not to be in some degree inter-subjective. It is in conscience that *knowledge of truth and sense of duty unite to become the normative force of truth*' (Person and Act, p. 161, Author's underlining).

47 Conversely, it is only through love, i.e. affirmation of the person, that chastity becomes a virtue. In St Augustine's definition *'caritas est forma virtutum'*.

48 In ethical discussions, and particularly in those which followed the publication of the encyclical *Humanae Vitae*, the aspiration to chastity, or more generally to the reconciliation of the demands of love with those of natural law, has often been defined as a manifestation of contempt for, or aversion from, the physical, a *'contemptus mundi'*, or quite simply a manifestation of Manicheism.

In this work the demand for chastity is taken to mean respect for the body and for human physical dynamism. At the same time, it is emphasized that this dynamism attains its full human expression by way of integration with the general dynamism of man, by means of its 'elevation' to the personal plane. For the dynamisms of the body are not an independent and self-contained phenomenon, but are naturally oriented to serving the good of the integral human person.

49 'These two norms – one deduced from the nature of the sexual urge and demanding respect for its purpose, and the other deduced from the dignity of the person, which entitles it to love – contain and condition each other in every interpersonal relationship in which there is a sexual factor. . . . The norm which derives from the order of nature and demands respect for the purpose of the urge is the more elementary and basic. The norm

which demands a proper attitude to the person in a sexual relationship is superordinate and, particularly in its scriptural form, it performs a perfectionist function. There can be no question of fulfilling the personalistic norm, especially in the concrete Christian version found in the Gospels, without respect for the purpose of the urge in relation to a person of the other sex.' ('The Problem of Catholic Sexual Morality', *Roczniki Filozoficzne* 13.1965, (2), p. 14.)

50 'Worthy of a human being' may be taken in two ways:

(1) In its broad sense it refers – as it does here – to rationality in action, understood in a non-utilitarian way, i.e. a *total rationality* for which utilitarian considerations are not the only nor the main ones.

(2) In the strictly personalistic sense the ethical qualification 'worthy of a human being' refers to the consonance of a moral act with the quite specific, unchanging and inalienable value which every person represents simply by being a person and not a thing – 'some-one to some-one', and not 'something for something'.

51 The concept of virtue in this context is closely bound up with that of transcendence, or the 'primacy of the person in relation to itself' and to its own dynamism. The person stands 'above' its action and 'above' the object of its action. It is this that makes possible the self-possession and self-control of the person, which are necessary conditions for the existence of virtue, or correctness in action. Transcendence so understood is an expression and a sign of the spirituality of man. Cf. 'Person and Act', (Part II – 'Transcendence of the Person in the Act'.)

52 Some values – moral values among them – are not values because some-one aspires to them; on the contrary, we aspire to them, and indeed feel it our duty to do so, because they are values. We have here something fundamentally different from conventional values, such as those which a collector attaches to the objects he seeks.

A value is not the same as the object which represents it; it constitutes a specific object-subject or subject-object relationship, an expression of a particular correspondence (of some-one to some-one, of something to some-one, or of something to something as it affects some-one). We do, however – as in this case – often, by metonymy, give the name of a value to an object representing it.

53 The author is here the spokesman for the view that moral duty owes its unconditional character not to the fact that it is prescribed (moral positivism, decretalism), nor to any authority external to the agent (heteronomic positivism), nor to any internal

authority such as 'practical reason', the function of which is sometimes identified with that of the will (Kant's autonomous positivism). For in any of these cases moral duty would be identified with external or internal compulsion, which would deprive the agent of his status of moral subject. The inalienable right to question moral duties is essential to this status of subject. The dignity of the person is the foundation on which moral duty is directly based.

54 Objectivization of the moral order in man takes place through his conception of truth – 'truth about the good' or 'axiological truth'. This truth is obtained by cognition, by reasoning about experience. The statement that something is really good and correct awakens a sense of duty in man and inspires him to act so as to realize that good. The superiority (transcendence) of the person in relation to its own dynamisms and the objects of its endeavours brings about a realization of the good and hence the 'self-fulfilling' of the person. Cf. 'Person and Act', Chapters I and IV.

55 An act of love, as an act of affirmation of the person to whom it is directed, is in respect for that person's dignity of its very nature a disinterested act. It possesses, in addition to its short-term consequences (it is an act of beneficence) some enduring consequences. It is a unique form of 'good deed' for the subject of action, who in performing an act of love fulfils himself or herself most fully. Love is at once 'disinterested and rewarded'. Cf. *'Il problema del costituirsi della cultura attraverso la Praxis umana'*, in 'Rivista di filosofia neoscolastica', 69.1977 (2–3), pp. 513–24.

56 Cf. Fr. Karol Wojtyła, 'Thoughts on Marriage', in *Znak* 7.1957, pp. 595–604.

57 *'The family is the place in which every human being appears in his or her uniqueness and unrepeatability.'* It is, and must be, a system of forces in which each member is important and necessary, because he is, and because he is what he is – a profoundly 'human' system, erected on the value of the person and completely oriented toward that value ('The Family as a Communio Personarum', in *Atenoum Kaplanskie* 66.1974, p. 348, [Author's underlining]).

58 Interpersonal 'communion' has as its foundation that 'capacity to give oneself, to become a gift for others' which is peculiar to man as a person, and which presupposes a structure of self-possession and self-control. ('Betrothed Love', p. 96). However, 'if this disinterested gift of self is to become effectively a gift in an interpersonal relationship . . . it must be *not only "given" but accepted in its true and authentic nature*' ('The Family as

"Communio"', p. 355 (Author's underlining). Part of the truth about it is that in giving himself – (which does not mean depriving himself of his ontological inseparability from himself – cf. 'Betrothed Love', pp. 95–100) – a man in some sense loses his right to himself for the benefit of the person to whom he has given himself. Hence 'encroachment on another person's property' (another person's husband or wife), or a second gift of self by a husband or wife to some-one to whom he or she is not married, is a specific form of theft, and does as much to damage the interpersonal communion of love as the gift of self does to create it in the first place.

'One cannot deprive a person of the gift he or she makes, cannot take away from the person as a gift of self is made that which the person really is and that which he or she means to express in this action' ('The Family As Communion', p. 355).

59 'Whenever we follow attentively the liturgy of this sacrament' [marriage – ed.] 'we see before us two people, a man and a woman, who have come to declare in the presence of God that they are establishing an objective situation in which they become, as spouses, each of them a gift to the other. Sexual intercourse is an essential part of the situation which here finds expression and is enabled to mature and take form as a sacrament. Sexual intercourse is part of the complex vocation which both of them embrace in the presence of God as their part together with Jesus Christ in the communion of the Church. And in embracing it they receive each other so to speak from the hands of God the Creator and Redeemer. They receive each other as a gift of each to the other, as husband and wife, and in this is the sacramental confirmation of their right to sexual intercourse, which cannot be justified as a way of exercising 'the right of giving' written into the being of the person by God except within a marital union ('On the Meaning of Married Love', p. 174).

60 'Justification through Grace', i.e. the release of man from his "original" debt, is basically accomplished by *baptism*. The rebellion of our first parents, however, so damaged the physical and moral nature of man that individuals are regularly impelled to offend against each other and to incur debts to each other, and above all to God, the lord of all being. People who for this reason need and long for justification also find it in Christ, for only through Him and in Him can man be 'all in order' with his Creator. This is accomplished basically through the *sacrament of penitence*, but also through the other sacraments, including the *sacrament of marriage*.

Neither of these forms of 'justification' should be confused with 'justification' of sexual intercourse within the objective and durable framework of the institution of marriage, as a *sacramentum naturae*, and as something legitimized by natural law.

61 The personalistic norm relates in the first place to the attitude of the subject (*benevolentia*): the subject must take steps to ensure the good of the other person, its object, and is certainly not free to subordinate the other entirely to its own ends. In putting this postulate into practice (*benficentia*) we cannot affirm the object in any way without assuring for that person pre-moral goods which are not in themselves moral goods (life, health, etc.), which have value to the extent that they serve the person; hence we may say that all norms affecting the realization of these goods have a teleological character: they are binding because and insofar as observation of them does more for the good of the object person than failure to observe them would. It does not follow from the fact that the value of the person is superior to the value of all goods other than moral goods that the norms which bid us realize those lesser goods admit of exceptions. Still less is it the case that the subject is empowered to determine for himself which norm is binding on him in a given situation. The way in which goods other than moral goods are bound up with the good of the person reveals to us a hierarchy of goods, which is constant to the extent that human nature is constant. Effective affirmation of the object-person demands, on the part of the subject, conscientious effort to determine the relative importance of the pre-moral goods involved in any situation. Respect for goods which are vitally bound up with the good and the development of the person is a test which shows how far the attitude of the subject is really one of love.

62 Cf. note 20.

63 The combination of these two orders, which is the essential characteristic of marital intercourse, is also emphasized by the Encyclical *Humanae Vitae* (see especially p. 12). The discussion to which the encyclical gave rise shows how difficult it is to grasp this idea that the marital act has a peculiar duality – an idea which derives from a definite vision of the human person and of married love, which in its basic features is common to the encyclical and to *Love and Responsibility*. Without going into the details of the discussion it is worth emphasizing the structural difference between the two orders pointed out by K. Wojtyla: the order of nature (understood here as the aggregate of more or less autonomous dynamisms instinctive in man) has as its object procreation, whereas the personal order expresses itself in the love of persons. The order of nature relates to the specific

result of the marital act (birth of a human being), whereas the personal order is concerned directly and above all with the expression of love towards one person by another. Since, however, the body is an integral part of the human person, and since the person expresses attitudes to other persons by means of the body, the way in which love is shown must respect the 'inner logic' by which nature is governed in man. For the specific characteristic of the human person – as K. Wojtyla shows in *Love and Responsibility*, and still more emphatically in *Person and Act* – is the ability to fit the order of nature into the framework of the personal order. The superiority of the latter does not confer any moral right to manipulate nature at will: on the contrary, observation of its basic laws is an indispensable condition of true and full realization of the personal order (cf. p. 215 below, and also the author's articles 'The Problem of Catholic Sexual Morality' and 'The Human Person and Natural Law'). The consequences of these anthropological premises in relation to marital ethics include the negative evaluation (which will be found both in *Love and Responsibility* and in *Humanae Vitae*, and which provokes particularly fierce controversy) of all methods of regulating conception which try to divorce the two orders and to realize interpersonal love by perverting the logic of nature.

The distinction drawn by the author between the order of nature and the order of the person recalls the differentiation, with which we are familiar in recent works on moral theology, between 'acts of performance' (*Erfullungshandlungen*) and 'acts of expression' (*Ausdruckshandlungen*). Contemporary writers tend to separate these two categories, but in K. Wojtyla's conception (and especially in relation to married love) it would be more accurate to speak of two 'dimensions' of the act: its 'consequential' aspect (which belongs to the order of nature) and its 'expressive' aspect (which is specific to the person). These two aspects – as we have said – must be properly harmonized.

64 'It is obviously not acceptable (except in cases of congenital or acquired sterility) for a man and a woman to marry primarily with the object of complementing or mutually completing each other (*mutuum adiutorium*), for that is not in accordance with the Creator's plan in the order of nature, as seen by the light of reason, or in the order of Grace as seen by the light of Revelation.' ('The Problem of Catholic Sexual Morality', p. 16.)

65 'Parenthood is an interior fact in husband and wife as father and mother, on whom the conception and birth of a child confers a new quality and a new condition.' ('Parenthood as "Communio Personarum"', p. 17) (*Ateneum Kaplanskie*, 84 (1975)). 'Children enter into the communion of husband and wife also in order

to confirm it, reinforce it, deepen it. Thus, their own *communio personarum* is enriched in this way. It is enrichment by a new person which originates entirely from the two of them and owes its existence to them' (ibid., p. 21).

66 Reason admits of only one view as to the Creator's attitude to such behaviour. It is as easy to divine as the reaction of a father who gives his child a piece of bread and jam, and sees him eating only the jam and throwing the bread away. If the child must not reject that which is necessary to sustain *life*, and grasp only at that which gives *pleasure*, how much less seemly is such conduct in adults?

67 Cf. note 20.

68 This is obviously not entirely correct. The birth of a new human being is the birth not only of 'another stomach to fill' but of another worker, perhaps even an inventor and a creator of the technical means for increasing many times over the productivity of labour.

69 Cf. Note 57.

70 Nature, it should be remembered, is meant here in the biological sense. The essential point is that the initiative of human persons should fall within the limits of that 'initiative' of which the creative order established by God is the expression. The initiative of people who use 'preventative' techniques to avoid the natural results of sexual intercourse quite clearly does not meet this requirement.

71 We refer here to conduct which lacks adequate moral grounds, and so has no objectively valid reasons dictated by the dignity of the person. This qualification deserves to be emphasized, so that no-one will jump to the conclusion that marital intercourse between persons incapable of having children cannot be virtuous.

72 'Avoidance of parenthood on a particular occasion of sexual intercourse cannot be equated with its avoidance or active prevention throughout a marriage. It is extremely important to take this into account' (*Love and Responsibility*, 1st Edition, Lublin 1960, p. 185).

73 We must remember that man is not only the object of concrete services on the part of God but that the very fact of the Creator's commitment to continually renewing his creature, endowing him with existence and with freedom, is a personal service of a particular kind. While purely material equality does not depend on the status of the contracting parties, equality in the exchange of personal services is very closely bound up with it.

74 The justice in question here is very clearly 'commercial' justice of the *'do ut des'* kind; but justice in the deeper, integral sense

also aims at a sort of 'equalization' in reciprocated love, in the 'giving of self'. The divergence between the two principles (justice and love) would disappear but for the fact that equality between the Creator and his creatures is unthinkable in this particular context: we are simply incapable of loving God as we are loved by Him.

INDEX